Dedicated to everyone who can remember
when toys didn't need a battery

CANCELLED.

The Toffs in the Towerblock

Contents

The Toffs in the Towerblock

Sct in October 1968 **The Toffs in the Towerblock** continues the story of **The Toffs in the Tenements'** Nairn family, a posh family from the affluent west end of Glasgow who, after losing all their money, end up living in the tenements of Bridgeton.

11 year old Rupert Nairn Private school educated until he was 9 years old; he now lives in a tenement with his family. Is highly intelligent, polite, observant and sensible, THIS IS HIS STORY...

Father Hubert was a bank manager, just like his dad before him, until he lost everything when money went missing at his bank; he worked in Arnotts and Simpsons menswear department until recently returning to banking with the help of his Father.

Mother Clarissa hates the fact they have no money, and still clings on to her past snobbish life any little way she can.

14 year old Wilhelmina is Rupert's big sister; She hates her flat, her brother, her school, her life and most off all her dad for bringing her to Brigton.

Enjoy a nostalgic trip back in time to the tenements of Heron St, Bridgeton in 1968, when kids knew how to make their own entertainment.

When the sun seemed to shine for 8 weeks of the school summer holiday, and you wouldn't dream of giving any cheek to an adult in fear of a kick up the backside.

A Time when everyone could leave their front door open, because they never had anything worth stealing. When everyone was in the same boat, struggling to make ends meet and living for a Friday (Payday).

When neighbours helped neighbours through trying times of poverty and hardship, and lifelong friendships were forged.

Join the posh Nairn's as they try to adapt to life in the tenements, in this funny and uplifting story that will make you laugh, cry and cringe as the Nairn's get ready for their move to the high flats in Ruby St.

Toffs Dictionary

Minging	Smelly
Narket	Stop it
Fankle/Fankled	Twisted and mixed up
Licees'	Off Sales
Manky	Dirty
Shebeen	Illegal drinking den
The Steamie	Place to wash clothes
The Barra's	Outdoor Market
The Booly	Waste ground used for play
Bools / Jorries	Marbles
Stank	Drain
Geeza song	It's your turn to sing
A Close	Entrance to flats
Cludgie	Outside shared toilet
Bo'z	Girls game bouncing balls
Moashie	Game with coins and 3 holes
Sidey	2 teams playing football
The Minors	Saturday cinema for kids
Merritt'	Married
Single End	One room flat
Midden	Dustbin
Lucky Midden	Dustbin behind shops
Furra	For a
Geeza	Give me
Gonny	Going to
Gettin' 'ra Malky	(See Chibbed)
Chibbed	Slashed in face with sharp instrument
Wisnae	Wasn't
Wiz	Was
Urny'	Are not
Aw'right	Good morning, how are you?
Squib or banger	Small explosive used at Guy Fawkes
Roon ra' back	Going round the backcourt
Geeza Brek	Cut me some slack
Provvie' Man	Provident check collection agent

The Toffs in the Towerblock

Ra baw's burst!

Sitting in the public library in Landressy St, I have just finished reading 'The autobiography of Andrew Carnegie', and coincidently my friend Sammy has just finished reading 'The Sparky'. I lean over towards Sammy and whisper "Father has been told we can move into our new flat in Ruby St this January". There is a pause before Sammy replies excitedly "'Rat means ye'll stull be here fur Hallo'een 'n Christmas". Before I can even nod in agreement the old man sitting at the opposite table shouts "Shoosh yooz two", as he stares right at us with his tobacco stained finger pressed against his pursed lips, and then to our amazement he puts his newspaper down and shouts at the lady behind the counter, "Hoi' hen, hiv ye goat yisterdays Evening Times?".

The rather strict looking lady with the horn rimmed glasses behind the counter is extremely annoyed and obviously not used to being shouted at. She raises her thin index finger up to her pursed lips which are covered in a little too much red lipstick, and angrily shakes her head. Meanwhile Sammy decides to get his own back and looks at the old man while mimicking his previous actions " Shoosh", he says to the old man, the old man is not very happy and shouts at Sammy " Ya cheeky wee bastard, I'll pit ma toe up yer arse". He then makes a feeble attempt to get out of his seat as Sammy grabs my arm and whispers, "C'moan let's get oot o'here 'afore 'ra old fart hiz a nanny rooney".

The old man notices us making our getaway and shouts "Aye ye better run ya wee buggers", he then starts shaking his fists at us before adding "See if ah wiz twenty years younger..". Sammy interrupts him by shouting "If ye wur twenty years younger ye'd stull be an auld crab". Sammy and I burst out laughing as all the other people in the library, including the lady behind the counter, turn to the old man and shout "Shhhhhhh".

We are still laughing as we run down the library stairs two at a time and out into Landressy St; we stop and look through the basement window of the snooker hall next door to the library, and notice there is a game in progress. We also notice there is quite a large crowd watching sitting on the benches at the back of the room. I am mesmerised by the thick cloud of cigarette and cigar smoke which is hovering above the snooker table like a ghostly spectre when Sammy turns to me and says "Get ready to run". I am a little confused as to why, but take a few steps towards James St just in case as I am not the fastest runner in the world.

While I am preparing to run, Sammy bends down at the open window just as one of the men leans over the snooker table and lines up a shot. I am a bag of nerves as I watch Sammy, wondering what he is up to. He waits until the man pulls his snooker cue back and is ready to hit the ball before screaming at the top of his voice "MISS IT". The man gets a fright and thrusts forward with his cue and misses the ball he was trying to hit, the cue flies out his hand and scatters all the other balls on the table. There is now total mayhem in the snooker hall as all the men start arguing and shouting.

Sammy turns to me and shouts "RUN", just as one of the men spots him at the window. "It wiz rat wee bastart 'it 'ra windae", he shouts as he points at Sammy. This shout is immediately followed by another more sinister shout of "Yooz ur gettin' chibbed by 'ra way". The purveyor of this message is encouraged to follow through with, what I presume is some sort of threat, by another man who bellows "Aye good on ye Razor, go an' get 'ra wee bastart's". Although I was really interested in finding out what 'Chibbed' meant, by taking into account the tone of the man's voice and the fact his name is Razor, I quickly conclude it isn't something I would particularly like, so we run along Dalmarnock Rd as fast as our legs will carry us towards the safe haven of Heron St.

"Stoap, slow doon" Sammy requests as we pass Woolworths. "Ah fink wur aw'right noo" he adds as we stop and catch our breath. I nervously glance towards Bridgeton Cross to check we haven't been followed by a mob before looking at Sammy and asking "What does 'chibbed' mean?". Sammy stands up straight and using his index finger, starts to make slicing gestures on his cheek as he replies "Slashed wi' a knife". As we start to walk towards Heron St, I shake my head in disbelief. It is hard to imagine I could have been scarred for life because of Sammy's childish bravado outside a snooker hall window.

"Haw! Lord Snooty.., stoap rat' ba'," shouts Jamie Mc Cabe as we turn the corner from Dalmarnock Rd into Heron St, I suddenly spot the ball in question across the road bouncing towards Sammy and I. Time seems to stand still as I think, "If I don't intercept that ball it will travel on to the busy Dalmarnock Rd and almost certainly be burst under the wheels of the cars and buses". I see this as an opportunity to endear myself to the McCabe twins because as Sammy immediately spots, this is no ordinary 2/-6d ball, this is *the* Reggy 5 the twins got for their birthday last week.

Sammy explained to me at the time that the Trophy Regulation 5 was only one step away from a Mouldmaster, or Mouldie as it is commonly known, and is quite expensive, so if I manage to save the day. The twins will be extremely grateful and forever indebted to me, I will have saved them from having to explain the demise of the Reggy 5 to their dad, and the verbal abuse and possible boot up the backside that would follow.

Quick as a flash I dart across the road as the rogue ball is now dangerously close to Dalmarnock Rd. "Yeess" shout the McCabe twins as I stretch out my leg to stop the ball. At this point I feel like Superman. To my horror the ball then hits a small stone on the road which changes its direction and it misses my outstretched leg by about half an inch and continues on its journey, I am absolutely panic stricken at this point as I turn round just in time to see Sammy stick out a leg and knock the ball back towards me like a professional footballer,"Yeess, ya dancer" the McCabe boys shout again, "Phew, that was close" I think to myself as I revert back to Superman mode ready to receive the acclamation of the McCabe twins.

My relief is short lived however as I step forward to pick the ball up and accidently kick it with my left toe. It shoots between Sammy's legs and heads right onto Dalmarnock Rd just in time to meet the 46 bus going to Castlemilk. What happens next seems to last an eternity, like slow motion. The ball hits the front wheel of the bus, bounces back off the kerb and heads right under the back wheel. From behind me I can hear the collective "Oohs!" and "Ahhs!" from the McCabe twins as the ball jumps about like a pinball for what seems like ages before we hear the inevitable BANG! The bus moves on and all that is left is a flat Reggy 5 lying there like a dead hedgehog. I gulp as I slowly get back on my feet, then as I nervously turn around I can see Sammy and the McCabe twins standing there with their hands on their heads and a look of horror on their faces. Time seems to stand still again, as I also notice a wee girl who was playing balls against the wall standing with both hands over her mouth and her wee shoulders raised up to her ears as if she has just witnessed a puppy getting run over.

Mrs Mc Kay breaks the uncomfortable silence from her ground floor flat when she shouts from her window, "If ah wiz you Rupert son, ah'd run like hell". At that moment there is a clap of thunder and the heavens open as the rain comes bucketing down.

In a matter of seconds Heron St is transformed into one giant puddle. Mrs Mc Kay retreats inside her house as the rain batters her now closed window and just when I thought things couldn't get any worse I hear a shout of "GET 'IM" as the McCabe twins decide to seek some retribution for their burst ball and come charging towards me like demented madmen.

My legs freeze as Sammy shouts "RUN RUPERT", but my legs won't listen to what my brain is telling them. The McCabe twins are now about ten yards from me and at this point I have given up all hope of being saved and I'm reconciled to the fact I am going to be beaten up by a miniature version of the Krays, then, just as the McCabe twins are within touching distance of my now shaking body, I hear a familiar voice shout "Rupert, come in out of the rain this instant". The McCabe's slide to a halt like the Keystone Kops when they hear Mother's voice as they realise there is now a potential adult witness to their impending dirty deed.

Mothers' voice is swiftly followed by Mrs McCabe, "Jamie, John get yer arses up the stair, move it," bellows Mrs McCabe at her two boys. The twins at this point are apoplectic with rage and staring right at me through screwed up eyes, pointing their fingers at me while mouthing the words *"Your gettin' it,"* as they reluctantly turn around and head for their close.

As I stand there whimpering and soaked to the skin, Sammy comes over and puts his hand on my still shaking shoulder as he whispers sympathetically "Ye better get up ra' stair and get dried oot". With the torrential rain still battering the pot holed strewn street, we walk along the pavement towards my close discussing how we are going to avoid the McCabe twins for the next twenty years, when an empty bus heading for Fordnuek St bus depot trundles past. It's wheels pass through a large puddle at the side of the kerb sending what seems like gallons of water right over Sammy and I, "Sorry lads," shouts the clippie, hanging from the pole at the back of the bus as it carries on towards its destination. We both look at each other standing there with our arms outstretched and absolutely soaked through.

The rain continues to batter the street, making it look even more grey and dank than usual. A worried Sammy says "Ma' maw's gonny kill me," I nod in agreement and reply "My Mother isn't going to be best pleased either," as I spit out water like a fountain in Glasgow Green.We reach my close first and I say cheerio to Sammy who slowly walks away towards his own close, his arms still outstretched and his legs apart at a funny angle as if he had just peed himself.

The dirty grey sandstone tenements of Heron St now look particularly old and gloomy as the water cascades down the face of the buildings from blocked or nonexistent guttering that has never been cleaned or repaired. The drainpipes outside some of the closes are burst sending a constant shower of water onto the uneven pavements from two storeys up, creating puddles and streams of water running along the kerb where the now blocked drains are already overflowing. I watch Sammy until he reaches his close, laughing at his unnatural walk, but I stop laughing immediately as I notice Mrs Kelly and her son Joe making their way towards me. You see Joe has a clubbed foot and walks with a pronounced limp. He wears one of those big heavy black shoes on his left foot which he swings forward in a semi circle like motion when he is walking; he is trying as hard as he can to walk faster so that his mother doesn't get soaked in the still pouring rain.

Joe always wears multi coloured tank tops that Mrs Kelly knits with left over wool along with a short sleeved grey shirt underneath. He also wears the same grey short trousers, and his short blond hair looks as if his mother cut it using a bowl. Needless to say the neanderthal McCabe twins have given him a really hard time since he arrived in Heron St.

Although he is small, Joe is about the same age as me and Sammy, but Mrs Kelly doesn't let him out to play on his own, Father told me to ask him out to play when they moved in, which I was more than happy to do as I know how it feels to be picked on, but Mrs Kelly looked horrified at the prospect and closed the door in my face when I asked.

They both moved in to our old single end flat about three weeks ago, but because of her very thick Irish accent, I find it difficult to understand Mrs Kelly. In saying that it took me nearly two years to understand Sammy and he's Scottish. When I first spoke to her I said "Good morning Mrs Kelly," as I passed her on the landing, I am not quite sure what she replied but it sounded like "Woojy betakin' the pissnow". I tried to reassure her I have never touched her 'pissnow', and I didn't know who took it. She then mumbled something else that sounded like "Rite ahlnobie takin' anyerlip now yawee shi..,"...I never heard the end as I quickly ran down the stairs and out the close.

When Mrs Kelly and Joe get a little nearer I notice they are carrying loads of stuff, Joe has a pillowcase in his right hand filled with something and he is holding his mother's hand with his left hand, Mrs Kelly is carrying a mop and bucket and a string bag full of potatoes in her left hand while holding on to Joe tightly with her right hand both trying to walk as fast as they can towards our close to escape the still pouring rain. I decide, as I am soaked through anyway, to run towards them and offer my services.

"Can I carry something for you?" I ask, as I waddle up beside them. "Bejeez yerah good boy, so ye are" I think she says, as she hands me the bucket and mop, and then the string bag as well. At this point I am now struggling to see in front of me, as she lifts up Joe as if he was a two year old boy and grabs the pillowcase before shooting away towards our close like an Olympic athlete.

When I eventually reach the close I am wobbling about trying to juggle the mop and bucket while being weighed down with the string bag full of potatoes. I am now even more wet if that's possible "Will ye be oright there Robert?", Mrs Kelly asks, The only word I caught was "Robert", as she speaks at a hundred miles an hour, "His name's Rupert mammy", Joe replies, in a soft spoken voice, "Areye sure there Joe?" Mrs Kelly asks, convinced her son is mistaken "Aye ah um", says Joe, "Well yer man's a good lad, so he is, no matter whiteze name is", I look at Joe for a translation as I try to work out who's man is a good lad, and he just shakes his head to indicate that everything is okay.

Mrs Kelly starts to help Joe climb the uneven stairs towards the outside toilet which is situated halfway down the stairs. I have to admire him as he manfully climbs the stairs without a moan or groan, swinging his bad leg out and up one stair at a time. Meanwhile I am following on behind, banging the mop off the landing wall as I can't see my feet and water is running down my face and into my eyes. Joe and Mrs Kelly eventually reach our landing and I am struggling up the last few stairs just behind them. I have about four stairs to go when Mr Campbell, our neighbour from across the landing appears from his front door with the obligatory newspaper under his arm, "*Just in the nick of time to help,*" I think to myself, no chance, he just barges past me shouting loudly "Move, move 'am touchin' cloth here,". He bangs off my shoulder in his rush to get to the toilet sending me spinning like a top. My grip on the metal mop bucket weakens and the bucket is sent flying down the stairs making an almighty racket as it bounces down every stair before coming to rest on the toilet landing, the string bag bangs off the wall and bursts, sending the potatoes through the air before they land and roll down all the stairs. The rogue Kerrs Pinks catch up with Mr Campbell and he stands on them, sending him off balance and his arms start spinning like a propeller on a spitfire as he tries desperately to regain his balance. The newspaper he is carrying under his arm is now sent skyward separating into individual pages and falling like very large confetti.

At this point Mr Campbell is heading straight for the open landing window and I am contemplating running away to avoid a manslaughter charge, but he manages to stop himself by grabbing the still open toilet door, but as he steps back from the door his hand slips on the wet handle and he falls backwards onto his posterior landing on top of the now settled potatoes, "Argh! ma arse", he shouts in agony, as a rather large potato disappears beneath him, at this point his wife Mrs Campbell arrives on the scene "Whit's o' the bloody racket ", she moans, as she approaches the top of the stairs, she is joined by Mother and Father "Oh dear what's happened here?", Father asks. "Are you okay Rupert?" Mother adds, I nod to let them know I'm fine, before turning back round to look down the stairs.

There is now a scene of total carnage. Newspaper pages and potatoes are strewn everywhere. I am left standing holding a mop, and Mr Campbell is sitting on the toilet landing obviously in some pain and holding a potato that's been somewhere it shouldn't. After surveying the scene and finally noticing her husband on the toilet landing Mrs Campbell shouts "Get yer arse aff ra' wummin's tottie's ya big fat lump". I look at Joe, who is trying not to laugh. Even Mrs Kelly and my parents are stifling their sniggers. Mrs Campbell looks at all of us one at a time before shaking her head and proclaiming to nobody in particular, " He canny even go furra shite withoot causin' a stooshie", as she makes her way back to her flat. That just tips us all over the edge and we burst out laughing. Mother invites Mrs Kelly and Joe in for a cup of tea, as I quickly gather up the stray potatoes. Just before we enter our flat I glance at Mr Campbell who is hobbling about trying to collect and piece together his Daily Record muttering out loud "Ah canny find ra' telly bit".

After getting dried and changed I join Mother and Father in the living room. There is a funny smell permeating around the room, Mother is standing at the sink washing some dishes and Father is sitting on the couch reading his newspaper, I meander over to the cooker and notice a pot of boiling water with what looks like a pair of cream coloured underpants floating around inside it, "What's for dinner?, I ask while staring at this revolting looking pot, "Tripe", Mother replies immediately, "Tripe ", I repeat back to her in a puzzled tone of voice, "Yes, Mrs Campbell gave me some to try", Mother continues, I didn't want to hurt Mother's feelings by letting her know that there was no way on earth, any of that slimy, horrible, disgusting looking stuff was passing my lips, so I just said " Smashing", as I sat down next to Father.

"What's tripe?" I ask, whispering to Father. He puts his paper down for a second and looks me in the eye before saying "It's er, um, it's, how can I put this?, it's the lining of er, a cow's stomach". On seeing the horrified expression on my face, he continues, "Mrs Campbell insists it's a real delicacy around these parts". He then goes back to reading his paper, leaving me totally dreading dinner. I am just about to question the sanity of eating this 'Delicacy' when there is a knock at the front door.

"I'll get it," I shout, as I run into the hall and open the door. Standing there are Mrs Kelly and Joe, both of them have changed into dry clothes but poor Joe is wearing another multi coloured tank top that looks like a stick of rhubarb with different shades of green and purple stripes. Mrs Kelly speaks first, at a hundred miles an hour, "Ye o'rite 'rer now Robert ?, its jist us," the only word I made out was Robert, Joe is just about to correct his Mother when I motion to him that it's okay, "Come in," I say, directing them into the living room.

After everyone says hello, Mrs Kelly sits next to Father on the couch as Mother asks "How do you take your tea Mrs Kelly?" Mrs Kelly looks at Joe and me with a confused expression on her face, after a short pause she slowly replies "Er, in a cup". Before Mother can say anything I announce that Joe and I are going to play in the room.

When Joe enters my bedroom his jaw drops. "Wow", he exclaims, as he slowly makes his way to the centre of the room. He then turns round 360° before proclaiming, "'Ris rooms massive". I had forgotten how small the single end we stayed in next door actually was, and that our room and kitchen must seem big in comparison.

The rain is still battering my bedroom window which shudders every now and then when a bus passes as Joe and I sit on the floor between the coal fire and the bunk beds. I reach under the bunk beds and pull out my toy box and as I open the lid Joe makes a beeline for my Famous Five books. It turns out Joe loves reading but Mrs Kelly can't afford to buy him any books. He can only read at school, but even then he doesn't get much time to finish a story.

We start to chat together like budgies and Joe tells me that he never knew his dad. He left Mrs Kelly when Joe was only two years old and they had to move in with his Grandmother who stayed in Cumberland St in the Gorbals, Joe goes on to tell me his Grandfather died during the war at the battle of El Alamein in the deserts of North Africa in 1942, and his Grandmother had to look after him so that Mrs Kelly could work in a pub called the Granite City. After his Grandmother died, Mrs Kelly couldn't work and look after Joe so they struggled to pay the rent, which led to them moving to Heron St as the rent for a single end was cheaper.

I sympathise with Joe and then proceed to tell him briefly about my past in the West end. How Father lost his job in the bank and we had to sell our big house. How my sister and I had to leave our school and friends and move here to Heron St. Joe's response however takes me aback as he declares, "'Am glad", after a short pause, as I think to myself, "Did he really say that", I am just about to challenge Joe about his hurtful comment when he continues, "Noo 'av goat 'ma furst pal". The frown I had on my face disappears and I smile at Joe as he puts the Famous Five book back in the toy box.

An hour later Joe and I are in the middle of a game of Super Soccer or magnetic fitba' as he calls it. The score is 3-3 and I am on the attack when the bedroom door opens and in comes Mrs Kelly. "Woojy look at 'rese two", she declares, as she sees me and Joe playing. She inches closer and points to the players, "An howizzit thit they wee men ur able tae move by thersel'" she asks. "It's the magnets Mrs Kelly" I reply holding the stick with the magnet on the end high in the air. "The polarity on the stick magnet is opposite to the one on the base of the players and.........", Father interrupts "That's enough Rupert", he says, "I don't think Mrs Kelly is really that interested in the workings of your football game".

Mrs Kelly looks at me with a grin on her face and laughingly says, "Rupert, izzit?, sure hiv ah no been calling ra' boy Roger". I then look at Mrs Kelly and say "Robert". Mrs Kelly looks at me with a confused expression on her face, "I t'ought ye sed it wiz Rupert", she says. "My name *is* Rupert", I reply, "But you have been calling me Robert". Mrs Kelly thinks for a second then asks, "Who is 'dis Roger then?". Joe looks at me and shakes his head as he notices the grin on my face. He starts to stand up and asks "Ur we gon' noo Mammy,?" Mrs Kelly lunges forward and grabs Joe trying to help him up on his feet. "I'm okay mammy," Joe declares indignantly, while shrugging away poor Mrs Kelly's' attempt to help.

Mrs Kelly stands upright and clasps her thin boney hands together nervously. She looks at Mother and Father before stuttering "Oh, right, well ah'll eh, jist, eh, get ye in the hoose then Joe". She then rushes past Mother and Father and heads for our front door. At this point she looks as if she ready to cry, she stops suddenly at the door and takes a deep breath before saying " Ah wid like tae t'ank ye fer yer hospitality Mr and Mrs Nairn," she then looks at me and adds " An' you as well young Robert," before rushing away to her flat.

"Ah better go," Joe declares as he limps towards the hall, Mother and Father have headed back into the living room at this point, so I accompany Joe out the front door onto the landing, "Thanks Rupert, that wiz great fun ra day," Joe says, placing his hand on his front door, "I had a great time too," I reply as Joe pushes his front door. "Ahh ma dose" comes the scream from Joe's flat as Mrs Kelly appears from behind the door holding her nose. She must have been standing right behind the door listening to us talking. Joe shakes his head again and squeezes past Mrs Kelly and into the flat. She then nods at me with her hand still covering her sore nose and closes the door. As I enter my flat I can hear Joe moaning "Ye'll need tae stoap mollycoddlin' me Mammy" as I close the door with a smile on my face.

The next day, Sammy and I are sitting at the front of my close, deciding what to do with ourselves. It isn't raining for a change and the sun is shining now and again between the gaps in the clouds, I am thinking hard what we can do on a limited budget when Sammy stands up quickly and asks "Muchyegoatoanye?". For the first time in a while I didn't understand what he said. It sounded like the name of some obscure Russian town. "Pardon?" I reply. Sammy looks exasperated, takes a deep breath and repeats slowly, "How much money huv ye goat oan ye?". He then digs deep into his trouser pockets as I stand up and search my own pockets.

We pull out our worldly goods to check, I have two yellow elastic bands, one marble, two small green plastic soldiers, and a ha'penny, Sammy's haul includes, two Mojo's stuck together, one small snuff tin containing 'Shuggie' his pet caterpillar, that's been dead for two weeks but I haven't plucked up the courage to tell him yet, two marbles and a penny.

"Ach!" Sammy moans, "Ah wiz wanty go tae ra puttin' o'er Richmond Park", he continues, we then sit back down at the mouth of the close and after a moment I ask Sammy "How much are we short?". He immediately starts to count on the fingers of both hands for what seems like ages before answering "Aboot a shullin'". We both then sit back against the wall and think how we are going to come up with a shilling. "Av goat it", Sammy shouts excitedly, "What?", I ask in anticipation, " We'll rake ra midgies fur gingie's", Sammy says as he stands up and pulls me to my feet. We have done this before and it involves trawling through the rubbish bins looking for empty ginger bottles we can take to the shop and get money back. We searched every bin in Heron St the last time and came up with nothing. "We'll start 'it ra boatum a' ra street an work wur wye up, c'mon"he says, as we start to run down Heron St towards Dalmarnock Rd.

"Hoi' werjifink yoor gon?" Mrs McKay shouts as we arrive at her close and disappear inside. We sheepishly come back out the close to her ground floor window and I say quickly "We are playing one man hunt Mrs Mc Kay, please don't give us away". She shuffles her ample cleavage to get more comfortable on the window ledge and replies "Naw yer awrite Rupert son, ah'll no' tell embday", as she gestures with her head that we can proceed.

We reach the bins at the back and notice they are overflowing with rubbish. The smell is disgusting and as we get nearer we both hold our noses as we approach, Sammy moves over to a bin with what seems like a million flies hovering above it, the stench is now overpowering as he leans closer and puts his hand on the lid while still holding his nose with his other hand, I am standing right behind him when he looks at me and starts a countdown "Three..Two..Wan," he then quickly lifts the lid "Aarghhh", we both scream, as a big black cat leaps out of the bin and over our shoulders, knocking us both over onto our backsides.

"Whit je let it oot fur?," a voice asks disappointedly, as I look up into the sun in the direction of this mysterious voice. I can see a silhouette of a boy that looks like Humpty Dumpty standing on top of the wall separating the back courts. As the sun disappears behind a cloud I can now clearly make out that he is about 12 years old but still in grey short trousers that are far too small for him and grip his flabby legs like a second skin. They are held up with a pair of fully extended braces over his stained blue shirt which was half in and half out of his trousers. I can't see his waist for his fat belly and his socks are down at his ankles, his shoes are filthy and the sole

has separated from the upper at the front, like two mouths open and his toes being the tongue. "It took me ages tae get 'rat cat in 'rer," he continues while walking along the wall towards us, I can now also clearly see his dirty round face with bright red cheeks barely visible below a mop of black curly hair. He sits down on the wall right above us before asking "Haud oan, yoos two urny looking fur gingie's ur ye?" Sammy and I get back on our feet and Sammy answers "Aye we ur," as he puts the lid back on the bin, "Yer wastin' yer time," Humpty says, "Av looked in 'orra bins in Heron St 'ris mornin'". He then stands back up on the wall as Sammy asks "Did ye get any gingie's?" Humpty starts to walk away as he replies,
"Na', 'ra nearest a goat wiz a Ferguzade boatle wi' nae label ful' a drippin'". Sammy and I watch Humpty as he nimbly walks along the Booly wall looking into the backcourts for anyone putting out rubbish.

"Well 'ats rat ren," Sammy proclaims, "That's that right enough," I concur. "Kin ye hear that?", Sammy asks as we prepare to leave Mrs McKay's backcourt, "Hear what?", I reply. "Shh, listen", Sammy continues. We both listen intently and after a few seconds I can clearly hear a girls voice singing, "Its comin' fae the next back", Sammy exclaims, as he starts to climb the wall containing the bins.

After we climb the wall we walk towards the next backcourt, we look down and there standing in the middle of the backcourt is a slim girl about the same age as Wilhelmina. She is wearing a black head scarf with a grey shawl covering her shoulders. her long black dress is nearly touching the muddy grass hiding her flat black shoes. She looks and dresses a lot older than her years, leading Sammy to ask "Is she wearing her grannies' clae's?". Before I can say anything the girl starts singing at the top of her voice, "*Speed bonny boat, like a bird on the wing......*". She has the voice of an angel and before long everybody is hanging out their window's listening to her. "*...carry the lad that's born to be king....*", she continues, Sammy and I watch and listen totally spellbound and intrigued. After she finishes the song everybody claps and whistles for a few seconds then disappear back inside their flats, but the girl just stands there motionless. One by one people come back to their windows and start throwing coins down towards her.

After the girl has picked up all the coins she walks over to the close. Standing there out of sight of the paying customers is a woman carrying a baby. She is dressed similar to the girl in all dark clothes with the baby inside a grey shawl. She collects the coins from the girl and kisses her on the head for a job well done as they make their way through the close towards the street.

Sammy and I climb down from the wall into the muddy backcourt, "Dae ye know any songs right through?" Sammy asks excitedly, "Not really", I reply, "Do you?" I retort. "Nah! Jist ten green boatles ur Happy Burthday", he replies, we agree that singing isn't going to accomplish the task of raising a shilling for the putting and decide to head back to my close to rethink our strategy.

We arrive just in time to meet Joe approaching the close carrying a bottle of Irn-Bru, "Hello Joe," I say cheerfully "O'rite Joe?" Sammy adds, "Hi Rupert...Sammy" Joe replies, "Ah wiz it ra shoap fur ma' Ma 'rer" he adds. "At's ra furst time 'av been tae ra shoap ma'sel," he says proudly with a look of satisfaction on his face "That's brilliant Joe", I say, "Aye, well done" Sammy adds. "Are you coming out to play?" I ask, "Kin ye haud oan a minute tae ah take 'ris boatle a' ginger up the stair an ah'll ask ma' Ma" Joe replies, before adding, "Dae ye want sum ginger?", "Yes please" I reply. Joe unscrews the lid of the Irn-Bru and hands it to me, "Ah kin only gie ye a toaty tate" he says apologetically, "Kin ah get a toaty tate tae?" Sammy asks as I take a mouthful of Irn-Bru, "Aye" Joe says as he hands the bottle to Sammy who gulps the Irn-Bru as if he hadn't had a drink in weeks. "Woa 'rer" Joe shouts as he grabs the bottle from Sammy's lips causing him to spill some ginger down his t-shirt. "Jeezo Sammy, ye put mer in 'ran ye took oot 'rer" Joe exclaims as we start laughing.

Sammy and I follow Joe as he slowly makes his way up the uneven stairs swinging his bad leg out and up one stair at a time, Sammy decides to rib Joe and says sarcastically "Fur God's sake Joe, it'll be time fur bed by ra time we get tae yoor hoose". Joe starts giggling as he tries to speed up with me and Sammy helping him. We reach Joe's flat and are still giggling just as Mrs Kelly opens the door, "Bejesus it's ra three musketeers" she jokingly proclaims. "'Am Porthos," Sammy shouts as he punches the air with a pretend sword, "I'm Aramis," I say punching the air also. We then turn to look at Joe waiting for him to join us as we pose with our hands in the air with pretend swords "Am, eh, am eh, oh! 'Am Spartacus," Joe shouts as he punches the air and bursts into hysterical laughter.

After a while we have stopped laughing long enough to ask Mrs Kelly if Joe can come out to play. There is a long pause as Mrs Kelly first looks at Joe, who has his best petted lip expression on his face, then Sammy, who is jumping up and down without actually moving and telepathically pleading "*Say yes*" and finally she looks at me as I subconsciously lean towards her slightly nodding my head with my eyes opened wide and an expectant expression on my face. She finally breaks the silence by saying "Ok". Sammy jumps in the air shouting "Yes", and I nearly fall into Mrs Kelly shouting "Yippee", as Joe just turns and says quietly "Thanks Mammy".

Sammy and I turn and run towards the stairs before we realise we have forgotten Joe, who is manfully trying to catch up with us. We turn back and help Joe down the stairs. Just as we are nearly at the entrance of the close we hear the dulcet tones of Mrs Kelly shouting "Jist play in da street now, ah'll be watching fae ra windae," as we head outside leaving the darkness of the close and into the brightness of the now bustling street.

"Jist da street now," Mrs Kelly reiterates from her first floor window. She must have run across her single end flat like Lachie Stewart to reach her window that quick, I thought to myself.

We are just about to sit down at the mouth of the close when I hear someone shout "Haw! Lord Snooty". I slowly turn round, and there walking towards us is the McCabe twins with four of their friends. "Aw naw" Sammy exclaims. "Whit's up?" Joe asks. We quickly fill Joe in on the earlier ball incident, "He disnae look very happy" Joe observes, looking over my shoulder. I slowly turn round again and the McCabe gang are about two closes away casually walking towards us,"Whits 'rat he's cerryin?'" Sammy asks. As I look closer I notice that Jamie McCabe is carrying a tennis racket. He is pointing it in my direction and making it clear that my head is going to be used as the ball.

When the McCabe's and their posse are about ten feet away from us, I turn away and shut my eyes and await the inevitable. I can hear Sammy gulp as I am pushed in the back with the racket and I screw up my face waiting on the impending pain, "Ah told ye, ye wur gonny get it, d'inta?" I can hear Jamie growl, my shoulders are now up at my ears and my legs are shaking.

"Ye o'rite rer lads?", Mrs Kelly asks from her first floor window. The McCabe's stare at all three of us in turn to let us know that any answer other than an affirmative would result in us being beaten up, "Fine Mammy" Joe says first followed by Sammy nervously responding "Great Mrs Kelly". After another prod in the back with the tennis racket I groan through clenched teeth "Smashing, Mrs Kelly" before returning my gaze to the ground "Whityeez o'daen, wid yeez be playin' a game?", Mrs Kelly enquires in her thick Irish brogue. Jamie takes a step back from us and looks up at Mrs Kelly, "Aye, we're gonny play a gemme o' rounder's Mrs.." Jamie answers with an evil grin on his face. Mrs Kelly accepts this explanation and goes back inside her flat leaving us at the mercy of the McCabe's.

"Rite yooz, 'ris is whit wur gonny dae" Jamie growls, "We'll play yeez a gemme o' rounders. If we win, yeez need tae buy us a new ba'. If yooz win...." he pauses for a moment and stares right at us before continuing "We'll no' gie yeez a doin'". This last statement is met by sarcastic laughter from the rest of the McCabe gang as they point at Joe's bad leg and a nervous silence from us.

With no option but to accept Jamie's offer we reluctantly agree. The McCabe's decide they will mark out the arena for our contest on the street, and all we have to do now is find another three people to make up our team. "Who are we going to ask to join our team?" I ask Sammy and Joe. After a short silence Joe shrugs his shoulders and replies, "Ah don't know e'mbday bit yooz two". We both turn to look at Sammy and he notices our anxiety as he screws up his face and thinks long and hard. After about thirty seconds he smiles broadly and shouts "Av goat it".... Ah'll be back in five minutes" before turning and running up Heron St towards Bernard St.

With Sammy away on his mission to recruit three new team members for our rounders challenge match, Joe and I are watching the McCabe's and their gang marking circles on the road and pavements with a piece of old slate, "There *is* one more small problem", I inform Joe as we both look at the McCabe's, "Whit's that?" Joe asks, as he stares blankly at the nearly finished arena. I look at my feet and mumble "I don't know how to play rounders". Joe slowly turns to face me with a look of disbelief on his face before repeating my words back to me in a high pitched screech *"Ye don't know how tae play rounders?"*. I notice the McCabe's and their cronies stop what they are doing on hearing Joe's pronouncement, then in unison they start howling with laughter. After a few seconds they return to marking the arena while Jamie McCabe smirks and declares "'Ris is gonny be a doddle".

Joe proceeds to give me a crash course on the rules of rounders. I have seen rounders being played on our street before but as I was never asked to take part I never payed much attention to it. As far as I can gather from Joe's brief description it is a bit like American baseball. There are four circles drawn in a diamond shape. Two down the centre of the road about forty feet apart. One on each pavement approximately half way between the circles on the road. This creates the diamond shape. The batsman stands in one of the circles on the road and the ball is thrown underhand from the bowler who is positioned in the middle of all the circles. He is trying to land the ball inside the circle that the batsman is standing in, and he/she has to bat the ball away. If they miss, and the ball lands inside the circle they are out. If they miss the ball but the ball lands outside the circle they have another two chances to bat.

If the batsman manages to bat the ball, they then have to run around all the circles in an anti- clockwise direction until they get back to where they started. If however, the other team manage to retrieve the ball quickly and hit the circle the batsman is running towards before he/she reaches it, they are out. Whichever team achieves the most complete runs before they are all out, wins.

I am still trying to digest this information when I turn around and notice Sammy coming down the street with our new teammates. My heart sinks when I see he is accompanied by his cousins the Murray twins Debbie and Daphne. "Who's that?" asks Joe. I explain to Joe that Debbie and Daphne are identical twins who live in Bernard St and are related to Sammy.

"Identical?" Joe asks with a puzzled look on his face. The reason for the quizzical expression is because, although they are indeed 12 year old twins, Daphne is about three stone heavier and six inches taller than Debbie, who is as thin as a rake.

Daphne is also very loud and has arms bigger than my Father. She is definitely not someone I would like to argue with. Debbie, on the other hand, is extremely timid and nervous and wears NHS prescription round glasses that don't fit properly and keep sliding down her nose. Despite the obvious difference in their appearance they dress exactly the same, and on this occasion it was navy blue pinafore dresses with white socks and blue plastic sandals; their pigtailed hair decorated with matching blue ribbons. I warn Joe not to mention the obvious differences in their appearance within earshot of Daphne, who insists the *only* difference between her and her sister is that Debbie wears glasses. Until now I haven't seen or heard of anyone who has been brave enough to disagree.

"Ye o'rite 'rer Rupert?" Daphne growls as she approaches us, "Er, hello Rupert" whispers Debbie, "Hello" I reply, "This is Joe", I continue as I nod in Joe's direction. With the introductions over I am about to point out to Sammy that we are still a man down for our team when I hear a voice say "Hi Rupert", I look down between Daphne and Debbie just as wee Tommy Ingles pushes his way through the girls. Wee Tommy is 10 years old but looks about 7. He just hasn't grown at all since I moved to Heron St nearly three years ago. He lives in wee Heron St above Walter's shop with his Grandmother or as he calls her "Ma' Grandy".

I stare at Sammy after looking at our team and he just shrugs his shoulders as if to say "*It's 'ra best ah could dae*". Meanwhile the McCabe's and their gang are across the road pointing and laughing at us as they obviously think they will win easily, and after looking again at our team I would find it difficult to argue with them.

Ra' big gemme a' rounders

"Heeds ur tails", Jamie asks Sammy as he tosses a halfpenny in the air. "Heeds", Sammy responds. The halfpenny lands on the road and Jamie steps on it, just in case it rolls into one of the overflowing drains and as he lifts his foot it reveals a "Tails". Jamie triumphantly returns to his gang punching the air as if he had just scored a goal for Scotland. After a short deliberation with his cohorts, he turns to us and informs us they will bat first.

Jamie takes up a position in the circle drawn on the road, his pals' line up behind him waiting on their turn to bat. He starts to swing the grubby tennis racket with hardly any strings from side to side in preparation. Meanwhile, Sammy has been elected captain of our team and decides he will bowl. He then positions the rest of us at various points along the street to try and catch the ball after Jamie has batted. " Where's ra' ba'?" Sammy asks, standing in the centre of the diamond with his arms outstretched, "Here, catch", shouts one of the McCabe gang as he tosses an old, threadbare tennis ball at Sammy. Sammy steps back and tries to catch it, but misses and falls over onto his posterior much to the delight of the McCabe gang who are laughing at Sammy's misfortune, "He couldnae catch a cauld", John McCabe quips, "We're gonny skoosh 'ris gemme", Jamie adds.

Sammy regains his composure and prepares to throw the first ball as I notice that we now have an audience. There are people leaning out their open windows all along the street, including Mrs Kelly, Mrs Campbell and Mrs McCabe, I look up to my window and can see the curtains moving as Mother and Father try to watch without being seen by anyone.

All along Heron St there are groups of adults and children standing at close mouths and sitting on the kerbs in anticipation of this game of rounders.

Sammy throws the first ball up the air towards Jamie and you can feel all the eyes of the street following the airborne ball in complete silence. Then Jamie swings and blasts the weakly delivered ball down the street towards Joe. Poor Joe makes a feeble attempt to catch it as it flies past him, he turns and chases the ball as fast as he can, limping and hopping after it. Eventually he stops the ball, but by this time Jamie has ran around all the circles and is standing laughing and celebrating with his cronies. Joe dejectedly throws the ball back to Sammy and then looks up at Mrs Kelly, who looks as if she is about to burst into tears. Joe limps back to his original position as Mrs Kelly can't hold back any longer and shouts "C'mon Joe". This is followed by Mrs Campbell shouting "C'mon wee man, get right intae them", Joe visibly straightens his posture after hearing these shouts of support. The McCabe's, on the other hand are not amused as John McCabe gets ready to bat.

Sammy decides to move Joe over to the opposite side of the street and replace him with Daphne. He then turns and throws the ball towards John McCabe, he swings his bat and thumps the ball down the street ,again towards Joe. He then starts laughing and pointing at poor Joe's efforts to stop the ball as he nonchalantly jogs around all the circles laughing sarcastically as he steps in each one, until finally walking back to his pals celebrating. The ball whizzes past Joe and I run after it, motioning towards Joe to stay where he is. This theme continues as Daphne, Debbie, weeTommy and I, become virtual spectators as the McCabe gang deliberately target Joe as the weakest link in our team. As the final member of the McCabe gang, big Malky, steps up to bat we are five runs down, I walk over to Sammy and whisper in his ear. Sammy then hands me the ball to bowl, and he takes up my old position halfway down the street.

By this time Mrs Kelly has come down to the front of the close for a better view along with Mrs Campbell, and standing just inside the close I can see Mother and Father. As I look at big Malky he is smiling confidently, waving the bat like a caveman with a club. I look round at my teammates who are poised and ready for action, except for Debbie who is cleaning her glasses with the hem of her dress.

I turn back and throw the ball up in the air towards big Malky, who takes a step back and smashes a forehand as hard as he can. This time however, the ball shoots off to the right high in the air and just misses old Mr Crawford who is watching from his second storey window at number 41. The ball hits the drainpipe next to his window and falls to earth like a brick before hitting Mrs Gaffney's window ledge on the first floor and bouncing outwards straight towards Debbie. She stands with her arms in the air trying to follow the trajectory of the ball while pushing her glasses up her nose every two seconds. Finally she decides that she isn't going to catch the ball using her hands so she grabs her pinafore with both hands at the hemline and to our astonishment she catches the ball with her dress before gently picking the ball out with her hands and triumphantly holding it up in the air.

"Yer oot, ya big fat bastart'", shouts Mrs Campbell pointing at big Malky, who is absolutely livid and smashes the racket face down in the street before turning to face the wrath of his pals. "Ya big diddy", Jamie shouts, "Whit wiz 'rat ya tadger?", John asks, as we all run to Debbie to congratulate her. Mrs Kelly is now jumping up and down with Mrs Campbell, and cheering can be heard all along the street from our ever expanding audience.

After things settle down a bit it is our turn to bat. All we have to do now is get six runs, a fact not lost on Jamie McCabe as he takes up his position to bowl, "C'mon lads", he shouts with his clenched fist waving in the direction of his team, "We'll stull skoosh 'ris gemme", he adds, "Whits hopalong an' 'ra incredible hulk gonny dae, eh!", he continues, smirking at his pals. This is obviously a reference to Joe and Daphne, but is also heard by Mrs Kelly who tries to make a dash towards Jamie while shouting " Ah'll gie' ye hopalong ya wee bastart'". Luckily for Jamie she is restrained by Mrs Campbell's arm around her neck who consoles her with the statement,

"Leave it 'ra noo Mrs Kelly, 'rat wee shite's two days 'aulder 'ran corn mutton". Mrs Kelly stops immediately and stares at Mrs Campbell with a confused expression on her face and slowly repeats back the last part of her sentence "Two days aulder 'ran...whit?", "Ach never mind", Mrs Campbell retorts, obviously realising that, just like me, Mrs Kelly hasn't a clue what she means.

Mrs Campbell has lots of sayings like that, but I am convinced only *she* knows what they mean. Like the time she was talking to Mother about a neighbour and she spouts "See 'rat wummin, she's as common as a shebeen in 'ra Gorbals". Or the time she found a penny in the close as I walked past and held it up saying something like "Many a machle makes a muckle", before putting the penny in the pocket of her apron.

To my surprise, Mother and Father have now come outside the close and are standing with Mrs Kelly and Mrs Campbell. Father has his unlit pipe in his mouth, which he uses now and again to point with as he explains to Mother the finer points of rounders. We are standing discussing the team batting order when Joe asks "Whit did you whisper tae Sammy 'afore ye bowled 'rat last baw?". I explain to Joe I told Sammy that at my old school in the West end I used to play cricket and knew a bit about spin bowling, which is why the ball shot up in the air when big Malky hit it instead of heading towards Dalmarnock Rd. What I didn't tell him was that I used to play tennis there as well.

"Right Rupert", Sammy says in his most commanding voice, "You furst, 'ren me, 'ren Tommy, Daphne, Debbie and Joe". As we line up in the agreed order I am standing inside the chalk circle with the bat in my hand ready to start, I look at Jamie who is doing all these stretching exercises with the ball in his hand, finally he looks at me and growls, "Ye ready bawheid?", I nod my head, and he lobs the ball in my direction. I turn sideways and open my stance then I swing through the ball sending it soaring into the grey, cloudy sky. "Wow", I can hear Sammy exclaim, as I set off running around the circles.

Jamie and John McCabe are standing open mouthed watching the ball as it falls to earth halfway down the street, "Get 'ra baw Malky", they shout in unison as poor Malky realises he is the nearest one to the ball. "Ah'll get it", he shouts belatedly, as he starts to run down the street holding up his trousers that are a couple of sizes too big. Just as he nears the now settled ball, disaster strikes. He trips on his shoelace and hurtles head first into a large filthy puddle. Unable to put out his hands to protect himself because of his trouser predicament, he lies there on his belly like a performing seal waiting on his fish treat for doing a trick. Jamie turns to the skies and shouts "O' fur fu...". Before he can finish his profane sentence, Mrs McCabe shouts from her window "JAMIE!, watch yer bloody language ya wee bastart". The whole street bursts out laughing at Mrs McCabe's warped logic, and much to John McCabe's annoyance, I am giggling myself as I safely arrive back into the arms of my celebrating teammates.

By this time big Malky is sheepishly walking back towards us with his head bowed and his eyes fixed on the ground with one hand still holding up his sodden trousers. "Geez 'ra baw ya diddy", John McCabe shouts at Malky, who throws the ball in the general direction of John without lifting his head. Meanwhile, Mrs Campbell is cackling with laughter while pointing at Malky. Mother is stifling her laughter while trying to look serious and Father is back inside the close with Mrs Kelly and they are both laughing out loud. Mrs Campbell stops laughing long enough to announce in a loud voice, "Ah've no' laughed so much since 'rat man o' mine sneezed, rifted and farted at 'ra same time in front a' 'ra Provvie man".

Sammy has now taken up his position to bat and does a couple of impressive practice swings which doesn't impress the still raging Jamie Mc Cabe who grunts at Sammy, "You've nae chance o' hittin' 'ris ba' ya bamstick". Sammy ignores Jamie and assumes the batting position with a look of determination etched across his face. This just annoys Jamie even more and he throws the ball right at Sammy's head, causing him to duck his head quickly to avoid the possibility of losing an eye, "Ooops", Jamie says sarcastically as the ball is returned to him. This time he bowls properly and Sammy swings and smashes the ball straight at Jamie's head. Jamie ducks and falls to the ground as the ball flies down Heron St being chased forlornly by John. Meanwhile Sammy is scampering around the circles with the applause of our expanding audience ringing in his ears.

A triumphant Sammy completes his circuit and we are waiting to celebrate with him. Mrs Kelly and Mrs Campbell have linked arms and are dancing a jig on the pavement outside my close, and the rest of the street are shouting and clapping their approval. The patrons of the Dog Leg pub on the corner of Heron St and Wee Heron St have come outside and are standing cheering while holding their drinks aloft. Two policemen on the beat have stopped about ten yards from Mother and Father to see what all the fuss is about. The police presence causes us to lose some dubious members of our audience as a few windows are closed immediately when it becomes clear they are stopping to watch the latter stages of our grudge game of rounders.

A short time later, Daphne, Debbie and Wee Tommy have eventually managed to hit the ball, *just*, and are dotted around on circles one, two and three. Much to the delight of the McCabe twins and their gang, this just leaves wee Joe standing between them and victory, the only way we can still win is if Joe can hit the ball far enough down the street to allow enough time for the rest of our team, including Joe, to complete their trip around all the circles.

As Joe limps up to bat the McCabe twins are already celebrating, laughing and sniggering as they point at Joe. Having seen everyone else have a practice swing Joe decides to do the same, but as he swings the bat a combination of his momentum and his club foot make him fall over. The McCabe gang burst out laughing, Mrs Kelly lets out a yell of "Joe" and dashes towards her son. Joe vigorously motions '*NO*' at her with his head and an extremely worried Mrs Kelly returns to the close and is comforted by Mrs Campbell, Mother and Father. Sammy and I help Joe up to his feet, "Are you okay Joe", I ask. Joe regains his composure and replies "I'm fine". Sammy then adds "Jist take yer time an' dae yer best Joe". Joe nods and we go back to our positions. Jamie McCabe is now standing ready to throw the ball and the rest of the McCabe gang have all moved closer to Joe, obviously expecting a weak hit from Joe. "Ur ye ready hopalong?", Jamie sneers at Joe as he gets ready to throw the ball. Joe's face can't hide his anger at Jamie as he assumes the batting position and to our surprise he responds through gritted teeth "Aye, am ready, go for it".

The whole street is now willing Joe to hit the ball. The two policemen are now standing watching intently. Mrs Kelly has turned her back and has her apron up at her mouth. Mrs Campbell, Mother and Father are standing at her side with Fathers pipe now lit. The men from the Dog Leg pub are gathered outside the pub with their beer and offering various shouts of "C'mon wee man", and "Ye kin dae it son".

There is a bus stopped at the bottom of the street on its way to the garage with the driver and conductress now standing at the front of the bus watching in eager anticipation. Even the dubious members of our audience have returned to their windows in spite of the police presence.

As Jamie throws the ball at Joe, there is an expectant mass intake of breath as the ball heads towards Joe who swings feebly and misses. A disappointed "Awww", is the collective reaction of the audience. "Yes", shouts the lone voice of John McCabe, but to his dismay the ball flies past the circle Joe is standing in, meaning Joe has another chance, "Ye wur lucky 'rer", Jamie taunts as he gets ready to throw again. Joe steadies himself again and stares right at Jamie before responding "It's no ma' fault yer rubbish at throwing". This response takes Jamie by surprise as he collects himself and mutters "Ya cheeky wee shite, ah'll show ye". He then proceeds to throw the ball a bit harder than the last time, Joe waits then swings as hard as he can without falling down, and misses. Again the collective "Awww", can be clearly heard, because Jamie threw the ball harder this time it was nowhere near the circle and now leaves Joe with one last chance to hit the ball.

Sammy and I are standing surveying the scene at this point. Big Malky is chatting up Daphne as she stands waiting in her circle. Debbie has sat down in her circle and is playing with two sticks having an imaginary conversation between them. Wee Tommy Ingles is walking around the perimeter of his circle as if it's a tightrope with his arms outstretched for balance. I look over at Mrs Kelly who is looking for some divine intervention as she faces the wall and repeats the words "Oh Jesus, Mary and Joseph". After we have taken in our surroundings Sammy looks at me and asks "How much is a Reggy 5?"

John McCabe shouts at his brother "Stoap fartin' aboot an' throw ra' ba' right". Jamie nods and prepares to throw. Joe adopts his batting stance once more and waits on the now deadly serious Jamie to pitch the ball towards him. You can hear a pin drop as everyone nervously waits. Rather than throw the ball at Joe, Jamie elects to lob the ball in the air making sure that if Joe misses this time the ball will land in the circle and Joe will be out. We all follow the path of the ball as it starts its descent towards Joe, who adjusts his position slightly in readiness to swing. As the ball drops to about head height Joe steps back again and swings the bat towards the ball. We all hold our breath as the bat just catches the ball on the wooden rim, which takes all the pace out of it, and it lands about two yards away and rolls towards the pavement next to the two policemen. "Aw Naw!", Sammy and wee Tommy cry in unison followed by a loud "Yes", by the McCabe twins. Collective "Aw naw's" and "Poor wee soul" comments, can be heard from all corners of Heron St. Daphne, Debbie and wee Tommy haven't moved from their circles because the ball is only a couple yards away.

We all watch as Jamie meanders over to collect it laughing out loud with his fist in the air celebrating his triumph. Joe is bent over leaning on the bat in despair and there is a look of disappointment on the faces of Mrs Kelly and Mrs Campbell. The ball at this point has settled at the feet of the policemen as Jamie leans over to pick it up and finish the game.

But as Jamie bends over to pick up the ball the older policemen stands on it. Jamie hesitates and looks tentatively at the policeman who then back heels the ball to his younger colleague before to turning to us and shouting, "Are you lot not meant to be running?". Jamie is trying to get past the policeman to get the ball but the older policeman is deliberately shifting his body in front of him while offering a fake apology. By this time Daphne, Debbie and wee Tommy have realised what is happening and start to run. Joe also drops the bat and starts to run swinging his bad leg out in a semi circle and hopping as fast as he can, he is now being cheered by our rejuvenated audience, Jamie meanwhile is franticly trying to get past the older policemen and shouts for help from his brother. John races over as Daphne arrives home to a cheer from the crowd. Joe meanwhile has reached the first circle where Mrs Kelly runs with him and tries to kiss him on the head while shouting "Come on Joe", as he heads for the second circle.

John manages to get round the older policeman only to see the younger policeman kick the ball full force down the street towards Dalmarnock Road which brings cheers from all corners of Heron St. "Get 'rat baw ya big diddy", John shouts to Malky who is standing cheering Daphne's arrival. Malky sets off after the ball clutching his trousers so they don't fall down, followed by the McCabe twins who are now turning the air blue with their profanities. They run past Malky shouting at him to go back to the home circle in readiness to catch the ball and get Joe out. Malky duly obliges and runs back. Meanwhile Debbie and wee Tommy have arrived home and are standing with Sammy and I cheering on Joe as he manfully hops towards circle two. His face has now lit up and he is smiling broadly as we all shout "C'mon Joe".

Malky is crouched at the home circle waiting on the ball as Joe approaches the third circle. He has to slow down to get his bad leg up on the pavement and is now looking very tired. The ball has stopped rolling at this point just in front of the bus that is parked at the bottom of Heron St and the McCabe twins are about twenty feet away. Joe has the screaming crowd willing him on as he nears the third circle but he catches his trailing foot on the pavement and falls to the ground. There is a huge groan from the assembled masses and Mrs Kelly is back eating her apron as Joe slowly picks himself up, Sammy and I run over to Joe to help. "Yer no' allowed tae help him", shouts Mrs McCabe from her window making it clear who's side she was on. Joe stands in the third circle and looks at the home circle ten yards away. He takes a deep breath and sets off . Sammy and I run at his side shouting words of encouragement. Meanwhile Jamie and John have reached the ball which has somehow landed under the bus as the driver and clippie unconvincingly deny all knowledge as to how it got there.

"GOT IT", shouts John as he appears from under the bus with the ball. "Geez it quick tae ah throw it tae Malky", orders Jamie. John does as he is told and Jamie launches a perfect throw towards Malky. Joe by this time is extremely tired and is trying to run as quick as can. His big heavy boot is swung out and in as he hops towards the home circle with the noise of the crowd ringing in his ears he is about three yards away as the ball heads toward Malky. Joe looks at the home circle now about two yards away, sweat is pouring from his forehead and his eyes are wide with excitement and determination as he hops along with his tongue hanging out the side of his mouth. The crowds of people, including the policemen, are shouting "C'mon Joe", as he stretches every muscle trying to reach home. The men from the pub have moved closer and are bellowing in unison "Gon yersel' wee man". Mrs Kelly is shouting "C'mon son". Malky looks at Joe and a smile starts to appear on his face as he puts his hands up for the easy catch that will finish this game. On seeing this, the excitement leaves an exhausted Joe's face, as he realises he isn't going to make it, and is replaced by a forlorn expression.

Mrs Kelly's apron is now over her head. Mrs Campbell and Mother are holding on to each other as Fathers pipe falls to the ground from his wide opened mouth. Sammy and I have also stopped shouting as we watch Malky about to make a catch that any two year old would make, but to our amazement Malky once again looks at Joe and winks as he deliberately drops the ball theatrically knocking it to the side. Joe's face lights up again as he steps onto the home circle to the cheers of the crowd. We all rush around him jumping up and down. Sammy and I, Daphne Debbie and somewhere in the middle wee Tommy Ingles all jump with delight as the two policemen come over to join in and ruffle Joe's hair. Mrs Kelly is now dancing a jig with Father as Mother and Mrs Campbell link arms and dance in circles. I look up just in time to see Mrs McCabe slamming her window shut in disgust just as her boys make their way towards Malky shouting abuse " Ya big diddy", Jamie shouts. "Ya big fat waste a' space", John adds, but their abusive shouts are drowned out by the men from the pub still shouting "Gon yersel' wee man" and "Gon ya dancer". Even the bus driver is tooting his horn as he passes by on his way to the garage.

When Jamie and John reach Malky they are still shouting abuse when out of the blue big Malky points his finger at the McCabe's and shouts "SHUT IT YOOS TWO". The McCabe's freeze as they stare at Malky. They think better of challenging him and duly oblige as they rather sheepishly head for their close mumbling under their breath about not playing with him again and something not being fair.

Sammy and I try feebly to lift Joe on to our shoulders but we are too weak, "Here let me dae it", Daphne growls as she pushes her way towards Joe. "Ah whit ra' hell", big Malky adds as he moves amongst the throng to help Daphne. The both of them effortlessly lift Joe onto their shoulders and Joe smiles the broadest smile I have ever seen as he waves to the crowd. Mrs Kelly's tearful face beams with a mixture of pride and trepidation as they carry a precariously balanced Joe towards our close with the cheers of the crowd still ringing around Heron St.

As the dust settles Malky and Daphne head towards Bernard St playfully pushing each other as they walk past the Dog Leg. Debbie and wee Tommy are a few yards behind them excitedly reliving every moment of our successful game of rounders by hitting imaginary balls with imaginary bats. A still beaming Mrs Kelly, Mother, Father and Mrs Campbell are huddled together all talking at the same time about the events they have just witnessed.

Sammy, Joe and I, sit down at the mouth of the close still smiling at our achievement as I notice Wilhelmina approaching the close from Dalmarnock Rd. She is walking slowly towards us with her head looking down at the pavement as she kicks a stone towards the road. "O'rite Wilhelmina", Sammy asks as she reaches the close. Wilhelmina doesn't even acknowledge Sammy as she sighs and walks past us and into the close, "Are you okay Wilhelmina?", a worried Mother asks as she passes, after a short pause Wilhelmina lifts her head and snaps " No, I'm not okay". Like a spoilt 5 year old she adds, " I hate this place", as she marches inside the close, before adding "Nothing exciting ever happens in this street". There is a moments silence as we all look at each other before bursting out laughing, hearing this outburst of laughter Wilhelmina pauses on the first stair and looks back at us with a confused look on her face before uttering a frustrated "Ohhhgh", as she stomps up the stairs.

A few minutes pass when Mrs Kelly announces loudly "To be sure, I won't betakin' no for an answer". As she starts to make her way inside the close she adds "Dat's it settled", in an even louder voice with her hand raised in the air just to reiterate her original point. She is followed up the stairs by Mrs Campbell who shouts "Don't you bo'rer yer erse Mrs Kelly, ah'll be rer wi' ma man". After recovering his now broken pipe from a puddle on the pavement Father also makes his way into the close as he tries half heartedly to join the two pieces of his broken pipe together, "Right –eee-ohh, I will see you lads later", he declares while pointing at us with a bit of his broken pipe before once again trying to miraculously bring the two pieces together again.

Sammy stands up and after saying "See yeez later" to Joe and I he starts to walk towards his close. I am helping Joe to his feet as Mother approaches us with a concerned look on her face. "What did Mrs Kelly mean when she said that's it settled then?" I ask as Joe stands beside me, "Well", my slightly worried looking Mother begins to answer. After a long pause her face now has a " How did that happen" expression as she continues, "We have been invited to a Halloween party at Mrs Kelly's tomorrow", before she slowly walks up the close towards the stairs in a trance like state. I am still trying to understand the reason for Mother's trepidation as Joe lets out a cry of "Yes" as he as he jumps for joy without actually leaving the ground.

"Whit ur ye gonny dress up izz?" Joe asks. It's only then I begin to understand Mother's anxiety because in the two years we have lived in Heron St we have never been invited to any social occasion by any of our neighbours, never mind a Halloween party.

The last Halloween party I attended was on the 28th October 1966. It was a charity event hosted by Father's work. I can remember clearly I was dressed in a tuxedo as a miniature James Bond and Wilhelmina was dressed as a flapper girl from the 1920's with lots of beads and feathers I can also remember Mother and Father coming down the stairs as we waited on our taxi. They were dressed as Robin Hood and Maid Marion. Father was all in green, with tights, a hat and a bow and arrow. Mother wore a long purple dress with a large thick gold necklace and a pointy hat with lilac chiffon falling from the tip of the hat over her shoulder and down over her arms. When the taxi arrived Father took Mother by the hand and bowed while saying in his best Robin Hood voice "Your carriage awaits m' lady". Mother nodded at him before answering "Well thank you kind sir" as we approached the bemused taxi driver who was holding open the door.

As Mother tried to get in the taxi she knocked her hat off. Father rushed over to help but only succeeded in tripping on his longbow before falling into Mother and pushing her head long inside the taxi and landing on top of her. As he tried to free himself, the longbow and satchel holding the arrows got caught in Mothers pointy hat and the more he struggled to free her the more he was strangling her. With every tug from Father, Mother's head was jerking forward causing her heavily hair sprayed hair to loosen and fall over her face. Father continued pulling her about like a ventriloquist's dummy until Mother's tenement upbringing surfaced and she yelled "Fur Christ's sake Hubert yer chokin'me".

Wilhelmina, the taxi driver and me couldn't control our laughter any longer, and much to Mothers chagrin we burst into hysterical laughter. When Father eventually freed himself he was wearing Mothers hat round his neck along with his longbow, and Mother had a satchel of arrows around her neck which was stuck fast to her gold necklace.

After ten minutes of frenzied activity Mother regained her composure and we were all sitting in our seats ready to go when the cabby asked "Right, where ur we offtay 'ren?". Father looked at Mother who in turn stared back at Father before snapping, "You have the invitations". Father coughed nervously while trying to find the invitations in the satchel of arrows as the taxi driver pulled away from our house. "Ahah!" Father proclaimed as he proudly held the invitations aloft. "Where we offtay 'ren Robin?", the taxi driver asked sarcastically, "its no 'ra Sherwood Hotel izzit?" he added while giggling like a schoolboy. Father paused as he read the invitations before uttering "Oh dear". Mother was getting more irritated by the minute before she eventually snapped "Well, tell the man where we are going or we'll be late". Father slowly looked at us all one at a time "I don't think we will be late dear" he mumbled under his breath. "What did you say?", Mother asked. He stared at the floor before lifting his head and sheepishly announcing "It's not till tomorrow night". I will never forget the look on Mother's face that night as we turned around and headed home.

"Well, whit ye gonny get dressed up izz?" Joe asks again. "I don't really know" I reply. "Ach it disnae matter cause it'll be a great party onyway" Joe concludes before we say our goodbye's and head up the stairs.

Hallo'een at 'ra Kelly's

"NUTS!" Father exclaims as we stop dead in our tracks at the bus stop outside Woolworths on Dalmarnock Rd. "What?"I respond with a confused expression on my face, "I forgot to get monkey nuts", he explains before asking me to go back to the fruit shop on Main St to pick them up. I am just about to go when a little old lady at the bus stop says "'Ra Countdown's goat hunners 'a rem". "Pardon", Father replies. The little old lady looks totally exasperated as she elaborates "'Ra Countdown, 'ra shoap across 'ra road, he's goat hunners a monkey nuts". Father looks at her with a smile on his face as he can't quite understand what she is saying. "Whit's the glaikit look fur?" she asks Father as she stares right at him "Ur ye tryin' tae take 'ra pish?" she continues. Father looks shocked as he quickly answers "No, no I'm not taking the pi.., eh the Countdown you say". The old lady shuffles forward towards us as she opens her string bag which is stuffed with monkey nuts. "Aye 'ra Countdown, he's daen 'rem 'it two bags furra shullin'", she says as she shows Father the open string bag. "Well thank you very much", Father responds. "We will eh, go to the Countdown right away". The old lady looks at Father as if he has just escaped from an asylum as she pushes between us saying " Aye nae bother, noo get oot ma' way 'rers ma bus cummin'", before adding " Ah wish a hudnae bother't ma erse".

After visiting the Countdown for our bargain monkey nuts, Father and I are standing outside the shop checking that we have everything for the party tonight at Mrs Kelly's. Father rhymes of the list and insists I say "Check" to every item he mentions which includes apples, scones, treacle and monkey nuts, "What's in the brown paper bag?" I ask, "Oh", says Father proudly as he opens the brown paper bag, "I bought two bottles of wine for tonight" He continues as he lifts one of the bottles out of the bag and stares at the label. "The man in the off sales told me they are very popular in this area", he continues as he reads the label. "What are they called?" I ask while lifting the other bottle out of the bag. "Well this one is called El dorado, and according to the man in the off sales is sometimes known affectionately as LD", he explains as he returns it to the bag "And that one you are holding is pronounced Lan- lee- kay", he adds as he takes the bottle from my hand and returns it to the bag. After reading the label I am not so sure that is how you pronounce Lanliq, but as Father looked happy with his new found knowledge of wine I didn't bother to raise the issue.

"Hello", Father shouts as we enter our house, after hanging up our coats Father tries again "Hello" he shouts as he opens the living room door and puts the bags down on the couch. As there is no one there we head towards the bedroom, "Hello" he shouts again as he opens the bedroom door "Have you seen my big string of pearls?", Mother asks as she lies on the floor with her arm beneath my bed searching blindly for the missing pearls. "No" we say in unison. Mother gets up from the floor just as we are joined by Mrs Campbell. "Whit huv ye loast?", she enquires, " My big string of pearls, I need them for tonight's party" Mother answers. "Huv ye tried ben 'ra skullery" Mrs Campbell asks. "Who's Ben The skullery?", Father replies,
"Eh" Mrs Campbell grunts as she stares at Father with a bemused expression on her face. "She means in the kitchen Hubert" Mother pronounces matter of factly while standing in the middle of the room with her hands on her hips. As we stand there impressed with Mothers grasp of Glasgow slang she adds "Right never mind I'll find them later". She makes her way towards us "Did you get everything at the shops" she asks Father as we make our way into the living room.

When we reach the living room Father opens the bags and puts the items on the couch. Mother notices Mrs Campbell watching intently as the items are laid out and decides to show off by looking at Mrs Campbell while asking Father "Did you remember the wine Hubert?". Mrs Campbell looks at Mother and crosses her arms below her chest as she looks away and mimics Mother's question whilst moving her shoulders from side to side and muttering under her breath *"Did ye remember 'ra wine Hubert?"*, "Sorry did you say something there?" Mother asks Mrs Campbell, "Naw, nuhin"; Mrs Campbell replies before adding quickly "Geeza look at yer nuts then Mr Nairn" as she leans over and lifts a bag of Monkey nuts out of the bag.

I am sure I saw Mother and Father sniggering as Mrs Campbell used her hand as an imaginary scale moving the bag of monkey nuts up and down. "Jeezo 'atsa good big bag 'a nuts 'rer Mr. Nairn whereje get 'rum?" she asks Father. "From the Countdown" Father replies before adding proudly "They were two bags for a shilling". Mrs Campbell thinks for a second before repeating "Two bags furra shullin'". After another short pause she looks at Mother and brazenly asks "Ah don't suppose ye could see yer way clear tae lending me a bag?". I was still trying to figure out what the benefit was of borrowing monkey nuts as you couldn't give them back after you have opened and eaten them when Mother replied "Okay Mrs Campbell go on take a bag".

Mrs Campbell turns to leave with a big smile on her face looking extremely happy with her free monkey nuts when Mother adds "Oh I believe it's my turn to wash the stairs Mrs. Campbell". Mrs Campbell stops dead in her tracks still looking at the door before slowly turning around to look at Mother. After a few seconds Mother lifts her eyebrows while still looking straight at Mrs Campbell as if to say "Well". Mrs Campbell relents and announces she will take Mother's turn of the stairs in return for the free nuts and heads out the front door muttering obscenities with every step.

"Is it okay if go out to play" I ask Mother as she lifts the wine bottles off the couch. She stares at the wine labels before turning to Father with a quizzical frown on her face that hinted she wasn't quite convinced of his choice of wine, before she eventually acknowledges my question. "Okay, but be back here in time for your tea, it's your favourite tonight", she replies without looking up from the wine labels. "What chips?" I ask excitedly. She finally stops staring at the wine labels long enough to look right at me with a blank expression on her face before replying sarcastically and slowly, " No, your other favourite, mince and doughballs". "Oh.. Right.., I see..." I stutter. The reason for the less than ecstatic response is that the last time we had this, Mrs Campbell suggested delicacy, the doughballs Mother made were rock solid. I actually used one to play tennis with Sammy round our backcourt using the washing line as a net. "Smashing", was all I could think of in reply before I hastily made my way out the flat and headed to Joe's next door.

After knocking on Joe's door I sat down on the ground, I had learned to be patient and allow Joe enough time to limp over to the door to answer my familiar knock. Eventually Joe opens the door, "I am going out to play, can you come?", I ask. Joe immediately looks back at Mrs Kelly while still holding the handle and shouts, " MA' KIN A' GO OOT WI' RUPERT?".

I can clearly see Mrs Kelly standing washing dishes at the sink, but she doesn't even acknowledge Joe. Joe looks at me with a perplexed expression on his face and shakes his head as he announces "Ma' maws deef, haud oan a minute". He lets go of the door and makes his way back inside.

With the door still opened a little I can still see Mrs Kelly and hear their conversation. "Ma'" Joe says as he reaches the sink. "Jesus Christ almighty" a startled Mrs Kelly exclaims as she jumps at Joe's touch. "Ye frightened da' shite outa me Joe", she says, as she holds her chest roughly where her heart is and breathes like a marathon runner after a race. "Sorry Ma'", Joe says sheepishly. "Kin ah go oot wi' Rupert?" he adds. "Yes, but make sure 'dat your back for your dinner now, it's your favourite tonight" she replies with her index finger waving in front of Joe's face. "Whit chips?", Joe asks excitedly. "No, its mince and doughballs" she replies with a confused expression on her face as she playfully slaps Joe about the head with a wet dish towel. Joe tries to swat away her unprovoked playful attack and then without saying anything starts limping towards the front door as he wipes his face with his sleeve. I can hear him muttering "'Ah hate doughballs" as he closes his front door and joins me on the landing

I suggest we go to ask Sammy if he is coming out to play. Before we can move Mr Campbell comes out of his flat in an almighty rush still putting on his jacket. He heads directly for the stairs growling in a loud voice "Ah told ye wummin' ah wiz gon furra pint". He is followed out by an irate Mrs Campbell who stands at the top of the stairs and shouts "You better no' be long ya bastart, 'am makin' yer favourite fur dinner". There is no response from Mr Campbell until he reaches the bottom stair where he stops and shouts back up the stair "'Av telt ye a hunner times, I hate mince and doughballs", before storming out the close.

Mrs Campbell turns to face Joe and I and talks to us as if we are Mr Campbell as she states matter of factly. "Am no' makin' mince and doughballs, 'am makin' chips and egg". This statement is followed by "So he kin get it right up 'im". Joe and I just stand there like statues until she makes her way back to her flat, and as soon as she closes the door we burst out laughing as we make our way down the stairs.

After meeting up with Sammy the three of us decide to use the time before the party by visiting Beatrice's newsagent on Dalmarnock Rd to look at the Halloween masks in the window." Whit ur yeez dressin' up iz 'ra night?" Joe asks excitedly as we make our way down Heron St towards Dalmarnock Rd. "A bloody Coalman", Sammy exclaims with a forlorn expression on his face. "Always a bloody Coalman" he sighs. He then continues to tell Joe and I that from about the age of four his mother has always dressed him up as a Coalman because it was simple and didn't involve any cost.

She would blacken his face with soot from the chimney in their living room, tie a handkerchief around his neck and make him put on his dad's donkey jacket and bunnet, and, hey presto, one miniature Coalman ready to meet his public. He was then paraded in front of all the neighbours in the close looking for treats in return for telling his one and only joke. "What's a cannibal's favourite game?" he would ask his bemused adult neighbours and when the answer came back "Don't know". He would respond. "Swallow my leader". After a few seconds of forced laughter the neighbour would then part with about a ton of monkey nuts and possibly a fruit pastille as a reward for his comedic talent.

"What about you Joe?" I ask as we reach Beatrice's shop. After thinking for a few seconds Joe's face lights up. He then stretches both arms out in front of him and shouts "Superman", before setting off limping around Sammy and I pretending to fly. "Hiv ye goat a costume Joe?" an obviously impressed Sammy asks. Joe suddenly stops and slowly lowers his arms "Naw", he replies looking totally dejected. "Ah'll probably be a Coalman a' naw", he adds dejectedly as he comes to terms with the fact that not having a costume could hamper his ambition to be Superman.

On seeing Joe's disappointment I try to cheer him up with my thoughts on Superman. I ask Sammy and Joe to picture this scene. Superman corners the baddie in an alley. The baddie pulls out his gun and starts blasting away at Superman. Sammy and Joe start nodding in agreement. Superman puffs out his chest as the bullets simply bounce off him without so much as a scratch. Sammy and Joe are still nodding. Then the baddie runs out of bullets and after a few desperate clicks of the trigger he throws the gun at Superman. My question is "Why does Superman duck when the gun comes towards him?". He has just let six bullets bounce of his chest no problem at all, surely a gun isn't going to hurt him. Sammy looks at Joe; they both review what I have just said in their minds, then thankfully, start to laugh out loud. Joe stops laughing long enough to exclaim " 'Av never thought a' 'rat afore" before continuing to laugh out loud with Sammy.

After looking at the plastic Dracula and Frankenstein masks in the window for about ten minutes Sammy asks me "Whit aboot you Rupert, whit ur you gonny dress up 'iz?". After a short pause I reply, "I really don't know". Before explaining that I have never dressed up since we moved to Heron St. "No doubt Mother will have something organised", I add as we head inside Beatrice's to buy something from the 'Penny Tray'.

Beatrice has a choice of a Penny Tray, a T'upenny Tray or a Thr'upenny Tray, each containing a various assortment of sweets. Sammy and I rummage in our trouser pockets and produce a penny each as we turn to face Joe who is still digging deep into both pockets of his short grey trousers.

He eventually accepts defeat as he pulls the pockets inside out and stands there holding the obviously empty pockets and shrugs his shoulders. "Don't worry wull share wurr sweeties" Sammy says to Joe who immediately cheers up as he stuffs the pockets back inside his trousers.

We move closer to the counter and when she notices our presence in the small shop Beatrice starts to slide off her stool in the corner like a walrus returning to the sea, and slowly makes her way towards us. When she reaches the counter she greets us with her usual cheery statement of "O'rite lads, whit yeez wanting 'ra day?". After a short debate with Sammy to clarify the negatives and positives between two things from the penny tray or one bigger thing from the tu'penny tray we both say at the same time "A penny tray". I am left on my own to say "Please". Beatrice bends down below the counter as she replies "Nae borra", before returning upright and sitting the penny tray on top the pile of newspapers on the counter. All three of us peruse the goodies on offer as the decision making process begins. "Get two dainties" Sammy says pointing to the small green tartan coloured toffees. "We kin break 'rem against 'ra wa' ootside" he continues. Joe is eager to contribute to this decision making process but due to his lack of funds he is holding himself back and says nothing. "What about the Swizzle's?", I ask my fellow decision makers. "We can share them easier than dainties", I add. "Aye right enough", Sammy responds before adding "Ah nearly broke ma' hon' oan 'ra coarner a'ah wa' tryin' tae brek a dainty".

Beatrice looks as if she is losing the will to live listening to our inane decision making process and finally interrupts with "Amuchyeezgoat?". I look at Sammy with a quizzical expression on my face as I never quite caught what she said, it sounded like she had randomly said "A small cheese goat". All becomes clear when Sammy announces "Tuppence", as he holds up his penny and grabs my wrist to show Beatrice my penny as well. I suddenly realise she is enquiring about our financial situation. After looking at our pennies she turns her attention to Joe who is now standing with his hands in his pockets and his head bowed looking at his feet. "Whit aboot you wee man?", she enquires. " Av no' goat anyfing", Joe responds in his best sad voice without looking up from his feet as he slowly sticks out his bad leg to show his big black boot. Beatrice stares at Joe and then looks down to his feet as she takes a deep breath. And then to our delight she announces "O'rite yeez kin hiv wan fing each". The three of us reply with a yell of "Yeess". Joe must have the Midas touch because Beatrice is notoriously tight fisted, as Sammy told me months ago "Beatrice widnae gie ye daylight in a dork corner".

As we make our way back up Heron St towards my close I am still eating my Swizzles, Sammy is chewing away on his dainty and Joe has a small bit of his banana sweet left. I have never liked the banana shaped sweets, it was like eating a small piece of polystyrene.

It was getting dark now as we approached my close at number 43 and there was a quiet eerie feeling as a fog descended on Heron St making it impossible to see the end of the street. The grey stone of the tenements looked even darker than normal with the dim hazy lights from the lamps in the closes illuminating through the fog offering a comforting glow. The only sound you could hear was the cascading water falling onto the pavement from a broken downpipe at number 45. The eerie silence is broken when a double decker bus, heading to the garage, rumbles past us and disappears into the fog like a ghost bus never to be seen again. As the red lights on the back of the bus fade in the distance the renewed silence is broken by Sammy. "See yeez ra'mora" Sammy grunts through a mouthful of toffee as we reach my close. "See you tomorrow", I reply. "Nae borra", Joe adds as we head up the stair to get ready for the Halloween party at Mrs Kelly's. Standing on our dimly lit landing I say cheerio to Joe who reminds me the party starts at 7.30pm as he enters his house and closes the door.

I am just about to enter chateau Nairn when I hear raised voices coming from Mrs Campbell's flat across the landing. I slowly tip toe over and listen at the door. "Whit dae ye mean ye hid nae money?" Mrs Campbell barks at Mr Campbell. "Ah telt ye ah must've drapt it ur sumfin'" is Mr Campbell's feeble response. "Drapt it... Drapt it, ye bloody drunk it dint ye ya big lump ah shite?". After a short pause Mr Campbell sheepishly replies "Ah only hud wan drink wummin'". On hearing this response Mrs Campbell's voice rises another notch. "Wan drink...WAN DRINK", she repeats". Look at ra' nick yer in, yer pissed as a fart ya waste a space". After a few deep breaths she continues her rant with "Noo whit ur we gonny dae furra' party ra' night eh?". Mr Campbell has learned quickly not to reply as she continues "Am no filling 'rat voddy boatle wi' water again, we nearly goat caught ra' last time at ra' Bains'".

Mr Campbell bravely tries to assert himself by shouting " Right wummin enough a' yer pish, ah'll jist go back doon ra' pub and get a hauf boatle". Mr Campbell's assertiveness doesn't last long as Mrs Campbell bellows "Aye so ye bloody wull ya big alky, sit oan yer arse". Mr Campbell obeys immediately as Mrs Campbell keeps her verbal onslaught going by asking "Ah thought ye said ye hid nae buroo money left, so yer a lying big bastart anaw?". An exasperated Mr Campbell reluctantly owns up to having "Ten bob" left from his unemployment benefit. "Geez 'rat money ya lazy bastart", Mrs Campbell screams as she snatches the money from her husband before adding "Thirty years av put wi' yer shite". I can clearly hear Mr Campbell's reply as he mutters "Aye so ye huv....ah canny remember breaking o' they mirrors ya bloody nag". Quick as a flash Mrs Campbell asks "Whit did you say 'rer?'", Mr Campbell nervously replies "Nuhin' hen", before adding "Er! Ah need tae go tae ra' toilet 'am burstin'".

On hearing this I quickly move away from the door towards my own flat but I can still hear Mrs Campbell shout "Don't you be long, je hear me, ah'll need tae go tae ra' licees' when ye come back?". The Campbell's door opens as Mr Campbell appears counting money he must have hidden from his wife, before he closes the door he shouts back "Nae problem hen". As he slams the door shut he turns round and sees me standing there as he buttons up his coat. "Listen tae me son", he says as he finishes the last button, "Never get merritt, aw wummin ur a pain in ra' arse". After conveying these words of wisdom he winks at me before he walks down the stairs two at a time and out the close obviously heading back to the Dog Leg pub at the bottom of Heron St. I was really curious to see what Mrs Campbell would do when she found out her husband wasn't in the toilet, but as Mr Campbell is renowned for being in the toilet for up to an hour I couldn't wait about to find out.

On entering chateau Nairn I walk into the living room to find Mother on her knees ironing a shirt on top of a towel on the floor. The iron is sitting on the flame of a gas ring on the cooker. Mother has done the ironing like this many times but never dressed as a Flapper Girl, she looked resplendent in her dress with a large string of pearls hanging round her neck. She had a tiara type thing on her head with a single feather sticking out of it. "Hello Rupert", Father says as he notices me and puts his newspaper down. Again this reveals the unexpected sight of Father with perfectly pressed black trousers, highly polished shoes and a white vest, his ensemble is completed by a black elasticated dickie bow around his neck.

"Here's your shirt Hubert", Mother announces as she finishes folding Fathers shirt on the towel. As she stands up to hand it over her knee gets caught in the large string of pearls. In order to stop her from snapping the pearls she tries to kneel back down but only proceeds to pull her neck down when her knee hits the floor. " Ma' Bloody knee", she shouts as her knee lands on a large pearl. She instinctively tries to get back up again but her knee is still trapped, and again preventing the pearls from snapping is of the utmost importance so she stays exactly where she is, hunched over with a knee trapped in the pearls pulling her head down. She is now keeping her balance with her outstretched arms on the floor. "Don't just sit there Hubert, Help me", she demands. Father and I run over to help but arrive too quickly. Both of us try to grab Mothers arm but only succeed in knocking her over on her side. With her knee still trapped inside the string of pearls she is now lying on her side.

We both try to help her by lifting her up "Watch the pearls!, Watch the pearls", she screams as we put her back down. Father leans over to lift the pearls off her knee but only succeeds in knocking her lovely tiara and feather over the side of her head .

During the melee no-one noticed Mrs Campbell walking into the living room, "Wur ye flashin' yer washin' there Mrs Nairn?" is a grinning Mrs Campbell's unhelpful observation. Eventually we manage to free Mother and she gingerly rises to her feet. She tries to straighten the tiara on her now dishevelled hair as she blows upwards to move the feather away from her face. She then barks at Mrs Campbell through clenched teeth "What can we do for you Mrs Campbell". Mother then regains her composure and flattens her slightly crumpled dress. Mrs Campbell hesitantly moves closer to us as she stares at Mother and stutters "Why ur ye? eh, whit ur ye dressed... eh, um?". Mother stares back at Mrs Campbell before asking sternly "Well?". Before Mrs Campbell can answer Father notices his own state of undress and hurriedly grabs his shirt while motioning that he is going into the bedroom, as he turns his back on Mrs Campbell and squeezes past her. Mrs Campbell looks at Father with a confused expression on her face, before shaking her head as he leaves the room. I'm sure I could hear Mrs Campbell mumbling "Idiot", under her breath.

Mrs Campbell regains her train of thought and continues to stare at Mother from head to toe before saying "Aye right, where wiz ah, Aye, Mrs Nairn ah wiz wondering if ye could see yer way clear to lend me ten bob tae next week?". Mother stares at Mrs Campbell making her feel slightly uncomfortable as a bit of revenge for her 'flashing your washing' quip. Mrs Campbell continues "That man o' mine has loast some money somewhere, and it wid really help me oot a hole". Mother decides she has had enough revenge and looks in my direction while saying "Rupert could you hand me that purse from the mantelpiece?". After I hand her the purse she opens it and pulls out a ten bob note and stretches out her hand towards Mrs Campbell. Mrs Campbell then reaches towards the ten bob note and just before she can take it Mother snatches it away while looking at Mrs Campbell with her eyebrows raised. "Okay, okay", Mrs Campbell reluctantly says before continuing "Ah'll take your turn o' ra' stairs next week". Mother then hands over the ten bob note with a grin on her face as Mrs Campbell walks away and mutters "Ah'll be daen ra' bloody stairs forever at 'ris rate".

"Right Rupert let's get you ready" Mother announces as she marches over and leads me by the shoulders into the hall. As we pass our front door en route to the bedroom we can clearly hear Mrs Campbell banging the toilet door outside as she shouts " Hurry up you, huv' ye fell doon ra pan ?".

She continues to bang the door as the toilet flushes and a clearly agitated Mrs Kelly emerges and states in her defence "Fur Christ's sake Mrs Campbell, sure av only been in here for two minutes".

There is complete silence as I imagine the look on Mrs Campbell's face on realising that she has been duped by her husband. "Er, naw, 'am sorry Mrs Kelly I thought 'rat man o' mine wiz in 'rer, er sorry" Mrs Campbell gushes as Mrs Kelly makes her way back up the stairs to her flat. She then shouts "Wait tae ah get ma hons oan 'rat big fat bastart". At this point Mother's hands move from my shoulders to my ears as we continue into the bedroom.

"How do I look?" Father asks as we enter the bedroom. He has put a jar of Brylcream on his hair which now looks wet and shiny with a middle parting. His black dinner suit highlights his recently ironed white shirt and dickie bow to great effect. His outfit is rounded off with a pair of the shiniest shoes I have ever seen. "I thought you were wearing your Spats" Mother asks. Father momentarily frowns in Mother's direction before proceeding to pose with his unlit pipe held up to his mouth. His right hand and four fingers of his left hand are tucked in the side pocket of his jacket with only the thumb hanging over the edge as he stares upwards towards the ceiling. "You look every inch the dapper gentleman", Mother eventually announces as she looks at Father from head to toe. "Now go away and let me help Rupert get ready" she demands as Father sheepishly grabs his top hat from the top bunk bed and heads towards the living room.

Mother opens the door of the small wardrobe and lifts out a hanger as I eagerly await beside my bed. I am totally underwhelmed as she slowly turns round to reveal my school uniform, she then opens the mirror section of the wardrobe and pulls out my school cap and tie. She walks into the centre of the room and holds up my uniform in her left hand and the cap and tie with her right hand "Well.. Well" she keeps saying as she nods at me wide eyed as if I should be guessing something. After a few seconds and noticing the blank expression on my face an exasperated Mother finally blurts out "Jimmy Clitheroe". She then continues with one of Jimmy's catchphrases "I'm all there with me cough drops" in a pretty good Lancashire accent I have to admit. "Ah! Jimmy Clitheroe" I slowly repeat back to Mother as I eventually realise who I will be dressing up as. My first thoughts were "Ooh! Flippin' Eck!" another one of Jimmy's catchphrases, but the more I thought about it the more the idea grew on me. Everybody loved Jimmy Clitheroe on the television in 'That's my boy' and 'Just Jimmy', Father and I still listen to him on the radio in 'The Clitheroe Kid'.

Mother leaves the room as I set about getting changed. I have just managed to strip off to my vest and pants when the front door is opened and a yell of "It's only me" echoes around the flat. I have one leg in my short grey trousers as the bedroom door flies open and in flounces Wilhelmina.

Before I can get my other leg in my trousers Wilhelmina pushes me as she shouts "Out of my way, I'm in a hurry". Luckily I spin round and land on the bottom bunk bed as she climbs the steps to the top bunk and grabs her nightdress. I have just regained my balance when she descends and bumps me again this time sending me spinning to the floor like Jackie Pallo, as she makes her way to the wardrobe. "Watch it" I feebly say as I stand up rubbing my elbow. "Where are you going in such a hurry?". She grabs her coat from the wardrobe and then turns to face me, she looks down her nose at me for a few seconds as if I have just broken wind before saying. "Not that it is any of your business, but I am going to stay with Veronica tonight". She then puts her coat on and stuffs her nightdress in a brown paper bag.

"Are you not coming to the party?" I ask, as she heads for the bedroom door. She suddenly stops before slowly turning round to look at me, at this point I wish I had never asked. She takes two steps towards me before saying through clenched teeth "I wouldn't be seen dead at a party in that hovel of a flat if it was the last place on earth". She then takes another step towards me as I step back and continues "They are old, dirty, smelly, common lowlifes". By this time I am backed against the bedroom wall as she pushes her index finger in my chest and declares. "I will never, ever associate with riff raff like the people next door or their smelly relatives", the word 'relatives' is followed by one final push in my chest with her index finger before she turns and heads into the living room.

"I take it that means No then" I whisper in case she hears me as I continue to get dressed in my Jimmy Clitheroe outfit. I can clearly hear her change her tone of voice as she enters the living room "Hello Mother you look lovely, Father you look just like James Bond" she gushes. Father then decides to treat Wilhelmina to his Sean Connery impression. "My name ish Bond, Jamesh Bond, double o sheven lishensed to kill". As Mother and Wilhelmina force out a laugh at Fathers effort there is a knock at the front door. "I'll get it", I shout as I open the front door to find a miniature coalman with a bad leg standing there. "Hi Rupert ur yeez ready yet?" Joe asks before pointing at me and shouting "Jimmy Clitheroe". I nod at Joe to come in and let him know we are nearly ready as we enter the living room.

"Well, well what do we have here?" asks Father as he looks at Joe. Joe stares at Father with a confused expression on his face "'Am Jock the coalman" Joe answers as he takes off his bunnet and then stares at Mother with the same confused look on his face. "You look every inch the coalman" Mother compliments Joe as she flicks the drooping feather hanging from her tiara from her face. Joe did look resplendent with his oversized donkey jacket, dirty neckerchief and black soot covered face all topped off with a greasy bunnet about five sizes too big.

Ten minutes later Mother is looking for her handbag as Father treats a clearly impressed Joe to his Sean Connery impression, when there is a knock on our front door. "I'll get it" I shout as I head towards the door. I open the door to be met by a young man about sixteen years old. "Is 'ra wee man 'rer?", he asks. After a short pause the young man notices the quizzical look on my face, "Wee Joe" he adds "'Am eez big cousin an' eez maw sent me tae get 'im". "Yes he's here come in" I reply as I snap back to reality. I show the young man into the living room and when Joe notices him he lets out a yell of "Sean" as he limps over towards us as quick as he can. "O'rite wee man" Sean says as he ruffles Joe hair "Yer maw wiz wunnerin' where ye wur" he continues. He then notices Mother and Father and just stares at them for what seems like an eternity, the uncomfortable silence is broken by Mother with the words "Good evening young man" as she makes her way towards us. At this point I can hear Joe quickly whisper to Sean "'Reez ur 'ra posh people a wiz tellin' ye aboot" Sean winks at Joe just as Mother approaches with her hand held out.

"I'm Mrs Nairn" Mother says as she shakes Sean by the hand she then looks in the direction of Father "That's Mr Nairn" she continues before turning towards me, "And that's Rupert". She then turns Sean around by the shoulder towards the couch where Wilhelmina is sitting with her head buried in an old copy of the Bunty. "And that's..", "Wilhelmina" Sean interrupts as he holds his hand out in Wilhelmina's direction.

Wilhelmina looks up from her comic and notices Sean for the first time. She quickly throws the comic down on the couch as she stands up and flattens her dress and fiddles with her hair. She then approaches Sean with a silly expression on her face. "Joe telt me a' aboot ye" Sean says to Wilhelmina before continuing " My name's Sean...Sean Connolly". Fathers face lights up as hears this and he is ready to do his James Bond impersonation when he is interrupted by Mother who looks him in the eye before sternly saying "The lad said Connolly". This tempers Father's enthusiasm and he continues loading a brown paper bag with monkey nuts and apples. But I did think to myself if there is ever a Chinese James Bond who better to play him than Sean Connolly. Wilhelmina regally stretches out her hand towards Sean as if she expects him to kiss it, but Sean shakes her hand so strongly her arm is nearly pulled from her shoulder. Every downward shake of her hand jerks her head and ruffles her perfectly kempt hair causing a multitude of kirbies to fall to the floor like confetti.

"Right everyone, we better get a move on" Mother orders like a Sergeant Major. "We'll see you tomorrow Wilhelmina" Mother continues as she gathers up a bunch of brown paper bags from the couch. "Er, um, I might as well just come to the party" Wilhelmina replies as she looks at Sean with that same silly expression on her face.

"Very well, let's go" Mother barks as she heads for the front door with her brown bags. "Let me gie ye a hon' rer Mrs Nairn" Sean offers as he grabs two of the bags from Mother. "Careful" Mother advises Sean "That bag has the wine in it". Sean looks inside before declaring "Gon ya dancer, a boatle o' Lanny n' LD". He then notices the concerned expression on Mother's face before adding nervously "'Am sure ma' aunty Jean loves LD". I felt like asking Sean if his aunty Jean Kelly was a good dancer but as he was a lot bigger than me I decided against it.

We make our way out of our flat and onto the landing. We can hear lots of loud voices and laughter coming from within Mrs Kelly's flat. There is also the sound of music courtesy of Tom Jones singing Delilah. As we wait on Mother locking the door Father turns to Sean and asks "Are you at the same school as Wilhelmina?". Sean's face has a look of indignation as he replies abruptly "'Am no' 'it school, am an apprentice Jiner". "A Jiner?" Father repeats. "Aye a Jiner" an annoyed Sean replies before adding "Whits up wi' 'rat?". "Nothing at all" Father mutters. After a few moments he adds "So what does a Jiner do?". Sean looks at Father to see if he is serious before saying slowly "Ah make hings oot o' wid". Father nods as if he understands and then asks curiously "Wid?". Sean sighs and then takes a deep breath in readiness to explain again but before he can say anything Mother finishes locking the door and joins the debate by saying "Joiner Hubert, he is a joiner who makes things out of wood okay?" Sean nods in agreement "Aye 'rats whit ah said".

Sean opens the door and enters the single end flat followed closely by Wilhelmina acting like a love struck puppy. Joe and I are next in with Mother and Father bringing up the rear. As Sean passes the coal bunker and comes into full view of the assembled throng there is a cacophony of hoots and cheers. The hoots and cheers continue when Joe and I enter with added shouts of "There's wee Jock the coalman" and "Look, Jimmy Clitheroe". This followed by loud laughter and chants of "Ooh! Flippin' eck" and "I'm all there with me cough drops". Joe and I are still giggling as Mother and Father enter the room with big smiles on their faces, "Hello everybody" Father shouts. I can hear the scratch of a needle across a record as the music comes to an abrupt halt and the room falls totally silent as the other party guests all stare at Mother and Father. It is only then that I realise that my parents are the only adults that have dressed up. After what seems like an eternity Mrs Kelly breaks the uncomfortable silence by walking over to my parents and saying in her best posh Irish voice " Wid je look who it is, Mr and Mrs Nairn, sure do ye no' look lovely, come in, come in and sit yersel doon".

Mrs Kelly holds out her arm to lead Mother and Father over to the crowded couch, Mother's face is bright red as she slowly makes her way through the guests, acknowledging eye contact with a forced grin through gritted teeth. Father meanwhile is oblivious to any embarrassment and says a cheery "Hello" to everyone he passes as he follows Mrs Kelly towards the couch.

"Right yooz two...UP!" Mrs Kelly barks towards two young girls as she reaches the couch. "Who are they?" I ask Joe. "'Rat's ma cousins" Joe replies before continuing "'Rat wan's Elaine Kelly, ma uncle Eddie's lassie" he says as he discreetly points to a girl about the same age as Wilhelmina. "'Innat wan's Elaine Crawford ma maw's sister's lassie" as he points to an angry young girl about my age who is not happy at all at being evicted from her space on the couch. " 'Ra pair o' rem canny ston' each other" he adds. Sure enough I notice that they are staring daggers at each other across the room as they take up their new positions, one at the sink and the other near the front door.

Meanwhile, Mrs Kelly has squeezed Mother and Father beside two other people on the couch and decides to do some introductions. "That's Eddie and George" she says as she points to the other occupants of the couch. The two gentlemen are definitely drunk as they raise their glasses to acknowledge the introduction followed by George's "'Orite, howzitgon?". Mother just does the grin again in response. Mrs Kelly continues as she points around the room. "The auld fella dozing at the fire, now dat's my uncle Pat and dat's his boy Dom sittin' next tae 'im, dat's ma niece Elaine at the sink, an' dat's ma 'ither niece Elaine 'it 'ra front door" she pauses for breath before continuing. "They two durty hingoot's winchin' at 'da tallboy, now dat's ma pals Mark n'Isobel, and ye already know young Sean". When she finishes she looks back towards Mother and Father who are busy declining 'A wee hauf' from Eddie. Again she tries to sound posh as she loudly asks my parents "Wid ye be wantin' an aperitif?". Before anyone can answer Uncle Pat sits bolt upright in his chair at the fire and shouts "'Av goat ma teeth, thir in ma poaket". This is met with howls of laughter as the music is restarted and the party resumes.

"its yersel Mrs Campbell" Mrs Kelly shouts above the dulcet tones of Matt Monro singing Born Free as a nervous Mrs Campbell enters the room. "Yer door wiz open, eh, um..." Mrs Campbell responds as she clutches a half bottle of vodka in the large front pocket of her grimy pinny. "Is yer man no wi' ye?" Mrs Kelly asks, as she walks towards Mrs Campbell. "Naw, eh, he hid sumfin', er, av brought ye 'ris", Mrs Campbell stutters as she pulls the vodka bottle from her pinny. "Wid ye look at 'rat?" Mrs Kelly exclaims as she takes the half bottle from Mrs Campbell. She holds the bottle up to her eye level before adding sarcastically "An' thirs a wee tait left tae". Mrs Campbell stares at her feet, as Mrs Kelly takes her arm and leads her over to the couch.

I notice Mrs Campbell is still wearing the same old slippers with the big furry strip across them. The flattened heels partially covered by the short nylon stockings with broken elastic around her ankles. "Right you..UP" Mrs Kelly barks, and it's George's turn to be evicted from the crowded couch. This seemed like the easiest option as Eddie is sitting holding a half bottle of whisky in one hand and a glass of whisky in the other having a one sided conversation with an imaginary adversary mumbling random threats like "Oh! Wull ye noo?" before adopting a conciliatory approach with "Fair do's... 'Nuff said". He then stares at both Mrs Kelly and Mrs Campbell in a trance like state with a big grin on his face while raising his glass to toast his imagined satisfactory conclusion with the words "See, ah knew it".

George leaves his seat to accommodate Mrs Campbell and at the same time responds to Eddie's "See, ah knew it" with a sarcastic "Aye, gonyersel son" as he shakes his head and pats Eddie on the knee. As Mrs Campbell takes her seat Eddie is happily repeating the words "Ah knew it....Ah, knew it" with a contented grin on his face.

I am still trying to work out what Eddie 'Knew' when the front door of the flat flies open and bangs of the wall as Mr Campbell staggers in knocking all the coats hanging up behind the door to the floor. He then tries to bend down to pick them up and falls backwards into the door of the coal bunker. As Joe and I watch intently we notice he is wearing a plastic Frankenstein mask held by elastic bands over his ears. He straitens himself up, hiccups loudly, and tries to walk in a straight line towards Mrs Kelly. He is now walking like a dressage horse stepping over invisible obstacles when his foot catches the corner of the tallboy. This sends him hurtling forward where he bumps into the record player cutting short The Rolling Stones singing *'Honky tonk woman'* and unintentionally replacing it with *'Tiptoe through the tulips'* by Tiny Tim.

As he regains his composure he surveys the room like a periscope on a submarine. On noticing his wife he points at her and tries to say something but instead burps loudly. After the longest burp I have ever heard he then tries to make it over to his wife a distance of about six feet. As he sets off he grabs the curtain that covers the recess bed, and again loses his balance. He then pulls the curtain off the pole as he falls to the floor crashing into a small wooden table filled with drinks and monkey nuts, sending glass and monkey nuts everywhere before he eventually lands at the feet of Mrs Campbell and Eddie.

Eddie calmly leans over and looks at Mr Campbell prostrate on the floor covered in a curtain and surrounded by broken glass and monkey nuts before promptly sitting back shaking his head and mumbling "Ah knew it...Ah knew it". Mr Campbell fights his way through the curtain and sits bolt upright on the floor. He removes the mask from his face and slides it up on top of his head.

After hiccupping and burping again he just smiles at his wife. "Where 'ra bloody hell huv you been?" an angry Mrs Campbell demands to know. Everyone in the room stares at Mr Campbell as he tries to focus his eyes on his wife before sarcastically replying in a drunken drawl "'Ra pictures". There is complete silence from everyone in the room as Mr Campbell then loudly breaks wind for about ten seconds and everyone bursts out laughing including Mrs Campbell. Eddie then joins Mr Campbell on the floor and hands him a glass of whisky before toasting the latest arrival at the party with a loud "Cheers" as the both of them join in the laughter.

After Mrs Kelly and Mrs Campbell have cleared up the debris from Mr Campbell's drunken entrance, the party continues. There is intermittent shouting and laughing accompanied by Tiny Tim still tip toeing through the tulips. Joe is away to get us more lemonade as I stand at the sink and survey the current scene of my first tenement party.

Even though we used to live in this single room flat I have never seen so many people in such a small space. It was now stifling hot with hardly any air in circulation and a large cloud of cigarette smoke is hovering above our heads making the room even duller than usual as it blocks the light from the uncovered 60 watt bulb in the centre of the ceiling. The only window in the room behind me at the sink is opened about six inches, and won't open any further. The street light outside the window provides some welcome light as it shines through the tatty net curtain, and the front door is ajar in a feeble effort to let in some fresh air. Old uncle Pat is still dozing in the chair by the fire with an unlit rolled up cigarette in his mouth and despite the intense sweaty atmosphere he still has his black suit jacket on with a woolly grey jumper underneath. As if that wasn't enough he also had a white shirt and grubby red tie on underneath the jumper. There is cigarette ash all over his black trousers that have risen above his black socks displaying his sock suspenders. His ensemble is completed by having one shoe on and one shoe off. He is still holding a glass of whisky at a precarious angle that looks as if it could fall onto the floor at any time as he snoozes peacefully unaware of the rabble around him.

Sitting next to Pat is his son Dom. Dom had the longest jet black hair I have ever seen on a man. His unkempt hair passed his shoulders and with a full black beard and moustache all you could see was two brown eyes squinting from below two bushy black eyebrows. He was wearing a multi coloured shirt that went all the way to his knees hiding a pair of denims with flared ragged bottoms and a pair of sandals on his bare feet. Dom didn't say much but when he did, every sentence ended with the word 'Man'.

On the couch Eddie had voluntarily evicted himself and retired to the recess bed to try and sober up. His replacement is a sleeping Mr Campbell sitting next to his wife, who every now and again took great delight in digging him in the ribs every time he snored. She was talking to Mother who had seemingly developed a taste for Eldorado wine and was slightly inebriated. I could tell she was drunk because she was slowly reverting back to her Partick tenement upbringing and starting to speak slang on a regular basis. The tiara had been discarded and Father was now wearing her large string of pearls while tickling Eddie's feet, with the feather from Mother's Tiara, which were sticking out the recess bed behind Father's shoulder.

Mark and Isobel had left the flat in a huff and headed for the landing outside to continue their kissing marathon after being berated by everyone for using words like 'Snookums' and 'Tiddums'. And Wilhelmina was at the coal bunker door talking to Sean, who was proudly holding open his grey jacket to show an impressed Wilhelmina the label and letting her know that he purchased his jacket from City Cash Tailors with his own money without the use of a "Provvie check". He was also wearing black drainpipe trousers with shiny black 'Winklepicker' pointy shoes. His jacket looked a couple of sizes too big with only the tips of fingers showing when he had his arms at his side. And with his 'Tony Curtis' haircut he looked like he was trying too hard to look older than he actually was.

Meanwhile, a drunken George is rifling through a meagre record collection looking for something to replace 'Hole in my shoe' by Traffic and finally settles for somebody called Jim Reeves singing Distant Drums. Eddie suddenly rises from his short five minute slumber and sits on the edge of the bed, gives himself a shake and makes a "Brrrrrrrrr" sound just as Jim Reeves velvet voice delivers the opening line of his song. "I hear the sound of distant drums..Far away, far away...". I have to assume Eddie isn't a big fan of Mr Reeves as he grumbles "Who pit 'rat shite oan?". George rebukes the now standing Eddie with the words "Whit dae you know, yer taste's in yer 'erse", as Jim Reeves continues in the background. The two Elaine's start arguing over the dregs of a blackcurrant cordial bottle, The childish argument is only halted when Mrs Kelly shouts a phrase that will live with me forever. "Leave Elaine 'alane Elaine" she poetically shouts without so much as a smirk, leaving the two girls none the wiser as to who is to leave who alone.

"Here's yer ginger" Joe says as he hands me a glass of lemonade. "By ra' way, ma maw's goat peeces 'n spam fur efter" he adds proudly. Spam was a popular delicacy around the East end of Glasgow and I have to admit I had grown to like a 'Spam fritter' now and again.

Jim Reeves finishes and there is a moments respite from any music as George frantically searches for something else to put on the record player. During this musical hiatus I can clearly hear snippets of the various conversations from around the room. Dom is speaking to Mother, Father and Mrs Campbell, regaling them with the tale of a wee black mongrel dog called 'Duke' that he found wandering in the street. "Cracking wee dug man" he drawls before sipping from a can of pale ale leaving white foam settled on his moustache and beard around his lips. "A wee black 'hing man" he continues. After another sip of pale ale he goes on " Aye man, licked ye an everyfin' man". After taking a large gulp of beer Dom takes a deep breath and with his voice now trembling, he drops a bombshell as he breathes out. "He's deed noo" . There is a sharp intake of breath from his audience as Dom, who now sounds close to tears continues."Aye man, knoaked doon wi' a Cellic supporters bus gon' tae Parkheed". He is now sobbing out loud as he finishes with "Ah luvved 'rat wee dug man". He then starts crying uncontrollably as he gets up and heads over to the sideboard for another can of pale ale, leaving his shell shocked audience sitting there open mouthed.

I am still trying to digest Dom's tragic tale when out of the blue uncle Pat wakes up, sits forward in his chair and starts singing. "*Ohhh Rose Marieeeee I luuuv yooooooo…*". This causes George to exclaim "Oh naw, ra' auld yins away again, 'am gon' furra pish" as he moves quickly towards the front door and heads for the outside toilet. This is automatically followed by random shouts of "Shhh" and "Gonyersel Pat" as everyone else in the room is immediately quiet and listens attentively to uncle Pat. "'Dat's yer Grannie's song" a beaming Mrs Kelly whispers to an unimpressed Joe as uncle Pat continues. "*I'mmm always dreaminnn' of yooo…*". As I look around the room there are random shouts of "Belt it oot Pat" and "'Eez sum' chanter intae?" and when uncle Pat finishes there is rapturous applause and whistling before he calmly sits back in his chair and immediately goes back to sleep.

Dom meanwhile has returned to his seat to be met by a concerned Mrs Campbell who offers her condolences for Dom's tragic loss. Dom seems to have quickly recovered from his loss as he replies while opening another can of beer. "Nae problem man, shit happens".

Eddie breaks the uncomfortable silence that follows Dom's heartless remark as he shouts "Right Herbert your turn tae geeza song". On hearing this request Wilhelmina suddenly appears from behind Sean with a look of horror on her face as Mother turns to Eddie and responds. "His name is Hubert, and he doesn't sing in public". She then turns to Father as she seeks confirmation of this fact only to be totally shocked as my drunk Father responds. "Well if truth be told no-one has ever asked me".

This is followed by "Why not" as he puts his glass of Eldorado wine down on the floor at the side of the couch and sits forward on the edge of his seat in preparation for his public singing debut. Before he can start Mother looks at Father and sarcastically comments "The only song you know all the words to is Happy Birthday". Father ignores Mother's unhelpful diatribe as he once again prepares to sing. It is at this point that , to my surprise, I find myself verbally supporting Father, "C'mon Father you can do it" I shout as everyone looks at me. Father looks over at me and winks."Kin yer da sing?" Joe asks. I quickly explain to Joe that I have never heard Father singing in my life, not even in the bath.

Everybody in the room is now looking at Father. Including Mother who has an apprehensive look on her face. Wilhelmina is cringing next to the coalbunker as she hides behind Sean. Father takes a final deep breath and starts to sing. ' Oh Danny Boy, the pipes the pipes are calling ..From glen to glen and down the mountain side' .There is complete silence as everyone sits open mouthed listening to Father's amazing baritone voice. Mother's face is a picture as she looks at Father with a stunned expression on her face. 'The summer's gone, and all the flow'rs are dying 'Tis you, 'tis you must go and I must bide'. As Father grows more confident he stands up as he sings 'But come ye back when summer's in the meadow..Or when the valley's hushed and white with snow' .I can clearly hear Mrs Kelly say to a now awake Uncle Pat "Jeezo, he sounds jist like 'dat fella Josef Locke". Uncle Pat nods in agreement as he sits forward in his chair and stares straight at Father with a look of admiration on his face. Father effortlessly continues. "Tis I'll be here in sunshine or in shadow..Oh, Danny boy, oh, Danny boy, I love you so'. There is premature applause and shouts of "More" at this point as Father continues to sing another two verses. He finishes with the line 'And I shall sleep in peace until you come to me'.

Everyone in the room stands and applauds loudly. Mother now has a proud look on her face as she cheers and claps her hands. This is a look I haven't seen on her face since Father emptied his first mouse trap the morning after we moved to Bridgeton. Wilhelmina has a big smile on her face and is clapping enthusiastically before she notices Sean looking at her which makes her stop and whisper under her breath "Brilliant". George, Eddie and Dom are standing with their fingers in their mouths whistling and shouting. Even Mark and Isobel have came in from the landing and have stopped kissing long enough to cheer appreciatively as Mrs Kelly helps old uncle Pat struggle from his chair and stand up to applaud Father's efforts.

Father loves the attention and places his right arm over his stomach and his left arm round his back as he bows to acknowledge the applause. Unfortunately the last bow me makes before sitting down causes him to break wind loudly which, after a moments silence, leads to more cheering and laughter.

Mrs Kelly has moved over to the wall at the side of the fire and is lowering the pulley used to dry clothes. "I t'ink it's time furra gemme o' treacle scones eh, now who'll be wantin' tae play?", she asks as she continues to lower the pulley. "Me" Joe shouts as he looks at me inviting me to agree with him "Yes please" I say to please Joe, although I don't have a clue what a game of treacle scones entails. "I remember 'ris fae when a wiz wee" shouts a slightly drunk Mother to the surprise of Mrs Kelly's family who had only ever heard her talking in a posh voice. "Geeza shout when yer ready" she continues before turning to Father and blurting "Hey Mario Lanza, 'ris wine's good innit?".

Mrs Kelly puts one end of a piece of string about three feet long through scones covered in treacle. She then ties the other end to the pulley and hoists it back up towards the ceiling. She secures the pulley rope on the hook at the fire leaving the treacle covered scones dangling from the string about my head height. "Right, Jock 'ra coalman an' Jimmy Clitheroe kin go first" Mrs Kelly announces As I stand there looking blankly at Joe with my shoulders hunched up to my ears indicating that I don't have a clue what to do, Joe declares he will go first and show me how it is done.

Joe manoeuvres into position standing, just below one of the three treacle scones and in between the feet of Uncle Pat who is still asleep on the chair below the pulley. Firstly he places his hands behind his back which provokes shouts of "Nae cheatin' noo" from the assembled throng. He then stands on his tip toes enabling him to reach the treacle covered scone and prepares to take a big bite. I am just thinking to myself that this looks relatively easy when Eddie shouts "Haud yer hoarses 'rer wee man" as he strides over to the dangling scones. "Yer no' gettin' 'it 'rat easy" he says as he pushes the scones making them sway from side to side. "Right, ye kin go noo" he adds laughing out loud. Joe prepares again and reaches up with his mouth to try and grab the scone, much to the amusement of the other party goers. The scone is swinging all ways and slaps Joe on the face a few times leaving his face covered in treacle. At this point I have changed my opinion about how easy it looks and I am now reticent to try this unusual game. Joe eventually completes his task and finishes the scone leaving the now empty string dangling. His face and hair is covered in treacle as he is ushered over to the sink by Mrs Kelly for the cleanup operation with the applause and cheers of everyone ringing in his ears.

"Right Mrs Nairn, you're up next", Eddie shouts in Mothers direction. Mother then attempts to get up from the couch holding a glass half full of wine. Her speech is now a mixture of posh, slang and drunk as she replies to Eddie "Okay dokey, haud oan a wee minute". I have often wondered why people say "A wee minute" surely a minute is a minute.

As my conscious wrestled with this dilemma, Mother has just about managed to stand up and is swaying from side to side. "Excuse me Hubert" she says politely, "Gonny haud ma' wine in case ah fall oan ma bahookie". She continues giggling like a schoolgirl and moves her hand towards Father. But before Father can reach the glass Mother drops it and it smashes on the floor. Mother looks aghast at the smashed glass on the floor and then turns towards Mrs Kelly and apologetically exclaims. "I am so, sooooooo sorry Mrs Kelly hic!, huv ye goat a bop and mucket and ah'll clean it up hic!?".

Mrs Kelly approaches Mother with a mop and bucket saying "Don't be daft now Mrs Nairn, sure it's not a problem, away ye go now and take yer shot". Trying to keep her balance Mother looks back down at the smashed glass as Mrs Kelly feverishly mops the floor at her feet and whispers "'Ris is the best party av' been tae in years hic! Yer a wovely lummin Mrs Kelly, ah mean, a lovely wummin, hic! So ye ur by the way". Mrs Kelly just smiles at Mother and finishes the mopping as Mother staggers over to the treacle scones.

"Ur ye ready ren Mrs Nairn?" Eddie asks as he pushes the scones making them sway and spin. "As ready as ah'll ever be" Mother answers as she watches the scones swaying and spinning. Her eyes are closely following the trajectory of the scones and her head is moving in unison with the swaying motion. Eventually her body starts to sway and she takes a small step back and stumbles. Suddenly the whole room becomes dark and the record player grinds to a halt just as Mary Hopkins was about to sing. " Awe fur Christ's sake" Mrs Kelly moans before adding, "Noo where did ah leave ma' purse?" as she fumbles around looking for a sixpence for the electric meter.

In the temporary darkness there are sniggers and random shouts of "Get yer hon' aff ma arse" by Eddie and "Keep yer hon' oan yer ha'penny" by Mrs Campbell. Finally George returns from the toilet and shouts "'Av goat a tanner here" and pops it in the meter.

The dim light from the bare light bulb once again fills the room and Mary Hopkins starts singing *'Those were the days my friend'*. This causes my slightly drunk Mother to stumble once again as she tries to re-focus her eyes on the swaying treacle scones. A sleeping Uncle Pat lets out an "Oooooomph!" sound as Mother lands on his lap. "I'm sooooo sorry" Mother screams as she tries to get back on her feet. On realising its Mother that has landed in his lap Uncle Pat suddenly has a big grin on his face. He places both his hands on Mother's posterior and pushes her back on her feet. Unsure whether to slap or thank him she glares at a smiling Uncle Pat as she nervously straightens her dress then her hair. When she has composed herself as best she can she looks at a still grinning Pat before pointing at his lap and saying "I think I might have broken that pipe in your trouser pocket". She then staggers back to the couch to be greeted by Mrs Campbell lying across her seat holding her stomach laughing hysterically.

Dom turns to his still smiling dad and says "You don't smoke a pipe ya durty auld bugger". On hearing this comment Uncle Pat grins even wider as he reaches into his trouser pocket and pulls out a packet of Mint Toffo and offers one to Dom as they both start laughing.

Meanwhile Mother has sat back down on the couch and is sitting with her back to Mrs Campbell pretending to talk to Father. George has resumed his disc jockey duties with the sound of Des o' Connor singing *'I Pretend'*. This selection however is met with some resistance. As Des starts singing Eddie shakes his head and leans over to Dom and moans "He's takin 'ra piss noo". Dom nods in agreement before adding "Ah know man, if he pits oan Sasha Distel 'am gon hame". The both of them are still chuckling at George's music selection as Mrs Kelly announces "Right Jimmy Clitheroe you're next" and leads me by the shoulders towards the pulley.

To my delight and Mrs Kelly's chagrin the last treacle covered scone has disappeared leaving three empty dangling bits of string. "Whit the...?" Mrs Kelly exclaims as everybody stares at the pulley. Mrs Campbell nudges Mother in the back and says "Widje look at 'rat, some bastart's stole ra' last scone". Mother turns around slightly and looks at me as I feign disappointment. Mrs Kelly looks up after checking the floor just in case it had fallen off the string and says forlornly "Sorry son, but ah only hid the three scones". Pretending to look disappointed I sigh before replying " It's okay Mrs Kelly" then I sit on the floor next to Joe.

Just as I sit down Dom stands up and shakes his head as he announces "Am away furra pish man" before adding with a smirk "Rat's heavy man, stealin' scones?". It is only then that I notice he has enough crumbs in his beard to feed a flock of birds for a week. As everyone else realizes Eddie is the culprit he is forced to break into a pretend jog to avoid the barrage of friendly abuse and monkey nuts aimed at him as he leaves the flat.

A few minutes later Mrs Campbell is helping Mrs Kelly make and distribute some spam sandwiches, when Uncle Pat opens his eyes and sits forward in his chair. After a few groans and moans he stands up and announces "'Am burstin'" before taking baby steps as he shuffles towards the front door. "Where ur you off tae auld yin?" asks George. "Ach 'am away furra three P's" an annoyed Uncle Pat answers. "Whit's the three P's?" George innocently enquires. "Fur Christ sake" Pat moans before growling at George "'Am away tae Point Percy tae 'ra Porcelain". This statement is met with howls of laughter from the men in the room and embarrassed smiles from the ladies.

Joe and I are sitting on the floor next to the fire enjoying our spam sandwiches as Mrs Kelly fills a basin with water at the sink and adds around half a dozen apples. "Right 'den, whose fur dookin' fur apples?" she shouts enthusiastically as she places the basin on the floor.

She then orders George to relinquish his chair at the record player and positions the back of the chair against the basin. The chair she was using looked distinctly like the chairs we used in school with its round green metal frame with a wooden seat and back. "Me, me" Joe responds with his right hand raised in the air. He looks at me with his eyes wide open and nodding his head at me to join him. "Me too" I shout much to Joe's delight. Mrs Kelly places a towel under the basin then looks at Joe and me and asks "Could yeez go an' get Mark and Isobel fae 'ra landing fur me?". We nod in agreement and immediately get up and make our way across the room towards the outside landing. We pass old uncle Pat on his way back from the toilet who playfully removes Joe's bunnet and ruffles his hair as he jokingly asks for a 'hunnerweight' bag of coal.

We continue towards the landing and pass Sean and Wilhelmina. "By 'ra way, leave 'rat tae Friday" Sean shouts at Joe as we approach the front door. A confused Joe stops and turns back round to look at Sean as he replies "Leave whit tae Friday?". Sean looks straight at Joe and sniggers as he responds "Robinson Crusoe's washin'". The joke seems to have been lost on Joe as he's obviously never read Robinson Crusoe.

When we reach the landing there is no sign of Mark and Isobel. "Whit's 'rat noise?" Joe asks. I listen intently and sure enough there is a funny sucking noise coming from the bottom of the stairs. "It sounds like sum'day suckin' purridge through a straw" is Joe's accurate description as we begin to follow the strange sound down the stairs. The sucking noise gets louder as we pass the toilet landing and head towards the bottom of the stairs. We are feeling a bit apprehensive as we continue slowly towards the entrance of the close. "Whit is 'rat noise?" a perturbed Joe asks as we stand at the close entrance.

It is really cold now and we can see our breath leave our mouths as Joe lightens the mood by pretending he is smoking. "Look at me wi' ma' Woodbine" he jokingly shouts as he puffs on an invisible cigarette. The fog is even thicker now and we can't even see thirty feet across the road to the wall of Martin's leather works. We forget the funny noise for a moment as we survey the eerie sight of our street shrouded in fog with the faint lights from the houses offering the only comforting glow. I can hear the muffled sound of occasional laughter from the open windows along the street and loud gruff voices emanating from the Dog Leg pub. The street itself is totally empty as Joe looks left and I look right from the edge of the close. "Scary lookin', intit?" Joe whispers. I have to agree as I reply "Very".

Suddenly the noise stops from the Dog Leg pub *and* from the open windows along the street. For a brief moment Heron St falls deathly quiet. I am looking at our shadows cast on the pavement from the dim light in the close when strangely; another shadow appears in between ours.

I whisper to Joe and nod towards the shadow as we watch it getting bigger and bigger. The strange sucking noise is now getting louder and louder "Mammy, Daddy" Joe quietly groans as I take a deep breath in readiness to turn round and run. The strange sucking noise suddenly stops as I nervously begin to turn around. My eyes follow the shadow from its head slowly down the close towards its origin. "Whit ur yooz two up tae?" Mark asks... Joe and I jump and grab each other as we scream like five year old girls. "Aw, did yeez get a fright 'rer?" Isobel adds in what can only be described as a very high pitched nasally voice.

Joe and I slowly separate and compose ourselves, "Ah knew it wiz you" a breathless Joe declares as he tries to save face, before adding quickly "Ma' maw wants yeez up 'ra stair". Mark and Isobel grin at Joe and arm in arm they start to make their way up the stair. Sure enough they start to kiss again as they climb the stair and it then becomes apparent what the funny sucking noise was.

"Take your time" I say to Joe as I help him up the stair. He is still annoyed after being frightened by Mark and Isobel as he lifts his bad leg out and up the uneven stairs. "Baldy bastart" Joe moans. He tells me Mark and Isobel were only married two weeks ago and have just returned from their honeymoon in a caravan in Saltcoats. He continues to tell me that they met when Isobel, who is a bus conductress, threatened to throw Mark off her bus in Sauchiehall St after he commented she had nice 'thr'upenny bits' as she handed him his change. They must have been shiny new coins I thought to myself but still couldn't work out why it would get you thrown off a bus.

We stop at the toilet landing to let Joe rest and he has now added the words 'wee fat' to his earlier expletive laden description of the follicley challenged Mark. I had to agree they were an odd looking match. Mark is about twenty five years old with very fine blond hair that he combs over from one side of his head to the other in order to cover the missing hair on top of his head, and quite frankly it just looked silly. He is wearing a fully buttoned grey waistcoat over a black shirt to cover his enormous belly which still manages to protrude from the gap between his waistcoat and the top of his tight grey trousers. To make matters worse he was only about five foot four inches tall with his shoes on. The buttons on his waistcoat look ready to pop at any time as they try their best to defy gravity.

Isobel on the other hand was twenty two years old but looked about fifteen. She reminded me of the girl in the 'Puppy Love' picture my Granny McDonald has hanging over her fireplace in Castlemilk. With her long black hair framing her beautiful face and skin like a porcelain doll she really was particularly stunning. She was wearing a white polo neck sweater and black hot pants. Like the ones Mother said Wilhelmina will only ever wear over her dead body. With her big black boots that reached all the way past her knee she was also about six inches taller than Mark.

It's often said in a lot of art books I have read that every work of art has at least one flaw. Well in the case of Isobel it was definitely her voice. When she speaks it is like listening to Pinky and Perky and I don't think I would like to be stuck in an elevator with her for too long.

"'Rer 'rur 'rer" Mrs Campbell shouts as Joe and I enter the flat to be met with the alien sight of Mother kneeling on a chair dressed as a 1920's flapper girl with a fork in her mouth getting ready to dook for apples. Everyone is gathered round watching as *'Mac the Knife'* by Bobby Darin belts out from the record player in the background. George stirs the basin of water with the apples in it and declares to Mother "Right ye kin go noo". Mother, still slightly drunk, leans over the edge of the chair which causes her tiara to fall off into the basin. George instinctively puts his hand in the water to retrieve the tiara just as Mother says "Oops", which releases the fork from her mouth and it falls towards the water. For a split second all eyes are on George's hand and an audible collective intake of breath can be heard, fortunately the fork misses his hand and to Mother's surprise lands right in the middle of an apple.

Mother's tenement upbringing in Partick comes to the fore once again as she lets out a yell of "Gonyersel!". She triumphantly parades the fork with the apple on it all the way back to her seat, to be met by my drunk Father who is slumped on the couch. He is clutching an empty bottle of Eldorado wine singing the wrong words to Mack the Knife. Mother plonks herself down on the couch beside Father and drunkenly waves the apple on a fork in his face as she drunkenly says "A' won an apple fur ye". Father tries to focus his bleary eyes on the apple Mother is waving like a hypnotist's watch and suddenly his body starts to heave. My confused Mother stops waving the apple as Father heaves again and this time his cheeks puff out. As everybody turns round to look at Father Eddie shouts "He's gonny be sick". My clueless Mother grabs Father's face with her hand and points it at her face while asking in a baby voice "Are you okay pumpkin?". Father is helpless to prevent nature taking its course as he heaves one last time and his cheeks puff out like a trumpet player and his eyes have a look of sheer panic.

I cover my eyes with my hands as he looks my unsuspecting Mother in the eye..... And thank God only belches, but with such ferocity it nearly blows Mother's wet tiara clean off her head. Eddie seems disappointed as he comments "A thought he wiz gonny be sick o' ower her 'rer". Father stops belching and just smiles like Stan Laurel as he drunkenly mumbles in a mock French accent "Pardonnay moi". Before Mother can give him a rollicking, Eddie interrupts as he claps his hands together and shouts "Right whose next fur 'ra dookin'?".

Everyone turns round to the basin just in time to see old Uncle Pat trying to climb up on the chair. There are moans of "Ooh! Ma' feckin' back" and "Ahh! Ma feckin' knees" but eventually he manages to assume the 'dookin' position. "Geeza fork 'ren" he demands as he kneels on the chair. Mrs Kelly hands him a fork as everyone starts to giggle, everyone except Dom who shows his admirable support by shouting "Gon yersel Da, show 'rum how it's done man" before muttering under his breath "Silly auld bastart'". He quickly turns his gaze in Mother's direction when he notices her opening a bottle of Lanliq, "Gonny geeza anither gless a' 'rat wine hen?" he asks as he holds his glass out towards Mother. Meanwhile Pat steadies himself as George stirs the basin. "Right on ye go auld yin" George announces. Pat leans out a bit further with the fork in his mouth watching the apples, after a few seconds he lets go the fork and it drops towards the apples. Unfortunately for Pat so does his false teeth as both upper and lower set race the fork towards the water, the fork wins but misses all the apples and, luckily for us that still had to 'dook', so does his teeth. "'Rat's cheatin'" George shouts sarcastically as Uncle Pat looks at everyone and gurns a smile which causes everyone to burst out laughing.

A couple of hours after we have all dooked for apples I am sitting on the floor with a very tired Joe and we are surveying the scene of my first tenement Halloween party. Mother and Father are sleeping on the couch with their heads leaning against each other. I wish I had a camera as Mother is wearing Father's top hat and has an empty bottle of Lanliq in her lap while Father is now wearing her tiara as well as her pearls. Wilhelmina and Sean are sitting on the floor at the coalbunker deep in conversation about what kind of music they like. Wilhelmina is pleading a case for Herman's Hermits which is met with derision from Sean who simply states " They're shite" and puts forward his case for a group called The Small Faces. Desperately trying not to be outdone poor Wilhelmina tamely retorts with, "They're even more poo". Sean just shakes his head and smiles at her feeble attempt to curse.

Meanwhile the two Elaine's are at opposite ends of the flat pointing and making threatening gestures at each other as Mr Campbell, Dom and Eddie have a heated debate about shipyards and unions. At first I thought they were talking about animal cruelty as I heard the words Swan Hunter, but it turns out that this is a ship building company who had stopped building ships at their Clydeholm yard in Whiteinch. Mr Campbell blamed the management, Eddie blamed the unions and for some strange reason Dom blamed the workers for wearing donkey jackets with the statement "They dunkey jaikets ur boufin man".

A contented Mrs Kelly is sitting on the arm of the chair next to a sleeping Uncle Pat, happy in the knowledge that everyone seems to be enjoying themselves. It's quite late in the evening now as Mrs Kelly enjoys a well earned drink. A drunken George is pretending to throw a basin of water over Mark and Isobel who are still kissing at the sink and I have come to the conclusion that Mark just keeps kissing her so that she doesn't have to talk to anyone with her funny voice. I also note that four of the overworked buttons on poor Mark's waistcoat had lost the battle with gravity resulting in even more of Mark's belly slowly making an appearance like that black oozy stuff from the film 'The Blob'.

Last but not least there was Mrs Campbell, during this lull in the party she seizes her opportunity as she sits forward on the edge of the couch closes her eyes and bursts into song. She proceeds to sing the saddest song I have ever heard in my life. "I once had a dear old motherrr..An' she wiz kind tae me...and when I was in trouble...She sat me oan her knee". At this point Mrs Kelly wipes a tear from her eye as she nods her head and acknowledges Mrs Campbell's song choice by saying "Gonyersel hen". Mrs Campbell continues to sing and the 'dear old mother' in the song ends up in heaven with the angels. By the time she finishes half the people in the room are sobbing, including the men, as they give her a rapturous round of applause interspersed with shouts of "She's sum chanter int she?"and "Ah luv 'rat song man".

The applause wakes Mother and Father from their drunken slumber and they automatically join in the applause even though they have no idea what they are applauding. Mother has sobered up slightly as she nudges Father and asks "What time is it Hubert?". Father looks at his pocket watch and tries to focus as he mumbles "It's eh, eh, um, eh" he then stares at Mother as he sheepishly replies "Oh dear! my watch has stopped at five o' clock". Mother just sighs and shakes her head. "'Dat's nearly midnight now Mrs Nairn" Mrs Kelly shouts over to Mother. "Nearly midnight" a shocked Mother repeats before adding "I think it's time we were off home". She quickly stands up and the bottle of Lanliq on her lap falls to the ground, much to Mothers relief it doesn't smash. She then stares at Father before saying "Would you mind taking off my tiara and pearls Hubert?". My embarrassed Father sits bolt upright as he fumbles about trying to remove Mother's jewellery. He then looks at Mother before truculently asking "Well can I have my top hat back then?".

After they have sorted themselves Mother orders Wilhelmina to get ready to leave. This request is met with groans from Wilhelmina and a plea for more time as we only live next door. Isobel takes a break from locking lips with Mark and decides to take Wilhelmina's side as she screeches at Mother "Don't worry yersel Mrs Nairn we'll keep an eye oan her fur ye".

Everyone in the room, except Mark, winces as they struggle with Isobel's high pitched squeak of a voice, including Mother, whose face is still contorted as she replies "No thank you dear, Wilhelmina will be coming with us". On realising that her reply might be deemed as quite curt she unfortunately follows it up with, "But it was very nice of you to squeak up and offer your assistance". She then turns to help Father put on his jacket totally unaware of her Freudian slip. Everyone in the room has stifled their laughter as Isobel stares daggers at Mother but isn't quite sure if she heard her correctly and thankfully returns to her kissing marathon with Mark.

When Mother is finally ready to leave, she motions with her head for me to join her at the front door as she starts to say cheerio to everyone. I say my goodbyes to Joe and arrange to meet up with him the next day. Mrs Kelly has joined us and opens her arms to hug Mother. Surprisingly Mother reciprocates and gives Mrs Kelly a genuinely warm hug. The reason I'm surprised is because she doesn't even hug Father. "We have had a wonderful time" Mother gushes to a smiling Mrs Kelly, "Well I'm glad dat ye enjoyed yersel" Mrs Kelly responds before adding "We'll need tae do dis again sometime". Without thinking Mother responds with "Why don't you all join us at the 'Bells'?". The first person to respond is Mrs Campbell who, without looking up, raises her glass in the air and shouts "Ah'll be 'rer". This opens the floodgates and eventually everyone in the room , apart from the two Elaine's, insist they will be there too.

We leave the flat and are standing in the cold dark landing waiting for a still drunk Father to locate the keyhole of our front door with his key. As I look out the landing window at the toilet I can see right across 'The Booly' towards London Rd. The fog has started to lift now and I can clearly see the lights on the top deck of the buses heading towards Auchenshuggle. Meanwhile Father is still trying to gain entry to our flat when it dawns on Mother what she has done. She looks back at the now closed door of the Kelly's with a worried expression on her face. She bites her bottom lip deep in thought just as the volume is increased on the record player and Andy Stewart, along with everybody else at the party, starts to sing *"I've jist came down fae the Isle o' Skye, am no very big....."*. Mother shrugs her shoulders and sighs loudly as she whispers "Oh well" just as Father manages to open the door and we all enter our flat singing *"Donald where's yer troosers?"*.

Penny Furra Guy?

After breakfast I return to my bedroom to finish reading a comic called 'The Beezer' that Sammy insists I read instead of Father's Glasgow Herald. My concentration is broken by the faint sound of someone calling my name. I get up from my bunk bed and open the bedroom door to see if it is my parents calling me only to hear Father singing 'Born Free' at the top of his voice. It's been five days now since Mrs Kelly's hallo'een party and Father hasn't stopped singing since. Thinking I must have imagined it I close my room door only to still hear someone shouting my name. I conclude it must be coming from outside and decide to open my bedroom window and have a look. I try with all my might to open the window, but it won't budge, there used to be two rings at the bottom of this old sash style window to lift it up, but these came off in Fathers hand just after we moved in here, so I now have to push the window up from the top. In the end I settle for rubbing a hole in the condensation covered windows with my sleeve and look down towards the street.

When I look left towards the 'Dog Leg pub' I can see the ragman getting ready to blow his trumpet, even though there is a queue of eager children already there. Just in front of him is the man selling hot coal brickets unsurprisingly there is lots of steam rising from the hot bricks as it's a very cold morning.

I then look right towards Dalmarnock Rd and can only see two girls playing hopscotch across the road. One of the girls is knocking an empty tin of 'Kiwi Crown' or 'Cherry Blossom' shoe polish with her foot as she hops between the numbered squares. "DOON HERE!" a voice shouts as I rub the bottom of the steamed up window and look directly below me. There is Sammy furiously gesticulating at me to join him in the street, I give him the thumbs up and head downstairs to join him.

After letting my parents know I am going out to play I open the front door and nearly knock over Joe. "Ah wiz jist cummin' in fur ye 'rer" a smiling Joe says with his hand still in the 'knock at the door' position. I return his hand to his side and finish putting on my anorak as I explain that Sammy is waiting for us and we make our way down the stairs.

"'Mon see 'rese two diddies" a sniggering Sammy says as we join him in the street. Sammy points at two young men carrying an old door about twenty yards away heading in our direction. "They've been tryin' tae humph 'rat door up 'ra street fur ages" Sammy continues as he starts to laugh out loud. As we look on they drop the door again and take another rest. We sit down at the close and Sammy pulls five stones from his pocket and we start to play. Sammy tells us that he knows the two men very well and they are friends of his big brother. One is called Chic and the other Billy. He goes on to tell us that they have never worked since leaving school and that the school they did attend was somehow 'Approved'.

Watching Chic and Billy's comical effort to transport the door to its destination was like watching an old Laurel and Hardy film. Chic stood about six foot tall but also had a six foot waist. He was wearing grubby, faded dungarees with a large brown belt around his waist below his belly. His dungarees were tucked into the large 'bovver' boots he was wearing on his feet and his chubby face had a large scar down the left side from just below his eye to his mouth, which added to his shaved head made him look really mean.

Billy on the other hand was about five foot tall; his small thin frame was covered by a boilersuit that looked about five sizes too big with rolled up legs and sleeves. His thin face was covered in acne and was just visible below his greasy long black hair. They both had a permanent rolled up cigarette dangling from their mouths that they would relight every now and again. I would suggest Billy was the brains of the outfit judging by the way he buzzed about the heavy door like the spiv in the St Trinian films, barking out orders to poor Chic. Who, although he didn't have a clue what Billy meant, would try his very best to carry them out.

" Fur Christ's sake ye nearly took ma' hon' aff 'rer ya fud" Billy screams at his apologetic friend as they pass us carrying the wooden front door with the doorframe still attached. The door in question keeps opening inside the frame and has just been dropped by Chic, much to Billy's consternation, enroute to the bonfire being erected on the spare ground known as the Booly behind the backcourts of Heron St.

The heavy door is now leaning against the wall a couple of yards from where we are sitting on the pavement as Billy and Chic discuss the various options available to deliver the heavy door to its destination. "Hey Sammy" Chic shouts "Gonny geeza hon here?". Sammy reluctantly gets up and walks over towards Chic. I say reluctantly because in our game of five stones he was in big twosy and well on his way to victory. "'Kin ye grab an end a' 'ris door 'n geeza hon' tae get it doon ra' Booly?" Chic asks Sammy. Chic, Sammy and Billy lift the door but only manage to carry it about five yards before it falls to the ground again and they all jump back. Billy looks back at Joe and me as he shouts "Yooz two anaw", and motions with his head for us to join him. We excitedly stand up, and that is when Billy notices Joe's bad leg with the big black boot on it. "Naw, naw wee man sit oan yer erse" Billy instructs Joe. A dejected Joe returns to the five stones just as Chic shouts "Cheers 'onyway wee man" this makes Joe feel slightly better.

"Right you grab 'rat end" Billy barks at me indicating the bottom of the door with his head. "Excuse me" I say, as I make my way to the bottom of the door next to Chic. "Is this door for the bonfire?" I ask. Billy looks at Chic and then they both look at Sammy and ask "Is he fur real?". Sammy sheepishly nods to indicate yes. Billy turns to me and sarcastically answers my question with "Naw, we're building a raft tae sail doon 'ra Clyde". Chic dutifully giggles and then slowly says in a mock posh voice "Yes, this door is indeed for 'ra bonfire, pray why dae ye ask?".

Billy and Chic start laughing at my expense as I ask Sammy to grab an end of the door and we lean the door against the wall about two feet up. A still laughing Billy folds his arms and Chic copies him like a five year old child as they stand watching me and relight their cigarettes. I indicate to Sammy to stand back and then I walk onto the road. As my audience watches me I turn and run towards the door and jump on it. This action manages to separate the door from the doorframe. I then pull the doorframe to one side and lean the door against the wall in the same position. At this point Chic looks at Billy as they stop laughing, unfold their arms and start to feel a bit stupid because they have carried this full door all the way from Muslin St.

I take one step back lift my leg and kick through one of the door panels. I repeat this for all four panels. After moving all the panel wood out of the way, I stand the skeleton of the door halfway across a high part of the pavement and the road. I tell Sammy to stand at one side of me and shout on Joe for the other side. I count down from three and we run towards the door and jump on it and it completely snaps in two. I pick up one half and hand it to a very happy Chic, and the other half to a dumbstruck Billy. Sammy, Joe and I pick up the rest of the wood as I say "Let's go then" and head off towards the Booly. "Haud oan, haud oan" Billy shouts as he catches up with me. He stares at me before saying " 'Am the wan 'rat says lets go then". We all stop and look at Billy who walks a couple of steps in front staring at all of us one at a time as he passes with a 'I'm the boss' look on his face before shouting "Let's go 'ren".

When we reach the Booly we are met with the impressive sight of a tower made up of doors and pallets, there is even an old armchair and mattress in the centre of the pile of wood. As we throw our door on the bonfire I innocently ask where the door came from, both Billy and Chic reply at the same time but with different answers. Billy replies "We funnit in 'ra street" while Chic replies "An empty hoose in Muslin St". Billy angrily shakes his head at Chic who belatedly bows his head and whispers like a scolded child "We funnit in 'ra street".

When it is time to say cheerio to Billy and Chic they tell us that they haven't got a 'Guy' yet for the top of the fire. This news sparks Sammy's entrepreneurial spirit as he decides that we will make a 'Guy' and sit outside the 'The Cactus' pub at Bridgeton Cross and make some money. With Sammy as project manager Joe is tasked with making a sign that simply reads: 'PENNY FOR THE GUY', while Sammy and I will make the actual 'Guy'. We agree that these tasks are to be completed within half an hour and arrange to meet up again outside my close.

Half an hour later we meet up as arranged. Joe reveals his impressive sign made from the inside of a cornflake box which reads: PENY FUR A GUY. As he looks down at his sign he proudly adds "Ah used ma' Ma's bingo pen". It is now the turn of Sammy and I to show Joe our 'Guy'. After looking at our creation for a few seconds Joe's critique consists of the statement "Jeezo, it's a wee bit wee izzit no'?". I have to admit Joe's observation was spot on. The hastily constructed 'Guy' consisted of an old pair of my short trousers, Sammy's old striped 'sloppy joe' t-shirt, a brown paper bag with a smiley face drawn on it for the head, all stuffed with the filling from an old urine stained mattress lying on the unlit bonfire. Joe also points out the shoes it is wearing, one wee black sandshoe and one old working boot, "We only hid haufanoor" a smirking Sammy offers in our defence and undeterred we head off to Bridgeton Cross to make our fortune.

Sammy is carrying 'Guy' like a small child in his arms as we make our way past Woolworths towards Bridgeton Cross. Just as we pass a small group of old ladies at the bus stop Guy's left leg falls off right at their feet. One of the ladies with thick glasses on screams and jumps back at the sight of Guy's left leg lying on Dalmarnock Rd. This causes the other old ladies to burst out laughing. On realising that it is only a dummy the little old lady places her hand on her heart as she sighs "Fur Christ's sake ah shat ma'sel 'rer". This causes her friends to laugh even louder as they watch us trying to stuff Guy's leg back into his shorts. "Sorry" I meekly say as we hurry the last few yards to the Cactus pub on the corner of Bridgeton Cross.

"Why are we rushing" I ask my two friends as we sit down outside the pub. "Cos it's nearly hauf two" Sammy replies as he sits Guy against the wall just outside the entrance. He then notices the blank expression on my face. "'Ra pubs shut at hauf two an' don't open again tae five 'ra night" an exasperated Sammy elaborates. He then places the sign on Guy's chest as we sit down and wait.

While we are waiting I pass the time surveying the scene of bustling Bridgeton Toll. The first thing that catches my attention is the almost hypnotic melodic beat created by the buses wheels passing over the old tram lines about ten feet away. Clouds of engine and cigarette smoke hang in the air above the heads of the throngs of chattering people going about their daily business, which coupled with the traffic noise creates a cacophony of unintelligible noise. As I look towards the Olympia picture house my view is temporarily obstructed by an old man and woman walking towards us pushing the skeleton of a pram carrying a roll of linoleum. It is only when they eventually pass I notice a small queue of adults and children waiting for the afternoon showing of Ice Station Zebra with Rock Hudson.

Suddenly the doors to the pub fly open and two men stagger out and stand beside us. One of the men is quite old with grey hair and the other is a young man with long hair who is trying to stand still with his hands in his pockets. I look up and can clearly see the words 'British Rail' on the back of their donkey jackets which is concealing the majority of their oil and grease stained overalls. "Where ur we gonny go noo smart arse?" the young man asks as he tries to stand upright with his left leg static and his right leg moving randomly to ensure he keeps his balance. "You wur 'ra wan 'rat wantit' a pass oot 'cos ye won a few bob oan 'ra hoarses" he continues. The older man, who is quite steady on his feet, calmly re-lights a rolled up cigarette in his mouth before announcing triumphantly "Av goat it!", as he points his tobacco stained fingers in the air.

"C'mere, jist you cum wi yer auld Da", he signals to the young man to follow him and they turn around. "Where ur we gon?" the young man asks. The older man puts his arm around his shoulders as he proudly says "We're gon tae see ma' pal Merlin who runs a wee shebeen in Muslin St". The young man stares at his friend with a bemused expression on his face as he asks "Whit dae ye call him Merlin fur?".The older man pulls his shoulder tightly as he replies "Cos when 'ra pubs ur shut.... his hoose is magic" he replies as they both start laughing.

It's at this point Sammy shouts "Penny fur the guy?". They look down towards us, smile profusely, and without uttering a word reach into their pockets and toss a thr'upenny bit each into the old bunnet Joe had brought to collect our earnings. The young man smiles as he reciprocates the old mans actions and puts his arm around his shoulders as they start to walk away stepping in unison. The old man bursts into a chorus of "We're off tae see 'ra wizard..." as the young man asks "Whits a shebeen?".

A few minutes later I look over at the clock on the 'Umbrella' at Bridgeton Cross just as it reaches 2.30pm. "'Rat's nearly two bob we've goat" Joe exclaims as he counts the money in the bunnet. The doors to the pub are wide open now with a barman standing there shouting "Time gentlemen please". Thinking that there won't be many more people inside the pub we get ready to leave. But just as Sammy helps Joe to his feet a steady procession of people start to leave the pub, they are all dressed in their Sunday best which leads Sammy to conclude that they must have been to a christening. We quickly sit down again and Joe and Sammy start shouting "Penny fur the guy". Our wee bunnet is inundated with coins, pennies, ha'pennies, and even the odd sixpence. As the last person leaves the barman slams the doors shut as we look in disbelief at the bounty we have accrued in such a short space of time. "We're rich" Joe shouts excitedly as he holds the bunnet in the air. "Let's go hame an' coont it" Sammy proclaims as we excitedly pick up 'Guy' and hurry back to Heron St.

"Seven shillings and sixpence" I announce as I place the last coin on the pile. Our earnings from 'Guy' are sitting on the bottom stair of my close as Sammy and Joe peer over my shoulder eagerly awaiting the final tally. "How much izzat each?" Joe asks as he leans further over my shoulder and looks at the pile of coins. "Two shillings and sixpence" I reply. Joe's eyes light up as he stands up straight and exclaims "Wow! 'rat must be nearly hauf a' croon". After clarifying it is indeed half a Crown Joe asks "Whit yeez gonny spend yours oan?". Right away Sammy replies "Bangers" Joe immediately concurs with Sammy's response as he shouts "Aye Bangers". I have to admit that I was taken aback by my friend's eagerness to spend our earnings on sausages. I was even more confused when Sammy intimated that he was looking forward to lighting them and throwing them into a close.

I am just about to question this weird decision to buy sausages when my blushes are saved as Joe adds "Whit other fireworks kin we get?". I then realise that bangers are some kind of firework.

After distributing our new found wealth Sammy suggests that, before we buy fireworks, we deliver Guy to the bonfire. As Mother frowns upon me climbing the wall in the backcourt to enter the Booly and Joe has a bad leg, Sammy informs us that "Thurs' a big hole in 'ra dyke" at number 49. We pick up Guy and with the coins jangling in our pockets make our way to the big hole.

We enter the close at number 49 and are met by the sound of a young girl singing. She has the most beautiful singing voice I have ever heard. Sammy and Joe continue through the close to the backcourt as I pause a moment at the bottom of the stairs. On the toilet landing I can see the girl with the angelic voice standing in a trance like state looking out of the landing window as she sings '*Sailor stop your roaming....Sailor, leave the sea*'. After a minute or two Sammy and Joe join me and they too look up at the girl. '*Sailor, when the tide turns ...Come home safe to me*' she continues as we stand mesmerised by her singing. Sammy eventually breaks the silence by whispering, "'Rat's Lizzie Boyle, she's sum singer intshe?". Joe and I nod our heads in agreement with Sammy's assessment as he continues "Ah know 'rat song". He then screws up his face as he looks up at the ceiling of the close struggling to remember the name or singer of the song in question. He starts to think out loud as he mutters to himself "Pet...eh, Pet...um..." eventually he has a 'Eureka' moment as he shouts "PETUNA CLERK". He looks relieved as he informs us that the song is called '*Sailor*' and that his Father bought it last year for his mum's birthday.

Lizzie turns around and abruptly stops singing as soon as she notices her new audience. She looks horrified and covers her face with her blue pinafore to hide her embarrassment before running up the stairs. Joe starts clapping his hands and Sammy and I join in applauding and whistling as loud as we can. When we realise that Lizzie won't be doing an encore Sammy jerks his head to indicate we better go. I'm still not totally convinced that there is a singer called 'Petuna Clerk' as we make our way through to the backcourt.

"Where's 'ra hole in 'ra wa'?" Joe asks as we enter the back court. "Haud oan" Sammy replies as we notice an old woman standing there. She looks like a clone of all the other old people in the East end of Glasgow. She is wearing a hairnet and a grease stained flowery pinafore. As well as the customary slippers with the fur across the top and the heels squashed flat. Her outfit is completed with the obligatory nylon stockings around her ankles. I am beginning to think that when woman reach a certain age in Bridgeton the government must issue them with this 'uniform'.

My attention is drawn towards an old carpet hanging over the washing line and some sort of guitar shaped object made out of bamboo lying on the ground. She has just lit a cigarette which is being feverishly sucked in her toothless mouth as she stands looking up at the sky. "What's she doing?" I whisper to my friends. "Dunno" Sammy replies. Joe just shrugs his shoulders.

The old woman then puts out her cigarette with her fingers and places it in the front pocket of her pinafore. She then bends down and picks up the bamboo guitar and holds it with her right hand at the neck end. We all curiously stare in her direction as she proceeds to batter the carpet with the bamboo guitar filling the air with clouds of dust. It's only when Joe starts coughing that she stops and turns to look right at us. Her scary face looks as if it has been beaten a few times with the bamboo guitar as she squints her eyes and screams in a high pitched whine, "Whit yooz wantin'?". I freeze on the spot and just stare at her, Joe decides looking at his feet is the best response while Sammy brazenly asks "Huv ye seen a wee broon cat Mrs?" The old woman looks confused for a second before replying "Naw av no' seen yer cat, noo bugger aff".

She then starts beating the carpet again with even more aggression causing the whole backcourt, and beyond, to fill with dust. Suddenly we hear a female voice coming from the backcourt at number 51, "Fur Christ's sake, geeza brek, av jist hung a washin' oot". The old lady stops and moves over to the wall separating the backcourts and shouts back "Away 'n geez peece ya clatty bizzum". This infuriates the woman at number 51 and she shouts back "Ah'll clatty bizzum ye ya auld bastart, am cummin' roon 'rer 'ra noo". On hearing this, the old woman has second thoughts about confronting her younger sounding adversary and scurries towards the close mumbling "Bitch" under her breath as she hurriedly passes us and enters the sanctuary of the close.

"Quick, let's go" Sammy shouts. But before we can move we hear a blood curling scream from within the close, we run inside and see the breathless old woman leaning against the wall with her left hand and her right hand over her chest. She starts to regain her composure as she points to the bottom stair and blurts out "Ah shat ma'sel 'rer". We look down at the bottom stair and there sitting quite comfortably is 'Guy'. We are still trying to stifle our laughter as Sammy stands with his hands on his hips before sarcastically pointing his finger and shouting at 'Guy' "There yer there ya wee bugger, where huv you been?", He then grabs 'Guy' and shouts "*RUN*" as we burst out laughing and quickly make our way through the backcourt with the old woman waving her fist and shouting "'Am tellin' yer maws oan yeez, ya wee bastart's".

We duck under the abused carpet and sure enough there is a large hole in the wall leading to the Booly which we hurriedly jump through, unfortunately leaving poor Guy's left leg behind in our haste.

Standing at the top of the grass hill that leads to the lower level of the Booly we are still laughing when an obviously worried Joe asks, "Dae ye 'fink 'rat auld wummin wull tell ma maw?". Sammy sniggers as he replies "Nah! She'll be too busy shiting 'ersel fae 'rat wummin 'it number 51".

We slide down the hill on our backsides and make our way over to the bonfire. It is only when we reach the bonfire that we notice Guy has lost another a couple of limbs. "Oh shite" Sammy exclaims as he holds up the remains of poor Guy which consist of a head, and a torso with one arm.

As we stand and lament the demise of poor Guy we are interrupted by two small boys about eight years old. One of the boys is slightly taller than the other and is wearing what looks like his big brothers' short trousers that hang midway between his feet and his knee with the waist nearly at his chest. His thick grey socks are around his ankles covering his torn sandshoes and his short black hair is neatly combed at the front but sticking out at the back like a burst mattress. His freckled filled dirty face contorts as he points at Guy and simply says "At's pish". His smaller ginger headed cohort tugs his arm and whispers "We need tae go". The taller boy rejects this advice shrugging off the smaller boy as he points to the top of the bonfire and continues, "Oor Guy's much better 'ran 'rat wee shitey 'hing". His wee pal tries again and pleads "C'mon we need tae go". We look up at the bonfire and notice a large Guy about six feet tall sitting proudly at the apex of the pile, fully stuffed and wearing long trousers and a shirt it made our effort seem pretty pathetic.

An irked Sammy turns his attention to the taller boy and barks "Dae whit yer wee pal says an' bugger aff". The taller boy defiantly smiles at Sammy his wee pal starts to get irritated as he pulls his friend by the arm and begs "We need tae go...right noo". The taller boy turns and looks his wee pal right in the eye and moans "Haud yer hoarses, 'am enjoying 'ris, whits 'ra rush". The smaller lad places both hands behind his rear end as he starts to jump up and down on the spot and his eyes begin to water, He eventually shouts "COS A' NEED A JOBBY", he then turns and runs as fast as his wee legs can carry him reluctantly followed by his taller pal.

Sammy waits until the lads are outside hearing range before shouting "Aye gon... get tae...".They disappear up the hill where the taller boy stands and sticks two fingers up from both hands as he wiggles his backside. We decide to ignore this blatant show of defiance and turn our attention to Guy who, after a count of three, is unceremoniously despatched somewhere in the middle of the bonfire.

"Hoi! Sammy, gonny geeza hon' here?" Billy shouts from over at the Dalmarnock Rd end of the Booly. We turn around to see Billy and Chic struggling with what seems like fifty long wooden poles. We run towards them just as Chic drops his bundle closely followed by Billy who deliberately throws his bundle to the ground. "Ma erms ur killin' me" Chic moans as we reach the struggling duo. "Whereje get 'rese?" Sammy asks. Chic is about to reply when he is interrupted by Billy who declares "We fun 'rem lyin' in Poplin St". He then glares at Chic who concurs by nodding his head and saying "Aye, Poplin St".

The pieces of wood are very long and flat with a 'V' shape cut out of end. "They look like claes poles" Joe states as he catches up with us. "Oh, dae they?" Billy replies as he and Chic furtively look up at the sky. There is about twenty of these poles now lying at our feet as Billy looks at us and asks "Kin ye geeza hon tae cerry 'rum tae 'ra bonfire?". He then looks directly at me before adding sarcastically "Or has Bamber Gascoigne goat any other ideas?", I just smile as we grab a bundle each and head for the bonfire.

Joe insists on carrying at least one pole as he follows behind us. I drop off my bundle at the bonfire and head back with Sammy for the rest of the poles and we pass poor Joe struggling with his pole, which is about five times his size, he refuses our offer of help and soldiers on. I now have this vision in my head of about twenty wee wifies in the backcourts of Poplin St scratching their heads at the sudden disappearance of their clothes poles. This vision is quickly replaced by one with loads of kids turning up at school on a nice sunny day wearing soaking wet clothes.

I am brought back to reality by Sammy who asks "Dae ye fink hoddit 'n doddit knocked they poles?". After taking a few seconds to decipher Sammy's question, I simply nod in reply as I can't imagine anyone throwing them out never mind twenty at the same time. We pass Joe again on our final journey with the remaining poles; he is still struggling and is now holding the pole like a jousting Ivanhoe without the horse, eventually he makes it to the bonfire.

Chic grabs the pole and places it upright against the bonfire, which now looks like a wigwam with all the clothes poles around the perimeter. "That'll dae nicely" Billy declares as he stands back admiring his handy work. "Magic" Chic adds as he looks on with his arms folded. After a few seconds Billy looks at Sammy and shouts "Right, we're off wee man, see yeez 'ra night" he then heads back towards Dalmarnock Rd closely followed by Chic who is rubbing his hands together in eager anticipation of the evenings events.

We make our way back up the hill and decide to use the hole in the wall again as we all agree that the wee angry old woman will still be in her house hiding from her irate neighbour. After climbing through the hole, we again duck under the carpet and head through the close. As we reach the bottom of the stairs Lizzie Boyle is once again in full voice, this time she is lending her dulcet tones to a song that even I knew, '*Rocking, rolling, riding, out along the bay, All bound for Morningtown, many miles away*' Lizzie's beautiful version of The Seekers, Morningtown Ride fades as we leave the close and enter a now busy Heron St.

"Hoi, Sammy" a female voice shouts as we walk along the street, Sammy immediately looks up to see his Mother leaning out of her window gesticulating at Sammy to approach her. Sammy walks the few yards to below his window as Joe and I wait outside our close. We watch as Sammy tries to catch the coins his Mother is dropping from the window, "Av tae go a message fur ma' Ma" a forlorn Sammy laments as he rejoins us, "Av tae get a packet o' lentils oot 'ra Grain Store fur ma Da's soup" he continues. Sammy cheers up slightly when Joe and I offer to accompany him, "We kin get wur bangers while we're roon 'rer" Joe says excitedly.

The Grain Store was on Old Dalmarnock Rd next to Doctors Lawton and Quigley's surgery and we arrive a few minutes later. The Grain Store has all sorts of hessian or gunny sacks outside filled with every imaginable seed or grain you could think of. Inside the shop the floor is covered in sawdust and the shelves are stacked with already weighed brown bags filled with the various stock available. We join the small queue and await our turn to be served. While we are waiting we can hear the two ladies in front of us talking "Aye sum bastart stole ma claes pole" moans the woman with the headscarf. "Nawww" her disbelieving friend sympathises. "Aye, ah kid you not'" she continues. "Jeezo" her friend commiserates, "Honesty God, ah wiz jist back fae 'ra steamie wi' two big bags a' washin' anaw" she elaborates. This time her friend just shakes her head and 'tuts' before asking "Whit ur ye gonny dae noo?" The woman with the headscarf takes a step forward in the queue before shrugging her shoulders and responding matter of factly, "Ah jist goat ma man tae knock me anither wan" to my surprise her friend responds "Oh 'rats good, honestly ye need eyes oan 'ra back o' yer heed, so ye dae". The old saying 'two wrongs don't make a right' obviously didn't ring any bells with these two ladies.

After purchasing the lentils for Sammy's' Mother we make our way down Muslin St to Main St. We are heading for a wee newsagent next to 'Galls' wool shop that Sammy insists we can purchase bangers and matches with no questions asked. On arrival at our destination Sammy declares "Right let me dae 'ra talkin'".

He steps up to the counter and asks the man behind the counter if he has any bangers, without a moment's hesitation the man bends down behind the counter and hands Sammy a cigarette sized box, "Two bob" is all the man says. Sammy hands over his money and then motions with his head for Joe and I to do the same. As we get ready to leave the man randomly shouts "Matches". Sammy stops and returns to the counter just as the man puts a box of matches on the counter and growls "Thru' pence". Sammy looks at the box of matches on the counter and then looks at the man "Huv ye no goat a book a' matches" he asks. The man sighs loudly as he bends down again and replaces the box with a book of matches, "Penny" he grunts, and again, Joe and I copy Sammy and we leave the shop.

I am just about to let Sammy know how impressed I was with his purchasing skills when he blurts out "'Rat wiz ma Uncle Jimmy", before Joe or I can say anything he continues "Grumpy bastart so he is'". It transpires that Jimmy hasn't had anything to do with Sammy's Mother for years ever since he was caught peeing in her rubber plant at a party in Sammy's house. It also didn't help that Sammy's dad thought it was hilarious and still insists to this day that's the reason the plant is now over four feet tall.

We make our way back to Heron St and Sammy delivers the lentils safely to his Mother then meets up with Joe and I and we head towards Baltic St to light our bangers. We stand outside the main door of Martins Leather Works, which is now closed for the day, and start to open our boxes of bangers. "Whit ur we gonny dae wi' o' 'rese squibs?" Joe asks as he opens his box. "Ah fink we should keep 'rum fur 'ra night" Sammy replies as he quickly opens his box. After a quick count they both exclaim "Whit the...". What's wrong I ask. "Av only goat four" Joe moans, "Me anaw" Sammy groans. I open mine, and sure enough only have four as well. "We should huv eight in each boax" Sammy seethes. His Uncle Jimmy had split the boxes knowing full well nobody can tell their parents as they shouldn't be buying fireworks in the first place, "'Rat ...Fat...Grumpy...Ugly... Bastart" Sammy growls, before vowing to seek revenge at a later date.

"C'mon an' let wan aff each" Joe suggests. Sammy and I agree and I watch closely as they take one banger each from their boxes. Sammy decides to go first, he holds the bottom of the banger as he opens his book of matches, and with great dexterity he tears off a match and strikes it. He moves the lit match towards the blue touch paper until it turns red, then he quickly throws the banger onto the road. The touch paper starts to fizz and a slow procession of sparks fly out the top of the banger. Sammy and Joe put their fingers in their ears anticipating the big bang. Unfortunately the banger just fizzes some more, makes a 'Phhhutttt' sound and goes out. Joe decides to try his but only achieves the same result as Sammy and it turns out all our bangers are literally 'damp squibs'.

An apoplectic Sammy reiterates his intent to get even with his Uncle as Joe and I pledge to help him in any way we can.

We trudge back to Heron St with a number of plans to gain revenge on Sammy's uncle at the embryonic stage and as we reach number 43 I notice Father walking up the street carrying a box under his arm. When he reaches us he says a cheery 'Hello' and shows us that he has bought a small box of fireworks he goes on to say that Sammy and Joe are welcome to join us round our backcourt tonight when we set them off. Unfortunately he also informs me its tea time, so I say cheerio to Sammy and arrange to meet him again at 7.30. Father disappears up the close as I help Joe up the stairs and when we reach the landing Father has already invited Mrs Kelly to our firework display.

Father has spent the last couple of hours reading the instructions on the back of the fireworks box, and with every passing minute his confidence is draining. "Some of these fireworks are highly dangerous" he observes before replacing the lid on the box for the umpteenth time.

We used to attend large organised displays when we lived in the West End, so Father has never lit a firework in his life. Eventually he asks me to bring my torch, before Mother squeezes my head into woolly hat that is obviously two sizes too small. She then proceeds to wrap one of Father's old scarves around my neck about three times which nearly chokes me in the process. With my Gloverall duffle coat buttoned all the way up and the hood pulled over the hat, she then tucks my trousers inside my wellies before finishing off my ensemble with a massive pair of woolly gloves. Finally she stands back to admire her work with the words "There, all done".

I now have enough insulation to undertake a trek to the North Pole, and have to rotate my whole body just to see where I'm going. "Whmm ummm" I mumble, to which Mother replies "Pardon". I mumble even louder "Whmmm Whmmmmm", Mother reaches over and removes the scarf from my mouth, "Where's Wilhelmina?", I ask. "Oh, she's staying over with her friend tonight" she replies before replacing the scarf back over my mouth and grabbing her coat. Making our way downstairs we can hear lots of laughter and chatter emanating from the backcourt and as we stop at the landing window and look down, the backcourt is filled with people, The Bains, The Kelly's, The Campbell's and the dreaded McCabe's, Fathers face turns grey as we continue down the stairs.

"Hullorerr" shouts Mrs Campbell as we enter the backcourt; she then raises the glass she is holding in our direction. After a few more "Hullorerr's" and "Howzitgon's" we integrate into the throng of people. The light at the entrance to the backcourt is flickering on and off so most of the light in the backcourt is coming from the flat lights which had been left on.

Mr Bain is throwing wood on a small fire he made using the bottom half of an old oil drum, and I can see a line of brown bags with cans of beer sitting against the wall next to a small selection of fireworks.

Like me, some of the other children had torches which shone in all directions including the sky. It reminded me of the war films on television when the soldiers were looking for German aeroplanes in the night sky. Mr Campbell was standing a clothes pole upright against the Booly wall and hammering a nail into it, while the McCabe twins sat on top of the Booly wall itching to throw the bangers they were holding in amongst the crowded backcourt.

Mother and Father are being encouraged to partake in some alcohol by the other adults in attendance with various shouts of "Gon, take a wee hauf" and "Huv a wee drink". They try to refuse the kind offers, with the memory of the Halloween party still fresh in their minds. Mr Bain thrusts a lit sparkler into my hand with the words "Here ye go wee man".

I look around our backcourt and everyone seems to be having a great time. Even Mother and Father seem relaxed and are laughing and joking with all our neighbours. I can't help but notice the difference to when we lived in our big house in the West End, then I didn't know any of our neighbours, they would very rarely speak to other adults never mind children. Yet here we are among people who are a genuine, tough, hard working bunch with very little in the way of material things, but who all help each other to get through tough times. I start to feel a tinge of sadness that we will be leaving here shortly to move into our new flat in Ruby St.

To the left of the bin shed I notice Joe standing with Mrs Kelly, the only reason I knew it was him was the big black boot on his bad leg. The rest of him was insulated in a similar fashion to me, except for the grey woollen trench coat he was wearing with the big belt. I remember him telling me he hated that coat, he got it from 'The Meanie' along with a navy blue suit with short trousers and only ever wore it if his Mother made him.

"BANG" Everyone jumps as the first banger is let off, except I notice, Mrs Kelly, who doesn't seem her usual cheery self. "What's the matter with your mum?" I ask Joe as we make our way over to the small oil drum fire. "Ah don't know, she's been' funny o' day" Joe replies, "She wiz in a right grumpy mood when a' went in fur ma dinner" he continues. We warm ourselves at the fire as the fireworks around Bridgeton are in full flow, there is even the whistling sound of the odd rocket now and again as they go off and light up the night sky.

Mr Bain starts the proceedings at our display by hanging a 'Catherine Wheel' on the nail in the clothes pole. "Ston' back everybody" he orders as he leans over and lights the blue touch paper.

The Catherine Wheel bursts into life and starts spinning furiously, suddenly the nail comes loose and the wheel falls to the ground and shoots sparks in all directions as it bounces across the grass. This sends everyone into a panic and mayhem ensues, some people head for the close and others hide in the bin shed as the rogue Catherine Wheel reeks havoc in the backcourt.

Eventually it stops and everyone returns to the backcourt, "Jeezo who pit 'rat nail in?" Mrs Campbell asks. Everyone looks around for Mr Campbell who is nowhere to be seen. I look up at the landing window just in time to see him entering the safe haven of the toilet. After being informed it was her husband who put the nail in, to everyone's amusement Mrs Campbell remarks "Ah widnae trust him tae hit the toilet pan wi' eez ain shite".

The rest of the evening is pretty uneventful but enjoyable. Joe and I are disappointed that Sammy never made it as the fireworks were brilliant. Even Father managed to let off his fireworks without killing anybody. Everyone is now milling around the backcourt as the dying embers of the oil drum fire start to fade. The torch batteries have long since died, and the alcohol is just about finished. Suddenly a high pitched siren can be heard in the distance.

The sound grows louder as the spinning blue lights of a fire engine reflect in the sky above the Booly. Joe and I rush over to the Booly wall at the bin shed, which has three bricks missing allowing a clear view of the Booly and the impending action. It turns out to be a bit of an anti climax as the bonfire that today stood majestic in the Booly, is now scattered across the ground setting fire to the dry grass. All the people who were in attendance at the bonfire have left and it doesn't take the firemen long to extinguish what's left of the fire and tackle the grass fires as well.

We make our way to the close just as a final rocket lights up the sky and signals the end of a great evening. "'Rat wiz a great night w'intit?" a smiling Joe says as he looks at the contents of the last rocket falling from the sky. I smile in agreement as we enter the close and I help Joe up the stairs. When we reach our landing I say goodnight to him as he follows, a still subdued, Mrs Kelly into their flat.

Should Auld Acquaintance Be Forgot

"Cheer up its Hogmanay" Father says enthusiastically as he tries to cheer me up. I am sitting on my bedroom floor playing five stones while still trying to get over the shock of Mrs Kelly, doing what Mrs Campbell described as a 'moonlight flit', after our Guy Fawkes party. In fact I was quite glad we spent Christmas at my Granny McDonald's house in Castlemilk as it just wasn't the same here without my wee pal Joe. The rumours going around the street range from, Mrs Kelly has moved to Ireland to Mrs Kelly has ran away with the 'Provvie' man, the latter courtesy of Mrs Campbell who doesn't like the new man who collects her Provident cheque money.

I can't help but feel sorry for Joe, who obviously didn't have a clue what was going on and would have needed to be helped down the stairs in the middle of the night. I have wondered every day since where he has ended up and if he is alright. "Why don't you play with your new racing track you got for Christmas" Father suggests, "Come on, I'll help you set it up" he continues as he drags the box from under the bed.

Luckily I am saved from Fathers attempts to keep a toy car on the track by a knock at the front door. "'Ur ye comin' oot tae play?" Sammy asks after I open the door. I grab my anorak and am just about to leave when Mother shouts from the living room, "Remember we'll need some help later to get ready for the party" I stick my head around the living room door and slowly say "Okay" before joining Sammy and running down the stairs.

After pooling our resources, which amounted to 8d, Sammy and I make our way to Walter's shop in Wee Heron St to buy some sweets. We pass number 51 just as a woman comes out the close carrying two big heavy bags and loads them into the back of a small Bedford van, "Right, 'rat's 'ra lot" she shouts to the driver as she gets in the passenger side.

Sammy informs me that the woman is Mrs Trainer and that two days ago her and her family moved to the new Bluevale Flats in Millerston St. Seemingly their new flat is twenty - eight stories up in this massive block of flats. "Wow" I think to myself, they will be looking down on the birds. Then just as we pass the van, Mrs Trainer rolls down the window and says cheerio to Sammy. When she starts to roll the window up again, we can clearly hear her say to the driver "Quick go...ah canny wait tae get away fae 'ris shitehole", and they drive away to their new life.

There seems to be quite a lot of people leaving Heron St at this time, especially from our close at number 43. We were moving shortly to Ruby St flats, old Mrs McLean had already moved to a maisonette in the Gallowgate, Mrs Kelly and Joe had gone, and the McCabe twins had moved to Drumchapel with their Father, after Mrs McCabe ran off with a bingo caller from the bingo hall on Dalmarnock Rd. Actually, I was quite happy about the McCabe's, but it did leave a lot of empty houses up our close.

"Did ye hear 'ra latest?" Sammy asks as we continue or journey to Walter's. I shake my head and he continues, "Martins Leather Works is shuttin' fur good". This was indeed big news, Martin's had been there for years and its buildings took up about three streets, Heron St, Bernard St and Baltic St, they had recently closed Baltic St and now the news that the rest is going to close will definitely have a huge impact on the local community. On the positive side I certainly won't miss the smell.

"Are you still coming to our party tonight?" I ask Sammy as we turn into Wee Heron St. "Aye, aye" he replies. Father had asked Sammy's parents to fill the void left by Mrs Kelly leaving, but it still left just The Campbell's as the other guests. After the great time we had at Halloween with the Kelly's I wasn't too optimistic that our party would be as enjoyable. Father had borrowed a record player and some records from Granny McDonald, but the record collection left a lot to be desired. It included such songs as 'For these are my mountains' by the Alexander Brothers and 'Gilly gilly ossenfeffer katzenellen bogen by the sea' by Max Bygraves. In some ways I was glad Eddie and George weren't going to be there as they would have verbally slaughtered Father if he put any of Granny's songs on.

Mother has spent all morning creating fancy nibbles, including vol au vents. She used to serve these using chicken and fish fillings when we stayed in the West end and she was having a dinner party. The sumptuous fillings for tonight's party included a jar of salmon spread and a jar of mixed pickles from Aldo's chip shop, undaunted, she is also attempting to make a steak pie, which I have to collect later from the butchers in Main St.

Eventually we reach Walter's just in time to see him being verbally attacked by an irate old woman, "Whitje mean yiv nae shortbreed eh! eh!?". The little old woman was obviously a bit deaf and leans over the counter with her head to the side trying to listen to Walter's reply. Walter leans over towards the old woman's ear and slowly shouts "'Thur's.. nane... left". The old woman jumps back and stares at Walter while growling "Ya cheeky bastart' whitje mean av goat bad breath?". Walter shakes his head and mouths the words "Naw, naw". The old woman concentrates hard and stares straight at Walter watching his lips and nodding after every word, he tries again by saying even more slowly "'Ra shortbreed's dun'...it's no more".

She looks at the floor for a couple of seconds with a confused expression on her face before returning her gaze back to Walter and angrily shouting "Dunn and Moore don't make shortbreed ya eejit". An extremely frustrated Walter turns his back and curses as the old woman shakes her head and barks "Never bloody mind 'ra shortbreed, jist geeza wee tin o' beans an' a tamata". Walter turns round to gather the requested items as the old woman leans against the counter and looks at us She nods her head in Walter's direction and whispers "Ah 'fink he's gon' deef".

The old woman leaves the shop uttering the words "Aye, aye shove it up yer arse" in response to Walter wishing her a happy new year. He then turns his attention to Sammy and I. "Right lads. Whit kin a get yeez?" Before me or Sammy can reply he says excitedly "Oh, here's wan' fur ye. Ye'll like 'ris". He then stands up straight and sniggers as he proceeds to tell us his latest joke. "Did ye hear aboot the auld guy wi' nay ears who went blind?". We stare blankly at him as he sniggers again with excitement, before continuing, "Eez bunnet kept falling o'er eez eyes". He then laughs heartily as Sammy looks at me and mouths the words "That wiz pish". We quickly buy four dainties each and head back to Heron St.

Everyone seems very cheery at this time of year, obviously except for one old woman, and as we pass the Dog Leg pub the doors are wide open and all the patrons seem in a really good mood. Everyone is wishing everyone else a happy new year when it comes. All except an old man and a young man sitting right at the front door playing cards. Each had a pile of coins sitting on the table in front of them and were holding some cards in their hands. Sammy says it reminds him of Maverick on the television as we stand and watch from just inside the entrance.

The old man is sitting with his back to the wall puffing on a cigarette and staring into the eyes of the young man, who is sitting on a stool facing him.
The younger man is fidgeting with his cards and his left leg is shaking nervously under the table as he says "Ah'll go a shullin'", and pushes a shilling into the centre of the table.

The old man looks again at his cards before replying "Ah'll go two bob". The young man immediately says "Ah'll go four bob". The old man thinks for a second and then responds "Ah'll go eight bob". Without any hesitation the young man confidently says "Ah'll go sixteen bob".

The older man once again looks at his cards then hesitates as he struggles to work out what he should say next. He starts to count on his fingers before removing his bunnet and scratching his head. Eventually the still confused and embarrassed old man stutters "Ah'll go eh, em, um", before replacing his bunnet and apologetically asking the young man "Is it o'rite if we start again son?". The younger man agrees as he grins and sympathetically shakes his head at the old man's lack of mental arithmetic skills. He then returns the old man's coins from the centre of the table.

After smiling condescendingly at the older man, he says again "Ah'll go a shullin'" before placing his cards face down on the table and confidently lighting a cigarette. The old man grins from ear to ear as he immediately says "Ah'll see ye". The stunned expression on the young man's face is priceless as he realises he has just been conned by his wily old adversary. After a few seconds he bursts out laughing and gets up from his stool, "Whit ye want tae drink ya cheatin' auld bastart, it's ma' round?" he asks the grinning old man, who just nonchalantly holds up his empty whisky glass in response before gathering the cards together.

"Right yooz two bugger off" the barmaid shouts as she marches towards us waving a tea towel. "Yooz 'urny allowed tae ston' 'rer, Shoo!" she screams again as if we are flies in a butter dish, "Aye o'rite, keep yer hair oan Mrs" Sammy retorts defiantly before we move back out onto the street.

"Rupert" Mother shouts as we approach number 43 "Can you please go to the butchers on Main St and pick up my steak pie?" she asks as I stand beneath the window with Sammy. After nodding, she throws down some coins wrapped in a ten shilling note before adding "Come straight back now do you hear, no dilly dallying". Sammy jokingly mimics Mother's words as we make our way down Heron St, "Hurry up now Rupert, there will be no dilly dallying today" he repeats in his best posh voice. I decide to get my own back by answering in my best slang voice "Okay Dokey, shift your 'erse then young man". We both keep this pretence going and laugh all the way to Main St.

When we arrive at the butchers it is extremely busy and there is quite a big queue in front of us. There are loud banging noises and endless chatter as the butcher and his staff busily chops huge slabs of meat and serve customers at the counter. "Next" the butcher shouts as he leans on the counter with both hands. He looks like your archetypal butcher with his round face and rosy red cheeks. He is also wearing the standard white hat with his ginger hair, that all butchers seem to have, sticking out the side. A blue and white stripy apron covered in blood, finishing off his outfit.

"Whit kin a get ye doll?" he confidently asks the next woman to approach the counter. "Hiv ye goat a big steak pie Tam?" she asks. He immediately walks away while shouting "Listen hen, oor steak pie's ur 'rat big ye could land a helicopter oan 'rem". This statement causes all the other woman in the shop to start laughing.

"Anyfin' else sweetheart?" he asks as he places an enormous steak pie on the counter. "Aye, huv ye goat any ham haughs fur ma' soup?" the woman replies. Immediately the butcher smiles again as he sarcastically quips "Naw, huv ye tried 'ra chemist". Again the other women in the queue start laughing as his customer grins and pretends to hit him with her right hand as she coyly mutters "Ach, see you". He wraps up the ham haughs and makes a note with his pencil on a blank sheet of wrapping paper before returning it behind his ear. The woman is now perusing the meat behind the glass fronted counter. Again the butcher looks out to his captive audience and moans, "Christ, dae ye want tae hurry up Ina afore we mis 'ra bells?". Again his appreciative audience reward him with a laugh. Eventually 'Ina' points to some square sausages behind the glass and asks "Ur 'rey fresh?". Not one to miss an opportunity the butcher responds sarcastically "Fresh? If ye listen close enough ye'll stull hear 'rem moo'in'?". After some more laughter Ina moans with mock reluctance "Gon 'ren, geeza hauf pun'". She then turns and looks at the rest of the woman in the queue and groans "Whit's he like by the way?". This relentless banter continues until Sammy and I reach the front of the queue.

"Next" the butcher shouts, I approach the counter and innocently say "Good afternoon, I believe you have a steak pie put aside for my Mother, Mrs Nairn". The butcher stares at me before realising he has an opportunity to secure another laugh from the new audience that have come in behind Sammy and I. He leans towards me, but looks at the woman in the queue, as he mimics my voice and replies loudly in a sarcastic tone "Good eftefnoon, I do believe ye might be right in yer assumption young man". There is a muted reaction from his audience of mainly woman who don't take too kindly to him trying to be smart with a young lad. Sammy just stares at him and shakes his head.

The butcher then walks away and returns a few seconds later with a steak pie already wrapped with our name written on the plain white wrapping paper, he places it on the counter and I hand him the money.

As he unravels and counts the money it obviously still irks him that he never got the reaction he wanted from his last attempt at humour so he decides to try again. I am struggling to lift the large steak pie from the counter as he again sarcastically quips in a mock posh voice " I have a coupla' pieces of 'ra finest venison in the back if you would like them?", he starts sniggering as he looks expectantly at his audience. Again the response is muted with some of the woman even shaking their heads in dismay.

Quick as a flash I respond "No thanks, they're too dear". The woman in the shop immediately burst into hysterical laughter interspersed with triumphant shouts of "Gonyersel wee man" and disparaging remarks of "Serves ye right ya big bully" and "'Rat put yer gas oan a peep ya big smart arse" aimed at the now raging butcher. Sammy is at a loss as to why everyone is laughing until I repeat to him "Too dear, get it?. Venison.. Two Deer". By the look on his face he still doesn't get it but starts to laugh anyway, much to the annoyance of the now uncharacteristically quiet butcher.

We are still discussing my quick witted reply in the butchers as we turn into Muslin St at the George Bar. Right in front of us is a drunk man standing sideways against the pub wall with his hands in his pockets. After a few seconds he leaves the stability of the wall and tries to stagger forward but only manages about two yards before returning to the comforting safety of the wall. We can clearly hear him talking to himself as he practices the excuses he will use when he reaches home, "Av only hid two drinks hen'" he mutters to himself. Obviously unconvinced he berates himself by saying "Nah, c'mon you, she's no' 'rat daft".

He then removes one hand from his pocket and wags his index finger in mid air while saying " Listen wummin' am 'ra man o' 'ra hoose" but then returns his hand to his pocket as he concludes "Nah she'll jist batter me an' throw me oot again". Once again he leaves the wall and staggers forward before trying to step over an invisible step; this only makes him trip and fall forward. He instinctively removes his hands from his pocket and breaks into a slight jog for about five yards, as if to indicate to anyone who might be watching that he meant to run all along and never tripped.

Sammy and I decide to follow him down Muslin St in case he falls over and he stops outside the first close we arrive at. He takes a deep breath and straightens himself up in readiness for what seems like the final leg of his journey. But before he can make a move, a portly woman with long grey hair wearing a brown raincoat staggers across the road from Reid St shouting "Oh, ho 'rer ma' Davie boy, howzitgon?". She is just as drunk as him, if not more so, as she proceeds to stagger diagonally across the road towards him.

He squints his eyes at the woman before shouting back "Brenda darlin'". He then takes the opportunity to seize the moral high ground by adding "Ah wiz jist comin' tae look fur ye 'rer". The poor woman bows her head slightly as she approaches him and contritely says "'Am sorry pet, ah ended up inra Red Lion wi' ma' Maw 'n never noticed 'ra time". In order to increase her feelings of guilt he gushes "Ah wiz worried aboot ye 'rer so ah wiz". The woman approaches him and gives him a big hug as she meekly says "'Am sorry pet".

The drunk man is still cuddling her and relishing his lucky escape when two young boys appear from the close aged about eight and ten. They walk up to the cuddling couple and the older boy shouts "Ho! Da, where huv you been 'am starvin'?", the younger boy then adds "We've bin waitin' here fur ages, gonny let us in 'ra hoose am burstin' furra jobby?".

With these two statements the drunk man's subterfuge is revealed and the drunk woman pushes him away as she sarcastically repeats his words back to him "Jist comin' tae look fur me eh!?". She then slaps him hard across the face, he puts his arms up to protect himself as she continues "Worried aboot me eh!?" as she hits him again. He tries to avoid her blows by turning his back while shouting "Brenda.... Darlin'...". She is having none of it as she aims a kick at his posterior and shouts "Don't you darlin' me ya lyin' bastart". They start to move in the direction of the close with the woman shouting in a robotic fashion "Wait... tae... ah... get... you... up... 'rat... stair... ya... durty... lyin'... toe rag..". She is now slapping the man once after every word she says which results in a melodic synchronistic assault. She only stops the assault to shout to her children "Right yooz two shift yer arses up 'rat stair... MOVE!". Needless to say the children obey immediately, before she turns her attention back to her husband and pushes him in the back while screeching "GET UP 'RAT STAIR YOU". We quickly walk past the close and glance at the poor man, who is now on all fours just inside the close entrance being repeatedly kicked in the posterior. Sammy shakes his head and remarks "Ah wouldnae like tae go hame tae her wi' a burst pay poke".

After safely delivering Mother's steak pie we are standing at the entrance of my close wondering what we can do to pass the time until the party starts. "Ah know" Sammy shouts, "Come wi' me" he adds and I follow him along Heron St. We arrive outside Sammy's close and he says "Wait here a wee minute tae ah nip up 'ra stair" he then runs inside as I stand and wait at the entrance.

While I'm waiting on Sammy, my attention is drawn towards the Dog Leg pub which is just closing. A crowd of drunk men are standing outside laughing and joking, and shouts of "Happy new year" reverberate around that end of the street as a procession of men leave the pub.

I particularly notice two young men holding up a much older man who can hardly stand because he is drunk. As they walk towards me one of the young men moans "Look 'it 'ra state o' him, ma maw's gonny kill us". The other young man adds "Ah know she is" before adding in his defence "Ah didnae know he hid a hauf boatle in eez poaket". The old man is mumbling to himself as he is unceremoniously dragged towards me and one of the young men attempts to humour him by saying "Ah know Da, Mickey Rooney wiz born in Polmadie".

This statement riles the old man who stops in his tracks right next to me and shakes his head as he shouts "Nawww, yeez urny listenin' tae me, it wiz Mickey Rooney's Da 'rat came fae Polmadie". The young men look at each other then both look up to the sky before one of them says sarcastically "Aye 'ra famous Mickey Rooney's Da came fae Polmadie. The other young man sniggers before adding, "Aye, an' Frank Sinatra's fae Maryhill".

The old man tries to lift his head to stare at the young men, but his head bounces around like a new born baby before he gives up and just whispers to himself "He did, ah know he did, ah saw 'im 'it 'ra Glesga Empire". One of the young men has had enough and barks "Enough aboot Mickey Rooney's Da, ma' Maw's gonny batter your melt in when she sees 'ra state o' ye". This only causes the old man to sigh and respond with "Aye yer wee Maw... ma' wee Kathleen". He then bursts into song singing *'I'll take you home again, Kathleen'* at the top of his voice. As they struggle past me I can hear one of the young men groan "Ah shite, 'ats o' we need". Before the other adds "Mi'be he'll fa' asleep oan 'ra bus?".

I am still watching the two young men struggle to carry their dad as they make their way down Heron St towards Dalmarnock Rd when Sammy appears from the close. "Ma' Da finishes eez work in hauf anoor, je want tae come wi' me tae meet 'im?" he asks. I nod in agreement and after I let Mother know where I am going, we set off for Nuneaton St.

Sammy's dad works as a plater in a large steel works called Sir William Arrol. It is a massive steel factory spread across Dunn St, Boden St and Nuneaton St. They build large steel structures like bridges and built the new Forth Road Bridge, which Sammy tells me was opened four years ago.

We walk along Bernard St and then Boden St which leads to Nuneaton St. And as we approach the first thing I see ahead is a large wooden double gate. "'At's where 'ra lorries deliver 'ra steel" Sammy tells me. We then turn the corner into Nuneaton St and Sammy points to two small openings about a hundred yards from the big gate. "'Ra wan oan 'ra right is where 'rey cloak' in, an' 'ra wan oan 'ra left is where 'rey cloak' oot", he says as we walk towards the small exit and wait across the road for Sammy's dad to appear.

For some reason there is a large crowd of woman waiting as well, all chattering to each other. "These women must really miss their husbands" I say to Sammy who sniggers and replies "Jist wait and see". The exit itself doesn't look much bigger than the small turnstiles at a football stadium with room for one person at a time. It must take ages for thousands of people to get out I think to myself.

From where we are standing I can see right into the exit where there is a clock machine on the wall and a queue of men in overalls patiently waiting holding cards. They are in a boisterous mood as they shout and joke with each other to pass the time.

Suddenly the deafening sound of a horn fills the air and the men spring into action. One by one and with lightening speed they insert their cards in the machine and place it in the cardholder on the wall. This deafening horn also has an amazing impact on the women who immediately stop talking and separate. They then stare at the exit like a bird of prey stalking its next victim. Their heads move from side to side as they scan everyone leaving the factory. Some of the men are drunk as they stagger out the exit and when I point this out to Sammy he explains that they are allowed to finish early on days like Christmas eve and Hogmanay and just sit with their friends drinking 'Cerry oots' they have brought in with them until it is time to clock out. They all look identical with their dirty navy overalls and oil covered bunnets on their heads as they file out and walk away in all directions. Most of them also seem to have some sort of green bag hanging from their shoulders. Again Sammy informs me that the bag is for their sandwiches, or as he says "Fur 'rer peeces".

I now know what Sammy was sniggering at when I mentioned the women missing their husbands. It's quite scary watching these snarling women pounce on their unsuspecting husbands like wild animals. They then frighten the life out them with shouts of "Right you! geez 'rat pay poke" and "You're 'gon naewhere tae ah get 'ma' money". The men's faces visibly contort with anguish at the sight of their 'loved' ones, and they meekly hand over little brown envelopes like scolded schoolboys.

There are now loads of bunnets filing through the exit like paratroopers jumping out a plane, as we look on waiting to spot Sammy's dad. Suddenly one old man, who is extremely drunk, struggles to insert his card in the machine. This enrages the waiting masses and they start to shout abuse in his direction. Derogatory shouts of "C'mon ya stupid auld bastart, hurry up", and "Shift yer 'erse 'Erchie, c'mon" are commonplace before the old man eventually manages to click his card. He then stands and checks it which infuriates the masses even more. "Whit ye daen ya auld bastart, move it" someone shouts. He then struggles to find a place for the card in the cardholder as he screws his eyes up and checks every number. The waiting crowd are apoplectic with rage now as someone screams, "Stick it anywhere ya auld bastart 'afore a' shove it up yer 'erse".
Eventually he slides the card in its place and walks outside. The rest of the men file out as they stare and shout abuse at the old man. He just defiantly smiles and wishes them all a happy new year.

"'Rers ma' Da 'rer" Sammy says as he points at the exit. "Ho, Da" he shouts. Mr Graham spots us and waves over. He then engages in conversation with some of the men before shaking their hands and wishing them a happy new year. A few of the men who are on bikes shout "'Orrabest when it comes Greggsy" and "Ho, Greggsy huv a guid new year" as they cycle past him on the road.

I look at Sammy and simply say "Greggsy?". Sammy explains that his dad's first name is Gregory, and when he was young he was called Greggsy by his friends and the name stuck to this day. This explanation just makes me so glad that no-one knows my middle name is Ninian. I am also extremely happy that it is not my first name. Living in Bridgeton with a name like Rupert Nairn is bad enough but I shudder to think what the McCabe twins would have done to me if I had been called Ninian Nairn.

Mr Graham eventually comes over and says "O'rite lads, howzitgon?" and leads us along Nuneaton St towards London Rd. "Ma' ma said she's gon' oot Da 'cos she hid a message tae go" Sammy informs his dad who replies "Aye ah know son. She'll be back afore we get hame". We turn into London Rd and Sammy starts sniggering as he tugs my shoulder and points at a pub. I look round and start to snigger too as I look at the 'Loughswilly' pub on London Rd. "Ah wunner' where 'ra rest o' him is?" Sammy chuckles as we continue down London Rd towards Bridgeton. Mr Graham stops outside a barbers shop and says "Ah need tae get ma' haircut fur 'ra party 'ra night. C'mon ah'll no' be long" and he leads us inside.

The barbers shop is quite small and dingy. The waiting area consists of eight old wooden school seats lined up against the wall at the entrance. Opposite the waiting area are three large mirrors with larger comfy chairs. These chairs are all occupied with barbers busily cutting hair and shaving the occupants. Everyone is smoking which has resulted in a large cloud of smoke hovering just above our heads. This includes the three old men sitting next to us who are obviously a bit deaf as they struggle to hear what each other is saying, resulting in constant shouts of "Eh!" and "Whitje say 'rer?". Next to them is an empty seat with a Daily Record newspaper on it, while the last chair is occupied by a very old man who is shoving snuff up his hairy nose while moaning and grumping to himself as he waits his turn.

One of the three old men next to us decides to try and make conversation with his friends by saying "Windy 'ra day 'intit?". The old man next to him replies "Naw its no' Wednesday, its Thursday". The third old man nods his head and retorts "Aye 'am thirsty, we'll go furra pint when wur' done".

Sammy, Mr Graham and I are trying to stifle our laughter as one of the barbers finishes with his customer. He brushes his neck with a soft brush and whips off of the large white cloth that is covering him like a Spanish matador. The customer poses in the mirror for a couple of seconds before handing over his money.

"Next" shouts the barber. The grumpy old man with the snuff and the hairy nose stands up and moans "Aboot bloody time" as he takes baby steps towards the available chair. " 'A much izza haircut?" he growls at the barber as he takes his seat. "Seven an' six" the barber replies as he places the large white cloth around the old man. "Fur Christ's sake son 'am no' made o' money" moans the old man before asking "'A much izza shave?".

The barber stands behind the old man and looks at him in the mirror as he sighs before replying "Hauf 'a croon". The old man shakes his head in disgust before moaning "Fine! Jist shave ma' heed". The three of us burst out laughing along with all the barbers, but the three old men sitting next to us just say "Eh!" and "Whit 'rey o' laughin' 'it?".

The three barbers are chatting and joking away to each other as they work which prompts Sammy to say "They're patter's brilliant, 'intit?". I had to agree they really are very funny. One of the barbers innocently asks "Did 'embday see Mission Impossible last night?". It obviously wasn't a rhetorical question as he continues "Did ye see 'rat new machine 'rey hid 'rat could tell when a person wiz tellin' lies?". Quick as a flash one of his colleagues retorts "Seen wan? Ah merrit wan". We are laughing constantly as the relentless banter continues. "Ah asked ma' burd tae merry me last night and dae ye know whit the cheeky bint said?", one of the barbers asks. The other two stop cutting hair and shake their heads as he puts on a female voice and answers "Naw! But ah'll always admire yer good taste".

It was like watching the comedians on the television as they kept going and we kept laughing. The oldest barber decides it's his turn as he says "Remember 'rat English guy we hid in here last week?". His colleagues answer "Aye" and "Awe 'rat smarmy git". He then looks at Mr Graham as he continues. "Honesty God, he says tae me…". He then puts on a posh voice before continuing. "… Yas, if you take away your Lochs, Glens and Mountains up here, then what have you got?". One of the other barbers immediately says "Tell 'rem whit ye said". After a short pause he calmly replies "Ah jist said *ENGLAND*". Again everyone laughs except the three old men who are still fidgeting and saying "Eh!".

The barber finishes with the grumpy old man and has given him a tidy short back and sides. After the old man has escaped the white cloth he stands and looks in the mirror before asking "A much izzat?". The barber smiles and replies "Seen its new year, hauf a croon". The old man seems happy as he hands over his money and leaves. The barber watches him all the way to the door and as soon as he is out of sight he groans, " He's 'rat auld he wiz probably aroon' when Long John Silver hid two legs 'n 'an egg oan eez shooder". He then cleans the seat and shouts "Next".

About twenty minutes and a hundred jokes later Mr Graham takes his seat in the barber's chair and it doesn't take him long to join in the festival of comedy. As his haircut gets underway he says to the barber, "Ah sayz tae 'ra wife, whitje want fur yer burfday, she sayz anyhin' wi' diamonds wid be nice, so ah goat 'er a pack a' cerds". The barber bursts out laughing along with Sammy and me. Then the barber momentarily stops cutting his hair and comes back with "Aye ah know whit ye mean, ah said tae 'ra wife. Its wur anniversary soon where wid ye like tae go? An' she sayz, somewhere 'av never been, so ah jist sayz tae her, try 'ra kitchen".

This particular jocular joust was turning into 'joke fight at the OK barbers' as Mr Graham and his barber tried to outdo each other. Mr Graham respectfully laughs at his barbers efforts before coming right back with "'Rat wife o' mine keeps biting 'er nails, but ah managed tae cure 'er dead quick". The barber plays his part by asking "How did ye manage 'rat", before Mr Graham sniggers as he replies "Ah planked 'er false teeth".

The barber takes a break from his verbal tennis and turns his attention to Sammy and me as he asks "Yeez o'rite 'rer lads? An' whit dae yooz want tae be when ye grow up". Thinking that he is actually interested and after a few seconds thought I reply "I would really like to go to university and study medicine". This reply leaves the barbers less than impressed as the older one contorts his face and mimics my response with his lips. The younger of the barbers then adds "Ah bet you're 'rat posh ye've goat ashtrays in 'ra hoose wi' nae adverts oan 'rem". His colleagues laugh out loud at this response with the older one adding the caveat "We're only kiddin' wi' ye son, it's nice hear sum'day talk proper furra change".

"Whit aboot you son?" he asks Sammy who just stares back at the barber. "Its o'rite son ye kin tell 'rem" Mr Graham shouts from the barber's chair. Sammy takes a deep breath and says "Ah want tae be an accountant or a chef". Immediately the younger barber quips "Izzat a turf accountant wee man?" as he laughs out loud. The older one adds "Why dae ye no' dae baith, 'rat way ye kin cook 'ra books". This statement causes even Sammy's dad to snigger. Sammy tries to get his own back by saying "Whit dae ye call a German barber". They all shake their heads "Herr- cut" Sammy shouts to raucous sympathetic laughter from the three barbers.

We eventually leave our new friends in the barbers shop, but not before one final remark from the youngest barber as we make our way to the door. "Whit dae ye call a sheep tied tae a lamp post in Aberdeen?" he asks. Mr Graham, Sammy and I all shake our heads. The three barbers all answer in unison as they shout "A Leisure Centre". Mr Graham bursts out laughing but Sammy and I just don't get it. Sammy asks his dad to explain it but he hurriedly changes the subject by saying "Never mind, let's get hame".

New Year At 'Ra Nairn's

Standing in my bedroom looking out the window I can see the top floors of Ruby St flats just above the roof of Martins Leather Works. The lights are on in all the flats as people get ready to celebrate the New Year. It's weird to think we will be living there soon and in some ways I will be sad to leave. I am going to miss seeing Mrs Campbell and hearing her cursing every day, and Sammy of course. Come to think of it, most of the neighbours in Heron St are great and I am not looking forward to starting again. On the plus side, I will have a room with a window that shuts properly, electric heating, instead of having to make up the fire every day. And I won't have to empty the mouse traps in the living room anymore or share a toilet with three other families, especially Mr Campbell.

Mother is busy in the living room making the final preparations for our New Year party. She has pulled out both wings of our small Formica topped table and has laid out a mouth watering array of nibbles and sandwiches. In fact she has laid out enough food for about twenty people, so with only the Grahams and the Campbell's coming to our party there is obviously far too much, but Mother remains convinced that the other neighbours in the close will drop in after the bells.

We are also waiting on Father and Wilhelmina to arrive back from Grandfather Nairn's. Wilhelmina was desperate to stay there for the 'Bells' but Mother was having none of it. She told Wilhelmina that, as this was going to be our last new year in Heron St, she was staying here to celebrate it as a family. This direct order didn't go down too well with my sister who commented as she left with Father "Well then, I'll just not shake anybody's hand, especially our smelly neighbours". The only thing missing from Mother's impressive spread was alcohol; Father was entrusted with the task of purchasing the alcohol on the way home from Grandfather's.

"Hello" Father shouts as he enters our flat. "Did you get the carry out?" my anxious Mother shouts as she rushes into the hall to meet him. "Yes, Yes" Father replies as he places two jangling brown bags on the couch.

Mother immediately investigates the contents as she lifts out a bottle of Eldorado, followed by a bottle of Lanliq. She places them on the table and returns to the bags. Next to make an appearance is a full bottle of 12 year old Glenfiddich malt whisky and Smirnoff vodka which she again places on the table. After fishing around the bottom of the bag her face up lights up as she reveals a bottle of Warninks Advocaat. She sighs and hugs the bottle before placing it at the forefront of the drinks display. She then turns her attention to the second bag but just peers inside at the cans of lager and pale ale. "Where are the mixers?" she asks in a panic.

"Help?" Wilhelmina squawks as she struggles in the door with another brown bag. Father just smiles at Mother who runs over to aid my big sister who can't see in front of her as she bangs the bag off the living door. Mother has a quick check inside the bag and returns to the table leaving Wilhelmina to fall onto the couch with the bag. "I've had to carry this bag all the way from Bridgeton Cross" she moans as she slumps on the couch next to her cargo.

Father is taking his coat and scarf off as he says, "Wait to I tell you what this cheeky bus conductress said to me". Wilhelmina huffs and raises her eyes to the ceiling before saying "I'm going to get ready" as she storms off into the bedroom. Mother isn't the slightest bit interested in Fathers story as she stares at her bottle of Advocaat and mutters "Yes dear". But Father continues anyway as he hangs his coat on the nail at the front door. "I got on the bus in Great Western Road and asked the conductress for a single and a half to Bridgeton...". He then sits on the couch and looks at Mother who is trying to open the Advocaat bottle, "Yes dear I'm listening" she pretends. "..This bus doesn't go to Bridgeton the conductress replied...". Mother now has the cork of the still sealed Advocaat bottle in her teeth as she mumbles "Yessh dear, go on". Father adopts a serious posture as he continues "Well I just said to her, it says Bridgeton on the front of the bus, does it not?" and do you know what the cheeky girl replied, eh?". Mother is now wrestling with the bottle under her arm trying to dislodge the cork as she responds "Er, no dear". Father walks over to her, takes the bottle from her, and quickly turns the cork and places it on the table. Mother stares at him with an admiring look on her face as he continues, "She said". Father then tries to speak slang, "Listen pal, it says Persil oan 'ra back of the bus, but we don't take in washin'". Mother and I are trying not to laugh, which is noticed by Father who then slowly changes his grimace to a smile as he relents and repeats the words "Don't take in washin'".

The small clock on the mantelpiece shows it's now 11.30pm as we sit and watch Andy Stewart singing 'Scottish Soldier' on the television. Mother has made me wear a shirt and tie and has put about two tons of brylcream in my hair which she has combed with a perfect side parting.

She is wearing her Sunday best and looks lovely with her long flowery dress and heavily lacquered hair. Her heavily made up face is dominated by her dark red lipstick. Father is wearing his navy blue suit with a shirt and tie while Wilhelmina is wearing her best black trousers with a red and cream coloured Fair Isle jumper. The table has been laid and re-laid until it meets with Mother's approval, and the tumblers and alcohol are sitting on the tallboy in readiness for our guests.

Mother nervously looks away from the television towards the clock every few seconds. She also checks her watch constantly as we watch a group of highland dancers performing the 'Dashing White Sergeant'; Every so often you can hear random shouts from the audience of 'Wheech' and 'Cheugh' as the kilted dancers cavort across the screen. Wilhelmina is sitting on the couch with her head down and her arms folded trying to pretend she isn't interested in anything, but I can clearly see her looking up every now and then, especially when Andy Stewart appears. As if to prove my point Andy Stewart starts to sing 'Donald where's yer troosers' and she immediately looks up. So just to annoy her, I deliberately look over, which makes her grunt and look down again immediately. Along with throwing peanuts in the air and catching them with my mouth, this is what I am reduced to in order to keep myself amused as we still await the arrival of our guests.

Mother nervously checks the clock again which is now showing 11.45pm. She sits forward in her chair and asks Father "Where is everybody?". Father, who is engrossed in the television, just shrugs his shoulders and continues to watch as Andy Stewart sings 'Donald where's yer troosers' like Elvis Presley. He then laughs out loud and looks at Mother as he points to the television, only to be met with an icy stare which makes him stop laughing and respond, "I'm sure they will be here soon".

No sooner had the words left Fathers lips when there is a knock at the door. Mother excitedly springs out of her seat as I shout "I'll get it" and jump up from the arm of the chair. Father stands up and straightens his tie as I pass him enroute to the door, and Wilhelmina clenches her arms together even tighter in defiance. I open the door and a chorus of "Happy New Year" fills the landing as a very drunk Mr and Mrs Campbell wave a half bottle of vodka each in the air. I invite them in and lead them into the living room. The cry of "Happy New Year" can be heard again as they hand Mother and Father their half bottles of vodka.

Mother invites the Campbell's to sit on the couch next to Wilhelmina, who looks horrified at the prospect as she moves her leg out a bit to mark her territory. It only takes a glare from Mother to make her grudgingly move along a bit as she places the vodka bottles on the tallboy with the rest of the alcohol.

I watch as Mother removes the cork from one of the vodka bottles and sniffs the contents. She is spotted by Mrs Campbell who rather than be annoyed, proudly shouts, "Ye'll no' fun' any watter in 'rey boatles". She looks at her husband for confirmation. He duly shakes his head and says "Nut' 'ra real McCoy 'ris time" without realising he was confirming the fact that there have been other times when water was used.

"Sorry wur' late Mrs Nairn but we couldnae get rid o' 'ra Exorcist" Mrs Campbell offers in her defence. "The Exorcist?" Mother repeats back to her with a confused expression on her face. Mr Campbell takes it upon himself to explain. "Aye she's tryin' tae be funny, she means ma' Da" he says before going on, "She calls him 'ra Exorcist 'cos every time he comes tae oor hoose, a' wur' spirits disappear" he then bursts out laughing along with Mrs Campbell. I am sure I saw Wilhelmina laugh as well because her shoulders were moving up and down. Still smiling, Father stands up at the tallboy and asks "What can I get you to drink Mr and Mrs Campbell". Right away Mr Campbell spots the whisky and replies "Eh, izzat whisky ah kin see up 'rer". Mrs Campbell joins her husband by saying "Aye, whisky's fine fur me tae".

Father hands the Campbell's a glass each and opens the whisky bottle. He pours a little into Mr Campbell's glass as he says "This is a 12 year old whisky you know". As he moves over to Mrs Campbell, Mr Campbell stares at the small amount of whisky in his glass then sarcastically says "It's a bit wee fur it's age intit?". Father takes the hint and pours some more whisky into both their glasses. "Never you mind him Mr Nairn, his family ur 'ra stingiest lot 'av ever met". Mr Campbell glares at his wife but before he can say anything she continues. "He wiz 'ra last o' five brothers tae get merritt". Mr Campbell looks indignantly at his wife and says "So!, whits 'rat goat tae dae wi' 'ra price o' fish?". She stares back at him and shouts "'Ra confetti wiz manky it hid been used 'rat many times". She then starts cackling with laughter as both my parents cover their mouths and snigger.

Mr Campbell leans over to his wife and purses his lips as he says "Aye, ye love me really daen't ye?" he then tries to kiss her on the cheek. "Get tae..." Mrs Campbell yells as she pulls away from him inadvertently leaning on a disgusted looking Wilhelmina's lap in the process.

After she sits upright she turns to her husband and says "How kin you no' be like 'rat young couple up 'ra next close?". Mr Campbell looks confused as she goes on "His wife sayz tae me 'rat every moarnin' he geez 'er a kiss afore he goes tae work, an' every night he geez 'er a bunch a floo'ers, how come you don't dae 'rat?" she pleads. "Cos ah don't know 'er 'rat well, dae ah?" he replies before laughing so hard he has a coughing fit.

With the time approaching midnight, everyone is sitting quietly waiting on the 'Bells'. "Everybody got a drink?" Father asks. "Aye" our guests respond as Wilhelmina and I hold up our sherry glasses filled with blackcurrant cordial. I look over at Mother who has a depressed look on her face caused by the poor turnout at her party.

Mr Campbell sits forward prompting Mother and Father to copy him thinking he is going to speak. Instead he just reaches down to the floor and helps himself to some peanuts from a saucer before sitting straight back again. "I suppose we better stand up for the Bells" Mother suggests, as everybody immediately gets to their feet. Except Wilhelmina who deliberately takes an eternity to get out of her seat. The television picture switches to Glasgow Cross where thousands of people have congregated to usher in the New Year. As the countdown to 1969 begins the enormous crowd join in. 10 - 9 - 8 -7 - 6, there is complete silence in our living room, so I decide to join in the countdown myself. 5 - 4 - 3 - 2 – 1 HAPPY NEW YEAR!, I excitedly shout at the top of my voice as the bells ring out on the television.

Everyone starts shaking hands and even Wilhelmina grudgingly offers her hand to me but quickly reverts back to form by saying "Yuck!" and wiping her hand on her jumper. Father hesitantly leans forward to kiss Mrs Campbell on the cheek but she moves back and offers her hand instead. This manoeuvre is copied by Mother as Mr Campbell moves forward towards her. After the ceremonial handshaking is complete everyone sits back down and the atmosphere reverts back to last minutes of 1968 with no-one speaking. Then to make matters worse the programme on the television finishes so Father switches it off and plugs in Granny McDonald's record player. It's not long until the sound of the Alexander Brothers singing *"These are my mountains"*, fills the room as he turns around and returns to his seat. He is met with comments of "Good song 'rat" from Mr Campbell and "Ur 'rey no' deed?" from Mrs Campbell. Wilhelmina responds with the uncharacteristically whimsical comment of "They sound as if their dead".

Mr Campbell starts to sing along but doesn't know the words as he sings *"Fur fame n' fur fortune... La da da da dee... ah la la ma' childhood...da dum dum da dee"*.

His effort is brought to an abrupt halt by his wife who barks "Fur Christ sake if ye don't know 'ra wurds jist shut yer geggay". Mr Campbell stops singing and looks at his wife and moans "You're stull in a bad mood aboot yesterday, 'int ye?", before adding "Fur God's sake it wiz only a joke". Mr Campbell then stands up and announces "'Am away furra pish" as he walks out the living room in a huff.

Mrs Campbell notices my parents looking at her and feels at liberty to explain. "We wur sitting last night an' bawheid goat up tae go furra pint. Then he said tae me, "Get yer coat an' hat wummin". So ah' said tae him. "Aw 'rats nice, ur ye takin' me wi' ye tae 'ra pub?'. 'Je know whit 'ra bastart sayz. 'Naw am jist turnin' 'ra fire aff while 'am oot'".

Mother and Father are trying not to laugh as they offer Mrs Campbell another drink and more nibbles. Mr Campbell returns and takes his seat while totally ignoring his wife and our living room is quieter than the library as Father swaps the records on the record player once again with the words "I remember this one". This statement doesn't fill me with confidence; in fact if the records get any older we'll soon be listening to a duet with Adam and Eve.

The song starts but the singer sounds like Pinky and Perky. Father apologises and changes the speed to 78rpm and we wait for the song to start again. There is a crackling sound coming from the record player as we patiently wait for it to start, it sounds like fish and chips frying in the chip shop. This crackling noise goes on for a long time before Mother looks at Father and nods her head in the direction of the record player indicating that she wants him to do something. He immediately obeys as he leans over and slaps the side of the record player which causes the needle to jump and Max Bygraves starts to sing *"There's a tiny house, by a tiny stream..."*.

Father sings along with Max and when the song reaches its chorus he shout's "All together now", and proceeds to sing words that sound like pure gobbledygook as he waves his hands in the air. The Campbell's obviously know the song as does Mother. They are all unsure of the words as they join in the chorus and the collaboration of voices sounds like they are singing *'Gilly Gilly hassenfefer ponsenella pokey by the sea'.*

The song reaches the chorus again just as Mrs Campbell accepts a handful of peanuts from her repentant husband and tosses them straight into her mouth. She tries to indicate that she likes this song as she excitedly points to the record player, but only succeeds in choking on a peanut. The battering she takes on her back from her overzealous husband doesn't seem to help. She pushes him away and stops coughing long enough to stare at him before the coughing starts again. She then jumps up and points to her throat before running out the room. Instead of following his stricken wife, Mr Campbell just sits there listening to Max Bygraves as he tries to sing along to *'Gilly Gilly ossenfeffer katzenellen bogen by the sea'.*

Mother glares at Mr Campbell and shakes her head. "You better go and see how old Mrs Campbell is" Mother whispers to Father, who dutifully follows Mrs Campbell out of the living room.

He returns about fifteen seconds later with a confused expression on his face and mumbles to Mother. "Mrs Campbell said it's none of your business how old she is". Mother then glares at Father and can't believe he has been that stupid. Mrs Campbell comes back in the living room behind Father with only the remnants of a cough. "Whit dae ye want tae know ma' age fur?" she asks Mother, who can't be bothered explaining and just shakes her head as she says, "Never mind, are you okay?". She then leads Mrs Campbell back to her seat. "Aye, 'am fine" Mrs Campbell replies.

Just before she sits down again she addresses the lack of support by her spouse by aiming a half hearted volley of blows at the unsuspecting Mr Campbell as she yells, "Aye you ya bastart, you're as much use as a chocolate fireplace" before finally sitting down and drinking a can of pale ale in one go.

Glen Miller's' 'In the mood' is now playing in the background, but the mood in our living room is more like a wake than a party. Everyone looks totally bored and it seems that this New Year's party has just about ran its course. I can hear Father whispering to Mother that when Glen Miller finishes we will be back to the Alexander Brothers. This statement results in Mother dejectedly looking at the food on the table, then glancing at the Campbell's before forlornly placing her hand on her forehead as if she has a migraine.

Suddenly there is a knock at the front door. Mother immediately snaps out of her depressed state as she stands up and flattens her crumpled dress. Father hurries to the door passing the Campbell's enroute, who look at each other and mouth the words "Thank God". Wilhelmina has fallen asleep on the arm of the couch which is now connected to her mouth with a saliva string, and I follow Father to the front door.

Father opens the door and standing there is Sammy with his mum and dad. Mr Graham is holding the hand of a small boy about three years old who is clinging to his leg for comfort. "Happy New Year", we all shout in unison as Father leads them into the living room. After the usual New Year pleasantries are completed everyone sits down with a drink. The small boy is leaning tightly against Mr Graham surveying the room with a look of trepidation in his eyes. "'Ris wee fella's ma nephew Alfie" Mr Graham says as he proudly looks down at the small boy. He then goes on to say "He's 'ra reason we're late".

Sammy and I sit down on the floor as Mr Graham elaborates by honestly explaining how his brother is an ex alcoholic whose wife left him with Alfie about a year ago. He goes on to say that he took ill earlier in the evening and was whisked in to the Royal Infirmary as a precaution.

He then tells us that his brother is fine now but won't get out of hospital until the morning.

Mother's maternal instinct kicks in as she walks over to Alfie and offers him a small glass of lemonade and a biscuit. Alfie visibly relaxes when he realises he is among friends. Alfie is slurping his lemonade as Father approaches him. "Hello Alfie, and how old are you" he asks. Mrs Campbell leans over to her husband and whispers "Whit izzit wi' 'rese people wantin' tae know everybody's age?". Alfie lowers the glass from his lips and replies to Father "'Am three, an' ah know a' ma' numbers". This response results in "Oohs" and "Ahhs" from all the adults in the room.

Alfie reacts to the attention he is receiving by becoming more confident as he adds proudly "Ma' Daddy showed me ma' numbers". Father then decides to test Alfie's numerical knowledge by asking "So what number comes after six?", quick as a flash Alfie answers "Seven". The adults in the room nod at each other and shout "Oh well done Alfie". This response makes him smile proudly as his confidence grows further. Father continues his grilling with the question "And what comes after eight?" the now supremely confident three year old answers immediately, "Nine". Again the shouts of "Well done" and "He's good fureez age intae?" fill the room.

Father is very impressed as he looks at Alfie and then Mr Graham and comments "Your Father has done an excellent job". At this point Alfie leaves Mr Graham's side and stands in front of Father, he starts shifting his weight from one leg to the other as if to say *'Go on give it your best shot'*.

Mrs Campbell remarks "Eez a gallus wee bugger intae?" Father rises to the challenge as he finally asks Alfie "And what comes after ten?" To the surprise of everyone in the room he replies "A Jack". Everyone bursts out laughing, including Alfie before Mr Graham picks him up and sits him on his knee.

"Kin ah tell 'rem yet?" Sammy pleads to his Father after the laughter subsides. Mr Graham nods his head and Sammy stands up and excitedly announces to his attentive audience, "Great news, we're movin' tae the flats anaw". There is a moments silence as this momentous news is digested. Mother looks at Mrs Graham who confirms the news by revealing that the Grahams have been offered a flat in Ruby St and will be moving shortly after us. "That's great news" Father gushes as he raises his glass and proposes a toast, "To Ruby St Flats". Everyone raises their glasses except Mrs Campbell who moans to her husband "We're gonny be 'ra only wan's left in 'ris street".

The party has certainly picked up and even the repeated music on the record player is providing laughter now instead of moans.

Everyone is having a great time, including Alfie who is trying to push a peanut up the still sleeping Wilhelmina's nose. Mother shouts above the din "Is that someone at the door?", The volume on the record player is turned down slightly and sure enough there is a loud knock at the door.

"Can you get that please Rupert?" Mother asks as she happily distributes more food and drink. I am still laughing at Alfie's antics as I open the door to be met with the most wonderful sight , "JOE" I shout as Mrs Kelly and her extended family shout back "HAPPY NEW YEAR". They all file into the flat laden with brown bags filled with alcohol. "HAPPY NEW YEAR" they shout again as they pass me in the hall and enter the living room. Nearly everyone from the Halloween party is here, Mrs Kelly, Joe and George, who thankfully has a bag full of records. He is followed in by Eddie, Sean Connolly, Mark and even old Uncle Pat.

Sammy joins me in the hall as we jump up and down together and wish Joe a happy new year. I can't help but notice the last person who enters the flat. He is totally bald wearing an orange tunic and sandals. He has two bells on the fingers of each hand which he is banging together as he chants something that sounds like 'Harry's cushion aff'.

After I close the door I turn to Joe and ask "Who is that". Joe looks at me as he replies "Dae ye remember Dom wi' 'ra beard an' dug 'rat died". I nod my head as Joe smiles and continues "'Rat's him". I shake my head in disbelief before asking "So he's Buddhist monk now?", Joe puts his arm over my shoulder and laughs before replying "Naw, no' a real wan, he didnae like 'ra bit aboot nae drink, so he still get's blootered".

Our living room is packed now with the overspill in the hall and my bedroom. George hasn't changed since Halloween and has thankfully taken over the disc jockey duties from Father as we listen to The Move singing *'Flowers in the rain'*. Wilhelmina has perked up and is talking to Sean in the hall who tells me he has signed a contract to play football for Partick Thistle. Poor Mark, who couldn't stop kissing Isobel at Halloween, is single again after she ran away to Paisley with a bus inspector. Eddie hasn't changed in the slightest and is still talking to himself as he sits on the couch alone shouting to fresh air "Whitje mean?".

The biggest surprise is Mrs Kelly. Joe tells me he was sworn to secrecy and that she did indeed get together with Gerry the 'Provvie man'. Gerry was a customer in the pub she worked in called the Granite City, and they now live in a cottage flat in Croftfoot. Joe is attending a new school which he loves and has made a lot of new friends in his street. When I asked why he had to move out of his flat so quickly he explained that, although Mrs Kelly had known Gerry for years, everything happened very quickly.

Mrs Kelly was so embarrassed she couldn't face the neighbours, so Gerry organised a van as quick as he could and helped them move before Mrs Kelly could change her mind.

Mrs Kelly did look very happy as she sat chatting to Mother like long lost friends. "I never expected you to turn up tonight" Mother says. "Sure, did we no' say we wid be here 'efter ye invited us" Mrs Kelly replies with a grin on her face. "Right everybody, oan yer feet, time furra dance" George shouts as he puts *'I'm a believer'* by the Monkees on the turntable and turns the volume up. Everybody gets on their feet and starts to dance, including Joe and Alfie. Dom dances alone in the centre of the room doing his 'Harry's cushion aff' chant as Wilhelmina and Sean dance in the hall. The Campbell's, for some unexplained reason, start to waltz across the living room floor. There are shouts of "Brilliant party intit'?" and "'Rat grub's magic" which brings a big smile to Mothers face as she dances with Father at the sink. All in all I have to say this is the best New Year I can ever remember.

We're Flittin' Tae 'Ra Flats

"The van will be here shortly Rupert" Mother shouts from the living room. Mrs Campbell and Mother are packing the last remaining items from under the sink, and Father is away to pick up the keys to our new flat. As I sit on a freshly packed and labelled box in my bedroom I can't believe that it's been three days now since our brilliant New Year party. As we come to the end of our stay in Heron St I am trying to stay positive and upbeat although inside my overwhelming emotion is sadness. At the end of the party there was a genuine show of friendship and affection as everyone hugged and kissed as we said our goodbyes. I will never forget the sight of Mrs Campbell and Mother crying as they hugged each other or Mrs Kelly wiping away tears as she swears to Mother that she will be up to see her as soon as she is settled in her new flat. It is only now that I have come to realise the true value of friends and family. It really doesn't matter how much money or things you have, as long as you have friends and family you are a very rich indeed.

It is heartening to know Sammy is moving to Ruby St too, but I'm dismayed at the thought of Joe being so far away in Croftfoot. I walk over to the bedroom window and look at the Flats we are moving to, they are only a few hundred yards away but I can feel myself becoming overwhelmed at the thought of leaving and tears start to well up in my eyes

I lean my head against the cold glass of the grubby window and stare down into the street remembering all the good times I have had there with Sammy and then Joe. "Ye a' rite 'rer son?" Mrs Campbell asks from the bedroom door. I keep staring out the window and use my sleeve to try and wipe away the evidence of tears from my eyes. "Yes, I'm fine thank you Mrs Campbell" I say through the sniffles.

She then comes over to me and turns me round and wipes my eyes with the hem of her apron, "Ach, ye'll be fine son" she says sympathetically as she gives me a big hug. I am treasuring this moment until she adds the caveat "Yer no' 'ra same wee snobby bastart ye wur when ye arrived here".

Our special moment is thankfully interrupted by Father, who arrives in the flat with a cheery "Hello" after picking up our new flat keys. He is followed in the open door by Mr Bain, Mr Campbell and Sammy's dad, who are here to give us a helping hand with our boxes. They congregate in the living room as there is another shout of "Hello" and Walter from our local shop appears at the door carrying a small box filled with some grocery essentials. He hands the box to Father and says "Jist a few wee 'hings fur yer new hoose". Then he spots me in the hall and comes over. "Here ye go wee man" he says as he hands me a massive Curly Wurly. "'Rat'll keep ye gon' tae dinner time" he adds. Before I can even say thank you there is the beep from a horn outside. "Oh 'rer yer van...'orrabest in yer new hoose" Walter says as Father stares at the groceries. He too is about to say thank you, but Walter raises his hand and mouths the words "It's okay", he then playfully ruffles my hair and leaves.

Walter's terrible jokes are immediately added to my mental list of things I'll miss as I watch him walk down the stairs. He is passed at the toilet landing by a familiar looking man who asks "The Nairn's?", After indicating that's us, he makes his way into the flat. I am still standing at the door and can hear Mother say "Gerry, come in". I look back down the stairs and can hear a familiar voice saying "Will ye take yer time now son, wan stair at a time". Mrs Kelly comes into view helping an eager Joe up the stairs. It turns out that Mrs Kelly had offered Mother the services of Gerry and his friend's van at the New Year party and deliberately didn't say anything to me as a surprise. It is indeed a brilliant surprise and to cap it all off Sammy has arrived to help as well.

Wilhelmina says goodbye as she leaves with her friend Constance who lives in Greenhead St and tells Mother she will see her at the new flat tonight. The men start to carry the furniture and beds down the stairs to the van, as Joe, Sammy and I are busy packing one final small box with the contents of the small wardrobe drawers.

"Whit's 'ris?" Sammy asks as he lifts a small black notebook out of the bottom drawer. I look over at the notebook and smile as I explain to Sammy and Joe that I used the book as a kind of diary when I first moved to Heron St. "Izzit o' right if ah hiv a wee look?" Sammy asks. I nod my head, as it was that long ago I have forgotten what I wrote in it. Sammy starts to flick through the pages before stopping at a particular page and reading out loud. "...*Starting new school tomorrow and I am really scared, Mother and Wilhelmina are always arguing and feel I sorry for Father who is trying his best to reassure all of us that this move is only temporary...*"

I immediately lean over and try to grab the notebook, but Sammy playfully turns his back and moves on a few pages before continuing to read. *"...I met a boy called Sammy Graham today, he seems really nice and I hope we can be friends as I really need a friend just now..."* Sammy looks at me and smiles before reading on. *"...The only problem is I can't understand a word he says..."* he then looks at me again before thankfully bursting out laughing.

"Let me see 'rat" Joe says as he takes the book from Sammy. He flicks to the back of the book and reads out a page heading "Questions That Need Answers". He reads a bit more and starts laughing to himself which arouses Sammy's curiosity as he shouts to Joe "Read it oot!". I start to recollect this section of the notebook and remember that it is filled with daft questions I used to ask myself to pass the time when I never had anyone to go out to play with. Joe composes himself with a little cough and duly obliges Sammy as he starts to read out loud as I playfully stick my head in the open box to hide my embarrassment.

"Why is abbrevi, abbrevia," he stammers. "Abbreviated" I shout from my box sanctuary. Joe continues *"Why is abbreviated such a long word?"*. He then looks at me with a confused expression on his face and asks "Whit dis abbreviated mean?". Before I can answer Sammy leans over and with a grin on his face, takes the notebook from Joe and says "Here let me read it".

He then continues to read out a list of my daft questions, *"Why is a boxing ring square?"* He just shakes his head before moving on. *"What would Geronimo shout if he jumped off a wall?"* They both start laughing at that one,. *"Why didn't Noah swat those two midges when he had them on the Ark?"* With my head still firmly in the box I can hear Joe laugh out loud and say "Ah know, ah goat ate alive 'ra last time ah wiz in 'ra Sonny pon'".

Sammy continues as I remove my head from the box feeling happy with myself that I am making them laugh. *"Why can't women put on mascara with their mouth closed?"*. Sammy laughs as he says "Aye 'rat's right ma' Maw always dis 'rat". He then treats us to an impersonation of his Mother putting on mascara before revealing one more daft question. *"Why don't you ever see the headline 'Psychic Wins Littlewoods Pools' in the newspaper?"*

He then reads the last one into himself before looking up at Joe and me and admitting "Nah, ah don't get 'rat wan". Joe leans over his shoulder and slowly reads before agreeing with Sammy as he shakes his head saying "Nah!". They hand me the book and I read aloud *"Why isn't the word phonetic spelt the way it sounds?*.

Luckily I am saved from having to provide an explanation by Mr Bain's 12 year old daughter Mary who sticks her head round the door and says "O' aye, ur ye flittin'?". Sammy and Mary have always had a mutual dislike for one another as Sammy sarcastically replies. "Naw, 'rey jist pack 'rer stuff up wance or twice a week tae see how minny boaxes it takes".

He then looks at Joe and me and shakes his head as he goes on to justify his response by adding, "Nae wunner. A big van doon 'ra stair... her Da's jist away oot 'ra hoose cerryin' a big wardrobe... an' 'rers loadsa boaxes o' o'r 'ra shoap" Mary just sticks her tongue out at Sammy and leaves as I quickly close the notebook and stuff it in the box.

The three of us venture into the living room and notice that there is a man standing on a stool emptying the electric meter. He quickly counts the sixpences and makes a note of the meter reading before saying "'At's us 'ren, orrabest in yer new hoose" and making his way to the landing. No sooner had he stepped outside when Mr Bain comments "Ye should huv pit a wee pin in 'ra meter, at's whit everybody dis". Father just smiles as he hasn't got a clue what Mr Bain means. Mr Graham agrees with Mr Bain as he says "Aye it stoaps 'ra wheel in 'ra meter fae turnin' roon' ah dae it tae". Again Father nods as if to say "I see" but still doesn't know what they mean and immediately changes the subject by proclaiming, "Well that's just about us finished". Mother looks around the empty living room and agrees "We better be on our way then" she says as she grabs her coat.

It's arranged that Sammy and I along with Father and Mr Graham will walk the few hundred yards to Ruby St, while Mrs Kelly, Joe and Mother will ride in the van. "Whit aboot me?" Mrs Campbell asks before adding "Ah wiz lookin' furrit' tae a hurrel inra van". Mother thinks for a moment but before she can say anything Joe offers to walk with me and Sammy. Mrs Kelly reluctantly agrees as a smiling Joe stands next to me as if he has just been picked for a game of one man hunt. After a final check to make sure we haven't missed anything, the ladies make their way downstairs as Sammy, Joe and the other men wait on the landing leaving me alone in the flat.

Standing there in the empty living room I wistfully look through the window across the Booly to London Rd as I try to embed the view in my mind. For the first time I can hear the whirring sound emanating from the electric meter along with the dripping tap in the sink below the window that Father was always going to fix. I look down at the floor and can now see the holes in the skirting board where all the mice live that were once hidden by our couch; the tears start to well up again in my eyes as the fact hits home that we really are leaving.

I look over to where our couch used to sit and remember Wilhelmina's last birthday when Mother presented her with a maxi leather coat from Reeta's which was laid out on the couch as she entered the living room. Rather worryingly my mind then switches to the time I came home early from school and walked into the living room only for Mother and Father to jump up and pretend they were looking for coins down the side of the couch.

I quickly place that memory to the back of my mind where it belongs and reach up towards the light switch, but before I get anywhere near it there is a single loud thumping noise as the living room light goes out and the whirring meter stops. As I stand there in the darkness I can only smile as I look upwards and say "Okay, I can take a hint, I'm leaving" and slowly make my way to the front door.

I join Father on the landing and he smiles as he ruffles my hair before locking our door for the last time. For a brief moment I forget my sadness at leaving Heron St as his act of affection replaces my sadness with the question "What is it with adults and ruffling children's hair?". He turns round after locking the door and looks at me before taking a deep breath and saying "Right, onwards and upwards".

We walk down the stairs and when we reach the toilet landing we can't help but notice the nauseating smell emanating from the toilet. The smell is so bad that both of us screw up our faces and pinch our noses. Father stops on the stair level with the toilet landing and winks at me as he shouts "Cheerio Mr Campbell". Mr Campbell replies from inside the toilet "Aye er, orrabest innat". We start laughing as we continue down the stairs and when we reach the entrance to the close we are surprised to find a small crowd gathered to wave us off.

Father notices Mr Mc Kay who is drunk as usual, he reaches out to shake Father's hand making Father feel as if he has to say something. "Er, you're looking great" is all Father can come up with. "Aye 'am oan a new Whisky diet" Mr Mc Kay replies as he taps his stomach. Father stares at him and hesitantly asks "Whisky diet?". Mr McKay laughs as he continues "Aye, 'av loast three days already". Father smiles and quickly moves away and helps Mother into the van. Standing at the side of the close is Walter who can't help himself as he says, "C'mere wee man, av goat wan fur ye afore ye go". He sniggers and goes on to tell me one of his jokes. "Did ye hear Roy Orbison goat a new cheese grater fur eez Christmas?" I shake my head as he delivers the punch line. "He said it wiz 'ra best book he hid ever read". Since this is the last time I would need to listen to his jokes, I decide to laugh heartily which makes him smile as he shakes me warmly by the hand.

After a while Gerry drives off with the ladies including Mrs Campbell who waves her hand out the van window like the Queen. There are random shouts of "Bye" and "'Orrabest" as the van makes it way down Heron St towards the Dog Leg pub. The rest of us start the short walk to Ruby St, and it only then that I notice Billy and Chic standing at the close of number 45. The both of them light up a cigarette as they look over at us and nod in our direction before turning their backs and pretending to speak to each other.

"Why are they here?" I ask Sammy, who looks a bit uncomfortable as he sheepishly replies "Thur gonny tan your hoose". After asking what he meant, Sammy explains that his big brother had mentioned to them that we were moving out and it was their intention to break in and remove all the copper and lead they could get their hands on before anyone else does it. "Gonny no' tell anybody ur ah'll get a doin'" Sammy pleads as we turn the corner into Baltic St. I thought about the amount of locks the previous occupants had fitted on our front door and came to the conclusion that they would never be able to get in anyway, so I agree not to mention our conversation to anyone.

When we arrive at Ruby St, the van is parked outside the middle of three blocks of flats and Gerry is standing at the back of the van smoking a cigarette. When he sees us come into view he throws away his cigarette and stands on it before pulling an armchair from the back of the van and making his way inside the flats. Sammy, Joe and I are ordered to wait at the van as Father and Mr Graham pull out the couch.

As we stand at the van looking up at the top of the flats Joe comments "Jeezo 'rat's high intit?". I am just about to say what floor number we are on when we are approached by a small woman, who looks like Mrs Campbell's twin sister, who says "Aw'right lads 'am Dolly Murphy, ah stay in 'ra furst block". Sammy just looks at his feet as usual while Joe offers a half hearted "Aye aw'right Mrs" before walking around the side of the van. It's left to me to say "Hello Mrs Murphy my names' Rupert and I'm very pleased to meet you". At first Mrs Murphy looks slightly wary of my posh accent, as if she can't decide if I'm taking a rise out of her, but her facial expression mellows after Sammy's well meaning comment of "He's no takin' 'ra piss Mrs, honesty God, he always talks like 'rat". She decides to accept my extended hand as she responds in her best posh accent "Well I'm very pleased tae meet ye son…its no' very often ah come across sum'day 'rats goat good manners an' kin talk good English". Just as she lets go of my hand, Father returns to the van with Mother and they both introduce themselves to our new neighbour Dolly before Mother tells us we can go up in the lift to our new flat.

"Whit number ur ye oan anyway?" asks Sammy as we wait on the lift to arrive. "The tenth floor" I reply. "Yeess" Joe shouts before adding "Ah thought ye wur gonny say ra second flair 'ur sumfin'". The lift arrives and the three of us step inside as Joe excitedly presses button ten. The lift starts to move and I look over at my friends who have a look of trepidation and excitement on their faces. As we pass the third floor they start to relax, and by the time we pass the fifth floor Sammy has a wicked grin on his face before deliberately breaking wind very loudly indeed.

Joe and I burst out laughing over the relentless sound of Sammy's bodily function, but by the time we reach the eighth floor the laughing has been replaced by a verbal assault on our friend Sammy. "You're boufin' by 'ra way" Joe states as he waves his hand in front of his face. Sammy just laughs as he says in his defence "Blame ma' Maw, she geid me beans oan toast fur ma' dinner". The lift has now been engulfed with an unimaginable aroma making the final leg of our journey highly uncomfortable. Eventually the lift makes a tinging noise as we arrive at floor ten. As soon as the doors open Joe and I exit in a theatrical manner coughing and spluttering, leaving Sammy to amble out the lift behind us grinning from ear to ear.

A little old lady is waiting to enter the now empty lift so Joe decides to offer her some advice, "Ye'll need a gas mask if yer gon 'rer Mrs" he shouts. She just shakes her head and enters the lift ignoring Joe's sound advice, as the doors close and the lift starts to descend the putrid aroma has obviously reached her nostrils as we hear her shout, "Awww Fur Christ's sake hiz sum'day died in here?".

"Whit wan's yours" Joe asks as we look along the landing. There are six flats on each landing and Father explained to me that they are a mixture of one, two and three bedroom flats. The one we have is a two bedroom flat, which I point to, just as Mr Graham and Gerry come out to head back down to the van. The three of us excitedly run along towards the open front door, which incurs the wrath of Sammy's dad who shout's "Haud yer hoarses yooz, watch ye don't fall oan yer arse". We respectfully slow down a little as we pass him and make our way inside the flat.

"Wow" Joe says as we enter the living room. We instinctively make our way over to the living room window, "Wow look 'it 'rat" Sammy says as we look out. The view is stunning and we can nearly see our old house in Heron St over the sloped glass roof of Martins Leather works. The top two storeys of Heron St are clearly visible but a hundred foot high giant brick chimney obscures the view of number 43.

To the right we can see all the way down Baltic St to Bernard St, and if we look beyond Heron St we can see a panoramic view of Glasgow with lots of smoking chimneys belonging to houses and industrial works. "'At's some view innit?" Joe says as Sammy and I nod our heads.

I leave my friends still looking out the window and decide to explore the rest of the flat. We now have an inside toilet and a separate kitchen which has an electric cooker fitted. The rooms all smell newly painted and clean and the views continue from the bedroom over towards the Glasgow Green. The bedrooms are a lot smaller than the tenement, but our bunk beds fit comfortably enough.

Mother and Father now have their own room and the toilet looks clean and fresh with its own brand new bath. I can't help but be impressed with the simple things, like the windows opening and shutting properly in every room. As I flush the toilet for the third time I can hear a familiar voice shout "Hello! Do I have a grandson living here?". I immediately rush out the toilet and into the arms of Granny and Granda McDonald from Castlemilk, "Granny...Granda" I shout excitedly before asking "What are you doing here?". Granda does the obligatory ruffling of my hair before saying "We're jist here tae dae wur nosey" followed by Granny, who can't resist cleaning my cheek with her thumb, as she adds "We couldnae miss seein' oor wee man flittin' intae his new hoose, could we?".

A short time later, I am giving Granda a guided tour of our new flat as Granny fills our new whistling kettle with water in the kitchen. The last boxes from the van have been delivered and Mother and Father are standing in the living room with the rest of the adults. "Hello" another familiar voice shouts as an exhausted Mrs Campbell walks into the flat. It turns out she was too scared to use the lift and decided to walk up the stairs. "Fur Christ's sake 'rey stairs ur a bastart so 'rey ur" she laments as she tries to catch her breath. Mother brings Mrs Campbell a glass of water before inviting her to look at the view. Mrs Campbell peers over in the direction of the window before declaring "Nah yer awrite, Ah'll jist sit here a minute 'ren ah'll gie ye a haun tae unpack yer boaxes" She then sits on top of a large box in the centre of the living room and sips her water, Mother smiles before joining Father in the hall to say goodbye to our helpers.

After all our helpers have left, including Sammy and Joe, Granny appears with a tray full of cups of tea and a plate of Abernethy biscuits. Suddenly we hear another familiar voice say "So this is the new chateau Nairn?" as Grandfather and Grandmother Nairn appear at the living room door with Wilhelmina, who had met them at the entrance of the flats.

After another round of pleasantries, Wilhelmina disappears to look at our new room as all my Grandparents sit down with a cup of tea. Mrs Campbell glares at Grandfather Nairn as she has never hidden her dislike for him. She tells everyone who will listen that he reminds her of the wee man on the Monopoly box. "So Hubert, how is your job at the bank coming along?" he asks .Father tells him that everything seems to be fine. Grandfather Nairn stands up and walks over to the window, "Lovely view you have here" he says before clearing his throat in readiness to speak.

Before he can say anything Mrs Campbell mumbles "Here we bloody go". Everyone stares at her as she adds "Nae wunner, it's like listenin' tae Perry bloody Mason every time he opens his mooth". Mother glares at Mrs Campbell as she moans "Ach! Where's yer toilet? 'Am away furra pish" and storms out into the hall.

Mrs Campbell is probably the only person in Glasgow who talks to Grandfather Nairn that way. He said to her the last time she spoke to him like that "I have a CBE madam". Mrs Campbell had everyone in the room laughing as she replied quick as a flash "Aye it probably stons' fur Crabbit Bloody Eejit".

Grandfather composes himself again and looks at Father as he goes on to say "Well my friends at the bank tell that everything isn't fine". Father looks at Mother with a concerned expression on his face as Grandfather continues, "In fact.... everything is much better than fine". Father lets out an audible sigh of relief as he watches Grandfather moving over to Grandmother and placing his hand on her shoulder. He then smiles at Father as he goes on to tell him that he is being promoted shortly to the position of bank manager and that his salary will be drastically increased with the added incentive of a preferential mortgage rate.

Mother is slightly confused as she looks at Grandfather and asks "What, er, when, er?". Grandfather walks over to Father and shakes him warmly by the hand as he says "Congratulation son, this means you can move back to your old house in the West End". There is a shout of "Yippee" from Wilhelmina who is listening in the hall. She is joined by Mrs Campbell who looks shocked as she mutters "Aw naw!". Father and Mother stand up and hug each other before Mother pulls back slightly and looks Father in the eye and says "You did it".

Granny and Granda McDonald politely smile and grudgingly say "Well done Hubert". At this point I am standing at the window looking towards Heron St still trying to digest this momentous news. I slowly turn and look at our new flat, and then look at my very happy parents who are still hugging and crying. I don't know whether to be happy or sad, before finally thinking "Oh no! What am I going to tell Sammy and Joe?".

THE END

Coming Soon: **The Toffs in the West End?**

Printed in Great Britain
by Amazon

36051241R00066

S0-BLL-354

BLACKMORE, R. D. (RICHARD
SLAIN BY THE DOONES.

[1969]
37565009111609   CENT

CENTRAL

C /

Blackmore, Richard Doddridge, 1825-1900.
  Slain by the Doones. Freeport N.Y. Books for
Libraries Press ₁1969₁
    244 p. 21 cm.
  Short story index reprint series
  Slain by the Doones.—Frida.—George
Bowring.—Crocker's Hole.

Short story Index Reprint series

    1. Short stories
    I. Title.

PZ3.B567S7ᵖR4132

823'.8

74-86137
MARC

Information Design

SLAIN BY THE DOONES

Slain by
the Doones

BY
RICHARD DODDRIDGE BLACKMORE

SONOMA CO. LiBRARY

Short Story Index Reprint Series

c/c

BOOKS FOR LIBRARIES PRESS
FREEPORT, NEW YORK

First Published 1895
Reprinted 1969

STANDARD BOOK NUMBER:
8369-3041-X

LIBRARY OF CONGRESS CATALOG CARD NUMBER:
74-86137

MANUFACTURED
BY
HALLMARK LITHOGRAPHERS, INC.
IN THE U.S.A.

CONTENTS

SLAIN BY THE DOONES.

CHAPTER I.

AFTER A STORMY LIFE.

To hear people talking about North Devon, and the savage part called Exmoor, you might almost think that there never was any place in the world so beautiful, or any living men so wonderful. It is not my intention to make little of them, for they would be the last to permit it; neither do I feel ill will against them for the pangs they allowed me to suffer; for I dare say they could not help themselves, being so slow-blooded, and hard to stir even by their own egrimonies. But when I look back upon the things that happened, and were for a full generation of mankind accepted as the will of God, I say, that the people who endured them must have been born to be ruled by the devil. And in thinking thus I am not alone; for the very best judges of that day stopped short of that end of the world, because the law would not go any further. Nevertheless, every word is true of what I am going to tell, and the stoutest writer of history cannot make less of it by denial.

My father was Sylvester Ford of Quantock, in the county of Somerset, a gentleman of large estate as well as ancient lineage. Also of high courage and resolution not to be beaten, as he proved in his many rides with Prince Rupert, and woe that I should say it! in his most sad death. To this he was not looking forward much, though turned of threescore years and five; and his only child and loving daughter, Sylvia, which is myself, had never dreamed of losing him. For he was exceeding fond of me, little as I deserved it, except by loving him with all my heart and thinking nobody like him. And he without anything to go upon, except that he was my father, held, as I have often heard, as good an opinion of me.

Upon the triumph of that hard fanatic, the Brewer, who came to a timely end by the justice of high Heaven—my father, being disgusted with England as well as banished from her, and despoiled of all his property, took service on the Continent, and wandered there for many years, until the replacement of the throne. Thereupon he expected, as many others did, to get his estates restored to him, and perhaps to be held in high esteem at court, as he had a right to be. But this did not so come to pass. Excellent words were granted him, and promise of tenfold restitution ; on the faith of which he returned to Paris, and married a young Italian lady of good birth and high qualities, but with nothing more to come to her. Then, to his great disappointment, he found himself left to live upon air—which, however distinguished, is not sufficient—and love, which, being fed so

easily, expects all who lodge with it to
live upon itself.

My father was full of strong loyalty ; and
the king (in his value of that sentiment)
showed faith that it would support him.
His majesty took both my father's hands,
having learned that hearty style in France,
and welcomed him with most gracious
warmth, and promised him more than he
could desire. But time went on, and the
bright words faded, like a rose set bravely
in a noble vase, without any nurture under
it.

Another man had been long established
in our hereditaments by the Commonwealth ; and he would not quit them of his
own accord, having a sense of obligation to
himself. Nevertheless, he went so far as
to offer my father a share of the land, if
some honest lawyers, whom he quoted,
could find proper means for arranging it.
But my father said : "If I cannot have my
rights, I will have my wrongs. No mixture
of the two for me." And so, for the last

few years of his life, being now very poor
and a widower, he took refuge in an outlandish place, a house and small property in
the heart of Exmoor, which had come to the
Fords on the spindle side, and had been
overlooked when their patrimony was confiscated by the Brewer. Of him I would
speak with no contempt, because he was
ever as good as his word.

In the course of time, we had grown used
to live according to our fortunes. And I
verily believe that we were quite content,
and repined but little at our lost importance.
For my father was a very simple-minded
man, who had seen so much of uproarious
life, and the falsehood of friends, and small
glitter of great folk, that he was glad to fall
back upon his own good will. Moreover he
had his books, and me; and as he always
spoke out his thoughts, he seldom grudged to
thank the Lord for having left both of these
to him. I felt a little jealous of his books
now and then, as a very poor scholar might
be; but reason is the proper guide for

women, and we are quick enough in discerning it, without having to borrow it from books.

At any rate now we were living in a wood, and trees were the only creatures near us, to the best of our belief and wish. Few might say in what part of the wood we lived, unless they saw the smoke ascending from our single chimney ; so thick were the trees, and the land they stood on so full of sudden rise and fall. But a little river called the Lynn makes a crooked border to it, and being for its size as noisy a water as any in the world perhaps, can be heard all through the trees and leaves to the very top of the Warren Wood. In the summer all this was sweet and pleasant ; but lonely and dreary and shuddersome, when the twigs bore drops instead of leaves, and the ground would not stand to the foot, and the play of light and shadow fell, like the lopping of a tree, into one great lump.

Now there was a young man about this time, and not so very distant from our place—as distances are counted there—who managed to make himself acquainted with us, although we lived so privately. To me it was a marvel, both why and how he did it ; seeing what little we had to offer, and how much we desired to live alone. But Mrs. Pring told me to look in the glass, if I wanted to know the reason ; and while I was blushing with anger at that, being only just turned eighteen years, and thinking of nobody but my father, she asked if I had never heard the famous rhymes made by the wise woman at Tarr-steps :

> " Three fair maids live upon Exymoor,
>   The rocks, and the woods, and the dairy-door.
>   The son of a baron shall woo all three,
>   But barren of them all shall the young man be."

Of the countless things I could never understand, one of the very strangest was how Deborah Pring, our only domestic, living in the lonely depths of this great wood, and seeming to see nobody but ourselves, in spite of all that contrived to know as much of the doings of the neigh-

bourhood as if she went to market twice a
week. But my father cared little for any
such stuff ; coming from a better part of the
world, and having been mixed with mighty
issues and making of great kingdoms, he
never said what he thought of these little
combings of petty pie crust, because it was
not worth his while. And yet he seemed
to take a kindly liking to the young De
Wichehalse ; not as a youth of birth only,
but as one driven astray perhaps by harsh
and austere influence. For his father, the
baron, was a godly man,—which is much to
the credit of anyone, growing rarer and
rarer, as it does,—and there should be no
rasp against such men, if they would only
bear in mind that in their time they had
been young, and were not quite so perfect
then. But lo ! I am writing as if I knew a
great deal more than I could know until
the harrow passed over me.

No one, however, need be surprised at
the favour this young man obtained with all
who came into his converse. Handsome,

and beautiful as he was, so that bold maids longed to kiss him, it was the sadness in his eyes, and the gentle sense of doom therein, together with a laughing scorn of it, that made him come home to our nature, in a way that it feels but cannot talk of. And he seemed to be of the past somehow, although so young and bright and brave ; of the time when greater things were done, and men would die for women. That he should woo three maids in vain, to me was a stupid old woman's tale.

"Sylvia," my father said to me, when I was not even thinking of him, "no more converse must we hold with that son of the Baron de Wichehalse. I have ordered Pring to keep the door ; and Mistress Pring, who hath the stronger tongue, to come up if he attempted to dispute ; the while I go away to catch our supper."

He was bearing a fishing rod made by himself, and a basket strapped over his shoulders.

"But why, father ? Why should such a

change be? How hath the young gentle
man displeased thee?" I put my face into
his beard as I spoke, that I might not
appear too curious.

"Is it so?" he answered, "then high
time is it.   No more shall he enter this "—
house he would have said, but being so
truthful changed it into—"hut.   I was
pleased with the youth.   He is gentle and
kind ; but weak—my dear child, remember
that.   Why are we in this hut, my dear?
and thou, the heiress of the best land in
the world, now picking up sticks in the
wilderness?   Because the man who should
do us right is weak, and wavering, and
careth but for pleasure.   So is this young
Marwood de Wichehalse.   He rideth with
the Doones.   I knew it not, but now that
I know, it is enough."

My father was of tall stature and fine
presence, and his beard shone like a
cascade of silver.   It was not the manner
of the young as yet to argue with their
elders, and though I might have been a

little fluttered by the comely gallant's lofty talk and gaze of daring melancholy, I said good-bye to him in my heart, as I kissed my noble father. Shall I ever cease to thank the Lord that I proved myself a good daughter then?

CHAPTER II.

BY A QUIET RIVER.

LIVING as we did all by ourselves, and five or six miles away from the Robbers' Valley, we had felt little fear of the Doones hitherto, because we had nothing for them to steal except a few books, the sight of which would only make them swear and ride away. But now that I was full-grown, and beginning to be accounted comely, my father was sometimes uneasy in his mind, as he told Deborah, and she told me ; for the outlaws showed interest in such matters, even to the extent of carrying off young women who had won reputation thus. Therefore he left Thomas Pring at home, with the doors well-barred, and two duck guns loaded, and ordered me not to quit the house until he should return with a creel of trout for supper. Only our little boy Dick Hutchings was to go with him, to help when his fly caught in the bushes.

My father set off in the highest spirits, as anglers always seem to do, to balance the state in which they shall return; and I knew not, neither did anyone else, what a bold stroke he was resolved upon. When it was too late, we found out that, hearing so much of that strange race, he desired to know more about them, scorning the idea that men of birth could ever behave like savages, and forgetting that they had received no chance of being tamed, as rough spirits are by the lessons of the battlefield. No gentleman would ever dream of attacking an unarmed man, he thought ; least of all one whose hair was white. And so he resolved to fish the brook which ran away from their stronghold, believing that he might see some of them, and hoping for a peaceful interview.

We waited and waited for his pleasant face, and long, deliberate step upon the

steep, and cheerful shout for his Sylvia, to
come and ease down his basket, and say—
"Well done, father!" But the shadows of
the trees grew darker, and the song of the
gray-bird died out among them, and the
silent wings of the owl swept by, and all the
mysterious sounds of night in the depth of
forest loneliness, and the glimmer of a star
through the leaves here and there, to tell us
that there still was light in heaven—but of
an earthly father not a sign; only pain, and
long sighs, and deep sinking of the heart.

But why should I dwell upon this? All
women, being of a gentle and loving kind,
—unless they forego their nature,—know
better than I at this first trial knew, the
misery often sent to us. I could not
believe it, and went about in a dreary haze
of wonder, getting into dark places, when
all was dark, and expecting to be called out
again and asked what had made such a fool
of me. And so the long night went at last,
and no comfort came in the morning. But
I heard a great crying, sometime the next

day, and ran back from the wood to learn
what it meant, for there I had been searching up and down, not knowing whither I
went or why. And lo, it was little Dick
Hutchings at our door, and Deborah Pring
held him by the coat-flap, and was beating
him with one of my father's sticks.

"I tell 'ee, they Doo-uns has done for
'un," the boy was roaring betwixt his sobs;
"dree on 'em, dree on 'em, and he've a
killed one. The squire be layin' as dead as
a sto-un."

Mrs. Pring smacked him on the mouth,
for she saw that I had heard it. What followed I know not, for down I fell, and the
sense of life went from me.

There was little chance of finding Thomas
Pring, or any other man to help us, for
neighbours were none, and Thomas was gone
everywhere he could think of to look for
them. Was I likely to wait for night again,
and then talk for hours about it? I recovered my strength when the sun went
low ; and who was Deborah Pring, to stop

me? She would have come, but I would not have it; and the strength of my grief took command of her.

Little Dick Hutchings whistled now, I remember that he whistled, as he went through the wood in front of me. Who had given him the breeches on his legs and the hat upon his shallow pate? And the poor little coward had skiddered away, and slept in a furze rick, till famine drove him home. But now he was set up again by gorging for an hour, and chattered as if he had done a great thing.

There must have been miles of rough walking through woods, and tangles, and craggy and black boggy hollows, until we arrived at a wide open space where two streams ran into one another.

"Thic be Oare watter," said the boy, "and t'other over yonner be Badgery. Squire be dead up there; plaise, Miss Sillie, 'ee can goo vorrard and vaind 'un."

He would go no further; but I crossed the brook, and followed the Badgery stream,

without knowing, or caring to know, where
I was.   The banks, and the bushes, and the
rushing water went by me until I came
upon—but though the Lord hath made us
to endure such things, he hath not com-
pelled us to enlarge upon them.

In the course of the night kind people
came, under the guidance of Thomas Pring,
and they made a pair of wattles such as
farmers use for sheep, and carried home
father and daughter, one sobbing and
groaning with a broken heart, and the other
that should never so much as sigh again.
Troubles have fallen upon me since, as the
will of the Lord is always ; but none that I
ever felt like that, and for months everything was the same to me.

But inasmuch as it has been said by
those who should know better, that my
father in some way provoked his merciless
end by those vile barbarians, I will put into
plainest form, without any other change,
except from outlandish words, the tale
received from Dick Hutchings, the boy,

who had seen and heard almost everything while crouching in the water and huddled up inside a bush.

"Squire had catched a tidy few, and he seemed well pleased with himself, and then we came to a sort of a hollow place where one brook floweth into the other. Here he was a-casting of his fly, most careful, for if there was ever a trout on the feed, it was like to be a big one, and lucky for me I was keeping round the corner when a kingfisher bird flew along like a string-bolt, and there were three great men coming round a fuzz-bush, and looking at squire, and he back to them. Down goes I, you may say sure enough, with all of me in the water but my face, and that stuck into a wutts-clump, and my teeth making holes in my naked knees, because of the way they were shaking.

"'Ho, fellow!' one of them called out to squire, as if he was no better than father is, 'who give thee leave to fish in our river?'

"'Open moor,' says squire, 'and belongeth to the king, if it belongeth to anybody. Any of you gentlemen hold his majesty's warrant to forbid an old officer of his?'

"That seemed to put them in a dreadful rage, for to talk of a warrant was unpleasant to them.

"'Good fellow, thou mayest spin spider's webs, or jib up and down like a gnat,' said one, 'but such tricks are not lawful upon land of ours. Therefore render up thy spoil.'

"Squire walked up from the pebbles at that, and he stood before the three of them, as tall as any of them. And he said, 'You be young men, but I am old. Nevertheless, I will not be robbed by three, or by thirty of you. If you be cowards enough, come on.'

"Two of them held off, and I heard them say, 'Let him alone, he is a brave old cock.' For you never seed anyone look more braver, and his heart was up with

righteousness. But the other, who seemed
to be the oldest of the three, shouted out
something, and put his leg across, and
made at the squire with a long blue thing
that shone in the sun, like a looking-glass.
And the squire, instead of turning round to
run away as he should have, led at him
with the thick end of the fishing rod, to
which he had bound an old knife of Mother
Pring's for to stick it in the grass, while he
put his flies on. And I heard the old knife
strike the man in his breast, and down he
goes dead as a door-nail. And before I
could look again almost, another man ran
a long blade into squire, and there he was
lying as straight as a lath, with the end of
his white beard as red as a rose. At that
I was so scared that I couldn't look no
more, and the water came bubbling into
my mouth, and I thought I was at home
along of mother.

"By and by, I came back to myself with
my face full of scratches in a bush, and the
sun was going low, and the place all as

quiet as Cheriton church. But the noise
of the water told me where I was; and I
got up, and ran for the life of me, till I
came to the goyal. And then I got into
a fuzz-rick, and slept all night, for I
durstn't go home to tell Mother Pring.
But I just took a look before I began to
run, and the Doone that was killed was
gone away, but the squire lay along with
his arms stretched out, as quiet as a sheep
before they hang him up to drain."

CHAPTER III.

WISE COUNSEL.

SOME pious people seem not to care how many of their dearest hearts the Lord in heaven takes from them. How well I remember that in later life, I met a beautiful young widow, who had loved her husband with her one love, and was left with twin babies by him. I feared to speak, for I had known him well, and thought her the tenderest of the tender, and my eyes were full of tears for her. But she looked at me with some surprise, and said: "You loved my Bob, I know," for he was a cousin of my own, and as good a man as ever lived, "but, Sylvia, you must not commit the sin of grieving for him."

It may be so, in a better world, if people are allowed to die there; but as long as we

are here, how can we help being as the Lord
has made us ?   The sin, as it seems to me,
would be to feel or fancy ourselves case-
hardened against the will of our Maker,
which so often is—that we should grieve.
Without a thought how that might be, I did
the natural thing, and cried about the death
of my dear father until I was like to follow
him.   But a strange thing happened in a
month or so of time, which according to
Deborah saved my life, by compelling other
thoughts to come.   My father had been
buried in a small churchyard, with nobody
living near it, and the church itself was
falling down, through scarcity of money on
the moor.   The Warren, as our wood was
called, lay somewhere in the parish of
Brendon, a straggling country, with a little
village somewhere, and a blacksmith's shop
and an ale house, but no church that anyone knew of, till you came to a place called
Cheriton.   And there was a little church
all by itself, not easy to find, though it
had four bells, which nobody dared to ring,

for fear of his head and the burden above it. But a boy would go up the first Sunday of each month, and strike the liveliest of them with a poker from the smithy. And then a brave parson, who feared nothing but his duty, would make his way in, with a small flock at his heels, and read the Psalms of the day, and preach concerning the difficulty of doing better. And it was accounted to the credit of the Doones that they never came near him, for he had no money.

The Fords had been excellent Catholics always; but Thomas and Deborah Pring, who managed everything while I was over-come, said that the church, being now so old, must have belonged to us, and there-for might be considered holy. The parson also said that it would do, for he was not a man of hot persuasions. And so my dear father lay there, without a stone, or a word to tell who he was, and the grass began to grow.

Here I was sitting one afternoon in May, and the earth was beginning to look lively;

when a shadow from the west fell over me, and a large, broad man stood behind it. If I had been at all like myself, a thing of that kind would have frightened me; but now the strings of my system seemed to have nothing like a jerk in them, for I cared not whither I went, nor how I looked, nor whether I went anywhere.

"Child! poor child!" It was a deep, soft voice of distant yet large benevolence. "Almost a woman, and a comely one, for those who think of such matters. Such a child I might have owned, if Heaven had been kind to me."

Low as I was of heart and spirit, I could not help looking up at him ; for Mother Pring's voice, though her meaning ,was so good, sounded like a cackle in comparison to this. But when I looked up, such encouragement came from a great benign and steadfast gaze that I turned away my eyes, as I felt them overflow. But he said not a word, for his pity was too deep, and I thanked him in my heart for that.

"Pardon me if I am wrong," I said, with my eyes on the white flowers I had brought and arranged as my father would have liked them; "but perhaps you are the clergyman of this old church." For I had lain senseless and moaning on the ground when my father was carried away to be buried.

"How often am I taken for a clerk in holy orders! And in better times I might have been of that sacred vocation, though so unworthy. But I am a member of the older church, and to me all this is heresy."

There was nothing of bigotry in our race, and we knew that we must put up with all changes for the worst; yet it pleased me not a little that so good a man should be also a sound Catholic.

"There are few of us left, and we are persecuted. Sad calumnies are spread about us," this venerable man proceeded, while I gazed on the silver locks that fell upon his well-worn velvet coat. "But of such things we take small heed, while we know that the Lord is with us. Haply even you, young maiden, have listened to slander about us."

I told him with some concern, although not caring much for such things now, that I never had any chance of listening to tales about anybody, and was yet without the honour of even knowing who he was.

"Few indeed care for that point now," he answered, with a toss of his glistening curls, and a lift of his broad white eyebrows. "Though there has been a time when the noblest of this earth—but vanity, vanity, the wise man saith. Yet some good I do in my quiet little way. There is a peaceful company among these hills, respected by all who conceive them aright. My child, perhaps you have heard of them?"

I replied sadly that I had not done so, but hoped that he would forgive me as one unacquainted with that neighbourhood. But I knew that there might be godly monks still in hiding, for the service of God in the wilderness.

"So far as the name goes, we are not monastics," he said, with a sparkle in his deep-set eyes; "we are but a family of ancient lineage, expelled from our home in these irreligious times. It is no longer in our power to do all the good we would, and therefore we are much undervalued. Perhaps you have heard of the Doones, my child?"

To me it was a wonder that he spoke of them thus, for his look was of beautiful mildness, instead of any just condemnation. But his aspect was as if he came from heaven; and I thought that he had a hard job before him, if he were sent to conduct the Doones thither.

"I am not severe; I think well of mankind," he went on, as I looked at him meekly; "perhaps because I am one of them. You are very young, my dear, and unable to form much opinion as yet. But let it be your rule of life ever to keep an open mind."

This advice impressed me much, though

I could not see clearly what it meant. But the sun was going beyond Exmoor now, and safe as I felt with so good an old man, a long, lonely walk was before me. So I took up my basket and rose to depart, saying, "Good-bye, sir ; I am much in your debt for your excellent advice and kindness."

He looked at me most benevolently, and whatever may be said of him hereafter, I shall always believe that he was a good man, overcome perhaps by circumstances, yet trying to make the best of them. He has now become a by-word as a hypocrite and a merciless self-seeker. But many young people, who met him as I did, without possibility of prejudice, hold a larger opinion of him. And surely young eyes are the brightest.

"I will protect thee, my dear," he said, looking capable in his great width and wisdom of protecting all the host of heaven. "I have protected a maiden even more beautiful than thou art. But now she hath unwisely fled from us. Our young men are thoughtless, but they are not violent, at least until they are sadly provoked. Your father was a brave man, and much to be esteemed. My brother, the mildest man that ever lived, hath ridden down hundreds of Roundheads with him. Therefore thou shalt come to no harm. But he should not have fallen upon our young men as if they were rabble of the Commonwealth."

Upon these words I looked at him I know not how, so great was the variance betwixt my ears and eyes. Then I tried to say something, but nothing would come, so entire was my amazement.

"Such are the things we have ever to contend with," he continued, as if to himself, with a smile of compassion at my prejudice. "Nay, I am not angry; I have seen so much of this. Right and wrong stand fast, and cannot be changed by any facundity. But time is short, and will soon be stirring. Have a backway from thy bedroom, child. I am Councillor Doone ; by birthright and in right of understanding, the captain of that pious family, since the return of the good Sir Ensor to the land where there are no lies. So long as we are not molested in our peaceful valley, my will is law; and I have ordered that none shall go near thee. But a mob of country louts are drilling in a farmyard up the moorlands, to plunder and destroy us, if they can. We shall make short work of them. But after that, our youths may be provoked beyond control, and sally forth to make reprisal. They have their eyes on thee, I know, and thy father hath assaulted us. An ornament to our valley thou wouldst be; but I would reproach myself if the daughter of my brother's friend were discontented with our life. Therefore have I come to warn thee, for there are troublous times in front. Have a back-way from thy bedroom, child, and slip out into the wood if a noise comes in the night."

Before I could thank him, he strode away, with a step of no small dignity, and as he raised his pointed hat, the western light showed nothing fairer or more venerable than the long wave of his silver locks.

CHAPTER IV.

A COTTAGE HOSPITAL.

MASTER PRING was not much of a man to talk. But for power of thought he was considered equal to any pair of other men, and superior of course to all womankind. Moreover, he had seen a good deal of fighting, not among outlaws, but fine soldiers well skilled in the proper style of it. So that it was impossible for him to think very highly of the Doones. Gentlemen they might be, he said, and therefore by nature well qualified to fight. But where could they have learned any discipline, any tactics, any knowledge of formation, or even any skill of sword or firearms? "Tush, there was his own son, Bob, now serving under Captain Purvis, as fine a young trooper as ever drew sword, and perhaps on his way at this very moment, under orders from the Lord Lieutenant, to rid the country of that pestilent race. Ah, ha! We soon shall see ! "

And in truth we did see him, even sooner than his own dear mother had expected, and long before his father wanted him, though he loved him so much in his absence. For I heard a deep voice in the kitchen one night (before I was prepared for such things, by making a backway out of my bedroom), and thinking it best to know the worst, went out to ask what was doing there.

A young man was sitting upon the table, accounting too little of our house, yet showing no great readiness to boast, only to let us know who he was. He had a fine head of curly hair, and spoke with a firm conviction that there was much inside it. "Father, you have possessed small opportunity of seeing how we do things now. Mother is not to be blamed for thinking that we are in front of what used to be.

What do we care how the country lies? We have heared all this stuff up at Oare. If there are bogs, we shall timber them. If there are rocks, we shall blow them up. If there are caves, we shall fire down them. The moment we get our guns into position——"

"Hush, Bob, hush! Here is your master's daughter. Not the interlopers you put up with; but your real master, on whose property you were born. Is that the position for your guns?"

Being thus rebuked by his father, who was a very faithful-minded man, Robert Pring shuffled his long boots down, and made me a low salutation. But, having paid little attention to the things other people were full of, I left the young man to convince his parents, and he soon was successful with his mother.

Two, or it may have been three days after this, a great noise arose in the morning. I was dusting my father's books, which lay open just as he had left them. There was "Barker's Delight" and "Isaac

Walton," and the "Secrets of Angling by J. D." and some notes of his own about making of flies; also fish hooks made of Spanish steel, and long hairs pulled from the tail of a gray horse, with spindles and bits of quill for plaiting them. So proud and so pleased had he been with these trifles, after the clamour and clash of life, that tears came into my eyes once more, as I thought of his tranquil and amiable ways.

"'Tis a wrong thing altogether to my mind," cried Deborah Pring, running in to me. "They Doones was established afore we come, and why not let them bide upon their own land? They treated poor master amiss, beyond denial ; and never will I forgive them for it. All the same, he was catching what belonged to them ; meaning for the best no doubt, because he was so righteous. And having such courage he killed one, or perhaps two; though I never could have thought so much of that old knife. But ever since

that, they have been good, Miss Sillie,
never even coming anigh us; and I don't
believe half of the tales about them."

All this was new to me; for if anybody
had cried shame and death upon that
wicked horde, it was Deborah Pring, who
was talking to me thus! I looked at her
with wonder, suspecting for the moment
that the venerable Councillor—who was
clever enough to make a cow forget her
calf—might have paid her a visit while I
was away. But very soon the reason of
the change appeared.

"Who hath taken command of the
attack?" she asked, as if no one would
believe the answer; "not Captain Purvis,
as ought to have been, nor even Captain
Dallas of Devon, but Spy Stickles by royal
warrant, the man that hath been up to
Oare so long! And my son Robert, who
hath come down to help to train them, and
understandeth cannon guns——"

"Captain Purvis? I seem to know that
name very well. I have often heard it

from my father. And your son under him! Why, Deborah, what are you hiding from me?"

Now good Mrs. Pring was beginning to forget, or rather had never borne properly in mind, that I was the head of the household now, and entitled to know everything, and to be asked about it. But people who desire to have this done should insist upon it at the outset, which I had not been in proper state to do. So that she made quite a grievance of it, when I would not be treated as a helpless child. However, I soon put a stop to that, and discovered to my surprise much more than could be imagined.

And before I could say even half of what I thought, a great noise arose in the hollow of the hills, and came along the valleys, like the blowing of a wind that had picked up the roaring of mankind upon its way. Perhaps greater noise had never arisen upon the moor; and the cattle, and the quiet sheep, and even the wild deer came bounding from unsheltered places into any offering of branches, or of other heling from the turbulence of men. And then a gray fog rolled down the valley, and Deborah said it was cannon-smoke, following the river course; but to me it seemed only the usual thickness of the air, when the clouds hang low. Thomas Pring was gone, as behooved an ancient warrior, to see how his successors did things, and the boy Dick Hutchings had begged leave to sit in a tree and watch the smoke. Deborah and I were left alone, and a long and anxious day we had.

At last the wood-pigeons had stopped their cooing,—which they kept up for hours, when the weather matched the light,—and there was not a tree that could tell its own shadow, and we were contented with the gentle sounds that come through a forest when it falls asleep, and Deborah Pring, who had taken a motherly tendency toward me now, as if to make up for my father, was sitting in the porch with my hands in her lap, and telling me how to behave hence-forth, as if the whole world depended upon that, when we heard a swishing sound, as of branches thrust aside, and then a low moan that went straight to my heart, as I thought of my father when he took the blow of death.

"My son, my Bob, my eldest boy!" cried Mistress Pring, jumping up and falling into my arms, like a pillow full of wire, for she insisted upon her figure still. But before I could do anything to help her——

"Hit her on the back, ma'am; hit her hard upon the back. That is what always brings mother round," was shouted, as I might say, into my ear by the young man whom she was lamenting.

"Shut thy trap, Braggadose. To whom art thou speaking? Pretty much thou hast learned of war to come and give lessons to thy father! Mistress Sylvia, it is for thee to speak. Nothing would satisfy this young springal but to bring his beaten captain here, for the sake of mother's management.

I told un that you would never take him in, for his father have taken in you pretty well! Captain Purvis of the Somerset I know not what—for the regiments now be all upside down. *Raggiments* is the proper name for them. Very like he be dead by this time, and better die out of doors than in. Take un away, Bob. No hospital here!"

"Thomas Pring, who are you," I said, for the sound of another low groan came through me, "to give orders to your master's daughter? If you bring not the poor wounded gentleman in, you shall never come through this door yourself."

"Ha, old hunks, I told thee so!"

The young man who spoke raised his hat to me, and I saw that it had a scarlet plume, such as Marwood de Wichehalse gloried in. "In with thee, and stretch him that he may die straight. I am off to Southmolton for Cutcliffe Lane, who can make a furze-fagot bloom again. My filly can give a land-yard in a mile to Tom Faggus and his Winnie. But mind one thing, all of you; it was none

of us that shot the captain, but his own
good men.   Farewell, Mistress Sylvia !"
With these words he made me a very low
bow, and set off for his horse at the corner
of the wood—as reckless a gallant as ever
broke hearts, and those of his own kin foremost; yet himself so kind and loving.

CHAPTER V.

MISTAKEN AIMS.

CAPTAIN PURVIS, now brought to the Warren in this very sad condition, had not been shot by his own men, as the dashing Marwood de Wichehalse said; neither was it quite true to say that he had been shot by anyone. What happened to him was simply this : While behaving with the utmost gallantry and encouraging the militia of Somerset, whose uniforms were faced with yellow, he received in his chest a terrific blow from the bottom of a bottle. This had been discharged from a culverin on the opposite side of the valley by the brave but impetuous sons of Devon, who wore the red facings, and had taken umbrage at a pure mistake on the part of their excellent friends and neighbours, the loyal band of Somerset. Either brigade had three culverins; and never having seen such things before, as was natural with good farmers' sons, they felt it a compliment to themselves to be intrusted with such danger, and resolved to make the most of it. However, when they tried to make them go, with the help of a good many horses, upon places that had no roads for war, and even no sort of road at all, the difficulty was beyond them. But a very clever blacksmith near Malmesford, who had better, as it proved, have stuck to the plough, persuaded them that he knew all about it, and would bring their guns to bear, if they let him have his way. So they took the long tubes from their carriages, and lashed rollers of barked oak under them, and with very stout ropes, and great power of swearing, dragged them into the proper place to overwhelm the Doones.

Here they mounted their guns upon cider barrels, with allowance of roll for recoil, and charged them to the very best of their knowledge, and pointed them as nearly as they could guess at the dwellings of the outlaws in the glen; three cannons on the north were of Somerset, and the three on the south were of Devonshire; but these latter had no balls of metal, only anything round they could pick up. Colonel Stickles was in command, by virtue of his royal warrant, and his plan was to make his chief assault in company with some chosen men, including his host, young farmer Ridd, at the head of the valley where the chief entrance was, while the trainbands pounded away on either side. And perhaps this would have succeeded well, except for a little mistake in firing, for which the enemy alone could be blamed with justice. For while Captain Purvis was behind the line rallying a few men who showed fear, and not expecting any combat yet, because Devonshire was not ready, an elderly gentleman of great authority appeared among the bombardiers. On his breast he wore a badge of office, and in his hat a noble plume of the sea eagle, and he handed his horse to a man in red clothes.

"Just in time," he shouted; "and the Lord be thanked for that! By order of His Majesty, I take supreme command. Ha, and high time, too, for it! You idiots, where are you pointing your guns? What allowance have you made for windage? Why, at that elevation, you'll shoot yourselves. Up with your muzzles, you yellow jackanapes! Down on your bellies! Hand me the linstock! By the Lord, you don't even know how to touch them off!"

The soldiers were abashed at his rebukes, and glad to lie down on their breasts for fear of the powder on their yellow facings. And thus they were shaken by three great roars, and wrapped in a cloud of streaky smoke. When this had cleared off, and they stood up, lo! the houses of the Doones were the same as before, but a great shriek arose on the opposite bank, and two good horses lay on the ground; and the red men were stamping about, and some crossing their arms, and some running for their lives, and the bravest of them stooping over one another. Then as Captain Purvis rushed up in great wrath, shouting: "What the devil do you mean by this?" another great roar arose from across the valley, and he was lying flat, and two other fine fellows were rolling in a furze bush without knowledge of it. But of the general and his horse there was no longer any token.

This was the matter that lay so heavily on the breast of Captain Purvis, sadly crushed as it was already by the spiteful stroke bitterly intended for him. His own men had meant no harm whatever, unless to the proper enemy; although they appear to have been deluded by a subtle device of the Councillor, for which on the other hand none may blame him. But those redfaced men, without any inquiry, turned the muzzles of their guns upon Somerset, and the injustice rankled for a generation between

two equally honest counties. Happily they
did not fight it out through scarcity of
ammunition, as well as their mutual desire
to go home and attend to their harvest
business.

But Anthony Purvis, now our guest and
patient, became very difficult to manage;
not only because of his three broken ribs,
but the lowness of the heart inside them.
Dr. Cutcliffe Lane, a most cheerful man
from that cheerful town Southmolton, was
able (with the help of Providence) to make
the bones grow again without much anger
into their own embraces. It is useless,
however, for the body to pretend that it is
doing wonders on its own account, and rejoicing and holiday making, when the thing
that sits inside it and holds the whip, keeps
down upon the slouch and is out of sorts.
And truly this was the case just now with
the soul of Captain Purvis. Deborah Pring
did her very best, and was in and out of his
room every minute, and very often seemed
to me to run him down when he deserved it

not; on purpose that I might be started to run him up. But nothing of that sort told at all according to her intention. I kept myself very much to myself; feeling that my nature was too kind, and asking at some little questions of behaviour, what sort of returns my dear father had obtained for supposing other people as good as himself.

Moreover, it seemed an impossible thing that such a brave warrior, and a rich man too—for his father, Sir Geoffrey, was in full possession now of all the great property that belonged by right to us—that an officer who should have been in command of this fine expedition, if he had his dues, could be either the worse or the better of his wound, according to his glimpses of a simple maid like me. It was useless for Deborah Pring, or even Dr. Cutcliffe Lane himself, to go on as they did about love at first sight, and the rising of the heart when the ribs were broken, and a quantity of other stuff too foolish to repeat. "I am

neither a plaster nor a poultice," I replied
to myself, for I would not be too cross
to them—and beyond a little peep at him,
every afternoon, I kept out of the sight of
Captain Purvis.

But these things made it very hard for
me to be quite sure how to conduct myself,
without father and mother to help me, and
with Mistress Pring, who had always been
such a landmark, becoming no more than a
vane for the wind to blow upon as it listed;
or, perhaps, as she listed to go with it.
And remembering how she used to speak of
the people who had ousted us, I told her
that I could not make it out.   Things were
in this condition, and Captain Purvis, as it
seemed to me, quite fit to go and make war
again upon some of His Majesty's subjects,
when a thing, altogether out of reason, or
even of civilisation, happened; and people
who live in lawful parts will accuse me of
caring too little for the truth.   But even
before that came about, something less
unreasonable—but still unexpected—befell

me. To wit, I received through Mistress Pring an offer of marriage, immediate and pressing, from Captain Anthony Purvis! He must have been sadly confused by that blow on his heart to think mine so tender, or that this was the way to deal with it, though later explanations proved that Deborah, if she had been just, would have taken the whole reproach upon herself. The captain could scarcely have seen me, I believe more than half a dozen times to speak of; and generally he had shut his eyes, gentle as they were and beautiful; not only to make me feel less afraid, but to fill me with pity for his weakness. Having no knowledge of mankind as yet, I was touched to the brink of tears at first; until when the tray came out of his room soon after one of these pitiful moments, it was plain to the youngest comprehension that the sick man had left very little upon a shoulder of Exmoor mutton, and nothing in a bowl of thick onion sauce.

For that I would be the last to blame

him, and being his hostess, I was glad to find it so. But Deborah played a most double-minded part ; leading him to believe that now she was father and mother in one to me ; while to me she went on, as if I was most headstrong, and certain to go against anything she said, though for her part she never said anything. Nevertheless he made a great mistake, as men always do, about our ways ; and having some sense of what is right, I said, " Let me hear no more of Captain Purvis."

This forced him to leave us ; which he might have done, for aught I could see to the contrary, a full week before he departed. He behaved very well when he said good-bye,—for I could not deny him that occasion,—and, perhaps, if he had not assured me so much of his everlasting gratitude, I should have felt surer of deserving it. Perhaps I was a little disappointed also, that he expressed no anxiety at leaving our cottage so much at the mercy of turbulent and triumphant outlaws. But it was not

for me to speak of that ; and when I knew
the reason of his silence, it redounded tenfold to his credit. Nothing, however, vexed
me so much as what Deborah Pring said
afterward : that he could not help feeling in
the sadness of his heart that I had behaved
in that manner to him just because his
father was in possession of our rightful
home and property.   I was not so small as
that ; and if he truly did suppose it, there
must have been some fault on my part,
for his nature was good to everybody, and
perhaps all the better for not descending
through too many high generations.

There is nothing more strange than the
way things work in the mind of a woman,
when left alone, to doubt about her own
behaviour.   With men it can scarcely be so
cruel ; because they can always convince
themselves that they did their best ; and if
it fail, they can throw the fault upon Providence, or bad luck, or something outside
their own power.   But we seem always to
be denied this happy style of thinking, and

cannot put aside what comes into our hearts
more quickly, and has less stir of outward
things, to lead it away and to brighten it.
So that I fell into sad, low spirits ; and the
glory of the year began to wane, and the
forest grew more and more lonesome.

CHAPTER VI.

OVER THE BRIDGE.

THE sound of the woods was with me now, both night and day, to dwell upon. Exmoor in general is bare of trees, though it hath the name of forest; but in the shelter, where the wind flies over, are many thick places full of shade. For here the trees and bushes thrive, so copious with rich moisture that, from the hills on the opposite side, no eye may pick holes in the umbrage; neither may a foot that gets amid them be sure of getting out again. And now was the fullest and heaviest time, for the summer had been a wet one, after a winter that went to our bones; and the leaves were at their darkest tone without any sense of autumn. As one stood beneath and wondered at their countless multitude, a quick breathing passed among them, not enough to make them move, but seeming rather as if they wished, and yet were half ashamed to sigh. And this was very sad for one whose spring comes only once for all.

One night toward the end of August I was lying awake thinking of the happier times, and wondering what the end would be—for now we had very little money left, and I would rather starve than die in debt —when I heard our cottage door smashed in and the sound of horrible voices. The roar of a gun rang up the stairs, and the crash of someone falling and the smoke came through my bedroom door, and then wailing mixed with curses. "Out of the way, old hag!" I heard, and then another shriek; and then I stood upon the stairs and looked down at them. The moon was shining through the shattered door, and the bodies and legs of men went to and fro, like branches in a tempest. Nobody seemed to notice me, although I had cast over my night-dress—having no more sense in the terror—a long silver coat of some animal shot by my father in his wanderings, and the light upon the stairs glistened round it. Having no time to think, I was turning to flee and jump out of my bedroom window, for which I had made some arrangements, according to the wisdom of the Councillor, when the flash of some light or the strain of my eyes showed me the body of Thomas Pring, our faithful old retainer, lying at the foot of the broken door, and beside it his good wife, creeping up to give him the last embrace of death. And lately she had been cross to him. At the sight of this my terror fled, and I cared not what became of me. Buckling the white skin round my waist, I went down the stairs as steadily as if it were breakfast time, and said :

"Brutes, murderers, cowards ! you have slain my father; now slay me !"

Every one of those wicked men stood up and fixed his eyes on me; and if it had been a time to laugh, their amazement might have been laughed at. Some of them took me for a spirit—as I was told long afterward—and rightly enough their evil hearts were struck with dread of judgment. But even so, to scare them long in their contemptuous, godless vein was beyond the power of Heaven itself; and when one of my long tresses fell, to my great vexation, down my breast, a shocking sneer arose, and words unfit for a maiden's ear ensued.

"None of that! This is no farmhouse wench, but a lady of birth and breeding. She shall be our queen, instead of the one that hath been filched away. Sylvia, thou shalt come with me."

The man who spoke with this mighty voice was a terror to the others, for they fell away before him, and he was the biggest monster there—Carver Doone, whose name for many a generation shall be used to frighten unruly babes to bed. And now, as he strode up to me and bowed,—to show some breeding,—I doubt if the moon, in all her rounds of earth and sky and the realms below, fell ever upon another face so cold, repulsive, ruthless.

To belong to him, to feel his lips, to touch him with anything but a dagger! Suddenly I saw my father's sword hanging under a beam in the scabbard. With a quick spring I seized it, and, leaping up the stairs, had the long blade gleaming in the moonlight. The staircase would not hold two people abreast, and the stairs were as steep as narrow. I brought the point down it, with the hilt against my breast, and there was no room for another blade to swing and strike it up.

"Let her alone!" said Carver Doone, with a smile upon his cold and corpselike face. "My sons, let the lady have her time. She is worthy to be the mother of many a fine Doone."

The young men began to lounge about in a manner most provoking, as if I had passed from their minds altogether; and some of them went to the kitchen for victuals, and grumbled at our fare by the light of a lantern which they had found upon a shelf. But I stood at my post, with my heart beating, so that the long sword quivered like a candle. Of my life they might rob me, but of my honour, never!

"Beautiful maiden! Who hath ever seen the like? Why, even Lorna hath not such eyes."

Carver Doone came to the foot of the stairs and flashed the lantern at me, and, thinking that he meant to make a rush for it, I thrust my weapon forward; but at the same moment a great pair of arms was thrown around me from behind by some villain who must have scaled my chamber window, and backward I fell, with no sense or power left.

When my scattered wits came back I felt that I was being shaken grievously, and the moon was dancing in my eyes through a mist of tears, half blinding them. I remember how hard I tried to get my fingers up to wipe my eyes, so as to obtain some

knowledge; but jerk and bump and helpless wonder were all that I could get or take;
for my hands were strapped, and my feet
likewise, and I seemed like a wave going
up and down, without any judgment, upon
the open sea.

But presently I smelled the wholesome
smell which a horse of all animals alone
possesses, though sometimes a cow is almost
as good, and then I felt a mane coming into
my hair, and then there was the sound of
steady feet moving just under me, with rise
and fall and swing alternate, and a sense
of going forward.   I was on the back of a
great, strong horse, and he was obeying the
commands of man.   Gradually I began to
think, and understood my awful plight.
The Doones were taking me to Doone Glen
to be some cut-throat's light-of-love; perhaps to be passed from brute to brute—me,
Sylvia Ford, my father's darling, a proud
and dainty and stately maiden, of as good
birth as any in this English realm.   My
heart broke down as I thought of that, and

all discretion vanished. Though my hands were tied my throat was free, and I sent forth such a scream of woe that the many-winding vale of Lynn, with all its wild waters could not drown, nor with all its dumb foliage smother it; and the long wail rang from crag to crag, as the wrongs of men echo unto the ears of God.

"Valiant damsel, what a voice thou hast! Again, and again let it strike the skies. With them we are at peace, being persecuted here, according to the doom of all good men. And yet I am loth to have that fair throat strained."

It was Carver Doone who led my horse; and his horrible visage glared into my eyes through the strange, wan light that flows between the departure of the sinking moon and the flutter of the morning when it cannot see its way. I strove to look at him; but my scared eyes fell, and he bound his rank glove across my poor lips. "Let it be so," I thought; "I can do no more."

Then, when my heart was quite gone in

despair, and all trouble shrank into a trifle, I heard a loud shout, and the trample of feet, and the rattle of arms, and the clash of horses. Contriving to twist myself a little, I saw that the band of the Doones were mounting a saddle-backed bridge in a deep wooded glen, with a roaring water under them. On the crown of the bridge a vast man stood, such as I had never descried before, bearing no armour that I could see, but wearing a farmer's hat, and raising a staff like the stem of a young oak tree. He was striking at no one, but playing with his staff, as if it were a willow in the morning breeze.

"Down with him! Ride him down! Send a bullet through him!" several of the Doones called out, but no one showed any hurry to do it. It seemed as if they knew him, and feared his mighty strength, and their guns were now slung behind their backs on account of the roughness of the way.

"Charlie, you are not afraid of him," I

heard that crafty Carver say to the tallest of his villains, and a very handsome young man he was ; "if the girl were not on my horse, I would do it. Ride over him, and you shall have my prize, when I am tired of her."

I felt the fire come into my eyes, to be spoken of so by a brute ; and then I saw Charlie Doone spur up the bridge, leaning forward and swinging a long blade round his head.

"Down with thee, clod !" he shouted ; and he showed such strength and fury that I scarce could look at the farmer, dreading to see his great head fly away. But just as the horse rushed at him, he leaped aside with most wonderful nimbleness, and the rider's sword was dashed out of his grasp, and down he went, over the back of the saddle, and his long legs spun up in the air, as a juggler tosses a two-pronged fork.

"Now for another !" the farmer cried, and his deep voice rang above the roar of Lynn ; "or two at once, if it suits you better. I will teach you to carry off women, you dogs !"

But the outlaws would not try another charge. On a word from their leader they all dismounted, and were bringing their long guns to bear, and I heard the clink of their flints as they fixed the trigger. Carver Doone, grinding his enormous teeth, stood at the head of my horse, who was lashing and plunging, so that I must have been flung if any of the straps had given way. In terror of the gun flash I shut my eyes, for if I had seen that brave man killed, it would have been the death of me as well. Then I felt my horse treading on something soft. Carver Doone was beneath his feet, and an awful curse came from the earth.

"Have no fear !" said the sweetest voice that ever came into the ears of despair. "Sylvia, none can harm you now. Lie still, and let this protect your face."

"How can I help lying still ?" I said, as a soft cloak was thrown over me, and in less than a moment my horse was rushing through branches and brushwood that swept his ears. At his side was another horse, and my bridle rein was held by a man who stooped over his neck in silence. Though his face was out of sight, I knew that Anthony Purvis was leading me.

There was no possibility of speaking now, but after a tumult of speed we came to an open glade where the trees fell back, and a gentle brook was gurgling. Then Captain Purvis cut my bonds, and lifting me down very softly, set me upon a bank of moss, for my limbs would not support me ; and I lay there unable to do anything but weep.

When I returned to myself, the sun was just looking over a wooded cliff, and Anthony, holding a horn of water, and with water on his cheeks, was regarding me.

"Did you leave that brave man to be shot ?" I asked, as if that were all my gratitude.

"I am not so bad as that," he answered,

without any anger, for he saw that I was not in reason yet. "At sight of my men, although we were but five in all, the robbers fled, thinking the regiment was there; but it is God's truth that I thought little of anyone's peril compared with thine. But there need be no fear for John Ridd; the Doones are mighty afraid of him since he cast their culverin through their door."

"Was that the John Ridd I have heard so much of? Surely I might have known it, but my wits were shaken out of me."

"Yes, that was the mighty man of Exmoor, to whom thou owest more than life."

In horror of what I had so narrowly escaped, I fell upon my knees and thanked the Lord, and then I went shyly to the captain's side and said: "I am ashamed to look at thee. Without Anthony Purvis, where should I be? Speak of no John Ridd to me."

For this man whom I had cast forth, with coldness, as he must have thought—

although I knew better, when he was gone —this man (my honoured husband now, who hath restored me to my father's place, when kings had no gratitude or justice), Sir Anthony Purvis, as now he is, had dwelled in a hovel and lived on scraps, to guard the forsaken orphan, who had won, and shall ever retain, his love.

FRIDA; OR, THE LOVER'S LEAP

FRIDA ; OR, THE LOVER'S LEAP.

A LEGEND OF THE WEST COUNTRY.

CHAPTER I.

On the very day when Charles I. was crowned with due rejoicings—Candlemas-day, in the year of our Lord 1626—a loyalty, quite as deep and perhaps even more lasting, was having its beer at Ley Manor in the north of Devon. A loyalty not to the king, for the old West-country folk knew little and cared less about the house that came over the Border ; but to a lord who had won their hearts by dwelling among them, and dealing kindly, and paying his way every Saturday night. When this has been done for three generations general and genial respect may almost be relied upon.

The present Baron de Wichehalse was fourth in descent from that Hugh de Wichehalse, the head of an old and wealthy race, who had sacrificed his comfort to his resolve to have a will of his own in matters of religion. That Hugh de Wichehalse, having an eye to this, as well as the other world, contrived to sell his large estates before they were confiscated, and to escape with all the money, from very sharp measures then enforced, by order of King Philip II., in the unhappy Low Countries. Landing in England, with all his effects and a score of trusty followers, he bought a fine property, settled, and died, and left a good name behind him. And that good name had been well kept up, and the property had increased and thriven, so that the present lord was loved and admired by all the neighbourhood.

In one thing, however, he had been unlucky, at least in his own opinion. Ten years of married life had not found issue in parental life. All his beautiful rocks and hills, lovely streams and glorious woods, green meadows and golden corn lands, must pass to his nephew and not to his child, because he had not gained one. Being a good man, he did his best to see this thing in its proper light. Children, after all, are a plague, a risk, and a deep anxiety. His nephew was a very worthy boy, and his rights should be respected. Nevertheless, the baron often longed to supersede them.

Of this there was every prospect now. The lady of the house had intrusted her case to a highly celebrated simple-woman, who lived among rocks and scanty vegetation at Heddon's Mouth, gathering wisdom from the earth and from the sea tranquillity. De Wichehalse was naturally vexed a little when all this accumulated wisdom culminated in nothing grander than a somewhat undersized, and unhappily female child—one, moreover, whose presence cost him that of his faithful and loving wife. So that the heiress of Ley Manor was greeted, after all, with a very brief and sorry welcome. "Jennyfried," for so they named her, soon began to grow into a fair esteem and good liking. Her father, after a year or two, plucked up his courage and played with her ; and the more he played the more pleased he was, both with her and his own kind self. Unhappily, there were at that time no shops in the neighbourhood; unhappily, now there are too many. Nevertheless, upon the whole, she had all the toys that were good for her ; and her teeth had a fair chance of fitting themselves for life's chief operation in the absence of sugared allurements.

A brief and meagre account is this of the birth, and growth, and condition of a maiden whose beauty and goodness still linger in the winter tales of many a simple homestead. For, sharing her father's genial nature, she went about among the people in her soft and playful way ; knowing all their cares, and gifted with a kindly wonder at them, which is very soothing. All the simple folk expected condescension

from her ; and she would have let them
have it, if she had possessed it.

At last she was come to a time of life
when maidens really must begin to consider
their responsibilities—a time when it does
matter how the dress sits and what it is
made of, and whether the hair is well
arranged for dancing in the sunshine and
for fluttering in the moonlight; also that
the eyes convey not from that roguish nook
the heart any betrayal of " hide and seek ";
neither must the risk of blushing tremble
on perpetual brinks ; neither must—but, in
a word, 'twas the seventeenth year of a
maiden's life.

More and more such matters gained on
her motherless necessity.   Strictly anxious
as she was to do the right thing always, she
felt more and more upon every occasion
(unless it was something particular) that
her cousin need not so impress his cousinly
salutation.

Albert de Wichehalse (who received that
name before it became so inevitable) was

that same worthy boy grown up as to whom the baron had felt compunctions, highly honourable to either party, touching his defeasance; or rather, perhaps, as to interception of his presumptive heirship by the said Albert, or at least by his mother contemplated. And Albert's father had entrusted him to his uncle's special care and love, having comfortably made up his mind, before he left this evil world, that his son should have a good slice of it.

Now, therefore, the baron's chief desire was to heal all breaches and make things pleasant, and to keep all the family property snug by marrying his fair Jennyfried (or " Frida," as she was called at home) to her cousin Albert, now a fine young fellow of five-and-twenty. De Wichehalse was strongly attached to his nephew, and failed to see any good reason why a certain large farm near Martinhoe, quite a huge cantle from the Ley estates, which by a prior devise must fall to Albert upon his own demise, should be allowed to depart in that way from his posthumous control.

However, like most of our fallible race, he went the worst possible way to work in pursuit of his favourite purpose. He threw the young people together daily, and dinned into the ears of each perpetual praise of the other. This seemed to answer well enough in the case of the simple Albert. He could never have too much of his lively cousin's company, neither could he weary of sounding her sweet excellence. But with the young maid it was not so. She liked the good Albert well enough, and never got out of his way at all. Moreover, sometimes his curly hair and bright moustache, when they came too near, would raise not a positive flutter, perhaps, but a sense of some fugitive movement in the unexplored distances of the heart. Still, this might go on for years, and nothing more to come of it. Frida loved her father best of all the world, at present

CHAPTER II.

THERE happened to be at this time an old fogy—of course it is most distressing to speak of anyone disrespectfully; but when one thinks of the trouble he caused, and not only that, but he was an old fogy, essentially and pre-eminently—and his name was Sir Maunder Meddleby. This worthy baronet, one of the first of a newly invented order, came in his sled stuffed with goose-feathers (because he was too fat to ride, and no wheels were yet known on the hill tracks) to talk about some exchange of land with his old friend, our De Wichehalse. The baron and the baronet had been making a happy day of it. Each knew pretty well exactly what his neighbour's little rashness might be hoped to lead to, and each in his mind was pretty sure of having the upper hand of it. Therefore both their hearts were open—business being now dismissed, and dinner over—to one another. They sat in a beautiful place, and drew refreshment of mind through their outward lips by means of long reeden tubes with bowls at their ends, and something burning.

Clouds of delicate vapour wandered round and betwixt them and the sea; and each was well content to wonder whether the time need ever come when he must have to think again. Suddenly a light form flitted over the rocks, as the shadows flit; and though Frida ran away for fear of interrupting them, they knew who it was, and both, of course, began to think about her.

The baron gave a puff of his pipe, and left the baronet to begin. In course of time Sir Maunder spoke, with all that breadth and beauty of the vowels and the other things which a Devonshire man commands, from the lord lieutenant downward.

"If so be that 'ee gooth vor to ax me, ai can zay wan thing, and wan oney."

"What one thing is it, good neighbour ? I am well content with her as she is."

"Laikely enough.   And 'e wad be zo till 'e zeed a zummut fainer."

"I want to see nothing finer or better than what we have seen just now, sir."

"There, you be like all varthers, a'most! No zort o' oose to advaise 'un."

"Nay, nay! Far otherwise. I am not by any means of that nature. Sir Maunder Meddleby, I have the honour of craving your opinion."

Sir Maunder Meddleby thought for a while, or, at any rate, meant to be thinking, ere ever he dared to deliver himself of all his weighty judgment.

"I've a-knowed she, my Lord Witcher, ever since her wore that haigh. A purty wanch, and a peart one. But her wanteth the vinish of the coort. Never do no good wi'out un, whan a coomth, as her must, to coorting."

This was the very thing De Wichehalse was afraid to hear of. He had lived so

mild a life among the folk who loved him
that any fear of worry in great places was
too much for him.   And yet sometimes he
could not help a little prick of thought
about his duty to his daughter.   Hence it
came that common sense was driven wild
by conscience, as forever happens with the
few who keep that gadfly.   Six great horses,
who knew no conscience but had more
fleshly tormentors, were ordered out, and
the journey began, and at last it ended.

Everything in London now was going
almost anyhow.   Kind and worthy people
scarcely knew the way to look at things.
They desired to respect the king and all his
privilege, and yet they found his mind so
wayward that they had no hold of him.

The court, however, was doing its best,
from place to place in its wanderings, to
despise the uproar and enjoy itself as it
used to do.   Bright and beautiful ladies
gathered round the king, when the queen
was gone, persuading him and one another
that they must have their own way.

Of the lords who helped these ladies to their strong opinions there was none in higher favour with the queen and the king himself than the young Lord Auberley. His dress was like a sweet enchantment, and his tongue was finer still, and his grace and beauty were as if no earth existed. Frida was a new thing to him, in her pure simplicity. He to her was such a marvel, such a mirror of the skies, as a maid can only dream of in the full moon of St. John.

Little dainty glance, and flushing, and the fear to look too much, and the stealthy joy of feeling that there must be something meant, yet the terror of believing anything in earnest and the hope that, after all, there may be nought to come of it; and when this hope seems over true, the hollow of the heart behind it, and the longing to be at home with anyone to love oneself—time is wasted in recounting this that always must be.

Enough that Frida loved this gallant from the depths of her pure heart, while he admired and loved her to the best of his ability.

CHAPTER III.

THE worthy baron was not of a versatile complexion. When his mind was quite made up he carried out the whole of it. But he could not now make up his mind upon either of two questions. Of these questions one was this—should he fight for the king or against him, in the struggle now begun? By hereditary instincts he was stanch for liberty, for letting people have their own opinions who could pay for them. And about religious matters and the royal view of them, he fell under sore misgiving that his grandfather on high would have a bone to pick with him.

His other difficulty was what to say, or what to think, about Lord Auberley. To his own plain way of judging, and that human instinct which, when highly culti-vated, equals that of the weaker dogs, also to

his recollection of what used to be expected
in the time when he was young, Viscount
Auberley did not give perfect satisfaction.

Nevertheless, being governed as strong
folk are by the gentle ones, the worthy
baron winked at little things which did not
please him, and went so far as to ask that
noble spark to flash upon the natives of
benighted Devon. Lord Auberley was glad
enough to retire for a season, both for
other reasons and because he saw that
bitter fighting must be soon expected.
Hence it happened that the six great
Flemish horses were buckled to, early in
September of the first year of the civil war,
while the king was on his westward march
collecting men and money. The queen
was not expected back from the Continent
for another month; there had scarcely been
for all the summer even the semblance of a
court fit to teach a maiden lofty carriage
and cold dignity ; so that Lord de Wichehalse thought Sir Maunder Meddleby an
oaf for sending him to London.

But there was someone who had tasted strong delight and shuddering fear, glowing hope and chill despair, triumph, shame, and all confusion of the heart and mind and will, such as simple maidens hug into their blushing chastity by the moonlight of first love. Frida de Wichehalse knew for certain, and forever felt it settled, that in all the world of worlds never had been any body, any mind, or even soul, fit to think of twice when once you had beheld Lord Auberley.

His young lordship, on the whole, was much of the same opinion. Low fellows must not have the honour to discharge their guns at him. He liked the king, and really meant no harm whatever to his peace of mind concerning his Henrietta ; and, if the worst came to the worst, everyone knew that out of France there was no swordsman fit to meet, even with a rapier, the foil of Aubyn Auberley. Neither was it any slur upon his loyalty or courage that he was now going westward from the world of camps and war. It was important to secure the wavering De Wichehalse, the leading man of all the coast, from Minehead down to Hartland ; so that, with the full consent of all the king's advisers, Lord Auberley left court and camp to press his own suit peacefully. What a difference he found it to be here in mid-September, far away from any knowledge of the world and every care; only to behold the manner of the trees disrobing, blushing with a trembling wonder at the freedom of the winds, or in the wealth of deep wood browning into rich defiance; only to observe the colour of the hills, and cliffs, and glens, and the glory of the sea underneath the peace of heaven, when the balanced sun was striking level light all over them! And if this were not enough to make a man contented with his littleness and largeness, then to see the freshened Pleiads, after their long dip of night, over the eastern waters twinkling, glad to see us all once more and sparkling to be counted.

These things, and a thousand others, which (without a waft of knowledge or of thought on our part) enter into and become our sweetest recollections, for the gay young lord possessed no charm, nor even interest. "Dull, dull, how dull it is!" was all he thought when he thought at all ; and he vexed his host by asking how he could live in such a hole as that. And he would have vexed his young love, too, if young love were not so large of heart, by asking what the foreign tongue was which "her people" tried to speak. "Their native tongue and mine, my lord!" cried Frida, with the sweetness of her smile less true than usual, because she loved her people and the air of her nativity.

However, take it altogether, this was a golden time for her. Golden trust and reliance are the well-spring of our nature, and that man is the happiest who is cheated every day almost. The pleasure is tenfold as great in being cheated as to cheat. Therefore Frida was as happy as the day

and night are long. Though the trees
were striped with autumn, and the green of
the fields was waning, and the puce of the
heath was faded into dingy cinamon;
though the tint of the rocks was darkened
by the nightly rain and damp, and the clear
brooks were beginning to be hoarse with
shivering floods, and the only flowers left
were but widows of the sun, yet she had
the sovereign comfort and the cheer of
trustful love. Lord Auberley, though he
cared nought for the Valley of Rocks or
Watersmeet, for beetling majesty of the
cliffs or mantled curves of Woody Bay,
and though he accounted the land a wilderness and the inhabitants savages, had
taken a favourable view of the ample spread
of the inland farms and the loyalty of the
tenants, which naturally suggested the raising of the rental. Therefore he grew more
attentive to young Mistress Frida ; even
sitting in shady places, which it made him
damp to think of when he turned his eyes
from her. Also he was moved a little by

her growing beauty, for now the return to
her native hills, the presence of her lover,
and the home-made bread and forest mutton, combining with her dainty years, were
making her look wonderful.   If Aubyn
Auberley had not been despoiled of all true
manliness, by the petting and the froward
wit of many a foreign lady, he might have
won the pure salvation of an earnest love.
But, when judged by that French standard
which was now supreme at court, this poor
Frida was a rustic, only fit to go to school.

There was another fine young fellow who
thought wholly otherwise.   To him, in his
simple power of judging for himself, and
seldom budging from that judgment, there
was no one fit to dream of in comparison
with her.   Often, in this state of mind, he
longed to come forward and let them know
what he thought concerning the whole of
it.   But Albert could not see his way
toward doing any good with it, and being
of a bashful mind, he kept his heart in
order.

CHAPTER IV.

THE stir of the general rising of the kingdom against the king had not disturbed these places yet beyond what might be borne with. Everybody liked to talk, and everybody else was ready to put in a word or two; broken heads, however, were as yet the only issue. So that when there came great news of a real battle fought, and lost by Englishmen against Englishmen, the indignation of all the country ran against both parties.

Baron de Wichehalse had been thinking, after his crop of hay was in,—for such a faithful hay they have that it will not go from root to rick by less than two months of worrying,—from time to time, and even in the middle of his haycocks, this good lord had not been able to perceive his proper course. Arguments there were that sounded quite as if a baby must be perfectly convinced by them; and then there would be quite a different line of reason taken by someone who knew all about it and despised the opposite. So that many of a less decided way of thinking every day embraced whatever had been last confuted.

This most manly view of matters and desire to give fair play was scorned, of course, by the fairer (and unfairer) half of men. Frida counted all as traitors who opposed their liege the king.

"Go forth, my lord; go forth and fight,' she cried to Viscount Auberley, when the doubtful combat of Edgehill was firing new pugnacity; "if I were a man, think you that I would let them do so?"

"Alas, fair mistress! it will take a many men to help it. But since you bid me thus away—hi, Dixon! get my trunks packed!" And then, of course, her blushing roses faded to a lily white; and then, of course, it was his duty to support her slender form; neither were those dulcet murmurs absent which forever must be present when the female kind begin to have the best of it.

So they went on once or twice, and would have gone on fifty times if fortune had allowed them thus to hang on one another. All the world was fair around them; and themselves, as fair as any, vouched the whole world to attest their everlasting constancy.

But one soft November evening, when the trees were full of drops, and gentle mists were creeping up the channels of the moorlands, and snipes (come home from foreign parts) were cheeping at their borings, and every weary man was gladdened by the glance of a bright wood fire, and smell of what was over it, there happened to come, on a jaded horse, a man, all hat, and cape, and boots, and mud, and sweat, and grumbling. All the people saw at once that it was quite impossible to make at all too much of him, because he must be full of news, which (after victuals) is the greatest need of human nature. So he

had his own way as to everything he
ordered; and, having ridden into much
experience of women, kept himself as warm
as could be, without any jealousy.

This stern man bore urgent order for
the Viscount Auberley to join the king at
once at Oxford, and bring with him all his
gathering.   Having gathered no men yet,
but spent the time in plucking roses and
the wild myrtles of Devonshire love, the
young lord was for once a little taken
aback at this order.   Moreover, though he
had been grumbling, half a dozen times a
day—to make himself more precious—
about the place, and the people, and the
way they cooked his meals, he really meant
it less and less as he came to know the
neighbourhood.   These are things which
nobody can understand without seeing
them.

"I grieve, my lord," said the worthy
baron, "that you must leave us in this hot
haste."   On the whole, however, this excellent man was partly glad to be quit of him.

"And I am deeply indebted to your lordship for the grievance; but it must be so. *Que voulez-vous?* You talk the French, *mon baron?*"

"With a Frenchman, my lord; but not when I have the honour to speak with an Englishman."

"Ah, there! Foreign again! My lord, you will never speak English."

De Wichehalse could never be quite sure, though his race had been long in this country, whether he or they could speak born English as it ought to be.

"Perhaps you will find," he said at last, with grief as well as courtesy, "many who speak one language striving to silence one another."

"He fights best who fights the longest. You will come with us, my lord?"

"Not a foot, not half an inch," the baron answered sturdily. "I've a-laboured hard to zee my best, and 'a can't zee head nor tail to it."

Thus he spoke in imitation of what his

leading tenant said, smiling brightly at himself, but sadly at his subject.

"Even so!" the young man answered; "I will forth and pay my duty.   The rusty weathercock, my lord, is often too late for the oiling."

With this conceit he left De Wichehalse, and, while his grooms were making ready, sauntered down the zigzag path, which, through rocks and stubbed oaks, made toward the rugged headland known, far up and down the Channel, by the name of Duty Point.   Near the end of this walk there lurked a soft and silent bower, made by Nature, and with all of Nature's art secluded.   The ledge that wound along the rock-front widened, and the rock fell back and left a little cove, retiring into moss and ferny shade.   Here the maid was well accustomed every day to sit and think, gazing down at the calm, gray sea, and filled with rich content and deep capacity of dreaming.

Here she was, at the present moment,

resting in her pure love-dream, believing all
the world as good, and true, and kind as
her own young self. Round her all was
calm and lovely; and the soft brown hand
of autumn, with the sun's approval, tem-
pered every mellow mood of leaves.

Aubyn Auberley was not of a sentimental
cast of mind. He liked the poets of the
day, whenever he deigned to read them;
nor was he at all above accepting the dedi-
cation of a book. But it was not the
fashion now—as had been in the noble time
of Watson, Raleigh, and Shakspere—for
men to look around and love the greater
things they grow among.

Frida was surprised to see her dainty lord
so early. She came here in the morning
always, when it did not rain too hard, to let
her mind have pasture on the landscape of
sweet memory. And even sweeter hope
was always fluttering in the distance, on the
sea, or clouds, or flitting vapour of the
morning. Even so she now was looking at
the mounting glory of the sun above the

sea-clouds, the sun that lay along the land, and made the distance roll away.

"Hard and bitter is my task," the gallant lord began with her, "to say farewell to all I love. But so it ever must be."

Frida looked at his riding-dress, and cold fear seized her suddenly, and then warm hope that he might only be riding after the bustards.

"My lord," she said, "will you never grant me that one little prayer of mine—to spare poor birds, and make those cruel gaze-hounds run down one another?"

"I shall never see the gaze-hounds more," he answered petulantly; "my time for sport is over. I must set forth for the war to-day."

"To-day!" she cried; and then tried to say a little more for pride's sake; "to go to the war to-day, my lord!"

"Alas! it is too true. Either I must go, or be a traitor and a dastard."

Her soft blue eyes lay full on his, and tears that had not time to flow began to spread a hazy veil between her and the one she loved.

He saw it, and he saw the rise and sinking of her wounded heart, and how the words she tried to utter fell away and died within her for the want of courage; and light and hard, and mainly selfish as his nature was, the strength, and depth, and truth of love came nigh to scare him for the moment even of his vanities.

"Frida !" he said, with her hand in his, and bending one knee on the moss ; "only tell me that I must stay ; then stay I will ; the rest of the world may scorn if you approve me."

This, of course, sounded very well and pleased her, as it was meant to do ; still, it did not satisfy her—so exacting are young maidens, and so keen is the ear of love.

"Aubyn, you are good and true. How very good and true you are! But even by your dear voice now I know what you are thinking."

Lord Auberley, by this time, was as well
within himself again as he generally found
himself ; so that he began to balance
chances very knowingly. If the king
should win the warfare and be paramount
again, this bright star of the court must
rise to something infinitely higher than a
Devonshire squire's child. A fine young
widow of a duke, of the royal blood of
France itself, was not far from being quite
determined to accept him, if she only
could be certain how these things would
end themselves. Many other ladies
were determined quite as bravely to wait
the course of events, and let him have
them, if convenient. On the other hand,
if the kingdom should succeed in keeping the king in order—which was the
utmost then intended—Aubyn Auberley
might be only too glad to fall back upon
Frida.

Thinking it wiser, up n the whole, to
make sure of this little lamb, with nobler
game in prospect, Lord Auberley heaved as

deep a sigh as the size of his chest could compass.   After which he spoke as follows, in a most delicious tone:

"Sweetest, and my only hope, the one star of my wanderings ; although you send me forth to battle, where my arm is needed, give me one dear pledge that ever you will live and die my own."

This was just what Frida wanted, having trust (as our free-traders, by vast amplitude of vision, have in reciprocity) that if a man gets the best of a woman he is sure to give it back.   Therefore these two sealed and delivered certain treaties (all unwritten, but forever engraven upon the best and tenderest feelings of the lofty human nature) that nothing less than death, or even greater, should divide them.

Is there one, among the many who survive such process, unable to imagine or remember how they parted ?   The fierce and even desperate anguish, nursed and made the most of ; the pride and self-control that keep such things for comfort afterward ; the falling of the heart that feels itself the true thing after all. Let it be so, since it must be ; and no sympathy can heal it, since in every case it never, never, was so bad before!

CHAPTER V.

Lovers come, and lovers go; ecstasies of joy and anguish have their proper intervals ; and good young folk, who know no better, revel in high misery. But the sun ascends the heavens at the same hour of the day, by himself dictated ; and if we see him not, it is our earth that spreads the curtain. Nevertheless, these lovers, being out of rule with everything, heap their own faults on his head, and want him to be setting always, that they may behold the moon.

Therefore it was useless for the wisest man in the north of Devon, or even the wisest woman, to reason with young Frida now, or even to let her have the reason upon her side, and be sure of it. She, for her part, was astray from all the bounds of reason, soaring on the wings of faith, and

hope, and high delusion. Though the
winter-time was coming, and the wind was
damp and raw, and the beauty of the
valleys lay down to recover itself ; yet with
her the spring was breaking, and the world
was lifting with the glory underneath it.
Because it had been firmly pledged—and
who could ever doubt it ?—that the best
and noblest lover in this world of noble
love would come and grandly claim and win
his bride on her next birthday.

At Christmas she had further pledge of
her noble lover's constancy. In spite of
difficulties, dangers, and the pressing need
of men, he contrived to send her by some
very valiant messengers (none of whom
would ride alone) a beautiful portrait of
himself, set round with sparkling diamonds;
also a necklace of large pearls, as white and
pure as the neck whose grace was to
enhance their beauty.

Hereupon such pride and pleasure
mounted into her cheeks and eyes, and
flushed her with young gaiety, that all who

loved her, being grafted with good superstition, nearly spoiled their Christmas-time
by serious sagacity. She, however, in the
wealth of all she had to think of, heeded
none who trod the line of prudence and
cold certainty.

"It is more than I can tell," she used to
say, most prettily, to anybody who made
bold to ask her about anything; "all
things go so in and out that I am sure of
nothing else except that I am happy."

The baron now began to take a narrow,
perhaps a natural, view of all the things
around him. In all the world there was for
him no sign or semblance of any being
whose desires or strictest rights could be
thought of more than once when set against
his daughter's. This, of course, was very
bad for Frida's own improvement. It
could not make her selfish yet, but it really
made her wayward. The very best girls
ever seen are sure to have their failings ;
and Frida, though one of the very best,
was not above all nature. People made too

much of this, when she could no more
defend herself.

Whoever may have been to blame, one
thing at least is certain—the father, though
he could not follow all his child's precipi-
tance, yet was well contented now to stoop
his gray head to bright lips, and do his best
toward believing some of their soft elo-
quence. The child, on the other hand, was
full of pride, and rose on tiptoe, lest anybody might suppose her still too young for
anything. Thus between them they looked
forward to a pleasant time to come, hoping
for the best, and judging everyone with
charity.

The thing that vexed them most (for
always there must, of course, be something)
was the behaviour of Albert, nephew to the
baron, and most loving cousin of Frida.
Nothing they could do might bring him to
spend his Christmas with them; and this
would be the first time ever since his long-
clothed babyhood that he had failed to be
among them, and to lead or follow, just as

might be required of him. Such a guest
has no small value in a lonely neighbourhood, and years of usage mar the circle of
the year without him.

Christmas passed, and New Year's Day,
and so did many other days. The baron
saw to his proper work, and took his turn
of hunting, and entertained his neighbours,
and pleased almost everybody. Much
against his will, he had consented to the
marriage of his daughter with Lord Auberley—to make the best of a bad job, as he
told Sir Maunder Meddleby. Still, this
kind and crafty father had his own ideas;
for the moment he was swimming with the
tide to please his daughter, even as for her
dear sake he was ready to sink beneath
it. Yet, these fathers have a right to form
their own opinions; and for the most part
they believe that they have more experience. Frida laughed at this, of course, and
her father was glad to see her laugh.
Nevertheless, he could not escape some
respect for his own opinion, having so

rarely found it wrong; and his own opinion was that something was very likely to happen.

In this he proved to be quite right. For many things began to happen, some on the right and some on the left hand of the baron's auguries. All of them, however, might be reconciled exactly with the very thing he had predicted. He noticed this, and it pleased him well, and inspired him so that he started anew for even truer prophecies. And everybody round the place was born so to respect him that, if he missed the mark a little, they could hit it for him.

Things stood thus at the old Ley Manor— and folk were content to have them so, for fear of getting worse, perhaps—toward the end of January, A. D. 1643. De Wichehalse had vowed that his only child—although so clever for her age, and prompt of mind and body—should not enter into marriage until she was in her eighteenth year. Otherwise, it would, no doubt, have all been settled long ago; for Aubyn Auberley sometimes had been in the greatest hurry. However, hither he must come now, as everybody argued, even though the fate of England hung on his stirrup-leather. Because he had even sent again, with his very best intentions, fashionable things for Frida, and the hottest messages; so that, if they did not mean him to be quite beside himself, everything must be smoking for his wedding at the Candlemas.

But when everything and even everybody else—save Albert and the baron, and a few other obstinate people—was and were quite ready and rejoicing for a grand affair, to be celebrated with well-springs of wine and delightfully cordial Watersmeet, rocks of beef hewn into valleys, and conglomerate cliffs of pudding; when ruddy dame and rosy damsel were absorbed in "what to wear," and even steady farmers were in "practice for the back step"; in a word, when all the country was gone wild about Frida's wedding—one night there happened to come a man.

This man tied his horse to a gate and sneaked into the back yard, and listened in a quiet corner, knowing, as he did, the ins and outs and ways of the kitchen. Because he was that very same man who understood the women so, and made himself at home, by long experience, in new places.   It had befallen this man, as it always befell any man of perception, to be smitten with the kindly loveliness of Frida. Therefore, now, although he was as hungry as ever he had been, his heart was such that he heard the sound of dishes, yet drew no nearer.   Experience of human nature does not always spoil it.

CHAPTER VI.

WHEN the baron at last received the letter which this rider had been so abashed to deliver, slow but lasting wrath began to gather in his gray-lashed eyes. It was the inborn anger of an honest man at villany mixed with lofty scorn and traversed by a dear anxiety. Withal he found himself so helpless that he scarce knew what to do. He had been to Frida both a father and a mother, as she often used to tell him when she wanted something; but now he felt that no man could administer the velvet touches of the female sympathy.

Moreover, although he was so kind, and had tried to think what his daughter thought, he found himself in a most ungenial mood for sweet condolement. Any but the best of fathers would have been delighted with the proof of all his prophecies and the riddance of a rogue. So that even he, though

dwelling in his child's heart as his own,
read this letter (when the first emotions had
exploded) with a real hope that things, in
the long run, would come round again.

"To my most esteemed and honoured
friend, the Lord de Wichehalse, these from
his most observant and most grateful Aubyn
Auberley,—Under command of his Majesty,
our most Royal Lord and King, I have this
day been joined in bands of holy marriage
with her Highness, the Duchess of B——,
in France. At one time I had hope of
favour with your good Lordship's daughter,
neither could I have desired more complete
promotion. But the service of the kingdom and the doubt of my own desert have
forced me, in these troublous times, to
forego mine own ambition. Our lord the
King enjoins you with his Royal commenda-
tion, to bring your forces toward Bristowe
by the day of St. Valentine. There shall I
be in hope to meet your Lordship, and
again find pleasure in such goodly com-

pany.   Until then I am your Lordship's poor and humble servant,

"AUBYN AUBERLEY."

Lord de Wichehalse made his mind up not to let his daughter know until the following morning what a heavy blow had fallen on her faith and fealty. But, as evil chance would have it, the damsels of the house—and most of all the gentle cook-maid—could not but observe the rider's state of mind toward them. He managed to eat his supper in a dark state of parenthesis; but after that they plied him with some sentimental mixtures, and, being only a man at best, although a very trusty one, he could not help the rise of manly wrath at every tumbler. So, in spite of dry experience and careworn discretion, at last he let the woman know the whole of what himself knew. Nine good females crowded round him, and, of course, in their kind bosoms every word of all his story germinated ninety-fold.

Hence it came to pass that, after floods of tears in council and stronger language than had right to come from under aprons, Frida's nurse (the old herb-woman, now called "Mother Eyebright") was appointed to let her know that very night the whole of it. Because my lord might go on mooning for a month about it, betwixt his love of his daughter and his quiet way of taking things; and all that while the dresses might be cut, and trimmed, and fitted to a size and fashion all gone by before there came a wedding.

Mother Eyebright so was called both from the brightness of her eyes and her faith in that little simple flower, the euphrasia. Though her own love-tide was over, and the romance of life had long relapsed into the old allegiance to the hour of dinner, yet her heart was not grown tough to the troubles of the young ones; therefore all that she could do was done, but it was little.

Frida, being almost tired with the bliss-

ful cares of dress, happened to go up that
evening earlier than her wont to bed.   She
sat by herself in the firelight, with many
gorgeous things around her — wedding
presents from great people, and (what
touched her more) the humble offerings of
her cottage friends.   As she looked on
these and thought of all the good will they
expressed, and how a little kindness gathers
such a heap of gratitude, glad tears shone
in her bright eyes, and she only wished
that all the world could be as blessed as
she was.

To her entered Mother Eyebright, now
unworthy of her name; and sobbing, writh-
ing, crushing anguish is a thing which even
Frida, simple and open-hearted one, would
rather keep to her own poor self.

CHAPTER VII.

Upon the following day she was not half so wretched and lamentable as was expected of her. She even showed a brisk and pleasant air to the chief seamstress, and bade her keep some pretty things for the time of her own wedding. Even to her father she behaved as if there had been nothing more than happens every day. The worthy baron went to fold her in his arms, and let her cry there; but she only gave him a kiss, and asked the maid for some salt butter. Lord de Wichehalse, being disappointed of his outlet, thought (as all his life he had been forced to think continually) that any sort of woman, whether young or old, is wonderful. And so she carried on, and no one well could understand her.

She, however, in her own heart, knew the

ups and downs of it. She alone could feel
the want of any faith remaining, the ache
of ever stretching forth and laying hold on
nothing. Her mind had never been encouraged—as with maidens nowadays—to
magnify itself, and soar, and scorn the
heart that victuals it. All the deeper was
her trouble, being less to be explained.

For a day or two the story is that she
contrived to keep her distance, and her own
opinion of what had been done to her.
Child and almost baby as her father had
considered her, even he was awed from
asking what she meant to do about it.
Something seemed to keep her back from
speaking of her trouble, or bearing to have
it spoken of. Only to her faithful hound,
with whom she now began again to wander
in the oak-wood, to him alone had she the
comfort of declaring anything. This was
a dog of fine old English breed and high
connections, his great-grandmother having
owned a kennel at Whitehall itself—a very
large and well-conducted dog, and now an

old one, going down into his grave without
a stain upon him.   Only he had shown such
foul contempt of Aubyn Auberley, proceeding to extremes of ill-behaviour toward his
raiment, that for months young Frida had
been forced to keep him chained, and take
her favourite walks without him.

"Ah, Lear!" now she cried, with sense
of long injustice toward him; "you were
right, and I was wrong; at least—at least
it seems so."

"Lear," so called whether by some man
who had heard of Shakspere, or (as seems
more likely) from his peculiar way of contemplating the world at his own angle,
shook his ears when thus addressed, and
looked too wise for any dog to even sniff
his wisdom.

Frida now allowed this dog to lead the
way, and she would follow, careless of
whatever mischief might be in the road for
them.   So he led her, without care or even
thought on her part, to a hut upon the
beach of Woody Bay; where Albert had set

up his staff, to think of her and watch her.
This, her cousin and true lover, had been
grieving for her sorrow to the utmost power
of a man who wanted her himself.   It may
have been beyond his power to help saying
to himself sometimes, "How this serves
her right, for making such a laughing-stock
of me!"   Nevertheless, he did his utmost
to be truly sorrowful.

And now, as he came forth to meet her,
in his fishing dress and boots (as different
a figure as could be from Aubyn Auberley),
memories of childish troubles and of strong
protection thrilled her with a helpless hope
of something to be done for her.   So she
looked at him, and let him see the state her
eyes were in with constant crying, when
there was not anyone to notice it.   Also,
she allowed him to be certain what her
hands were like, and to be surprised how
much she had fallen away in her figure.
Neither was she quite as proud as might
have been expected, to keep her voice
from trembling or her plundered heart from

sobbing. Only, let not anybody say a word to comfort her. Anything but that she now could bear, as she bore everything. It was, of course, the proper thing for everyone to scorn her. That, of course, she had fully earned, and met it, therefore, with disdain. Only, she could almost hate anybody who tried to comfort her.

Albert de Wichehalse, with a sudden start of intuition, saw what her father had been unable to descry or even dream. The worthy baron's time of life for fervid thoughts was over; for him despairing love was but a poet's fiction, or a joke against a pale young lady. But Albert felt from his own case, from burning jealousy suppressed, and cold neglect put up with, and all the other many-pointed aches of vain devotion, how sad must be the state of things when plighted faith was shattered also, and great ridicule left behind, with only a young girl to face it, motherless, and having none to stroke dishevelled hair, and coax the troubles by the firelight. However, this good fel-

low did the utmost he could do for her.
Love and pity led him into dainty loving
kindness ; and when he could not find his
way to say the right thing, he did better—
he left her to say it.   And so well did he
move her courage, in his old protective
way, without a word that could offend her
or depreciate her love, that she for the moment, like a woman, wondered at her own
despair.   Also, like a woman, glancing into
this and that, instead of any steadfast gazing, she had wholesome change of view,
winning sudden insight into Albert's
thoughts concerning her.   Of course, she
made up her mind at once, although her
heart was aching so for want of any tenant,
in a moment to extinguish any such pre-
sumption.   Still, she would have liked to
have it made a little clearer, if it were for
nothing else than to be sure of something.

Albert saw her safely climb the steep and
shaly walk that led, among retentive oak
trees, or around the naked gully, all the
way from his lonely cottage to the light,

and warmth, and comfort of the peopled Manor House. And within himself he thought, the more from contrast of his own cold comfort and untended state:

"Ah ! she will forget it soon; she is so young. She will soon get over that gay frippard's fickleness. To-morrow I will start upon my little errand cheerfully. After that she will come round; they cannot feel as we do."

Full of these fond hopes, he started on the following morning with set purpose to compel the man whom he had once disliked, and now despised unspeakably, to render some account of despite done to such a family. For, after all, the dainty viscount was the grandson of a goldsmith, who by brokerage for the Crown had earned the balls of his coronet. In quest of this gay fellow went the stern and solid Albert, leaving not a word about his purpose there behind him, but allowing everybody to believe what all found out. All found out, as he expected, that he was gone to sell his hay, perhaps as far as Taunton; and all the parish, looking forward to great rise of forage, felt indignant that he had not doubled his price, and let them think.

Alack-a-day and all the year round ! that men perceive not how the women differ from them in the very source of thought. Albert never dreamed that his cousin, after doing so long without him, had now relapsed quite suddenly into her childish dependence upon him. And when she heard, on the following day, that he was gone for the lofty purpose of selling his seven ricks of hay, she said not a word, but only felt her cold heart so much colder.

CHAPTER VIII.

She had nothing now to do, and nobody to speak to ; though her father did his utmost, in his kind and clumsy way, to draw his darling close to him. But she knew that all along he had disliked her idol, and she fancied, now and then, that this dislike had had something perhaps to do with what had befallen her. This, of course, was wrong on her part. But when youth and faith are wronged, the hurt is very apt to fly to all the tender places. Even the weather also seemed to have taken a turn against her. No wholesome frost set in to brace the slackened joints and make her walk until she began to tingle ; neither was there any snow to spread a new cast on the rocks and gift the trees with airiness ; nor even what mild winters, for the most part, bring in counterpoise—soft, obedient skies, and trembling pleasure of the air and earth. But—as over her own love—over all the country hung just enough of mist and chill to shut out cheerful prospect, and not enough to shut folk in to the hearth of their own comfort.

In her dull, forlorn condition, Frida still, through force of habit or the love of solitude, made her daily round of wood and rock, seashore and moorland. Things seemed to come across her now, instead of her going to them, and her spirit failed at every rise of the hilly road against her. In that dreary way she lingered, hoping nothing, fearing nothing, showing neither sigh nor tear, only seeking to go somewhere and be lost from self and sorrow in the cloudy and dark day.

Often thus the soft, low moaning of the sea encompassed her, where she stood, in forgotten beauty, careless of the wind and wave. The short, uneasy heave of waters in among the kelpy rocks, flowing from no swell or furrow on the misty glass of sea,

but like a pulse of discontent, and longing
to go further ; after the turn, the little
rattle of invaded pebbles, the lithe relapse
and soft, shampooing lambency of oarweed,
then the lavered boulders pouring gritty
runnels back again, and every basined outlet wavering toward another inlet ; these,
and every phase of each innumerable to-
and-fro, made or met their impress in her
fluctuating misery.

"It is the only rest," she said ; "the
only chance of being quiet, after all that I
have done, and all that people say of me."

None had been dastard enough to say a
syllable against her ; neither had she, in
the warmest faith of love, forgotten truth ;
but her own dejection drove her, not to
revile the world (as sour natures do con-
sistently), but to shrink from sight, and
fancy that the world was reviling her.

While she fluttered thus and hovered
over the cold verge of death, with her sore
distempered spirit, scarcely sure of anything, tidings came of another trouble, and

turned the scale against her. Albert de
Wichehalse, her trusty cousin and true
lover, had fallen in a duel with that
recreant and miscreant Lord Auberley.
The strictest orders were given that this
should be kept for the present from Frida's
ears ; but what is the use of the strictest
orders when a widowed mother raves?
Albert's mother vowed that "the shame-
less jilt" should hear it out, and slipped
her guards and waylaid Frida on the morn
of Candlemas, and overbore her with such
words as may be well imagined.

"Auntie !" said the poor thing at last,
shaking her beautiful curls, and laying one
little hand to her empty heart, "don't be
cross with me to-day. I am going home to
be married, auntie. It is the day my
Aubyn always fixed, and he never fails me."

"Little fool !" her aunt exclaimed, as
Frida kissed her hand and courtesied, and
ran round the corner ; "one comfort is to
know that she is as mad as a mole, at any
rate."

CHAPTER IX.

FRIDA, knowing—perhaps more deeply than that violent woman thought—the mischief thus put into her, stole back to her bedroom, and, without a word to anyone, tired her hair in the Grecian snood which her lover used to admire so, and arrayed her soft and delicate form in all the bridal finery. Perhaps, that day, no bride in England—certainly none of her youth and beauty—treated her favourite looking-glass with such contempt and ingratitude. She did not care to examine herself, through some reluctant sense of havoc, and a bitter fear that someone might be disappointed in her. Then at the last, when all was ready, she snatched up her lover's portrait (which for days had been cast aside and cold), and, laying it on her bosom, took a snatch of a glance at her lovely self.

After some wonder she fetched a deep

sigh—not from clearly thinking anything, but as an act of nature—and said, "Good-by!" forever, with a little smile of irony, to her looking-glass, and all the many pretty things that knew her.

It was her bad luck, as some people thought thereafter—or her good luck, as herself beheld it—to get down the stairs and out of the house without anyone being the wiser. For the widow De Wichehalse, Albert's mother, had not been content with sealing the doom of this poor maiden, but in that highly excited state, which was to be expected, hurried into the house, to beard the worthy baron in his den. There she found him; and, although he said and did all sympathy, the strain of parental feelings could not yield without "hysterics."

All the servants, and especially Mother Eyebright (whose chief duty now was to watch Frida), were called by the terrified baron, and with one unanimous rush replied; so that the daughter of the house left it without notice, and before any glances was out of sight, in the rough ground where the deer were feeding, and the umber oak-leaves hung.

It was the dainty time when first the year begins to have a little hope of meaning kindly—when in the quiet places often, free from any haste of wind, or hindrances of pattering thaw, small and unimportant flowers have a little knack of dreaming that the world expects them. Therefore neither do they wait for leaves to introduce them, nor much weather to encourage, but in shelfy corners come, in a day, or in a night—no man knows quite which it is; and there they are, as if by magic, asking, "Am I welcome?" And if anybody sees them, he is sure to answer "Yes."

Frida, in the sheltered corners and the sunny nooks of rock, saw a few of these little things delicately trespassing upon the petulance of spring. Also, though her troubles wrapped her with an icy mantle, softer breath of Nature came, and sighed for her to listen to it, and to make the best of all that is not past the sighing. More than once she stopped to listen, in the hush of the timid south wind creeping through the dishevelled wood ; and once, but only once, she was glad to see her first primrose and last, and stooped to pluck, but, on second thoughts, left it to outblossom her.

So, past many a briered rock, and dingle buff with littered fern, green holly copse where lurked the woodcock, and arcades of zigzag oak, Frida kept her bridal robe from spot, or rent, or blemish. Passing all these little pleadings of the life she had always loved, at last she turned the craggy corner into the ledge of the windy cliff.

Now below her there was nothing but repose from shallow thought; rest from all the little troubles she had made so much of; deep, eternal satisfaction in the arms of something vast. But all the same, she did not feel quite ready for the great jump yet.

The tide was in, and she must wait at least until it began to turn, otherwise her white satin velvet would have all its pile set

wrong, if ever anybody found her.   There
could be no worse luck than that for any
bride on her wedding-day; therefore up the
rock-walk Frida kept very close to the land-
ward side.

All this way she thought of pretty little
things said to her in the early days of love.
Many things that made her smile because
they had gone so otherwise, and one or two
that would have fetched her tears, if she
had any.   Filled with vain remembrance
thus, and counting up the many presents
sent to her for this occasion, but remaining
safe at home, Frida came to the little
coving bower just inside the Point, where
she could go no further.   Here she had
received the pledges, and the plight, and
honour ; and here her light head led her on
to look for something faithful.

"When the tide turns I shall know it.
If he does not come by that time, there will
be no more to do.   It will be too late for
weddings, for the tide turns at twelve
o'clock.   How calm and peaceful is the

sea! How happy are the sea gulls, and how true to one another !"

She stood where, if she had cared for life, it would have been certain death to stand, so giddy was the height, and the rock beneath her feet so slippery. The craggy headland, Duty Point, well known to every navigator of that rock-bound coast, commands the Channel for many a league, facing eastward the Castle Rock and Countisbury Foreland, and westward High-veer Point, across the secluded cove of Leymouth. With one sheer fall of a hundred fathoms the stern cliff meets the baffled sea—or met it then, but now the level of the tide is lowering. Air and sea were still and quiet; the murmur of the multitudinous wavelets could not climb the cliff; but loops and curves of snowy braiding on the dark gray water showed the set of tide and shift of current in and out the buried rocks.

Standing in the void of fear, and gazing into the deep of death, Frida loved the pair of sea gulls hovering halfway between her and the soft gray sea. These good birds had found a place well suited for their nesting, and sweetly screamed to one another that it was a contract. Frida watched how proud they were, and how they kept their strong wings sailing and their gray backs flat and quivering, while with buoyant bosom each made circles round the other.

As she watched, she saw the turning of the tide below them. The streaky bends of curdled water, lately true as fairy-rings, stopped and wavered, and drew inward on their flowing curves, and outward on the side toward the ebb. Then the south wind brought the distant toll of her father's turret-clock, striking noon with slow deliberation and dead certainty.

Frida made one little turn toward her bower behind the cliff, where the many sweet words spoken drew her to this last of hope. All was silent. There was no one. Now was the time to go home at last.

Suddenly she felt a heavy drag upon her velvet skirt. Ancient Lear had escaped from the chain she had put on him, and, more trusty than mankind, was come to keep his faith with her.

"You fine old dog, it is too late! The clock has struck. The tide has turned. There is no one left to care for me ; and I have ruined everyone. Good-by, you only true one !"

Submissive as he always was, the ancient dog lay down when touched, and drew his grizzled eyelids meekly over his dim and sunken eyes. Before he lifted them again Frida was below the sea gulls, and beneath the waves they fished.

Lear, with a puzzled sniff, arose and shook his head, and peered, with his old eyes full of wistful wonder, down the fearful precipice. Seeing something, he made his mind up, gave one long re-echoed howl, then tossed his mane, like a tawny wave, and followed down the death-leap.

Neither body was ever found ; and the whole of this might not have been known so clearly as it is known, unless it had

happened that Mother Eyebright, growing
uneasy, came round the corner just in time
to be too late.   She, like a sensible woman,
never dreamed of jumping after them, but
ran home so fast that she could not walk
to church for three months afterward ; and
when her breath came back was enabled to
tell tenfold of all she had seen.

.   .   .   .   .

One of the strangest things in life is the
way in which we mortals take the great and
fatal blows of life

For instance, the baron was suddenly
told, while waiting for Frida to sit beside
him, at his one o'clock dinner :

"Plaize, my lard, your lardship's darter
hath a been and jumped off Duty Point."

"What an undutiful thing to do!" was
the first thing Lord de Wichehalse said ;
and those who knew no better thought that
this was how he took it.

Aubyn Auberley, however, took a different measure of a broken-hearted father's
strength.   For the baron buckled on the

armour of a century ago, which had served
his grandsire through hard blows in foreign
battles, and, with a few of his trusty servants, rode to join the Parliament. It happened so that he could not make redress of
his ruined life until the middle of the summer. Then, at last, his chance came to him,
and he did not waste it. Viscount Auberley, who had so often slipped away and
laughed at him, was brought to bay beneath
a tree in the famous fight of Lansdowne.

The young man offered to hold parley,
but the old man had no words. His snowy
hair and rugged forehead, hard-set mouth
and lifted arm, were enough to show his
meaning. The gallant, being so skilled of
fence, thought to play with this old man as
he had with his daughter ; but the Gueldres
ax cleft his curly head, and split what little
brain it takes to fool a trusting maiden.

So, in early life, deceiver and deceived
were quit of harm ; and may ere now have
both found out whether it is better to
inflict the wrong or suffer it.

GEORGE BOWRING

GEORGE BOWRING.

A TALE OF CADER IDRIS.

CHAPTER I.

When I was a young man, and full of spirits, some forty years ago or more, I lost my best and truest friend in a very sad and mysterious way. The greater part of my life has been darkened by this heavy blow and loss, and the blame which I poured upon myself for my own share in the matter.

George Bowring had been seven years with me at the fine old school of Shrewsbury, and trod on my heels from form to form so closely that, when I became at last the captain of the school, he was second to me. I was his elder by half a year, and "sapped" very hard, while he laboured little; so that it will be plain at a glance, although he never acknowledged it, that he was the better endowed of the two with

natural ability. At that time we of Salop
always expected to carry everything, so
far as pure scholarship was concerned, at
both the universities. But nowadays I am
grieved to see that schools of quite a
different stamp (such as Rugby and Harrow, and even Marlborough, and worse of
all peddling Manchester) have been running our boys hard, and sometimes almost
beating them. And how have they done
it? Why, by purchasing masters of our
prime rank and special style.

George and myself were at one time
likely, and pretty well relied upon, to keep
up the fame of Sabrina's crown, and hold
our own at Oxford. But suddenly it so
fell out that both of us were cut short of
classics, and flung into this unclassic world.
In the course of our last half year at school
and when we were both taking final polish
to stand for Balliol scholarships, which we
were almost sure to win, as all the exam-
iners were Shrewsbury men,—not that they
would be partial to us, but because we knew

all their questions,—within a week, both George and I were forced to leave the dear old school, the grand old town, the lovely Severn, and everything but one another.

He lost his father; I lost my uncle, a gentleman in Derbyshire, who had well provided my education; but, having a family of his own, could not be expected to leave me much. And he left me even less than could, from his own point of view, have been rational. It is true that he had seven children; but still a man of £15,000 a year might have done, without injustice— or, I might say, with better justice—something more than to leave his nephew a sum which, after much pushing about into divers insecurities, fetched £72 10s. per annum.

Nevertheless, I am truly grateful; though, perhaps, at the time I had not that knowledge of the world which enlarges the grateful organs. It cannot matter what my feelings were, and I never was mercenary. All my sentiments at that period ran in Greek senarii; and perhaps it would show how good and lofty boys were in that ancient time, though now they are only rude Solecists, if I were to set these verses down—but, after much consideration, I find it wiser to keep them in.

George Bowring's father had some appointment well up in the Treasury. He seems to have been at some time knighted for finding a manuscript of great value that went in the end to the paper mills. How he did it, or what it was, or whether he ever did it at all, were questions for no one to meddle with. People in those days had larger minds than they ever seem to exhibit now. The king might tap a man, and say, " Rise, Sir Joseph," and all the journals of the age, or, at least, the next day, would echo " Sir Joseph ! " And really he was worthy of it. A knight he lived, and a knight he died; and his widow found it such a comfort!

And now on his father's sudden death, George Bowring was left not so very well off. Sir Joseph had lived, as a knight should do, in a free-handed, errant, and chivalrous style; and what he left behind him made it lucky that the title dropped. George, however, was better placed, as regards the world, than I was; but not so very much as to make a difference between us. Having always held together, and being started in life together, we resolved to face the world (as other people are always called) side by side, and with a friendship that should make us as good as one.

This, however, did not come out exactly as it should have done. Many things arose between us—such as diverse occupation, different hours of work and food, and a little split in the taste of trowsers, which, of course, should not have been. He liked the selvage down his legs, while I thought it unartistic, and, going much into the graphic line, I pressed my objections strongly.

But George, in the handsomest manner— as now, looking back on the case, I acknowledge—waived my objections, and insisted as little as he could upon his own.

And again we became as tolerant as any two men, at all alike, can be of one another.

He, by some postern of influence, got into some dry ditch of the Treasury, and there, as in an old castle-moat, began to be at home, and move, gently and after his seniors, as the young ducks follow the old ones. And at every waddle he got more money.

My fortune, however, was not so nice. I had not Sir Joseph, of Treasury cellars, to light me with his name and memory into a snug cell of my own. I had nothing to look to but courage, and youth, and education, and three-quarters of a hundred pounds a year, with some little change to give out of it. Yet why should I have doubted? Now, I wonder at my own misgivings; yet all of them still return upon me, if I ever am persuaded just to try Welsh rabbit. Enough, that I got on at last, to such an extent that the man at the dairy offered me half a year's milk for a sketch of a cow that had never belonged to him.

George, meanwhile, having something

better than a brush 'for a walking stick and
an easel to sit down upon, had taken unto
himself a wife—a lady as sweet and bright
as could be—by name Emily Atkinson. In
truth, she was such a charming person that
I myself, in a quiet way, had taken a very
great fancy to her before George Bowring
saw her; but as soon as I found what a
desperate state the heart of poor George was
reduced to, and came to remember that he
was fitted by money to marry, while I was
not, it appeared to me my true duty toward
the young lady and him, and even myself, to
withdraw from the field, and have nothing
to say if they set up their horses together.

So George married Emily, and could not
imagine why it was that I strove in vain
to appear as his "best man," at the rails
where they do it.

For though I had ordered a blue coat
and buttons, and a cashmere waistcoat
(amber-coloured, with a braid of peonies),
yet at the last moment my courage failed
me, and I was caught with a shivering in

the knees, which the doctor said was ague. This and that shyness of dining at his house (which I thought it expedient to adopt during the years of his married life) created some little reserve between us, though hardly so bad as our first disagreement concerning the stripe down the pantaloons.

However, before that dereliction I had made my friend a wedding present, as was right and proper—a present such as nothing less than a glorious windfall could have enabled me to buy. For while engaged, some three years back, upon a grand historical painting of "Cœur de Lion and Saladin," now to be seen—but let that pass; posterity will always know where to find it —I was harassed in mind perpetually concerning the grain of the fur of a cat. To the dashing young artists of the present day this may seem a trifle; to them, no doubt, a cat is a cat—or would be, if they could make it one. Of course, there are cats enough in London, and sometimes even a few to spare; but I wanted a cat of peculiar order, and of a Saracenic cast. I walked miles and miles; till at last I found him residing in a very old-fashioned house in the Polygon, at Somers Town. Here was a genuine paradise of cats, carefully ministered to and guarded by a maiden lady of Portuguese birth and of advanced maturity. Each of these nine cats possessed his own stool—a mahogany stool, with a velvet cushion, and his name embroidered upon it in beautiful letters of gold. And every day they sat round the fire to digest their dinners, all nine of them, each on his proper stool, some purring, some washing their faces, and some blinking or nodding drowsily. But I need not have spoken of this, except that one of them was called "Saladin." He was the very cat I wanted. I made his acquaintance in the area, and followed it up on the knife-boy's board. And then I had the most happy privilege of saving him from a tail-pipe. Thus my entrance was secured into this feline Eden; and the lady was so well pleased that she gave me an order for nine full-length cat portraits, at the handsome price of ten guineas apiece. And not only this, but at her demise—which followed, alas! too speedily—she left me £150, as a proof of her esteem and affection.

This sum I divided into three equal parts—fifty pounds for a present for George, another fifty for a duty to myself, and the residue to be put by for any future purposes. I knew that my friend had no gold watch; neither, of course, did I possess one. In those days a gold watch was thought a good deal of, and made an impression in society, as a three-hundred-guinea ring does now. Barwise was then considered the best watchmaker in London, and perhaps in the world. So I went to his shop, and chose two gold watches of good size and substance—none of your trumpery catchpenny things, the size of a gilt pill trodden upon—at the price of fifty guineas each. As I took the pair, the foreman let me have them for a hundred pounds, including also in that figure a handsome gold key for each, of exactly the same pattern, and a guard for the fob of watered black-silk ribbon.

My reason for choosing these two watches, out of a trayful of similar quality, was perhaps a little whimsical—viz., that the numbers they bore happened to be sequents. Each had its number engraved on its white enamel dial, in small but very clear figures, placed a little above the central spindle; also upon the extreme verge, at the nadir below the seconds hand, the name of the maker, "Barwise, London." They were not what are called "hunting watches," but had strong and very clear lunette glasses fixed in rims of substantial gold. And their respective numbers were 7777 and 7778.

Carrying these in wash-leather bags, I gave George Bowring his choice of the two; and he chose the one with four figures of seven, making some little joke about it, not good enough to repeat, nor even bad enough to laugh at.

CHAPTER II.

For six years after this all went smoothly with George Bowring and myself. We met almost daily, although we did not lodge together (as once we had done) nor spend the evening hours together, because, of course, he had now his home and family rising around him. By the summer of 1832 he had three children, and was expecting a fourth at no very distant time. His eldest son was named after me, "Robert Bistre," for such is my name, which I have often thought of changing. Not that the name is at all a bad one, as among friends and relations, but that, when I am addressed by strangers, "Mr. Bistre" has a jingling sound, suggestive of childish levity. "Sir Robert· Bistre," however, would sound uncommonly well; and (as some people say) less eminent artists—but perhaps, after

all, I am not so very old as to be in a
hurry.

In the summer of 1832—as elderly people
will call to mind, and the younger sort will
have heard or read—the cholera broke over
London like a bursting meteor.   Such panic
had not been known, I believe, since the
time of the plague, in the reign of Charles
II., as painted (beyond any skill of the
brush) by the simple and wonderful pen of
Defoe.   There had been in the interval
many seasons—or at least I am informed
so—of sickness more widely spread, and of
death more frequent, if not so sudden.
But now this new plague, attacking so
harshly a man's most perceptive and valued
part, drove rich people out of London
faster than horses (not being attacked)
could fly.   Well, used as I was to a good
deal of poison in dealing with my colours, I
felt no alarm on my own account, but was
anxious about my landlady.   This was an
excellently honest woman of fifty-five sum-
mers at the utmost, but weakly confessing

to as much as forty. She had made a point of insisting upon a brisket of beef and a flat-polled cabbage for dinner every Saturday; and the same, with a "cowcumber," cold on Sunday; and for supper a soft-roed herring, ever since her widowhood.

"Mrs. Whitehead," said I—for that was her name, though she said she did not deserve it; and her hair confirmed her in that position by growing darker from year to year—"Madam, allow me to beg you to vary your diet a little at this sad time."

"I varies it every day, Mr. Bistre," she answered somewhat snappishly. "The days of the week is not so many but what they all come round again."

For the moment I did not quite perceive the precision of her argument; but after her death I was able to do more justice to her intellect. And, unhappily, she was removed to a better world on the following Sunday.

To a man in London of quiet habits and regular ways and periods there scarcely can

be a more desperate blow than the loss of
his landlady. It is not only that his conscience pricks him for all his narrow,
plagiaristic, and even irrational suspicions
about the low level of his tea caddy, or a
neap tide in his brandy bottle, or any false
evidence of the eyes (which ever go spying
to lock up the heart), or the ears, which are
also wicked organs—these memories truly
are grievous to him, and make him yearn
now to be robbed again; but what he feels
most sadly is the desolation of having
nobody who understands his locks. One of
the best men I ever knew was so plagued
with his sideboard every day for two years,
after dinner, that he married a little new
maid-of-all-work—because she was a blacksmith's daughter.

Nothing of that sort, however, occurred
in my case, I am proud to say. But finding
myself in a helpless state, without anyone
to be afraid of, I had only two courses
before me : either to go back to my former
landlady (who was almost too much of a

Tartar, perhaps), or else to run away from my rooms till Providence provided a new landlady.

Now, in this dilemma I met George Bowring, who saw my distress, and most kindly pressed me to stay at his house till some female arose to manage my affairs for me. This, of course, I declined to do, especially under present circumstances; and, with mutual pity, we parted. But the very next day he sought me out, in a quiet nook where a few good artists were accustomed to meet and think; and there he told me that really now he saw his way to cut short my troubles as well as his own, and to earn a piece of enjoyment and profit for both of us. And I happen to remember his very words.

"You are cramped in your hand, my dear fellow," said he (for in those days youths did not call each other "old man"—with sad sense of their own decrepitude). "Bob, you are losing your freedom of touch. You must come out of these stony holes, and look at a rocky mountain."

My heart gave a jump at these words ; and yet I had been too much laid flat by facts—"sat upon," is the slang of these last twenty years, and in the present dearth of invention must serve, no doubt, for another twenty—I say that I had been used as a cushion by so many landladies and maids-of-all-work (who take not an hour to find out where they need do no work), that I could not fetch my breath to think of ever going up a mountain.

"I will leave you to think of it, Bob," said George, putting his hat on carefully ; "I am bound for time, and you seem to be nervous. Consult your pillow, my dear fellow ; and peep into your old stocking and see whether you can afford it."

That last hit settled me. People said, in spite of all my generous acts—and nobody knows, except myself, the frequency and the extent of these—without understanding the merits of the case—perfect (or rather imperfect) strangers said that I was stingy! To prove the contrary, I resolved to launch into great expenditure, and to pay coach fare all the way from London toward the nearest mountain.

Half the inhabitants now were rushing helter-skelter out of London, and very often to seaside towns where the smell of fish destroyed them. And those who could not get away were shuddering at the blinds drawn down, and huddling away from the mutes at the doors, and turning pale at the funeral bells. And some, who had never thought twice before of their latter end, now began to dwell with so much unction upon it, that Providence graciously spared them the waste of perpetual preparation.

Among the rest, George Bowring had been scared, far more than he liked to own, by the sudden death of his butcher, between half a dozen chops for cutlets and the trimming of a wing-bone. George's own cook had gone down with the order, and meant to bring it all back herself, because she knew what butchers do when left to consider their subject. And Mrs. Tompkins was so alarmed that she gave only six hours' notice to leave, though her husband was far on the salt-sea wave, according to her own account, and she had none to make her welcome except her father's second wife. This broke up the household ; and hence it was that George tempted me so with the mountains.

For he took his wife and children to an old manor-house in Berkshire, belonging to two maiden aunts of the lady, who promised to see to all that might happen, but wanted no gentleman in the house at a period of such delicacy. George Bowring, therefore, agreed to meet me on the 12th day of September, at the inn in Reading— I forget its name—where the Regulator coach (belonging to the old company, and leaving White Horse Cellars at half-past nine in the morning) allowed an hour to dine, from one o'clock onward, as the roads might be. And here I found him, and we supped at Oxford, and did very well at the Mitre. On the following morning we took coach for Shrewsbury, as we had agreed, and, reaching the town before dark, put up at the Talbot Inn, and sauntered into the dear old school, to see what the lads had been at since our time ; for their names and their exploits, at Oxford and Cambridge, are scored in large letters upon the panels, from the year 1806 and onward, so that soon there will be no place to register any more of them ; and we found that though we ourselves had done nothing, many fine fellows had been instituted in letters of higher humanity, and were holding up the old standard, so that we longed to invite them to dinner. But discipline must be maintained ; and that word means, more than anything else, the difference of men's ages.

Now, at Shrewsbury, we had resolved to cast off all further heed of coaches ; and knowing the country pretty well, or recalling it from our childhood, to strike away on foot for some of the mountain wildernesses. Of these, in those days, nobody

knew much more than that they were high
and steep, and slippery and dangerous, and
much to be shunned by all sensible people
who liked a nice fire and the right side of
the window. So that when we shouldered
staves with knapsacks flapping heavily, all
the wiser sort looked on us as marching off
to Bedlam.

In the morning, as we were starting, we
set our watches by the old school dial, as I
have cause to remember well. And we
staked half a crown, in a sporting manner,
each on his own watch to be the truer by
sun upon our way back again. And thus
we left those ancient walls and the glancing of the river, and stoutly took the
Welshpool road, dreading nought except
starvation.

Although in those days I was not by any
means a cripple, George was far stronger
of arm and leg, having always been famous,
though we made no fuss about such things
then, for running and jumping, and lifting
weights, and using the boxing-gloves and

the foils.   A fine, brave fellow as ever lived, with a short, straight nose and a resolute chin, he touched the measuring-bar quite fairly at seventy-four inches, and turned the scales at fourteen stone and a quarter. And so, as my chattels weighed more than his (by means of a rough old easel and material for rude sketches), he did me a good turn now and then by changing packs for a mile or two.   And thus we came in four days' march to Aber-Aydyr, a village lying under Cader Idris.

CHAPTER III.

IF any place ever lay out of the world, and was proud of itself for doing so, this little village of Aber-Aydyr must have been very near it. The village was built, as the people expressed it, of thirty cottages, one public-house, one shop universal, and two chapels. The torrent of the Aydyr entered with a roar of rapids, and at the lower end departed in a thunder of cascades. The natives were all so accustomed to live in the thick of this watery uproar that, whenever they left their beloved village to see the inferior outer world, they found themselves as deaf as posts till they came to a weir or a waterfall. And they told us that in the scorching summer of the year 1826 the river had failed them so that for nearly a month they could only discourse by signs; and they used to stand on the bridge and point at the shrunken rapids, and stop their ears to exclude that horrible emptiness. Till a violent thunderstorm broke up the drought, and the river came down roaring; and the next day all Aber-Aydyr was able to gossip again as usual.

Finding these people, who lived altogether upon slate, of a quaint and original turn, George Bowring and I resolved to halt and rest the soles of our feet a little, and sketch and fish the neighbourhood. For George had brought his rod and tackle, and many a time had he wanted to stop and set up his rod and begin to cast; but I said that I would not be cheated so: he had promised me a mountain, and would he put me off with a river? Here, however, we had both delights; the river for him and the mountain for me. As for the fishing, all that he might have, and I would grudge him none of it, if he fairly divided whatever he caught. But he must not expect me to follow him always and watch all his dainty manœuvring; each was to carry and eat his own dinner, whenever we made a day of it, so that he might keep to his flies and his water, while I worked away with my brush at the mountains. And thus we spent a most pleasant week, though we knew very little of Welsh and the slaters spoke but little English. But—much as they are maligned because they will not have strangers to work with them—we found them a thoroughly civil, obliging, and rather intelligent set of men; most of them also of a respectable and religious turn of mind; and they scarcely ever poach, except on Saturdays and Mondays.

On September 25, as we sat at breakfast in the little sanded parlour of the Cross-Pipes public house, our bedroom being overhead, my dear friend complained to me that he was tired of fishing so long up and down one valley, and asked me to come with him further up, into wilder and rockier districts, where the water ran deeper (as he had been told) and the trout were less worried by quarrymen, because it was

such a savage place, deserted by all except
evil spirits, that even the Aber-Aydyr slaters
could not enjoy the fishing there.   I promised him gladly to come, only keeping the
old understanding between us, that each
should attend to his own pursuits and his
own opportunities mainly; so that George
might stir most when the trout rose well,
and I when the shadows fell properly.   And
thus we set forth about nine o'clock of a
bright and cheerful morning, while the sun,
like a courtly perruquier of the reign of
George II., was lifting, and shifting, and
setting in order the vapoury curls of the
mountains.

We trudged along thus at a merry swing,
for the freshness of autumnal dew was
sparkling in the valley, until we came to
a rocky pass, where walking turned to
clambering.   After an hour of sharpish
work among slaty shelves and threatening
crags, we got into one of those troughlike
hollows hung on each side with precipices,
which look as if the earth had sunk for the

sake of letting the water through. On our left hand, cliff towered over cliff to the grand height of Pen y Cader, the steepest and most formidable aspect of the mountain. Rock piled on rock, and shingle cast in naked waste disdainfully, and slippery channels scooped by torrents of tempestuous waters, forbade one to desire at all to have anything more to do with them— except, of course, to get them painted at a proper distance, so that they might hang at last in the dining rooms of London, to give people appetite with sense of hungry breezes, and to make them comfortable with the sight of danger.

"This is very grand indeed," said George, as he turned to watch me; for the worst part of our business is to have to give an opinion always upon points of scenery. But I am glad that I was not cross, or even crisp with him that day.

"It is magnificent," I answered; "and I see a piece of soft sward there, where you can set up your rod, old fellow, while I get my sticks in trim. Let us fill our pipes and watch the shadows; they do not fall quite to suit me yet."

"How these things make one think," cried Bowring, as we sat on a stone and smoked, "of the miserable littleness of men like you and me, Bob!"

"Speak for yourself, sir," I said, laughing at his unaccustomed, but by no means novel, reflection. "I am quite contented with my size, although I am smaller than you, George. Dissatisfied mortal! Nature wants no increase of us, or she would have had it."

"In another world we shall be much larger," he said, with his eyes on the tops of the hills. "Last night I dreamed that my wife and children were running to meet me in heaven, Bob."

"Tush! You go and catch fish," I replied; for tears were in his large, soft eyes, and I hated the sentimental. "Would they ever let such a little Turk as Bob Bistre into heaven, do you think? My godson would shout all the angels deaf and outdrum all the cherubim."

"Poor little chap! He is very noisy; but he is not half a bad sort," said George. "If he only comes like his godfather I shall wish no better luck for him."

These were kind words, and I shook his hand to let him know that I felt them; and then, as if he were ashamed of having talked rather weakly, he took with his strong legs a dangerous leap of some ten or twelve feet downward, and landed on a narrow ledge that overhung the river. Here he put his rod together, and I heard the click of reel as he drew the loop at the end of the line through the rings, and so on; and I heard him cry "Chut!" as he took his flies from his Scotch cap and found a tangle; and I saw the glistening of his rod, as the sunshine pierced the valley, and then his tall, straight figure pass the corner of a crag that stood as upright as a tombstone; and after that no more of any live and bright George Bowring.

CHAPTER IV.

SWIFT is the flight of Time whenever a man would fain lay hold of him. All created beings, from Behemoth to a butterfly, dread and fly (as best they may) that universal butcher—man. And as nothing is more carefully killed by the upper sort of mankind than Time, how can he help making off for his life when anybody wants to catch him ?

Of course, I am not of that upper sort, and make no pretence to be so ; but Time, perhaps, may be excused for thinking—having had such a very short turn at my clothes—that I belonged to the aristocracy. At any rate, while I drew, and rubbed, and dubbed, and made hieroglyphics, Time was uneasily shifting and shuffling the lines of the hills, as a fever patient jerks and works the bed-clothes. And, worse than that, he was scurrying westward (frightened, no doubt, by the equinox) at such a pace that I was scared by the huddling together of shadows. Awaking from a long, long dream—through which I had been working hard, and laying the foundations of a thousand pounds hereafter—I felt the invisible damp of evening settling in the valleys. The sun, from over the sea, had still his hand on Cader Idris ; but every inferior head and height was gray in the sweep of his mantle.

I threw my hair back—for an artist really should be picturesque ; and, having no other beauty, must be firm to long hair, while it lasts—and then I shouted, "George !" until the strata of the mountain (which dip and jag, like veins of oak) began and sluggishly prolonged a slow zig-zag of echoes. No counter-echo came to me ; no ring of any sonorous voice made crag, and precipice, and mountain vocal with the sound of "Bob !"

"He must have gone back. What a

fool I must be never to remember seeing him! He saw that I was full of rubbish, and he would not disturb me. He is gone back to the Cross-Pipes, no doubt. And yet it does not seem like him."

"To look for a pin in a bundle of hay" would be a job of sense and wisdom rather than to seek a thing so very small as a very big man among the depth, and height, and breadth of river, shingle, stone, and rock, crag, precipice, and mountain. And so I doubled up my things, while the very noise they made in doubling flurried and alarmed me; and I thought it was not like George to leave me to find my way back all alone, among the deep bogs, and the whirlpools, and the trackless tracts of crag.

When I had got my fardel ready, and was about to shoulder it, the sound of brisk, short steps, set sharply upon doubtful footing, struck my ear, through the roar of the banks and stones that shook with waterfall. And before I had time to ask, "Who goes there?"—as in this solitude one might do—a slight, short man, whom I knew by sight as a workman of Aber-Aydyr, named Evan Peters, was close to me, and was swinging a slate-hammer in one hand, and bore in the other a five-foot staff. He seemed to be amazed at sight of me, but touched his hat with his staff, and said : "Good-night, gentleman !" in Welsh; for the natives of this part are very polite. "Good-night, Evan !" I answered, in his own language, of which I had picked up a little; and he looked well pleased, and said in his English: " For why, sir, did you leave your things in that place there ? A bad mans come and steal them, it is very likely."

Then he wished me "Good-night" again, and was gone—for he seemed to be in a dreadful hurry—before I had the sense to ask him what he meant about " my things." But as his footfall died away a sudden fear came over me.

"The things he meant must be George Bowring's," I said to myself ; and I dropped

my own, and set off, with my blood all tin-
gling, for the place toward which he had
jerked his staff. How long it took me to
force my way among rugged rocks and
stubs of oak I cannot tell, for every
moment was an hour to me. But a streak
of sunset glanced along the lonesome gorge,
and cast my shadow further than my voice
would go; and by it I saw something long
and slender against a scar of rock, and
standing far in front of me. Toward this I
ran as fast as ever my trembling legs would
carry me, for I knew too well that it must
be the fishing-rod of George Bowring.

It was stuck in the ground—not care-
lessly, nor even in any hurry; but as a
sportsman makes all snug, when for a time
he leaves off casting. For instance, the
end fly was fixed in the lowest ring of the
butt, and the slack of the line reeled up so
that the collar lay close to the rod itself.
Moreover, in such a rocky place, a bed to
receive the spike could not have been found
without some searching. For a moment I

was reassured. Most likely George himself was near—perhaps in quest of blueberries (which abound at the foot of the shingles and are a very delicious fruit), or of some rare fern to send his wife, who was one of the first in England to take much notice of them. And it shows what confidence I had in my friend's activity and strength, that I never feared the likely chance of his falling from some precipice.

But just as I began, with some impatience—for we were to have dined at the Cross-Pipes about sundown, five good (or very bad) miles away, and a brace of ducks was the order—just as I began to shout, "George! Wherever have you got to?" leaping on a little rock, I saw a thing that stopped me. At the further side of this rock, and below my feet, was a fishing basket, and a half-pint mug nearly full of beer, and a crust of the brown, sweet bread of the hills, and a young white onion, half cut through, and a clasp-knife open, and a screw of salt, and a slice of the cheese, just dashed with goat's milk, which George was so fond of, but I disliked; and there may have been a hard-boiled egg. At the sight of these things all my blood rushed to my head in such a manner that all my power to think was gone. I sat down on the rock where George must have sat while beginning his frugal luncheon, aud I put my heels into the marks of his, and, without knowing why, I began to sob like a child who has lost his mother. What train of reasoning went through my brain—if any passed in the obscurity—let metaphysicians or psychologists, as they call themselves, pretend to know. I only know that I kept on whispering, "George is dead! Unless he had been killed, he never would have left his beer so!"

I must have sat, making a fool of myself, a considerable time in this way, thinking of George's poor wife and children, and wondering what would become of them, instead of setting to work at once to know what was become of him. I took up a piece of cheese-rind, showing a perfect impression of his fine front teeth, and I put it in my pocketbook, as the last thing he had touched. And then I examined the place all around and knelt to look for footmarks, though the light was sadly waning.

For the moment I discovered nothing of footsteps or other traces to frighten or to comfort me. A little narrow channel (all of rock and stone and slaty stuff) sloped to the river's brink, which was not more than five yards distant. In this channel I saw no mark except that some of the smaller stones appeared to have been turned over ; and then I looked into the river itself, and saw a force of water sliding smoothly into a rocky pool.

"If he had fallen in there," I said, "he would have leaped out again in two seconds ; or even if the force of the water had carried him down into that deep pool, he can swim like a duck—of course he can. What river could ever drown you, George ?"

And then I remembered how at Salop he used to swim the flooded Severn when most of us feared to approach the banks ; and I knew that he could not be drowned, unless something first had stunned him.   And after that I looked around, and my heart was full of terror.

"It is a murder!" I cried aloud, though my voice among the rocks might well have brought like fate upon me.   "As sure as I stand here, and God is looking down upon me, this is a black murder !"

In what way I got back that night to Aber-Aydyr I know not.   All I remember is that the people would not come out of their houses to me, according to some superstition, which was not explained till morning ; and, being unable to go to bed, I took a blanket and lay down beneath a dry arch of the bridge, and the Aydyr, as swiftly as a spectre gliding, hushed me with a melancholy song.

CHAPTER V.

Now, as sure as ever I lay beneath the third arch of Aber-Aydyr Bridge, in a blanket of Welsh serge or flannel, with a double border, so surely did I see, and not dream, what I am going to tell you.

The river ran from east to west ; and the moon, being now the harvest moon, was not very high, but large and full, and just gliding over the crest of the hill that over-hangs the quarry-pit; so that, if I can put it plainly, the moon was across the river from me, and striking the turbulent water athwart, so that her face, or a glimmer thereof, must have been lying upon the river if any smooth place had been left for it. But of this there was no chance, because the whole of the river was in a rush, according to its habit, and covered with bubbles, and froth, and furrows, even where it did not splash, and spout, and leap, as it loved to do. In the depth of the night, when even the roar of the water seemed drowsy and indolent, and the calm trees stooped with their heavy limbs overhanging the darkness languidly, and only a few rays of the moon, like the fluttering of a silver bird, moved in and out the meshwork, I leaned upon my elbow, and I saw the dead George Bowring.

He came from the pit of the river toward me, quietly and without stride or step, gliding over the water like a mist or the vapour of a calm white frost ; and he stopped at the ripple where the shore began, and he looked at me very peacefully. And I felt neither fear nor doubt of him, any more than I do of this pen in my hand.

"George," I said, "I have been uneasy all the day about you and I cannot sleep, and I have had no comfort. What has made you treat me so ?"

He seemed to be anxious to explain, having always been so straightforward ;

but an unknown hand or the power of death held him, so that he could only smile. And then it appeared to me as if he pointed to the water first and then to the sky, with such an import that I understood (as plainly as if he had pronounced it) that his body lay under the one and his soul was soaring on high through the other ; and, being forbidden to speak, he spread his hands, as if entrusting me with all that had belonged to him ; and then he smiled once more, and faded into the whiteness of the froth and foam.

And then I knew that I had been holding converse, face to face, with Death; and icy fear shook me, and I strove in vain to hide my eyes from everything. And when I awoke in the morning there was a gray trunk of an alder tree, just George Bowring's height and size, on the other side of the water, so that I could have no doubt that himself had been there.

After a search of about three hours we found the body of my dear friend in a deep black pool of the Aydyr—not the first hole below the place in which he sat down to his luncheon, but nearly a hundred yards farther down, where a bold cliff jutted out and bent the water scornfully. Our quarrymen would not search this pool until the sunlight fell on it, because it was a place of dread with a legend hovering over it. "The Giant's Tombstone" was the name of the crag that overhung it; and the story was that the giant Idris, when he grew worn out with age, chose this rock out of many others near the top of the mountain, and laid it under his arm and came down here to drink of the Aydyr. He drank the Aydyr dry because he was feverish and flushed with age; and he set down the crag in a hole he had scooped with the palms of his hands for more water; and then he lay down on his back, and Death (who never could reach to his knee when he stood) took advantage of his posture to drive home the javelin. And thus he lay dead, with the crag for his headstone, and the weight of his corpse sank a grave for itself in the channel of the river, and the toes of his boots are still to be seen after less than a mile of the valley.

Under this headstone of Idris lay the body of George Bowring, fair and comely, with the clothes all perfect, and even the light cap still on the head. And as we laid it upon the grass, reverently and carefully, the face, although it could smile no more, still appeared to wear a smile, as if the new world were its home, and death a mere trouble left far behind. Even the eyes were open, and their expression was not of fright or pain, but pleasant and bright, with a look of interest such as a man pays to his food.

"Stand back, all of you!" I said sternly; "none shall examine him but myself. Now all of you note what I find here."

I searched all his pockets, one after another; and tears came to my eyes again as I counted not less than eleven of them, for I thought of the fuss we used to make with the Shrewsbury tailor about them. There

was something in every pocket, but nothing
of any importance at present, except his
purse and a letter from his wife, for which
he had walked to Dolgelly and back on the
last entire day of his life.

"It is a hopeless mystery!" I exclaimed
aloud, as the Welshmen gazed with super-
stitious awe and doubt. "He is dead as if
struck by lightning, but there was no storm
in the valley!"

"No, no, sure enough; no storm was
there. But it is plain to see what has
killed him!" This was Evan Peters, the
quarryman, and I glanced at him very sus-
piciously. "Iss, sure, plain enough," said
another; and then they all broke into Welsh,
with much gesticulation; and "e-ah, e-ah,"
and "otty, otty," and "hanool, hanool,"
were the sounds they made––at least to an
ignorant English ear.

"What do you mean, you fools?" I
asked, being vexed at their offhand way of
settling things so far beyond them. "Can
you pretend to say what it was?"

"Indeed, then, and indeed, my gentleman, it is no use to talk no more. It was the Caroline Morgan."

"Which is the nearest house?" I asked, for I saw that some of them were already girding up their loins to fly, at the mere sound of that fearful name; for the cholera morbus had scared the whole country; and if one were to fly, all the rest would follow, as swiftly as mountain sheep go. "Be quick to the nearest house, my friends, and we will send for the doctor."

This was a lucky hit; for these Cambrians never believed in anyone's death until he had "taken the doctor." And so, with much courage and kindness, "to give the poor gentleman the last chance," they made a rude litter, and, bearing the body upon sturdy shoulders, betook themselves to a track which I had overlooked entirely. Some people have all their wits about them as soon as they are called for, but with me it is mainly otherwise. And this I had shown in two things already; the first of which came to my mind the moment I pulled out my watch to see what the time was. "Good Heavens!" it struck me, "where is George's watch? It was not in any of his pockets; and I did not feel it in his fob."

In an instant I made them set down the bier; and, much as it grieved me to do such a thing, I carefully sought for my dear friend's watch. No watch, no seals, no ribbon, was there! "Go on," I said; and I fell behind them, having much to think about. In this condition, I took little heed of the distance, or of the ground itself; being even astonished when, at last, we stopped; as if we were bound to go on forever.

CHAPTER VI.

WE had stopped at the gate of an old farmhouse, built with massive boulder stones, laid dry, and flushed in with mortar. As dreary a place as was ever seen; at the head of a narrow mountain-gorge, with mountains towering over it. There was no sign of life about it, except that a gaunt hog trotted forth, and grunted at us, and showed his tusks, and would perhaps have charged us, if we had not been so many. The house looked just like a low church-tower, and might have been taken for one at a distance if there had been any battlements. It seemed to be four or five hundred years old, and perhaps belonged to some petty chief in the days of Owen Glendower.

"Knock again, Thomas Edwards. Stop,

let me knock," said one of our party impatiently. "There, waddow, waddow, waddow!"

Suiting the action to the word, he thumped with a big stone heavily, till a middle-aged woman, with rough black hair, looked out of a window and screamed in Welsh to ask what this terrible noise was. To this they made answer in the same language, pointing to their sad burden, and asking permission to leave it for the doctor's inspection and the inquest, if there was to be one. And I told them to add that I would pay well—anything, whatever she might like to ask. But she screamed out something that sounded like a curse, and closed the lattice violently. Knowing that many superstitions lingered in these mountains—as, indeed, they do elsewhere plentifully—I was not surprised at the woman's stern refusal to admit us, especially at this time of pest; but I thought it strange that her fierce black eyes avoided both me and the poor rude litter on which the body of George lay, covered with some slate-workers' aprons.

"She is not the mistress!" cried Evan Peters, in great excitement, as I thought. "Ask where is Hopkin—Black Hopkin—where is he?"

At this suggestion a general outcry arose in Welsh for "Black Hopkin"; an outcry so loud and prolonged that the woman opened the window again and screamed—as they told me afterward—"He is not at home, you noisy fools; he is gone to Machynlleth. Not long would you dare to make this noise if Hopkin ap Howel was at home."

But while she was speaking the wicket-door of the great arched gate was thrown open, and a gun about six feet long and of very large bore was presented at us. The quarrymen drew aside briskly, and I was about to move somewhat hastily, when the great, swarthy man who was holding the gun withdrew it, and lifted his hat to me, proudly and as an equal.

"You cannot enter this house," he said

in very good English, and by no means rudely. "I am sorry for it, but it cannot be. My little daughter is very ill, the last of seven. You must go elsewhere."

With these words he bowed again to me, while his sad eyes seemed to pierce my soul; and then he quietly closed the wicket and fastened it with a heavy bolt, and I knew that we must indeed go further.

This was no easy thing to do; for our useless walk to "Crug y Dlwlith" (the Dewless Hills), as this farm was called, had taken us further at every step from the place we must strive for after all— the good little Aber-Aydyr. The gallant quarrymen were now growing both weary and uneasy; and in justice to them I must say that no temptation of money, nor even any appeal to their sympathies, but only a challenge of their patriotism held them to the sad duties owing from the living to the dead. But knowing how proud all Welshmen are of the fame of their race and country, happily I exclaimed at last, when fear was getting the mastery, "What will be said of this in England, this low cowardice of the Cymro?" Upon that they looked at one another and did their best right gallantly.

Now, I need not go into any further sad details of this most sad time, except to say that Dr. Jones, who came the next day from Dolgelly, made a brief examination by order of the coroner. Of course, he had too much sense to suppose that the case was one of cholera; but to my surprise he pronounced that death was the result of "asphyxia, caused by too long immersion in the water." And knowing nothing of George Bowring's activity, vigour, and cultivated power in the water, perhaps he was not to be blamed for dreaming that a little mountain stream could drown him. I, on the other hand, felt as sure that my dear friend was foully murdered as I did that I should meet him in heaven—if I lived well for the rest of my life, which I resolved at once to do—and there have the whole thing explained, and perhaps be permitted to glance at the man who did it, as Lazarus did at Dives.

In spite of the doctor's evidence and the coroner's own persuasion, the jury found that "George Bowring died of the Caroline Morgan"—which the clerk corrected to cholera morbus—"brought on by wetting his feet and eating too many fish of his own catching." And so you may see it entered now in the records of the court of the coroners of the king for Merioneth.

And now I was occupied with a trouble, which, after all, was more urgent than the enquiry how it came to pass. When a man is dead, it must be taken as a done thing, not to be undone; and, happily, all near relatives are inclined to see it in that light. They are grieved, of course, and they put on hatbands and give no dinner parties; and they even think of their latter ends more than they might have desired to do. But after a little while all comes round. Such things must be happening always,

and it seems so unchristian to repine; and
if any money has been left them, truly
they must attend to it. On the other
hand, if there has been no money, they
scarcely see why they should mourn for
nothing; and, as a duty, they begin to
allow themselves to be roused up.

But when a wife becomes a widow, it
is wholly different. No money can ever
make up to her the utter loss of the love-
time and the loneliness of the remaining
years; the little turns, and thoughts, and
touches—wherever she goes and whatever
she does—which at every corner meet her
with a deep, perpetual want. She tries to
fetch her spirit up and to think of her
duties to all around—to her children, or
to the guests whom trouble forces upon
her for business' sake, or even the friends
who call to comfort (though the call can
fetch her none) ; but all the while how
deeply aches her sense that all these duties
are as different as a thing can be from her
love-work to her husband!

What could I do? I had heard from
George, but could not for my life remember, the name of that old house in Berkshire where poor Mrs. Bowring was on a
visit to two of her aunts, as I said before.
I ventured to open her letter to her husband, found in his left-hand side breast-
pocket, and, having dried it, endeavoured
only to make out whence she wrote; but
there was nothing. Ladies scarcely ever
date a letter both with time and place, for
they seem to think that everybody must
know it, because they do. So the best
I could do was to write to poor George's
house in London, and beg that the letter
might be forwarded at once. It came,
however, too late to hand. For, although
the newspapers of that time were respect-
ably slow and steady, compared with the
rush they all make nowadays, they generally managed to outrun the post, especially
in the nutting season. They told me at
Dolgelly, and they confirmed it at Machynlleth, that nobody must desire to get

his letters at any particular time, in the months of September and October, when the nuts were ripe. For the postmen never would come along until they had filled their bags with nuts, for the pleasure of their families. And I dare say they do the same thing now, but without being free to declare it so.

CHAPTER VII.

THE body of my dear friend was borne round the mountain slopes to Dolgelly and buried there, with no relative near, nor any mourner except myself; for his wife, or rather his widow, was taken with sudden illness (as might be expected), and for weeks it was doubtful whether she would stay behind to mourn for him. But youth and strength at last restored her to dreary duties and worldly troubles.

Of the latter, a great part fell on me; and I did my best—though you might not think so, after the fuss I made of my own—to intercept all that I could, and quit myself manfully of the trust which George had returned from the dead to enjoin. And, what with one thing and another, and a sudden dearth of money which fell on me (when my cat-fund was all spent, and my gold watch gone up a gargoyle), I had such a job to feed the living that I never was able to follow up the dead.

The magistrates held some enquiry, of course, and I had to give my evidence ; but nothing came of it, except that the quarryman, Evan Peters, clearly proved his innocence. Being a very clever fellow, and dabbling a bit in geology, he had taken his hammer up the mountains, as his practice was when he could spare the time, to seek for new veins of slate, or lead, or even gold, which is said to be there. He was able to show that he had been at Tal y Llyn at the time of day when George would be having his luncheon ; and the people who knew Evan Peters were much more inclined to suspect me than him. But why should they suspect anybody, when anyone but a fool could see "how plain it was of the cholera ? "

Twenty years slipped by (like a rope paid out on the seashore, "hand over hand," chafing as it goes, but gone as soon as one looks after it), and my hair was gray, and my fame was growing (slowly, as it appeared to me, but as all my friends said "rapidly"; as if I could never have earned it !) when the mystery of George Bowring's death was solved without an effort.

I had been so taken up with the three dear children, and working for them as hard as if they were my own (for the treasury of our British empire was bankrupt to these little ones—"no provision had been made for such a case," and so we had to make it)—I say that these children had grown to me and I to them in such degree that they all of them called me "Uncle !"

This is the most endearing word that one human being can use to another. A fellow is certain to fight with his brothers and sisters, his father, and perhaps even his mother. Tenfold thus with his wife ; but whoever did fight with his uncle ? Of course I mean unless he was his heir. And the tenderness of this relation has not escaped *vox populi*, that keen discriminator.

Who is the most reliable, cordial, indispensable of mankind—especially to artists—in every sense of the word the dearest? A pawnbroker; he is our uncle.

Under my care, these three children grew to be splendid "members of society." They used to come and kick over my easel with legs that were quite Titanic; and I could not scold them when I thought of George. Bob Bistre, the eldest, was my apprentice, and must become famous in consequence; and when he was twenty-five years old, and money became no object to me (through the purchase by a great art critic of the very worst picture I ever painted; half of it, in fact, was Bob's!), I gave the boy choice of our autumn trip to California, or the antipodes.

"I would rather go to North Wales, dear uncle," he answered, and then dropped his eyes, as his father used when he had provoked me. That settled the matter. He must have his way; though as for myself, I must confess that I have begun, for a long time now, upon principle, to shun melancholy.

The whole of the district is opened up so by those desperate railways that we positively dined at the Cross-Pipes Hotel the very day after we left Euston Square. Our landlady did not remember me, which was anything but flattering. But she jumped at Bob as if she would have kissed him ; for he was the image of his father, whose handsome face had charmed her.

CHAPTER VIII.

THE Aydyr was making as much noise as ever, for the summer had been a wet one; and of course all the people of Aber-Aydyr had their ears wide open. I showed Bob the bridge and the place of my vision, but did not explain its meaning, lest my love for him should seem fiduciary; and the next morning, at his most urgent request, we started afoot for that dark, sad valley. It was a long walk, and I did not find that twenty years had shortened it.

"Here we are at last," I said, "and the place looks the same as ever. There is the grand old Pen y cada, with the white cloud rolling as usual; to the left and right are the two other summits, the arms of the chair of Idris; and over the shoulder of that crag you can catch a glassy light in the air—that is the reflection of Tal y Llyn."

"Yes, yes!" he answered impatiently. "I know all that from your picture, uncle. But show me the place where my father died."

"It lies immediately under our feet. You see that gray stone down in the hollow, a few yards from the river brink. There he sat, as I have often told you, twenty years ago this day. There he was taking his food, when someone—— Well, well! God knows, but we never shall. My boy, I am stiff in the knees; go on."

He went on alone, as I wished him to do, with exactly his father's step, and glance, figure, face, and stature. Even his dress was of the silver-gray which his father had been so fond of, and which the kind young fellow chose to please his widowed mother. I could almost believe (as a cloudy mantle stole in long folds over the highland, reproducing the lights, and shades, and gloom of that mysterious day) that the twenty years were all a dream, and that here was poor George Bowring going to his murder and his watery grave.

My nerves are good and strong, I trow ; and that much must have long been evident. But I did not know what young Bob's might be, and therefore I left him to himself. No man should be watched as he stands at the grave of his wife or mother : neither should a young fellow who sits on the spot where his father was murdered. Therefore, as soon as our Bob had descended into the gray stone-pit, in which his dear father must have breathed his last, I took good care to be out of sight, after observing that he sat down exactly as his father must have sat, except that his attitude, of course, was sad, and his face pale and reproachful. Then, leaving the poor young fellow to his thoughts, I also sat down to collect myself.

But before I had time to do more than wonder at the mysterious ways of the world, or of Providence in guiding it ; at the manner in which great wrong lies hidden, and great woe falls unrecompensed ; at the dark, uncertain laws which cover (like an indiscriminate mountain cloud) the good and the bad, the kind and the cruel, the murdered and the murderer—a loud shriek rang through the rocky ravine, and up the dark folds of the mountain.

I started with terror, and rushed forward, and heard myself called, and saw young Bowring leap up, and stand erect and firm, although with a gesture of horror. At his feet lay the body of a man struck dead, flung on its back, with great hands spread on the eyes, and white hair over them.

No need to ask what it meant. At last the justice of God was manifest. The murderer lay, a rigid corpse, before the son of the murdered.

" Did you strike him ? " I asked.

"Is it likely," said the youth, "that I would strike an aged man like that ? I assure you I never had such a fright in my life. This poor old fellow came on me quite suddenly, from behind a rock, when all my mind was full of my father ; and his eyes met mine, and down he fell, as if I had shot him through the heart ! "

"You have done no less," I answered ; and then I stooped over the corpse (as I had stooped over the corpse of its victim), and the whole of my strength was required to draw the great knotted hands from the eyes, upon which they were cramped with a spasm not yet relaxed.

"It is Hopkin ap Howel ! " I cried, as the great eyes, glaring with the horror of death, stood forth. "Black Hopkin once, white Hopkin now ! Robert Bowring, you have slain the man who slew your father."

"You know that I never meant to do it," said Bob. "Surely, uncle, it was his own fault ! "

"How did he come ? I see no way. He was not here when I showed you the place, or else we must have seen him."

"He came round the corner of that

rock, that stands in front of the furze-
bush."

Now that we had the clue, a little examination showed the track. Behind the
furze-bush, a natural tunnel of rock, not
more than a few yards long, led into a narrow gorge covered with brushwood, and
winding into the valley below the farmhouse of the Dewless Crags. Thither we
hurried to obtain assistance, and there the
whole mystery was explained.

Black Hopkin (who stole behind George
Bowring and stunned, or, perhaps, slew him
with one vile blow) has this and this only to
say at the Bar—that he did it through love
of his daughter.

Gwenthlian, the last of seven, lay dying
on the day when my friend and myself
came up the valley of the Aydyr. Her
father, a man of enormous power of will
and passion, as well as muscle, rushed forth
of the house like a madman, when the doctor from Dolgelly told him that nothing
more remained except to await the good

time of heaven. It was the same deadly
decline which had slain every one of his
children at that same age, and now must
extinguish a long descended and slowly
impoverished family.

"If I had but a gold watch I could save
her!" he cried in his agony, as he left the
house. "Ever since the old gold watch
was sold, they have died—they have died!
They are gone, one after one, the last of all
my children!"

In these lonely valleys lurks a strange old
superstition that even Death must listen to
the voice of Time in gold; that, when the
scanty numbered moments of the sick are
fleeting, a gold watch laid in the wasted
palm, and pointing the earthly hours, com-
pels the scythe of Death to pause, the time-
less power to bow before the two great
gods of the human race—time and gold.

Poor George in the valley must have
shown his watch. The despairing father
must have been struck with crafty madness
at the sight. The watch was placed in his

daughter's palm; but Death had no regard for it. Thenceforth Black Hopkin was a blasted man, racked with remorse and heart-disease, sometimes raving, always roving, but finding no place of repentance. And it must have been a happy stroke—if he had made his peace above, which none of us can deal with—when the throb of his long-worn heart stood still at the vision of his victim, and his soul took flight to realms that have no gold and no chronometer.

CROCKER'S HOLE

CROCKER'S HOLE.

PART I.

THE Culm, which rises in Somersetshire, and hastening into a fairer land (as the border waters wisely do) falls into the Exe near Killerton, formerly was a lovely trout stream, such as perverts the Devonshire angler from due respect toward Father Thames and the other canals round London. In the Devonshire valleys it is sweet to see how soon a spring becomes a rill, and a rill runs on into a rivulet, and a rivulet swells into a brook; and before one has time to say, "What are you at?"—before the first tree it ever spoke to is a dummy, or the first hill it ever ran down has turned blue, here we have all the airs and graces, demands and assertions of a full-grown river.

But what is the test of a river? Who shall say? "The power to drown a man," replies the river darkly. But rudeness is not argument. Rather shall we say that the power to work a good undershot wheel, without being dammed up all night in a pond, and leaving a tidy back-stream to spare at the bottom of the orchard, is a fair certificate of riverhood. If so, many Devonshire streams attain that rank within five miles of their spring; aye, and rapidly add to it. At every turn they gather aid, from ash-clad dingle and aldered meadow, mossy rock and ferny wall, hedge-trough roofed with bramble netting, where the baby water lurks, and lanes that coming down to ford bring suicidal tribute. Arrogant, all-engrossing river, now it has claimed a great valley of its own; and whatever falls within the hill scoop, sooner or later belongs to itself. Even the crystal "shutt" that crosses the farmyard by the woodrick, and glides down an aqueduct of last year's bark for Mary to fill the kettle from; and even the tricklets that have no organs for telling or knowing their business, but only get into unwary oozings in and among the water-grass, and there make moss and forget themselves among it—one and all, they come to the same thing at last, and that is the river.

The Culm used to be a good river at Culmstock, tormented already by a factory, but not strangled as yet by a railroad. How it is now the present writer does not know, and is afraid to ask, having heard of a vile "Culm Valley Line." But Culmstock bridge was a very pretty place to stand and contemplate the ways of trout; which is easier work than to catch them. When I was just big enough to peep above the rim, or to lie upon it with one leg inside for fear of tumbling over, what a mighty river it used to seem, for it takes a treat there and spreads itself. Above the bridge the factory stream falls in again, having done its business, and washing its hands in the innocent half that has strayed down the meadows. Then under the arches they both rejoice and come to a slide of about two feet, and make a short, wide pool below, and indulge themselves in perhaps two islands, through which a little river always magnifies itself, and maintains a mysterious middle. But after that, all of it used to come together, and make off in one body for the meadows, intent upon nurturing trout with rapid stickles, and buttercuppy corners where fat flies may tumble in. And here you may find in the very first meadow, or at any rate you might have found, forty years ago, the celebrated "Crocker's Hole."

The story of Crocker is unknown to me, and interesting as it doubtless was, I do not deal with him, but with his Hole. Tradition said that he was a baker's boy who, during his basket-rounds, fell in love with a maiden who received the cottage-loaf, or perhaps good "Households," for her master's use. No doubt she was charming, as a girl should be, but whether she encouraged the youthful baker and then betrayed him with false *rôle*, or whether she "consisted" throughout,—as our cousins across the water express it,—is known to their *manes* only. Enough that she would not have the floury lad ; and that he, after giving in his books and money, sought an untimely grave among the trout. And this was the first pool below the bread-walk deep enough to drown a five-foot baker boy. Sad it was ; but such things must be, and bread must still be delivered daily.

A truce to such reflections,—as our foremost writers always say, when they do not see how to go on with them,—but it is a serious thing to know what Crocker's Hole was like ; because at a time when (if he had only persevered, and married the maid, and succeeded to the oven, and reared a large family of short-weight bakers) he might have been leaning on his crutch beside the pool, and teaching his grandson to swim by precept (that beautiful proxy

for practice)—at such a time, I say, there
lived a remarkably fine trout in that hole.
Anglers are notoriously truthful, especially
as to what they catch, or even more fre-
quently have not caught. Though I may
have written fiction, among many other sins,
—as a nice old lady told me once,—now I
have to deal with facts; and foul scorn
would I count it ever to make believe that
I caught that fish. My length at that time
was not more than the butt of a four-
jointed rod, and all I could catch was a
minnow with a pin, which our cook Lydia
would not cook, but used to say, "Oh,
what a shame, Master Richard! they would
have been trout in the summer, please
God! if you would only a' let 'em grow
on." She is living now, and will bear me
out in this.

But upon every great occasion there arises
a great man; or to put it more accurately,
in the present instance, a mighty and distinguished boy. My father, being the parson of the parish, and getting, need it be

said, small pay, took sundry pupils, very pleasant fellows, about to adorn the universities. Among them was the original "Bude Light," as he was satirically called at Cambridge, for he came from Bude, and there was no light in him. Among them also was John Pike, a born Zebedee, if ever there was one.

John Pike was a thick-set younker, with a large and bushy head, keen blue eyes that could see through water, and the proper slouch of shoulder into which great anglers ripen; but greater still are born with it; and of these was Master John. It mattered little what the weather was, and scarcely more as to the time of year, John Pike must have his fishing every day, and on Sundays he read about it, and made flies. All the rest of the time he was thinking about it.

My father was coaching him in the fourth book of the Æneid and all those wonderful speeches of Dido, where passion disdains construction; but the only line Pike cared for was of horsehair. "I fear, Mr. Pike,

that you are not giving me your entire attention," my father used to say in his mild
dry way; and once when Pike was more
than usually abroad, his tutor begged to
share his meditations. "Well, sir," said
Pike, who was very truthful, "I can see a
green drake by the strawberry tree, the first
of the season, and your derivation of 'bar-
barous' put me in mind of my barberry
dye." In those days it was a very nice
point to get the right tint for the mallard's
feather.

No sooner was lesson done than Pike,
whose rod was ready upon the lawn, dashed
away always for the river, rushing headlong
down the hill, and away to the left through
a private yard, where "no thoroughfare"
was put up, and a big dog stationed to en-
force it. But Cerberus himself could not
have stopped John Pike; his conscience
backed him up in trespass the most sinful
when his heart was inditing of a trout upon
the rise.

All this, however, is preliminary, as the

boy said when he put his father's coat upon his grandfather's tenterhooks, with felonious intent upon his grandmother's apples ; the main point to be understood is this, that nothing—neither brazen tower, hundred-eyed Argus, nor Cretan Minotaur—could stop John Pike from getting at a good stickle. But, even as the world knows nothing of its greatest men, its greatest men know nothing of the world beneath their very nose, till fortune sneezes dexter. For two years John Pike must have been whipping the water as hard as Xerxes, without having ever once dreamed of the glorious trout that lived in Crocker's Hole. But why, when he ought to have been at least on bowing terms with every fish as long as his middle finger, why had he failed to know this champion ? The answer is simple— because of his short cuts. Flying as he did like an arrow from a bow, Pike used to hit his beloved river at an elbow, some furlong below Crocker's Hole, where a sweet little stickle sailed away down stream, whereas for the length of a meadow upward the water lay smooth, clear, and shallow; therefore the youth, with so little time to spare, rushed into the downward joy.

And here it may be noted that the leading maxim of the present period, that man can discharge his duty only by going counter to the stream, was scarcely mooted in those days. My grandfather (who was a wonderful man, if he was accustomed to fill a cart in two days of fly-fishing on the Barle) regularly fished down stream; and what more than a cartload need anyone put into his basket?

And surely it is more genial and pleasant to behold our friend the river growing and thriving as we go on, strengthening its voice and enlargening its bosom, and sparkling through each successive meadow with richer plenitude of silver, than to trace it against its own grain and good-will toward weakness, and littleness, and immature conceptions.

However, you will say that if John Pike

had fished up stream, he would have found this trout much sooner. And that is true; but still, as it was, the trout had more time to grow into such a prize. And the way in which John found him out was this. For some days he had been tormented with a very painful tooth, which even poisoned all the joys of fishing. Therefore he resolved to have it out, and sturdily entered the shop of John Sweetland, the village blacksmith, and there paid his sixpence. Sweetland extracted the teeth of the village, whenever they required it, in the simplest and most effectual way. A piece of fine wire was fastened round the tooth, and the other end round the anvil's nose, then the sturdy blacksmith shut the lower half of his shop door, which was about breast-high, with the patient outside and the anvil within; a strong push of the foot upset the anvil, and the tooth flew out like a well-thrown fly.

When John Pike had suffered this very bravely, "Ah, Master Pike," said the blacksmith, with a grin, "I reckon you

won't pull out thic there big vish,"—the
smithy commanded a view of the river,—
"clever as you be, quite so peart as
thiccy."

"What big fish?" asked the boy, with
deepest interest, though his mouth was
bleeding fearfully.

"Why that girt mortial of a vish as hath
his hover in Crocker's Hole. Zum on 'em
saith as a' must be a zammon."

Off went Pike with his handkerchief to
his mouth, and after him ran Alec Bolt, one
of his fellow-pupils, who had come to the
shop to enjoy the extraction.

"Oh, my!" was all that Pike could utter,
when by craftily posting himself he had
obtained a good view of this grand fish.

"I'll lay you a crown you don't catch
him!" cried Bolt, an impatient youth, who
scorned angling.

"How long will you give me?" asked the
wary Pike, who never made rash wagers.

"Oh! till the holidays if you like; or, if
that won't do, till Michaelmas."

Now the midsummer holidays were **six** weeks off—boys used not to talk of "vacations" then, still less of "recesses."

"I think I'll bet you," said Pike, in his slow way, bending forward carefully, with his keen eyes on this monster; "but it would not be fair to take till Michaelmas. I'll bet you a crown that I catch him before the holidays—at least, unless some other fellow does."

PART II.

THE day of that most momentous interview must have been the 14th of May. Of the year I will not be so sure; for children take more note of days than of years, for which the latter have their full revenge thereafter. It must have been the 14th, because the morrow was our holiday, given upon the 15th of May, in honour of a birthday.

Now, John Pike was beyond his years wary as well as enterprising, calm as well as ardent, quite as rich in patience as in promptitude and vigour. But Alec Bolt was a headlong youth, volatile, hot, and hasty, fit only to fish the Maëlstrom, or a torrent of new lava. And the moment he had laid that wager he expected his crown piece; though time, as the lawyers phrase it, was "expressly of the essence of the contract."

And now he demanded that Pike should spend the holiday in trying to catch that trout.

"I shall not go near him," that lad replied, "until I have got a new collar." No piece of personal adornment was it, without which he would not act, but rather that which now is called the fly-cast, or the gut-cast, or the trace, or what it may be. "And another thing," continued Pike; "the bet is off if you go near him, either now or at any other time, without asking my leave first, and then only going as I tell you."

"What do I want with the great slimy beggar?" the arrogant Bolt made answer. "A good rat is worth fifty of him. No fear of my going near him, Pike. You shan't get out of it that way."

Pike showed his remarkable qualities that day, by fishing exactly as he would have fished without having heard of the great Crocker-ite. He was up and away upon the mill-stream before breakfast ; and the forenoon he devoted to his favourite course—first down the Craddock stream, a very pretty confluent of the Culm, and from its junction, down the pleasant hams, where the river winds toward Uffculme. It was my privilege to accompany this hero, as his humble Sancho; while Bolt and the faster race went up the river ratting. We were back in time to have Pike's trout (which ranged between two ounces and one-half pound) fried for the early dinner; and here it may be lawful to remark that the trout of the Culm are of the very purest excellence, by reason of the flinty bottom, at any rate in these the upper regions. For the valley is the western outlet of the Black-down range, with the Beacon hill upon the north, and Hackpen long ridge to the south; and beyond that again the Whetstone hill, upon whose western end dark port-holes scarped with white grit mark the pits. But flint is the staple of the broad Culm Valley, under good, well-pastured loam; and here are chalcedonies and agate stones.

At dinner everybody had a brace of trout—large for the larger folk, little for the little ones, with coughing and some patting on the back for bones. What of equal purport could the fierce rat-hunter show? Pike explained many points in the history of each fish, seeming to know them none the worse, and love them all the better, for being fried. We banqueted, neither a whit did soul get stinted of banquet impartial. Then the wielder of the magic rod very modestly sought leave of absence at the tea time.

"Fishing again, Mr. Pike, I suppose," my father answered pleasantly; "I used to be fond of it at your age; but never so entirely wrapped up in it as you are."

"No, sir ; I am not going fishing again. I want to walk to Wellington, to get some things at Cherry's."

"Books, Mr. Pike? Ah! I am very glad of that. But I fear it can only be fly-books."

"I want a little Horace for eighteen-pence—the Cambridge one just published, to carry in my pocket—and a new hank of gut."

"Which of the two is more important? Put that into Latin, and answer it."

"Utrum pluris facio? Flaccum flocci. Viscera magni." With this vast effort Pike turned as red as any trout spot.

"After that who could refuse you?" said my father. "You always tell the truth, my boy, in Latin or in English."

Although it was a long walk, some fourteen miles to Wellington and back, I got permission to go with Pike; and as we crossed the bridge and saw the tree that overhung Crocker's Hole, I begged him to show me that mighty fish.

"Not a bit of it," he replied. "It would bring the blackguards. If the blackguards once find him out, it is all over with him."

"The blackguards are all in factory now, and I am sure they cannot see us from the windows. They won't be out till five o'clock."

With the true liberality of young England, which abides even now as large and glorious as ever, we always called the free and enlightened operatives of the period by the courteous name above set down, and it must be acknowledged that some of them deserved it, although perhaps they poached with less of science than their sons. But the cowardly murder of fish by liming the water was already prevalent.

Yielding to my request and perhaps his own desire—manfully kept in check that morning—Pike very carefully approached that pool, commanding me to sit down while he reconnoitred from the meadow upon the right bank of the stream. And the place which had so sadly quenched the fire of the poor baker's love filled my childish heart with dread and deep wonder at the cruelty of women. But as for John Pike, all he thought of was the fish and the best way to get at him.

Very likely that hole is "holed out" now, as the Yankees well express it, or at

any rate changed out of knowledge.   Even
in my time a very heavy flood entirely
altered its character; but to the eager eye
of Pike it seemed pretty much as follows,
and possibly it may have come to such a
form again:

The river, after passing though a hurdle
fence at the head of the meadow, takes a
little turn or two of bright and shallow
indifference, then gathers itself into a good
strong slide, as if going down a slope
instead of steps.   The right bank is high
and beetles over with yellow loam and
grassy fringe; but the other side is of flinty
shingle, low and bare and washed by floods.
At the end of this rapid, the stream turns
sharply under an ancient alder tree into a
large, deep, calm repose, cool, unruffled, and
sheltered from the sun by branch and
leaf—and that is the hole of poor Crocker.

At the head of the pool (where the hasty
current rushes in so eagerly, with noisy
excitement and much ado) the quieter
waters from below, having rested and

enlarged themselves, come lapping up round either curve, with some recollection of their past career, the hoary experience of foam. And sidling toward the new arrival of the impulsive column, where they meet it, things go on, which no man can describe without his mouth being full of water. A "V" is formed, a fancy letter V, beyond any designer's tracery, and even beyond his imagination, a perpetually fluctuating limpid wedge, perpetually crenelled and rippled into by little ups and downs that try to make an impress, but can only glide away upon either side or sink in dimples under it. And here a gray bough of the ancient alder stretches across, like a thirsty giant's arm, and makes it a very ticklish place to throw a fly. Yet this was the very spot our John Pike must put his fly into, or lose his crown.

Because the great tenant of Crocker's Hole, who allowed no other fish to wag a fin there, and from strict monopoly had grown so fat, kept his victualing yard—if so low

an expression can be used concerning him
—within about a square yard of this spot.
He had a sweet hover, both for rest and
recreation, under the bank, in a placid antre,
where the water made no noise, but tickled
his belly in digestive ease. The loftier the
character is of any being, the slower and
more dignified his movements are. No true
psychologist could have believed—as Sweetland the blacksmith did, and Mr. Pook the
tinman—that this trout could ever be the
embodiment of Crocker. For this was the
last trout in the universal world to drown
himself for love ; if truly any trout has
done so.

"You may come now, and try to look
along my back," John Pike, with a reveren-
tial whisper, said to me. "Now don't be
in a hurry, young stupid; kneel down. He
is not to be disturbed at his dinner, mind.
You keep behind me, and look along my
back ; I never clapped eyes on such a
whopper."

I had to kneel down in a tender reminiscence of pasture land, and gaze carefully; and not having eyes like those of our Zebedee (who offered his spine for a camera, as he crawled on all fours in front of me), it took me a long time to descry an object most distinct to all who have that special gift of piercing with their eyes the water. See what is said upon this subject in that delicious book, "The Gamekeeper at Home."

"You are no better than a muff," said Pike, and it was not in my power to deny it.

"If the sun would only leave off," I said. But the sun, who was having a very pleasant play with the sparkle of the water and the twinkle of the leaves, had no inclination to leave off yet, but kept the rippling crystal in a dance of flashing facets, and the quivering verdure in a steady flush of gold.

But suddenly a May-fly, a luscious gray-drake, richer and more delicate than canvas-back or woodcock, with a dart and a leap and a merry zigzag, began to enjoy a little game above the stream. Rising and falling like a gnat, thrilling her gauzy wings, and arching her elegant pellucid frame, every now and then she almost dipped her three long tapering whisks into the dimples of the water.

"He sees her! He'll have her as sure as a gun!" cried Pike, with a gulp, as if he himself were "rising." "Now, can you see him, stupid?"

"Crikey, crokums!" I exclaimed, with classic elegance; "I have seen that long thing for five minutes; but I took it for a tree."

"You little"—animal quite early in the alphabet—"now don't you stir a peg, or I'll dig my elbow into you."

The great trout was stationary almost as a stone, in the middle of the "V" above described. He was gently fanning with his large clear fins, but holding his own against the current mainly by the wagging of his broad-fluked tail. As soon as my slow eyes had once defined him, he grew upon

them mightily, moulding himself in the
matrix of the water, as a thing put into
jelly does. And I doubt whether even
John Pike saw him more accurately than
I did. His size was such, or seemed to be
such, that I fear to say a word about it;
not because language does not contain the
word, but from dread of exaggeration.
But his shape and colour may be reasonably
told without wounding the feeling of an
age whose incredulity springs from self-
knowledge.

His head was truly small, his shoulders
vast; the spring of his back was like a rain-
bow when the sun is southing; the generous sweep of his deep elastic belly, nobly
pulped out with rich nurture, showed what
the power of his brain must be, and seemed
to undulate, time for time, with the vibrant
vigilance of his large wise eyes. His latter
end was consistent also. An elegant taper
run of counter, coming almost to a cylinder,
as a mackered does, boldly developed with
a hugeous spread to a glorious amplitude

of swallow-tail. His colour was all that can well be desired, but ill-described by any poor word-palette. Enough that he seemed to tone away from olive and umber, with carmine stars, to glowing gold and soft pure silver, mantled with a subtle flush of rose and fawn and opal.

Swoop came a swallow, as we gazed, and was gone with a flick, having missed the May-fly. But the wind of his passage, or the skir of wing, struck the merry dancer down, so that he fluttered for one instant on the wave, and that instant was enough. Swift as the swallow, and more true of aim, the great trout made one dart, and a sound, deeper than a tinkle, but as silvery as a bell, rang the poor ephemerid's knell. The rapid water scarcely showed a break; but a bubble sailed down the pool, and the dark hollow echoed with the music of a rise.

"He knows how to take a fly," said Pike; "he has had too many to be tricked with mine. Have him I must; but how ever shall I do it?"

All the way to Wellington he uttered not a word, but shambled along with a mind full of care. When I ventured to look up now and then, to surmise what was going on beneath his hat, deeply-set eyes and a wrinkled forehead, relieved at long intervals by a solid shake, proved that there are meditations deeper than those of philosopher or statesman.

PART III.

SURELY no trout could have been misled by the artificial May-fly of that time, unless he were either a very young fish, quite new to entomology, or else one afflicted with a combination of myopy and bulimy. Even now there is room for plenty of improvement in our counterfeit presentment ; but in those days the body was made with yellow mohair, ribbed with red silk and gold twist, and as thick as a fertile bumble-bee. John Pike perceived that to offer such a thing to Crocker's trout would probably consign him—even if his great stamina should overget the horror—to an uneatable death, through just and natural indignation. On the other hand, while the May-fly lasted, a trout so cultured, so highly refined, so full of light and sweetness, would never demean himself to low bait, or any coarse son of a maggot.

Meanwhile Alec Bolt allowed poor Pike no peaceful thought, no calm absorption of high mind into the world of flies, no placid period of cobblers' wax, floss-silk, turned hackles, and dubbing. For in making of flies John Pike had his special moments of inspiration, times of clearer insight into the everlasting verities, times of brighter conception and more subtle execution, tails of more elastic grace and heads of a neater and nattier expression. As a poet labours at one immortal line, compressing worlds of wisdom into the music of ten syllables, so toiled the patient Pike about the fabric of a fly comprising all the excellence that ever sprang from maggot. Yet Bolt rejoiced to jerk his elbow at the moment of sublimest art. And a swarm of flies was blighted thus.

Peaceful, therefore, and long-suffering, and full of resignation as he was, John Pike came slowly to the sad perception that arts avail not without arms. The elbow, so often jerked, at last took a voluntary jerk from the shoulder, and Alec Bolt lay prostrate, with his right eye full of cobbler's wax. This put a desirable check upon his energies for a week or more, and by that time Pike had flown his fly.

When the honeymoon of spring and summer (which they are now too fashionable to celebrate in this country), the hey-day of the whole year marked by the budding of the wild rose, the start of the wheatear from its sheath, the feathering of the lesser plantain, and flowering of the meadow-sweet, and, foremost for the angler's joy, the caracole of May-flies—when these things are to be seen and felt (which has not happened at all this year), then rivers should be mild and bright, skies blue and white with fleecy cloud, the west wind blowing softly, and the trout in charming appetite.

On such a day came Pike to the bank of Culm, with a loudly beating heart. A fly

there is, not ignominious, or of cowdab
origin, neither gross and heavy-bodied,
from cradlehood of slimy stones, nor yet of
menacing aspect and suggesting deeds of
poison, but elegant, bland, and of sunny
nature, and obviously good to eat. Him
or her—why quest we which?—the shep-
herd of the dale, contemptuous of gender,
except in his own species, has called, and
as long as they two coexist will call, the
"Yellow Sally." A fly that does not waste
the day in giddy dances and the fervid
waltz, but undergoes family incidents with
decorum and discretion. He or she, as the
case may be,—for the natural history of the
river bank is a book to come hereafter, and
of fifty men who make flies not one knows
the name of the fly he is making,—in the
early morning of June, or else in the
second quarter of the afternoon, this Yellow Sally fares abroad, with a nice well-
ordered flutter.

Despairing of the May-fly, as it still may
be despaired of, Pike came down to the

river with his master-piece of portraiture. The artificial Yellow Sally is generally always—as they say in Cheshire—a mile or more too yellow. On the other hand, the "Yellow Dun" conveys no idea of any Sally. But Pike had made a very decent Sally, not perfect (for he was young as well as wise), but far above any counterfeit to be had in fishing-tackle shops. How he made it, he told nobody. But if he lives now, as I hope he does, any of my readers may ask him through the G. P. O., and hope to get an answer.

It fluttered beautifully on the breeze, and in such living form, that a brother or sister Sally came up to see it, and went away sadder and wiser. Then Pike said : "Get away, you young wretch," to your humble servant who tells this tale ; yet being better than his words, allowed that pious follower to lie down upon his digestive organs and with deep attention watch. There must have been great things to see, but to see them so was difficult. And if I huddle up what happened, excitement also shares the blame.

Pike had fashioned well the time and manner of this overture. He knew that the giant Crockerite was satiate now with May-flies, or began to find their flavour failing, as happens to us with asparagus, marrow-fat peas, or strawberries, when we have had a month of them. And he thought that the first Yellow Sally of the season, inferior though it were, might have the special charm of novelty. With the skill of a Zulu, he stole up through the branches over the lower pool till he came to a spot where a yard-wide opening gave just space for spring of rod. Then he saw his desirable friend at dinner, wagging his tail, as a hungry gentleman dining with the Lord Mayor agitates his coat. With one dexterous whirl, untaught by any of the many books upon the subject, John Pike laid his Yellow Sally (for he cast with one fly only) as lightly as gossamer upon the rapid, about a yard in front of the big trout's head. A moment's pause, and then, too quick for words, was the things that happened.

A heavy plunge was followed by a fearful rush. Forgetful of current the river was ridged, as if with a plough driven under it ; the strong line, though given out as fast as might be, twanged like a harp-string as it cut the wave, and then Pike stood up, like a ship dismasted, with the butt of his rod snapped below the ferrule. He had one of those foolish things, just invented, a hollow butt of hickory; and the finial ring of his spare top looked out, to ask what had happened to the rest of it. "Bad luck !" cried the fisherman; "but never mind, I shall have him next time, to a certainty."

When this great issue came to be considered, the cause of it was sadly obvious. The fish, being hooked, had made off with the rush of a shark for the bottom of the pool. A thicket of saplings below the alder tree had stopped the judicious hooker from all possibility of following; and when he strove to turn him by elastic pliance, his rod broke at the breach of pliability. "I have learned a sad lesson," said John Pike, looking sadly.

How many fellows would have given up this matter, and glorified themselves for having hooked so grand a fish, while explaining that they must have caught him, if they could have done it! But Pike only told me not to say a word about it, and began to make ready for another tug of war. He made himself a splice-rod, short and handy, of well-seasoned ash, with a stout top of bamboo, tapered so discreetly, and so balanced in its spring, that verily it formed an arc, with any pressure on it, as perfect as a leafy poplar in a stormy summer. "Now break it if you can," he said, "by any amount of rushes; I'll hook you by your jacket collar; you cut away now, and I'll land you."

This was highly skilful, and he did it many times; and whenever I was landed well, I got a lollypop, so that I was careful not to break his tackle. Moreover he made him a landing net, with a kidney-bean stick, a ring of wire, and his own best nightcap of strong cotton net. Then he got the farmer's leave, and lopped obnoxious bushes ; and now the chiefest question was : what bait, and when to offer it ? In spite of his sad rebuff, the spirit of John Pike had been equable. The genuine angling mind is steadfast, large, and self-supported, and to the vapid, ignominious chaff, tossed by swine upon the idle wind, it pays as much heed as a big trout does to a dance of midges. People put their fingers to their noses and said : "Master Pike, have you caught him yet ?" and Pike only answered : "Wait a bit." If ever this fortitude and perseverance is to be recovered as the English Brand (the one thing that has made us what we are, and may yet redeem us from niddering shame), a degenerate age should encourage the habit of fishing and never despairing. And the brightest sign yet for our future is the increasing demand for hooks and gut.

Pike fished in a manlier age, when
nobody would dream of cowering from a
savage because he was clever at skulking ;
and when, if a big fish broke the rod, a
stronger rod was made for him, according
to the usage of Great Britain.   And though
the young angler had been defeated, he did
not sit down and have a good cry over it.

About the second week in June, when
the May-fly had danced its day, and died,—
for the season was an early one,—and
Crocker's trout had recovered from the
wound to his feelings and philanthropy;
there came a night of gentle rain, of
pleasant tinkling upon window ledges, and
a soothing patter among young leaves, and
the Culm was yellow in the morning.   "I
mean to do it this afternoon," Pike
whispered to me, as he came back panting.
"When the water clears there will be a
splendid time."

The lover of the rose knows well a gay
voluptuous beetle, whose pleasure is to lie
embedded in a fount of beauty.   Deep

among the incurving petals of the blushing
fragrance, he loses himself in his joys
sometimes, till a breezy waft reveals him.
And when the sunlight breaks upon his
luscious dissipation, few would have the
heart to oust him, such a gem from such a
setting. All his back is emerald sparkles ;
all his front red Indian gold, and here and
there he grows white spots to save the eye
from aching. Pike put his finger in and
fetched him out, and offered him a little
change of joys, by putting a Limerick hook
through his thorax, and bringing it out
between his elytra. *Cetonia aurata* liked it
not, but pawed the air very naturally, and
fluttered with his wings attractively.

"I meant to have tried with a fern-web,
said the angler; "until I saw one of these
beggars this morning. If he works like
that upon the water, he will do. It was
hopeless to try artificials again. What a
lovely colour the water is ! Only three days
now to the holidays. I have run it very
close. You be ready, younker."

With these words he stepped upon a branch of the alder, for the tone of the waters allowed approach, being soft and sublustrous, without any mud. Also Master Pike's own tone was such as becomes the fisherman, calm, deliberate, free from nerve, but full of eye and muscle. He stepped upon the alder bough to get as near as might be to the fish, for he could not cast this beetle like a fly; it must be dropped gently and allowed to play. "You may come and look," he said to me; "when the water is so, they have no eyes in their tails."

The rose-beetle trod upon the water prettily, under a lively vibration, and he looked quite as happy, and considerably more active, than when he had been cradled in the anthers of the rose. To the eye of a fish he was a strong individual, fighting courageously with the current, but sure to be beaten through lack of fins; and mercy suggested, as well as appetite, that the proper solution was to gulp him.

"Hooked him in the gullet. He can't get off!" cried John Pike, labouring to keep his nerves under; "every inch of tackle is as strong as a bell-pull. Now, if I don't land him, I will never fish again !"

Providence, which had constructed Pike, foremost of all things, for lofty angling— disdainful of worm and even minnow— Providence, I say, at this adjuration, pronounced that Pike must catch that trout. Not many anglers are heaven-born; and for one to drop off the hook halfway through his teens would be infinitely worse than to slay the champion trout. Pike felt the force of this, and rushing through the rushes, shouted: "I am sure to have him, Dick ! Be ready with my nightcap."

Rod in a bow, like a springle-riser ; line on the hum, like the string of Paganini ; winch on the gallop, like a harpoon wheel, Pike, the head-centre of everything, dashing through thick and thin, and once taken overhead—for he jumped into the hole, when he must have lost him else, but the fish too impetuously towed him out, and made off in passion for another pool, when, if he had only retired to his hover, the angler might have shared the baker's fate—all these things (I tell you, for they all come up again, as if the day were yesterday) so scared me of my never very steadfast wits, that I could only holloa! But one thing I did, I kept the nightcap ready.

"He is pretty nearly spent, I do believe," said Pike; and his voice was like balm of Gilead, as we came to Farmer Anning's meadow, a quarter of a mile below Crocker's Hole. "Take it coolly, my dear boy, and we shall be safe to have him."

Never have I felt, through forty years, such tremendous responsibility. I had not the faintest notion now to use a landing net; but a mighty general directed me. "Don't let him see it; don't let him see it! Don't clap it over him; go under him, you stupid! If he makes another rush, he will get off, after all. Bring it up his tail. Well done! You have him!"

The mighty trout lay in the nightcap of Pike, which was half a fathom long, with a tassel at the end, for his mother had made it in the winter evenings. "Come and hold the rod, if you can't lift him," my master shouted, and so I did. Then, with both arms straining, and his mouth wide open, John Pike made a mighty sweep, and we both fell upon the grass and rolled, with the giant of the deep flapping heavily between us, and no power left to us, except to cry, "Hurrah!"

THE END.

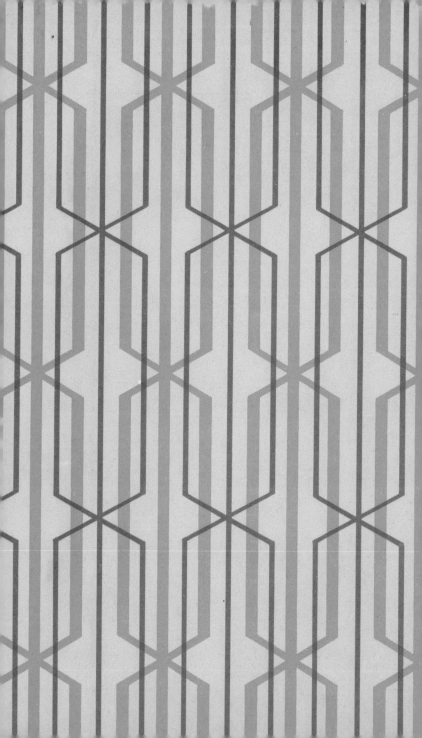